"I am coming for you, Demon," Malak said, his voice level but threatening. "I will reach the Celestial Tower by dark moon."

Lilith smiled callously. "You poor child. You will do exactly as I wish you to. Try to reach the Tower, and you will perish in the Wyrmspine Mountains. Your soul will then reside in my domain forever. Do nothing, and I will smash through your mind at dark moon. Once again, your soul will eternally abide in the qlippoth. There is no escape."

Malak glared at her, and their inhuman eyes clashed in a contest of wills. He knew that he could not hope to win such a mental confrontation: already he could feel her essence crushing him, even at full moon.

But he would not submit ever again.

Author's Note

Darkness and Light is a fantasy trilogy set within the doctrine of the Hebrew Qabalah, a work of fiction entwined with a factual philosophy. *Darkness and Light* is composed of three novels: *Lilith*, *Ronin*, and *Magus*. The trilogy follows Malak, an Adept of the White School of Magick. His story is analogous to the evolution of man, relating his Fall, Regeneration, Rebirth (self-realization), and God-realization. It is a tale related in many mythologies, most notably in Christ, but also in Osiris, the Phoenix, Krishna, Lugh, Baldur, and many others.

The glossary at the end of *Ronin* lists words the reader may be unfamiliar with. Also there is an essay on the Qabalah for those interested in the philosophy behind *Darkness and Light*, and a recommended reading list. These may be of interest to the open-minded reader.

I am always ready to accept any questions or comments from readers. I can be reached via the publisher or by Internet e-mail at dheeley@kether.demon.co.uk. For information on the status of my books see my web page at http://www.kether.demon.co.uk/.

Other Books by D. A. Heeley

Lilith

Ronin

Darkness and Light: Book II

D. A. Heeley

1997
Llewellyn Publications
St. Paul, MN 55164-0383

FIRST EDITION
First Printing, 1997

Cover art by Michael Kucharski
Cover design by Tom Grewe
Book design and editing by Darwin Holmstrom
Layout by Virginia Sutton

Library of Congress Cataloging-in-publication Data
Heeley, D. A. (David Anthony), 1971–
Ronin / D. A. Heeley — 1st ed.
p. cm. (Darkness and light : bk. 2)
Includes bibliographical references.
ISBN 1-56718-356-5 (pbk.)
1. Mythology, Semitic—Fiction. I. Title. II. Series: Heeley, D. A. (David Anthony), 1971– Darkness and light : bk 21
PR6058.E32R66 1997
823'.914—dc21 97-14408
CIP

Printed in the United States of America

Llewellyn Publications
A Division of Llewellyn Worldwide, Ltd.
P.O. Box 64383, St. Paul, MN 55164-0383

Dedication

For my parents: Jan and Tom.

A mention for Manjit, Harpy, Linda and John, Marc and Mel,
Tim, Maria, and especially Pally.

Genealogy

Original name	Present incarnation
Bal	Bal
Dethen	Jaad
Felmarr	Kalinda
Jeshua	Jeshua
Lena	Fiona
Malak	Shadrack

Recap of Minor Characters

Bal—An Adept of the Black School, and originally Dethen's father. Bal attempted to become Dethen's father again by copulating with Yhana. However, their child turned out to be Fiona, the next incarnation of Lena.

Ekanar—The sage that educated Shadrack on Tellus.

Felmarr—An Adept of the Black School, originally Dethen's personal apprentice. He was the only Black Adept to survive the evocation of Lilith.

Ghalan—Originally the Master of the Yellow School and Magus of Enya.

Jeshua—An ancient Adept of the White School. Jeshua has survived over a thousand years in the same incarnation. He once lived in Oaklan village, where Malak and Lena visited him.

Mendaz—A bandit leader and father of Jaad, the next incarnation of Dethen. A tortured man, Mendaz still mourns the death of his wife from over twenty years ago.

Yhana—A female Adept of the Yellow School. Drawn into a relationship with Bal, she gave birth to Fiona (Lena). She is Mendaz's mortal enemy, after murdering his wife.

Synopsis

Lilith

Ghalan, the Magus and protector of Enya, is dying. Without Ghalan the plane of Enya will disintegrate into the astral plane, killing everyone on it. A new Magus is required, someone to protect and nurture Enya through another Aeon.

The only two men able to assume the position are Malak and Dethen, once sons to Ghalan and still karmic twins, but now deadliest of enemies.

Malak is an Adept of the White School of Magick. He seeks the Seat of Magus to protect those he loves, especially his wife, Lena. Yet despite being a great warrior in his previous incarnations, Malak has yet to mature. He is content to live in a gullible paradise with his beautiful wife.

Dethen is Master of the Black School of Magick, and despite being defeated by Malak in a feud three lifetimes ago, he has extended his power tenfold since that time. He seeks the Seat of Magus to destroy Enya and the Tree of Life, for everywhere he looks he sees the pain and suffering of life: beauty does not exist for him.

Ghalan summons the two karmic brothers to him. As his body is consumed by fire, he whispers his last words: "Only through death can the twins be reunited...."

Determined to cross the Abyss and become the new Magus, Dethen wrestles with Arch-Demon Chronzon but is defeated. Unperturbed, he agrees to a plan to summon the Queen of the

Night, the Arch-Demon Lilith, knowing the result will be the destruction of Enya and the universe.

He dispatches his apprentice, Felmarr, to annihilate the White School. This is achieved, but Dethen is unexpectedly confronted by Malak as he prepares for his diabolical ritual. Malak is no match for Dethen's awesome power; Dethen leaves Malak wounded and performs his evocation of Lilith at the Rose Circle.

Lilith's incredible power is unleashed as she is summoned, killing Dethen and everyone in the Black School (except his apprentice Felmarr). Yet the Rose Circle constrains her form for a short while, giving Enya a few hours to survive.

Still injured from their confrontation with Dethen, Malak and Lena realize that only an act of self-sacrifice can banish Lilith back into the depths of Hell. Before her husband can react, Lena murmurs her vow of sacrifice and steps into the circle. Lilith's power rips her body and mind apart but the Demon is banished back into Hell, and Lena's soul is trapped with her.

Malak cannot live with the loss of his wife and the knowledge of her eternal torture. Against his instincts, he summons Lilith in a restrained form and bargains with her for his wife's soul. Lilith asks for the Celestial Tower, the traditional domain of the White School. Malak accepts and Lena's soul is released, but in making the bargain, Malak forsakes his own soul and Lilith devours him.

The shock of his death is enough to send Malak's soul plummeting back in time, and he is reincarnated on Earth in the icy land of Nippon as the child Shadrack. He is adopted by the ronin Ieyasu Tanaka, who is a renegade samurai, hunted by the Shogun. Tanaka raises him as his own son and teaches him the Bushido, the Way of the Warrior. The sage Ekanar educates the child. As he grows he begins to recall fragments of his life as Malak, and he begins to realize that a dark part of his soul is possessed by Lilith.

Meanwhile Dethen's father, Bal, is reincarnated on Enya and he copulates with Yhana, a young and cynical initiate of the Yellow School. He hopes the child will be the next incarnation of Dethen. However, Bal and Yhana run into a group of bandits lead by the capricious Mendaz, whose wife is also pregnant. Mendaz orders the pair killed, but Bal escapes, using his magick to trigger the childbirth of Mendaz's wife. Yhana is left behind and only survives by offering to deliver the baby. She delivers the baby safely but has no option but to allow the mother to die as the birth has complications.

Mendaz returns and is furious, but Yhana is aided in her escape by Bast, once Malak's familiar. In a rage, Mendaz crashes the dagger against his newborn son's head, permanently damaging his brain. The child is named Jaad, and ironically turns out to be the next incarnation of Dethen. Meanwhile Yhana has a daughter named Fiona, and this turns out to be Lena. Bal has lost contact with Yhana, and never discovers that his child wasn't Dethen.

On Earth, Shadrack grows to adulthood and becomes a samurai like Tanaka, learning his adopted father's formidable martial arts and sword skills, but the demon within him makes him a brutal and ruthless killer. When three samurai capture Tanaka, Shadrack automatically kills them, even though Tanaka forbids him to interfere. For breaking his pacifist vows, Tanaka disowns him. Shadrack becomes a fugitive like his father and is sentenced to death alongside him by the Shogun. Unable to stop himself, Shadrack becomes possessed by the full power of Lilith. As an unthinking creature of hatred, he kills over twenty samurai before being cut down. Beside him, Ieyasu Tanaka lies dead, killed by his own hand in the ritual of *hari-kari*.

On Enya, Fiona grows to adulthood and begins to recall her identity as Lena. She constantly dreams of Shadrack and Jaad, feeling love for one and terrible hatred for the other. Because of the trauma of her death caused by Lilith, the hatred she feels is so much stronger that she decides to seek out Jaad and kill him. Her mother, Yhana, tries to stop her, but Fiona is saved as Bast intervenes, horribly wounding her mother.

Fiona finds Jaad and viciously attacks him. He refuses to fight back and she knocks him unconscious. Driven by her hatred, she draws a dagger and prepares to kill him, yet feels constrained by her morals not to murder him. Unable to make a decision, she externalizes her hatred by projecting it into a huge wolf, giving it a life of its own. This renders her unconscious, and when she awakens she has full memories of being Lena.

Jaad is pursued by the wolf to the Rose Circle, where he trips and finds Dethen's sword *Widowmaker*. As he touches the weapon, his memories come flooding back and the wolf trembles before Dethen as it catches him.

With her memories returned, Lena begins to seek her husband, while Dethen's mind turns to revenge….

Part I

Regeneration

Inheritor of a dying world, we call thee to the living beauty.
Wanderer in the wild darkness, we call thee to the gentle light.
Child of Earth, long hast thou dwelt in darkness.
Quit the night and seek the day!

—Neophyte Ritual of the Golden Dawn

Child of Earth and Starry Heaven, thou who seekest this day the experience of the Mysteries, who seekest a clearer vision of Truth; thou who seekest worlds within worlds until for thee all worlds are one in eternity: the High Company of the Glorious Star greets thee.

Before we proceed, know this. Whoso enters the Mysteries can nevermore return to the evening world of unenlightened selfhood. To take the first step upon the sacred Way of Return is to be committed to it for ever. To enter upon this path is to find New Life in the morning world of Divine Inspiration, until all shall be caught up and assumed into the transforming Fire of Godhead.

I ask thee most seriously, therefore, art thou determined to make this venture and to undergo this transformation?

—Neophyte Ritual of the Aurum Solis

Let them hate, so long as they fear.

—Doctrine of the Black School

Prologue

Enya
Yesod of Yetzirah
Black School
subterranean lair
[Aeon of Despair]

"You are reporting failure?" The Warlock's voice sheared through the tenebrous chamber. Greshwin shuddered at the menace in the voice and quickly knelt.

"My lord, Sophia still stands. Prince Cassius Hawkin is too powerful an opponent."

"Cassius Hawkin still lives!"

Anger rippled from the Demon. Greshwin felt the air tighten around him. He stared at his Master, transfixed. Despite the Warlock's awesome size and fearsome skeletal face, his eyes usurped all attention. They burned like azure suns, a color so vivid and beautiful it took the breath away.

"Hawkin is strong, lord. He has combat skills that make him difficult to kill. He has neutralized my three best assassins, single-handedly." Greshwin's voice tremored. "Hawkin and his daughter still rule Sophia."

"I do not tolerate failure."

"No, Master." Greshwin closed his eyes, prepared for the blast that would rend his flesh from his bones. He had seen it many times before; no man ever survived. First the Demon's staff would glow; then would come the terrible pain.

The moment of tension lasted several seconds.

"You have tried magick against him?"

---

1 Lucius Accius 170–85 B.C.

Greshwin hesitated, surprised to find himself still alive. "I have tried death rituals, Master, but they do not seem to affect Cassius Hawkin. Those around him die, but he survives."

He felt the Warlock's emotions fluctuate, moving from anger through disbelief to slight confusion.

"But Hawking is not a magician. How can he deflect your ritual?"

"No, Master. Hawkin has less magical ability than a rock. We have never seen an aura so devoid of magick. It is something of a joke amongst the Adepts." Greshwin chuckled nervously; the laugh died in his throat as the Warlock's gaze dissected him.

"Then he should be very susceptible to magick, should he not? Only your incompetence can be to blame?"

Beads of sweat formed on Greshwin's brow. "Yes, Master."

"I want Cassius Hawkin dead! Sophia is the only city that still stands against me. Once it falls, the whole of Enya is mine. Hawkin is the last of my enemies."

"I will see to it personally, Master."

"Yes." The Warlock leaned forward on his throne; Greshwin suddenly noticed how vicious were the twin horns that sprouted from his head. "You *will* see to it personally. Or I will see to *you* personally."

Greshwin felt the full focus of the Demon's gaze on his face. His skin itched as if trying to escape the scrutiny.

"Yes, Master."

The Warlock dismissed the Adept with an impatient wave of a skeletal hand.

Suddenly a Black Guard lieutenant rushed into the chamber, almost knocking Greshwin over. He knelt quickly as the Warlock's eyes scathed across him.

"Master, we have taken a man prisoner in the wilderness. He wishes to see you."

"So? Why hasn't he been killed?"

The Warlock's eyes flamed brighter. He fingered his staff as though ready to shatter the lieutenant's skull. The staff never left the demon's hand; it was almost a part of him. The large gem on top glowed the same intense color as the Warlock's eyes.

"He…he is a Black Adept, Master," the lieutenant stuttered. "And he doesn't bear your mark."

"You captured him?" The Warlock radiated curiosity, something unusual in itself.

"He put up no resistance, Master. He claims he is here to see you."

The Demon's eyes dimmed. "Bring him before me!"

The lieutenant bowed and shouted to his men. Four soldiers entered nervously. Wedged between them was a short, somewhat overweight figure in black robes. His face was concealed within the recesses of his hood, and on his breast was the distorted symbol of a lightning bolt: mark of the Black School.

"He bore only this weapon, Master," the lieutenant said, showing a *wakizashi*.

The Warlock seemed disinterested in the sword. "Stand back and give him room."

The soldiers immediately moved away from the stranger. The man stood confidently alone, neither bowing nor kneeling.

"Why is it you wish to be in my presence, stranger, when all of Enya flees from it? And why do you wear the robes of a Black Adept?"

The figure had an aura of self-righteous arrogance around him. He chuckled.

"I come to bring you a warning, mighty Warlock." The voice was not that of a young man; there was a great deal of experience within it.

"Remove your hood when you address me, peasant!"

Another short laugh came from the figure.

"I have no allegiance to you, Warlock. I have been an Adept longer than you think."

The Warlock's aura rippled with amusement: it was rare he had such entertainment.

"Then reveal yourself, stranger! Let us all see this great Adept who thinks to challenge my authority!"

With a smooth movement, the man brushed back the hood of his robe. The Warlock would have raised an eyebrow if he possessed one, for the face was well known from the Second Aeon. It was middle-aged and dark skinned. The eyes were sharp and intelligent, the head shaved bald.

"I am Bal of the Black School. And I bring you a dire warning, Warlock."

The Warlock's dead grin seemed to widen slightly. "I am listening, Bal of the Old Time."

"You have taken the rightful place of another, Warlock. I know not whether you fare from Enya or beyond the Boundary, but you have usurped the true Master."

The Warlock laughed; the chamber shook with the sound. "You mean the weakling Felmarr?"

Bal shuddered visibly as the laugh washed over him.

"No, not Felmarr," he said dismissively. "I speak of the true Master. I mean Dethen."

The Warlock inclined his head. "Dethen? Another Adept from the Old Time. A man of considerable power and will."

Bal smiled humorlessly. "Quite considerable, Warlock...."

"I have waited a long time for this." The Warlock's eyes dimmed so much it seemed their light would be extinguished. "Longer than anyone can imagine..."

He stroked the gem of his staff. The gem vibrated urgently; Bal thought he saw something moving within it, seeking to escape.

"He comes to cast you down, Warlock."

"Perhaps once he would have succeeded." The Demon's orbs brightened. "But I anticipated his return long ago. Now no mortal can possibly stand against me." He stroked his staff lovingly.

Bal's eyes locked with the Warlock's. Bal shuddered and broke the gaze immediately, almost crushed by the Demon's will.

"Do we have any other business, mortal?"

Bal smiled thinly. "Only this."

He formed the attacking sign of Horus, hurling every ounce of his power at the Demon. The Warlock raised a hand and the energy bounced harmlessly away. It struck the four Black Guard soldiers, blasting them in all directions.

The Warlock laughed at his guest's audacity. Bal could only stare in amazement; he knew he had forfeited his life.

"Dethen may not have an equal among men, but I am an opponent of another magnitude entirely."

The Warlock's black aura became so intense it seemed he would suck the life from Enya. Bal stared in horror, awed by the Demon's power. For the first time in four lifetimes, he began to doubt his Master's power. How could Dethen stand against such a creature?

"Tell me, Bal. Have you ever seen flesh stripped from bone?"

The Warlock's staff began to glow.

1

Enya
Yesod of Yetzirah
City of Sophia

The voice of my higher soul said unto me, Let me enter the Path of Darkness, per adventure thus shall I obtain the Light. I am the only being in an abyss of darkness. From the darkness came I forth ere my birth, from the silence of a primal sleep, and the Voice of the Ages answered unto my soul:
I am he that formulates in darkness. Child of Earth; the Light shineth in the darkness, but the darkness comprehendeth it not.

—Neophyte Ritual of the Golden Dawn

Pale moonlight gently cascaded into the royal bed chamber, its cold rays casting an unholy shimmer across the dark ebony floor. Half-perceived etheral entities skulked around the room, a maleficent chill following their twisted paths. In the corner a solitary white candle burned, the flame dancing precariously on the whirling air currents; it gave out a pitiful amount of light.

Prince Cassius Hawkin knelt in *motsu* before the open veranda, enjoying the breath of the wind on his naked torso. Almost fifty winters of age, his hair and moustache had turned a distinguished silver-gray. Despite this, his body was hard and lean; the muscles of his abdomen and torso stood out conspicuously in the cold light.

Cassius felt the ethereal entities weaving around him in a hypnotic dance like half-formed shadows. He paid them no attention, enjoying a rare moment of peace.

"Father? Are you listening to me?" Kira's voice shattered the silence.

"What now?" Cassius didn't try to hide his irritation.

"The rationing, father. You have to end it. The people are becoming restless. You are becoming unpopular."

Cassius grunted. "Ah, what a crime. Kira, I don't need to be popular with the people. I just need to keep them alive and keep Sophia standing. Besides, you are popular enough. You're always ready to make the easy decisions."

Kira glowered. "I've assumed all your civil duties because you're so damned obsessed with your 'military strategy.' The people suffer more hardships each month because you're so convinced the Warlock seeks to subjugate us. Where will it end?"

"We are at war! We must be prepared!" Cassius snapped.

He turned to face her. As ever she wore chain mail armor, a scarlet cape hanging from her shoulders. Her long fiery red hair, tied back from her face, contrasted with her vivid green eyes.

"The Warlock has not moved against us in two years! How long will it take you to realize the war is over! It's time to cease the rationing."

Cassius' voice became quiet. "We are outnumbered twenty to one by the Warlock's forces. If he lays siege to Sophia, and we don't have enough supplies, we will not survive."

"The Warlock has no more interest in us!" Kira shouted, her face reddening. She cursed her lack of control; only her father could make her behave like this. "We must think of the people's needs."

"That is exactly what I'm thinking of. I don't expect you to understand. You're a woman. It's time you thought about marriage. Warfare is not a subject for a woman."

Kira seethed, but she would not lose control again. "I am captain of the guard. I won that right by combat, with no help from you. I beat every damned soldier you threw at me, so don't tell me I don't understand combat or warfare."

The room fell silent again. Cassius stared through the veranda. In the distance, the Boundary flickered like the aurora borealis. Every day it crept closer to his city, and he was defenseless against its power. He hated being helpless; he hated passivity, having to wait for events to unfold. The Boundary was gradually contracting, strangling Enya. It mirrored Cassius' own life; each day he felt more choked by limitations. He sought to escape. He wanted to escape from Kira, from Sophia, even from Enya. Most of all he yearned to escape his past.

He sighed. "You are a good soldier, Kira." The admission was grudgingly given. "But still, combat is not for women. You should think about marriage, and bearing children."

"I don't want to bear children," Kira said, shuddering. "That's not for me."

Cassius shrugged. "I do not agree with your choices, but I have never stopped you following your will."

"I know, father," Kira said quietly. "You never interfere with my life. In fact you have almost nothing to do with it. Are you so ashamed of me? Ashamed because I was born a daughter and not a son?"

Cassius appeared startled for a moment. "Ashamed? No. No, I'm not ashamed of you, Kira." He seemed about to add something else, then quickly changed his mind. "Since your mother left me, you are all I have." His voice was sorrowful, hinting at a wound that had never healed.

Kira studied him carefully. "Then why is it you push me away from you?"

"I loved your mother very much, when she left. . . ."

"Don't use her as an excuse, father," Kira interrupted. "The reason she left you was that you never reached out to her. You pushed her away as you do to me."

Cassius turned away from his daughter, annoyed.

"It's something from your past, isn't it? Something that happened to you?" Kira's emerald eyes were intense.

The silence was a great tension between them now. Cassius's emotions fluctuated wildly; despite his dedication to discipline, he had never learned to control them properly. Confusion was constantly with him. He badly wanted to reach out to his daughter, but the fear of loss was too great. Yet he knew that if he didn't reach out, eventually he would lose her, just as he had lost his wife many years ago.

Perhaps now is the time, he thought. He took a deep breath and held it for a few moments, trying to calm his hammering heart.

"Kira, there *is* something important I need to tell you about my past." His voice choked with emotion. "But it is not something that belongs to this life, not even to this plane." He took another breath. "In my last life. . . ."

Suddenly he lifted a finger to his lips and tilted his head, listening intently. Kira recognized the urgency of the gesture and stood silently waiting. Her father had a warrior's sixth sense.

Cassius moved fluently across the bedroom. His scarred hand reached for the hilt of his katana.

Kira inhaled sharply as a black-robed figure suddenly materialized on the moonlit veranda. She reached for her sword even before she noticed the Warlock's mark on his forehead.

"Father!"

A blast of astral energy collided with her, cutting short her warning. She gave a strangled cry as she crashed forcefully into the wall behind. She slumped to the floor, no longer breathing.

The Black Adept stepped into the bedroom. Cassius stared at his daughter, horror transforming to anger. The Adept turned to face him, his weasel-like face set with an oily smile.

"I am Greshwin," he said, giving a mock bow. "Please do not grieve for your daughter, for you are the next to die. It is the Warlock's bidding."

Cassius raised his *katana* and slid into a ready stance. The Adept seemed amused.

"You are an optimist, Prince Cassius Hawkin. Unfortunately my magick is quicker, and most definitely reaches further than your sword arm."

He formed the attacking sign of Horus, focusing every ounce of magick into a single blast. The wave hit Cassius at speed. But it deflected around his aura like liquid, colliding with the bed, which exploded into splinters.

Greshwin stared in utter amazement: he had never seen an aura so resistant to magick. It defied logic. His shoulders sagged in defeat: he had expended almost all his energy. He had only his sword left to attack with. Reluctantly he drew the blade.

Cassius felt his conflicting emotions flow away, as if doused with water. The anger, confusion, and frustration disappeared, replaced with complete focus. He felt balanced, whole. Only in combat did he feel like this.

"I'm afraid you've discovered something quite unfortunate," he said. "I can't allow the Warlock to learn of this."

He advanced on the Adept. Greshwin backed away, his haughty manner gone with his magick.

"How do you do it, Hawkin?" He licked his lips nervously and they began to circle each other. "You didn't use magick. Yet what else could it be? How did you deflect me?"

Cassius' eyes were glazed; though he stared at Greshwin, it was as if the Adept was insubstantial.

"Call it a surprise for the Warlock. Only he won't find out until it's too late," Cassius said. He knew the game Greshwin played, and he didn't allow the talk to distract him.

"I see now why my death rituals against you failed." Greshwin's voice was bitter. "They never had a chance. Well I supp—"

Suddenly he exploded into action. Cassius fully anticipated the attack. His katana sliced down on the attacking blade, cleaving it in two. He moved with incredible speed, made deceptive by the gracefulness of his movement.

Shocked by his opponent, Greshwin tried to take advantage of the close range. He dropped his useless weapon and grabbed for Cassius. Always reacting to his enemy's movements, Cassius slipped quickly from the intended headlock. His katana clattered to the floor as his arms locked around Greshwin's neck in a throat hold.

The Adept struggled wildly, crashing his elbow into Cassius's stomach. It was like striking iron. Cassius absorbed the blows without a sound, and in a few seconds Greshwin went limp. Cassius maintained the sleeper hold a moment longer, then allowed Greshwin to fall to the floor.

He retrieved his katana, slashing his finger on the blade.

"Why didn't you kill him?"

Cassius turned around to see Kira watching him from the floor.

"I thought you were dead," he said, his voice flat.

He walked over to her and reached out a hand to help her up. She stubbornly waved him away and tried to push herself up. Panic appeared in her eyes and she suddenly vomited over the floor, clutching her stomach. Cassius averted his eyes to spare her dignity. He knew the blast she had received from the Adept had been intense; it would take her several days to recover.

He stared at the Adept's unconscious body.

"I don't know," he said a few moments later.

"Don't know what?" Kira said, her voice hoarse.

"Why I didn't kill him. If I'd thought about it, I would have done it. He deserved it. But there is no time for thought in combat. I only react to my enemy." He nodded his head, as if he had just discovered a profound truth.

"Prince Cassius!" a guard shouted, running toward the bedchamber.

Cassius quickly moved to the door. "What is it?"

The guard was about to speak, then his eyes opened wide with shock. "You have been attacked!"

He leaned forward to gain a better view of the bedchamber. Cassius moved to block his view.

"What is it?" he asked again, irritated.

"Sire, it is Jeshua, the sage. He wishes to see you."

Cassius frowned. "Jeshua? You're sure?"

"Yes, Sire. He said it is most urgent."

Cassius's eyes were troubled. "It seems I am in for more excitement this night."

"Sire?"

"Oh, nothing. You're dismissed."

The guard saluted and resisted a last attempt to see past the prince before leaving.

Cassius crossed over to his daughter. Kira looked up, her face pale.

"Thank you," she said.

"For what?"

"For not letting my men see me in this state."

Cassius tentatively reached out to touch her hair, a gesture of affection, yet painfully self-conscious. He pulled his hand back quickly.

"I would have done the same for anyone."

Kira cast her eyes to the floor, and he immediately regretted his words.

"Did you hear the guard?" he asked, eager to shift her attention. "Jeshua has summoned me."

She looked up, shocked. "That bodes ill. The old sage has not summoned you in all the time I've been alive."

Cassius nodded, suddenly intense. "It has been nearly thirty years. Something is about to happen. Something important. I feel it in the air."

"About to happen? I don't understand."

Cassius's lips twisted into a half-smile; it looked strange, as if his facial muscles weren't used to the gesture.

"He is coming back to me," he said. "Shadrack is coming back to me."

Cassius ascended the tower stairs, following the path the Hawkin family had climbed for thirty generations. The stairs' edges had been completely rounded through a thousand years of use.

As he walked it was hard to differentiate between the dancing shadows from the torch and the ancient tower guardians that slunk back from the light. He knew he had nothing to fear; as a child, his aura had been imprinted with the necessary ward.

In a few minutes, he reached the top of the tower. There was no door to separate the sage's chamber from the stairwell; warm light spilled out of it. Cassius passed through the archway that led into the room. His body tingled as he passed through the intense astral screen used to block out uninvited entities.

The chamber was packed with assorted junk, much of it ancient and now unique. There were beautiful paintings and maps, books and scrolls, crystals, clocks and idols of gods from Egyptian, Babylonian and Assyrian pantheons. A coating of dust covered many parts of the room.

Standing at the far side of the room was Jeshua, his back to the entrance as he stared out the tower's arched window. Dressed in white robes, he leaned heavily on an ancient, gnarled walking stick. His back was bent and half-crippled: he had lost almost a foot in height since his days of youth, but he had forgotten his youth many centuries ago.

Cassius bowed as he entered. He placed his torch in a spare bracket and moved closer to the old man.

"Curious, isn't it, Cassius? Windows are such small things. We use them to cut the outside world down to a manageable size."

Cassius frowned, uncertain. "You are feeling philosophical, Jeshua?"

Jeshua sighed. "I'm always philosophical in these late days. What has been done has been done. And I can only watch the result of my labors now as time draws to an end."

He stared at the flickering colors of the ever-advancing Boundary.

"You know, in my day, the Boundary was a two-day ride from Sophia. And look now! If it continues to quicken its pace, it will swallow the city within a couple of years."

"Yet perhaps within that time, our plight will have been decided," Cassius said.

Jeshua chuckled and turned to face the warrior. His fingers played nervously with his white beard, which reached beyond his knees. Cassius noticed his eyes were more washed out than before. Centuries ago they had been a vivid blue, but the color had been gradually bleached away.

"Very astute, Cassius," he said. "The final wrestle for the control of Enya is about to begin."

He motioned his guest to a seat.

"A thousand years…" he said, shaking his head. "Perhaps now I have earned my rest. The final battle will begin, and because of my work, we will be in a position of strength."

Cassius frowned. "Will you not be with us for the final conflict?"

Jeshua grunted. "You know I hate this window. I hate it with every fiber of my being."

"The window?" Cassius couldn't hide the confusion on his face.

Jeshua continued as if he didn't hear the prince: "Every time I look out, I see a figure far below. He lies on the ground. His body is smashed and broken, his life extinguished."

Cassius heard the emotion in the old man's voice, and he stayed silent. When Jeshua turned from the window he painfully seated his aged body in his rocking chair. There was a single tear in his eye.

"You know, he is there every time I look. The vision has haunted me for a thousand years."

"Then why do you look?"

Jeshua smiled, a self-deprecating gesture. "In the hope that he won't be there. If the body wasn't there just once, I would be happy for the rest of my days."

Cassius nodded, though he didn't understand. An uncomfortable silence descended.

"You are wondering why I called you here?" Jeshua asked.

Cassius shrugged. "Of course. You haven't summoned me for thirty years. I was barely a man the last time we talked."

Jeshua nodded. "My task is coming to an end, but yours is just beginning, Cassius Hawkin. You are not on Enya in this time period by coincidence, Cassius. You know the importance of your last life."

Cassius grimaced; the mere mention of his last incarnation tasted like bile in his mouth.

"They have begun to return, Cassius. All the characters of the Summoning. They return from the Second Aeon."

"Shadrack?" Cassius asked, hope kindling within him.

"No, not yet. But soon. You know his situation better than anyone. His wife, Lena, has returned."

"Where is she? Do you want me to return her to Sophia?" Cassius' heart pumped faster. At last, the waiting was about to end.

Jeshua nodded. "She grew up within a Yellow School temple in the Enchanted Forest. She is now an outcast from their order, journeying northward. It is possible she is en route to the Celestial Tower. You must intercept her at the Gorom, for she will not know her friends from her enemies."

New life appeared in Cassius' eyes. "I ride at dawn, Jeshua."

"Good, good. You will have no problem recognizing her; her appearance is almost identical in this incarnation, and you have seen portraits aplenty."

"Then anyone might recognize her, and the Black School…."

"…must not find her," Jeshua finished.

Cassius nodded in understanding.

"You know, I met her several times at Oaklan village in the Enchanted Forest," Jeshua said. "That was in her last life, of course, before the Summoning in the Aeon of Dreams. She was the most lovely creature, full of courage and fire, yet also graceful and elegant. She loved nature and beauty with a passion."

The old man smiled, lost in his memories. He snapped back to reality with a start.

"One other thing, Cassius. Beware, for the enemy has returned…"

Cassius frowned. "The Warlock?"

Jeshua grunted. "The Warlock is a powerful being, but one has returned who will challenge him. He is the only mortal who might defeat the Demon, for even among demon-kind this man is feared."

Cassius grimaced. "Dethen."

"Your paths may cross, and you may be forced to confront the Black Master. Beware, he is the most deadly opponent. I doubt I could have matched him, even in my prime. His *budo-kai* and *iai-jitsu* may even match your own. And he is an Adept, a magician of tremendous power, whereas magick is forever forbidden to you."

Cassius didn't seem perturbed. "I know of Dethen. I know the pain he caused Shadrack. If he crosses my path, rest assured I will deal with him." He rested his hand on his sword hilt, his eyes steely.

"Be careful, Cassius. Avoid the conflict if possible, for it is Malak who must face the might of his twin brother."

Jeshua studied the eyes of his guest. They were pale blue, yet deep and profound. There was a depth and strength of character that few men could match. Jeshua realized that though he might conceivably be defeated, Cassius would not shrink from any kind of danger.

Jeshua nodded with satisfaction, and said, "If it becomes necessary, and it is possible for anyone to stand against Dethen, no one else has a better chance than you."

Cassius scowled, unused to accepting compliments. "And what of the Knights Templar? The Warlock may already know of my resistance to magick. Are we to lose our veil of secrecy?"

"Soon, Cassius, soon. As their leader, that decision will be yours to make. But do not unveil our secret too soon. Surprise will be our weapon."

Something moved in Cassius' peripheral vision, and he turned sharply. Sitting on one of the tables was a small, pudgy gnome. It was a mottled brown and orange with two horns, one of them broken. The eyes were twin pieces of coal, brimming with mischief. It idly kicked its legs back and forth as it watched the two men.

"How did that get in here?" Cassius asked.

Jeshua chuckled. "I'm not really sure. He turned up yesterday, bold as brass. But he's not your average elemental: this one's smart. He used to belong to Lena. His name is Squint."

Cassius raised an eyebrow, and as if to confirm his identity, the gnome winked several times.

"I've seen it all now," Cassius muttered.

"He phases in and out of the plane, but I think that he'll lead you to Lena if you can stand his company. He can't talk, but he can understand simple instructions," Jeshua said. "Not that he's obedient by any means. But I think I've made him understand what we want him to do."

"What do I do with him? I hardly think that throwing him in a saddle bag is practical."

"Don't worry. He'll trail you in his own way. He can travel anywhere almost instantly."

"I travel with Squint then," Cassius said, his voice unhappy but resigned.

"Good. Now I must sleep. My energy wanes quickly these days. It takes every scrap of magick and willpower just to cling to life."

Cassius rose and bowed. As he turned to leave the chamber he briefly wondered whether he would see the sage again.

"One other thing," Jeshua said. "Learn to find peace with yourself, and you will find the peace you seek with others, including your daughter. You must overcome the guilt you bear within, or it will be the cause of your premature death. Avoid self-pity and rid yourself of these feelings of worthlessness. Forgive yourself for your crimes."

Cassius paused, his shoulders tense.

"Only Shadrack may do that," he muttered before passing through the archway.

Nature fails unaided.

—Alchemical Truism

2

Tellus
Malkuth of Assiah
Saxon mid-lands

Ekanar wearily scanned the concrete rubble for marks that would jog his memory. Behind him, four knights plodded after him, like mobile fortresses in their plate mail armour. Between them they carried the stretcher that supported Shadrack, now drugged as well as tightly chained. He moaned softly to himself, semi-delirious in the oppressive, heavy atmosphere of late evening.

Ekanar wiped his brow, his face screwed up in annoyance. He had been away from his homeland for too long: he found the heat extremely tiring. The temperature was well above zero, far exceeding that reached in the Nipponese Empire. The air was extremely humid, and left a faint metallic taste on the tongue.

With resolve, Ekanar put the discomfort out of his mind and concentrated on the chore at hand.

He had been anxious about an attack from bandits, but he knew that they were now safe from that danger at least. No bandit would dare to enter the city through which they now wandered.

The city was huge, sprawling across the face of the earth like an ugly broken stone blanket. The buildings were shattered, most of them reduced to rubble from the massive shock blast of the Cataclysm. Those few that survived were dilapidated and unsafe, crumbling as they stood.

Ekanar had been through the city many times in his youth, yet he still found its sheer scale intimidating. Prenzlau had been a relatively small town in the Old Time, a prospect that was frightening. Truly, men had been like gods in the Old Time.

He signaled to the knights and then continued his labored walk forward, uncertain which direction he should take: it had been over twenty years since his last visit. The knights were obviously fearful about entering the forbidden city: they stared in awe as they passed burnt-out metal shells on the uneven, decrepit roads. They eyed the unearthed steel cables with suspicion, expecting them to strike with fangs at any moment. It was only their noble birth and faith in Ekanar's knowledge that forced them to stand their ground.

The sage himself knew that there was little to fear. Many of the encounters told in folklore through the land had occurred due to the power of the people he now sought. They wished no one to trespass on their territory, and the superstition surrounding the city aided them greatly.

Ekanar's mind suddenly snapped into alertness. The familiar sound of running water brought a flood of relief to his old bones, and he set off with new energy. The knights plodded on behind him, almost exhausted from the combined weight of their armour and the stretcher.

Soon Ekanar was looking down the miniature valley at the slow-running stream below him. It was much more feeble than he remembered it; once it had been a small river, providing the great town of Prenzlau with its water supply. Now it was barely a trickle, and the sage realized that the huge glaciers to the north were increasing in size. If they did not stop soon, within a lifetime the whole of the continent would be gripped by their icy embrace.

He leaned heavily on his staff, gathering strength for the last stretch. He now knew where he was, and his destination was close by. The knights stopped behind him, gently lowering the stretcher to gain a breather.

"Half a mile," Ekanar said, pointing along the course of the stream.

The men nodded, relief on their faces. Ekanar smiled to himself, realizing how long he had been in the Nipponese Empire. The ways of his homeland were strange and alien to him now, even though they were distantly familiar. After being in the company of samurai, the knights seemed like giants; some of them were six feet tall. Their faces seemed white and unhealthy, the eyes wide and strange.

Thinking of the samurai of the East caused him to suddenly dwell upon his old friend Ieyasu Tanaka, and of his recent death. The whole episode was a tragedy he wished to leave behind him, but could never forget. He sighed mournfully and signaled to the knights to continue.

They followed the meandering path of the stream for a quarter of an hour, passing shattered bridges and beached, dilapidated boats. Ekanar was sure of his route now; this part of the city had changed very little in twenty years, except for signs of further weathering.

Eventually, their destination loomed ominously into sight in the failing light. The sage barely discerned the hesitation in the step of the men behind as they saw it.

The wall was a mixture of gray and ebony blocks, towering into the sky. Looming behind the wall the tip of the city's derelict cathedral could just be discerned.

The wind whistled ominously as they advanced, and the air tightened about them. Ekanar wasn't sure whether it was imagination, but such things had always occurred when he approached the Temple.

Within a minute, they stood before the forbidding barrier. The knights lowered the stretcher, their hands flexing nervously near their long swords. Their apprehension reminded Ekanar of his own first view of the wall as a young man. In those days it had been the explorer in him that pushed him on—he had had an insatiable thirst for knowledge. Thinking back, he reflected how foolish, arrogant, and obnoxious he had been in those days. It brought a wry smile to his face.

Before him, set solidly into the wall, was a huge iron door. It was over six feet wide, and its height was much greater. Its surface was studded with rounded bolts, and the metal was covered with a barely perceptible oil film to prevent corrosion. The door was obviously maintained regularly to prevent rusting and dilapidation. Ekanar felt greatly relieved; despite its age, he had feared that somehow the Order might have ceased to exist in the last twenty years.

Set in the center of the door was a small hexagram, inconspicuous unless searched for. Above it was written: "Know thyself."

He raised his staff and hammered on the great door. The dull metallic noise rang out offensively, and for a few moments the atmosphere became incredibly tense; the city held its breath. The door hadn't been disturbed in many years.

For several minutes, nothing happened, and Ekanar was forced to strike the door once again. There seemed to be invisible entities in the air closing in on him. He shuddered as he remembered what he knew of the Order: there was almost certainly a host of invisible guardians around him.

Suddenly a small hatch opened in the door to show the face of an old, scowling man.

"What do you want? Leave me in peace!" he snarled viciously.

He moved to slam the hatch, but Ekanar was quick enough to catch it.

"I seek entrance to the Temple," he said, in a voice that the knights wouldn't overhear.

"Temple! What're you talking about, man?!" The old man's eyes flicked slightly to the side in nervousness.

Ekanar gave him a frank stare.

"I am Frater Scienta of the nought equals nought grade, and I seek entry!"

The old man looked surprised.

"Password?"

"Lux."

"That's an old one!" he shouted in triumph, slamming the hatch shut. Ekanar yanked his fingers away and cursed viciously.

A few seconds later the door cracked open a few inches.

"Why do you seek entrance, Neophyte?"

"It is important that I see the Frater Superior."

The old man scowled unappreciatively. "I suppose you have the right. But mayhap he can't see you for a while," he gestured at the knights, "and they can't enter."

Ekanar shook his head.

"No. It's important that he comes with me." He pointed to Shadrack. "He's the reason I need to see the Hierophant. Please, this is extremely important."

The old man grumbled to himself and slid the huge door shut with surprising ease. Ekanar turned and gave the knights an encouraging wink. None of them reacted; they stood completely motionless, but perhaps more relaxed than they had been. Despite his aching body, the sage found it difficult to suppress a smile: the knights were so serious, they were almost amusing.

The party waited a few minutes as the blood-red sun sank behind the horizon of rubble. The temperature was now becoming more comfortable to the old sage. It seemed strange to him how his body was completely adjusted to the ways of the East.

The great door swung open again, and the old man reappeared.

"Frater Superior has given you all permission to enter the Temple. Please step through."

Ekanar signaled to the resting knights, who again took up Shadrack's stretcher, and they all passed through the huge gate.

He scanned the ground around him and breathed in deeply. The gardens of the cathedral were covered in flowers of exotic colors, and with rare plants and trees. There were deep purples, greens, and blues, complemented by bright reds, yellows, and white. The sight was quite breathtaking.

A yellow-robed initiate walked towards them, carrying a small tray.

"I am the Sentinel," said the old man, his tone slightly more amicable. "You have been warded against the guardians?"

Ekanar nodded.

"Then only these five will need protecting," the Sentinel said, pointing to Shadrack and the knights.

He turned to face the initiate who now stood beside them.

"This is Frater Scienta. The others will require temporary wards for the Outer Temple. Frater Superior will greet Frater Scienta later."

The initiate bowed his head slightly and crossed over to the knights. He indicated that they should remove their helmets. They did so reluctantly, unsure whether they were to be blessed or cursed.

The initiate handed the tray he carried to the Sentinel and dipped his right index finger in a cup of water. With the wet index finger he traced an inverted equilateral triangle over the forehead of the first knight. He then picked up the censor and traced an upright triangle over the knight's forehead to form a hexagram. Finally, he picked up a rod that was decorated with twelve bands of color, and traced the sigil of the Order.

"You are now purified," he stated, before moving on to the second knight.

The first knight bowed his head in gratitude, his tired body feeling more relaxed.

Ekanar and the Sentinel watched impassively as the initiate baptized each of the knights in turn. Eventually, he stooped over the sleeping form of Shadrack.

"Sentinel, this man has already been initiated," he said with surprise.

The Sentinel frowned and looked at Ekanar.

"Is it a baptism from our School?"

The initiate shook his head, confused.

"It is beyond my power. He may be an Adept of some kind, but I'm not sure. His aura is black and purple and the centers of power are disaligned. He is not a natural man."

Shadrack murmured incoherently as the initiate scrutinized him.

"That is why he must see the Frater Superior," Ekanar interjected. "Surely, the sanctity of the Temple will protect him from possession while he is here."

The Sentinel looked at the initiate for a response, his eyes narrowed in distrust. The initiate shrugged and nodded his head.

"Very well," the Sentinel said, reluctance in his voice. "Follow me."

Nothing can resist the Human that will stake even its existence on its stated purpose.

—Doctrine of the Black School[2]

3

Enya
Yesod of Yetzirah
The Enchanted Forest

"I'm going to Gorom. Who's coming with me?" Mendaz asked.

The men looked up in surprise; they exchanged apprehensive glances.

"You've been drinking again," Raahd growled.

Mendaz glared at him and took another drink from his liquor.

"Why do you go to Gorom, Mendaz?" asked a voice from the black depths of the cavern. "Dark Moon is almost upon us. We should stay in the caves for shelter. If you must make a journey, it would be better to wait for the new moon."

Mendaz shook his head and slid down the wall to sit on the cavern floor.

"Two weeks," he said. "Two weeks since Jaad disappeared. Either dead or kidnapped, but whichever it is, I intend to find out. I won't wait for the new moon."

"And by what form of alcoholic reasoning did you come to the goal of Gorom?" Raahd asked, leering. "The only things you'll find in Gorom are the arena, whore houses, and Lilith's temples."

Mendaz hurled his bottle of liquor at Raahd. Raahd dodged; it narrowly missed his head to shatter against the wall. He glared at

2 Benjamin Disraeli

Mendaz, but didn't dare to retaliate. Mendaz pushed himself unsteadily to his feet and swaggered over to him.

"I go to Gorom because I know who took my son. It was those scum from the Yellow School. A woman. Janus saw her. Didn't you, Janus?"

"Yes, Mendaz." The voice was hesitant. "A dark-haired woman with the robes of a Yellow School initiate."

"See!" Mendaz pushed his face within an inch of Raahd's "See!"

Raahd stepped back and found himself pinned against the wall. "If it was an initiate, she'll be from the temple in the forest, not from Gorom."

"Idiot!" Mendaz cursed. "I'll never find the temple in the forest. It's concealed, and in thirty years we've never found it. We won't find it now. But the temple in Gorom isn't hidden."

"You really think they let anyone inside? You're a bandit. A criminal, not an Adept. Your brain is pickled by that booze."

The tension in the cavern multiplied; the men followed the conversation closely. Mendaz pulled out his dagger.

"Are you challenging me, Raahd?" he whispered menacingly. "Do you want to play with me?" He twisted the dagger so that the firelight glittered off its surface.

Raahd swallowed, his eyes fixed on the dagger.

"I didn't think so," Mendaz whispered. He turned around and shouted: "I can take any of you men. Yes, I'm drunk. I'm drunk and I'll still take any man in this cave. If anyone thinks differently, then step forward!"

The men exchanged glances but no one moved.

"They may fear you, Mendaz. But they don't respect you," Raahd said. "We all used to respect you, and that was why we followed you. You and I were once friends, but now your only friend lives in a bottle."

Mendaz glared at him for several long seconds and then turned away. "I go to Gorom," he said. "I go to Gorom to find out what happened to my son. By the gods, I may have mistreated him in life but I won't dishonor him in death." A look of guilt crossed over his face. "Twenty years ago a Yellow Adept killed my wife. I won't allow them to kill or kidnap my son and get away with it. Who goes with me?"

"Stay seated," said Raahd. "Stay seated and I will lead this band as it should have been led for the past score years."

"What do you say, Fenrin?" Mendaz asked. "Have you seen the future? Have you had a vision?"

The men fell quiet as they listened.

Fenrin grunted. "What any of you choose does not matter. Within three days every man in this cavern will be dead. Except for two. Only two men will survive. I suggest each man make peace with himself before death."

The silence intensified.

"Ah, horse shit!" Raahd bellowed. "Each of you make your choice, but if you stand and leave with him, there is no returning."

The men muttered to each other, and slowly half of them got to their feet. Mendaz ran his eyes sadly over the seated ones. They were the men who had enjoyed taunting Jaad, making his life a living hell. Some of the men standing had not been kind, but Jaad's apparent death had caused a great deal of guilt.

"Do you not journey with me, Fenrin?" Mendaz asked.

Fenrin shook his head. "Our crimes have caught up with us. I have seen what is to come. I am to meet my fate here, not in Gorom." He laughed. "I'm not sure which fate is worse."

Mendaz looked thoughtful. "Then we part company here, Fenrin. We go to find Jaad. I'll make my peace with him before I die, whether he's living or dead. You men standing, gather your belongings."

Raahd snickered. "Good riddance to the lot of you. It's a mad quest. You never know. A bad penny always turns up. If he's alive, and you're unlucky enough, Jaad just might find you."

Rain and wind slashed viciously across the ancient black megaliths of the Rose Circle, stinging the motionless sentries with a numbing chill. Near the tree-line horizon, the dirty puce-colored globe of the Enyan sun edged lower. A human figure knelt within the three circles of standing stones, dressed in ragged black robes. His head was bowed in deep, timeless contemplation, oblivious to the shrieking wind and lashing rain. He was as motionless as the huge sentinels about him as he pondered his situation.

Dethen stared into the dark pool of water before him; though his body shielded it, the pool rippled gently, disturbed by rogue drops of water. He studied his face carefully. Many of the vicious scars had followed him through from his previous incarnation, and the hawk-like resemblance to Ghalan was still present. His face was slightly different, as would be expected, but the fathomless black eyes were still there, even more haunted if anything.

He had been mentally marred by the experiences of Jaad—being a half-wit for twenty five years. How typical for humans to bully and despise him, rather than aid him. It strengthened his resolve to achieve the Purpose.

His mind was a bizarre cacophony of thoughts: Jaad's confused emotions and views had survived within him. And the half-wit's mingled, incoherent memories were far fresher than his own. It was only Dethen's iron willpower that made him the dominant personality.

It would take time to fully assimilate Jaad into his psyche. This task had to be his first priority: until it was achieved, he would gain no peace. At heart, both he and Jaad were the same essence. And until they were forged into a single identity, Dethen would be divided against himself.

Events had worked out reasonably considering the nature of his previous death, and the lack of subsequent preparations for his return. His body was large and strong, though presently lacking in stamina and muscle tone. He had been able to choose his own incarnation to an extent, but he had not foreseen he would incarnate within the body of an idiot child. He suspected that his arch-enemy had something to do with it: it was the twisted sense of humor that the Arch-Demon Chronzon possessed.

Looking up at the dirty purple sky, he felt an incredible difference in the plane: it was almost beyond belief. It was dark and cold, almost malignant through the absence of a Magus for many years. Despite the unwholesome atmosphere, he felt more at home on Enya than he ever had.

Around him, Dethen felt dark creatures prowling. Even though he was still growing in power he knew they wouldn't be foolish enough to attack. They could sense that he wasn't a normal man, not even a normal Adept. Here was one who had wrestled with the mighty Chronzon, and survived. Only those with the sublime title of Magus had ever achieved this before.

The Rose Circle was an easy point of access to other planes. Here in the center Dethen could feel other, more subtle dimensions pressing in upon him. He also felt a remnant of the dark force he had once summoned; Lilith had somehow maintained a foothold on Enya. He frowned as he struggled to order his deranged memories. A chaotic haze possessed his mind.

He knew that his ritual to summon the Demon Lilith had been successful, but that somehow the Rose Circle had contained her force, saving the plane from certain doom. He was also vaguely aware of the banishing of Lilith, achieved through his brother's wife Lena; he had learned of this after his physical death.

As he recalled her name, an involuntary sympathy flowed from him. He now remembered: she had voluntarily sacrificed herself to banish the Arch-Demon, thereby condemning herself to an eternity of torture in the Infernal Habitations. His feelings about Lena were very confused; though in one sense he hated her for luring his brother away from the Black School, in another way he felt affection for her. It was an alien emotion to Dethen, but Lena reminded him so much of Anya, a love he could never retain. He would ensure the glimmer of compassion he felt for her did not become a weakness, nor would he allow her to revive the terrible guilt buried deep within him.

He wondered what had become of Malak; he knew that his twin would have been crushed by the death of his wife. He remembered visiting Malak in astral form at the Celestial Tower after his physical death, but he recalled none of the details. He had been rapidly drawn into the Life Cycle after that, losing consciousness to reincarnate as Jaad.

Dethen sighed somberly; he had much to attend to. He had to rapidly improve his physical condition and harmonize his personality with the elements once again. Once his mind and body were balanced, he could concern himself with other things. In the meantime, he would have to scry as much of the plane as possible. He had to become familiar with any changes in geography and learn of any political considerations. Groups of significant power would have to be identified, and eventually he would seek out the rags of the Black School. He vaguely remembered that his apprentice, Felmarr, had survived the holocaust of the Summoning. The young magician might have preserved some semblance of the Order, which was all but destroyed in the evocation of Lilith.

There was also a vague recollection of a being called the Warlock. It was one of Jaad's memories, however, and quite confused. Jaad's mind had never made much sense of the world about him; it had absorbed only fragments of information.

Though he knew he was in the Enchanted Forest, he had no idea of what year it was, or even what Aeon. He knew there couldn't be a Magus on Enya, because only Malak or he could assume that position.

Suddenly a low, threatening growl came from behind him. Dethen lifted his head and turned slowly. Behind him loomed the wolf-like shadow of Graymist, the creature Lena had unwittingly created. Its soulless red eyes stared at its master, its huge jaws salivating with hunger.

Dethen gave it permission with a casual gesture of his hand.

"Go. Satisfy your appetite."

The demon loped off into the forest. A minute later, its shriveling howl sliced through the night atmosphere.

Dethen knew he had been fortunate to survive the ghastly pursuit through the forest. Graymist had existed for only one reason: to destroy him, but the Black Master had bent its essence to his will, and now the creature would be very useful.

He banished future concerns from his mind; as ever, he was more interested in the present. He had a debt to repay.

An old relative was about to receive a visit. He was integrating Jaad into his personality, and it was something he had to do, for the less dominant part of his split personality sensed its new-found power, and it desired vengeance against those who had mistreated him for so long. The anger and hatred, bottled up for twenty-five years, released itself like the breaking of a dam. Instead of the feeble and weak mind of a half-wit, the full wrath of a mighty Adeptus Major had been provoked.

Dethen's black eyes burned with fury; he slid his hand to *Widowmaker's* hilt. "Mendaz, I am coming for you, father."

Enya
City of Sophia

Cassius silently watched from the entrance to the family *dojo*, where Kira practiced her *kata*. Sweat dripped from her body and she wheezed as she moved, but she would not submit even when she staggered on her unsteady legs. Cassius observed his daughter with sadness. She reminded him so much of himself in some ways, but though she considered herself to be a man, she was not. In some ways, he knew he was to blame. His desire for a son made her try to fill the gap.

Kira formed the *kiash* of a side kick and her supporting leg suddenly buckled. She landed hard on the floor, grimacing.

"You should rest more before you push yourself so hard," Cassius said; he bowed in respect as he stepped into the *dojo*. "The blast you received from the Black Adept was severe. You should be in bed."

Kira's eyes narrowed in annoyance. "How long have you been standing there?"

"Long enough to know you are not fit enough for *kata*."

"And how many times have you taken bed-rest after an injury, Father?"

"Twice, actually." Cassius reached out his hand to help her up.

Kira looked suspiciously at the hand, but grasped it. Cassius hauled her to her feet, but Kira's expression did not soften.

"And as I remember, you were on the verge of death on both occasions. And you still tried to crawl from your bed. The healer had to sedate you because his healing magick could not affect you."

Cassius shrugged. "You do not have to emulate my foolishness, Kira. Besides, you are...."

"A woman," Kira interjected bitterly. "And we are not meant for combat." Her tone was heavy with sarcasm.

Cassius almost retorted, but resisted the temptation. "It is an old argument. And I did not come here to argue."

"What did you come here for, Father? To insult my *kata?*" Kira's vivid green eyes were challenging.

"No. I came to tell you that I'm leaving Sophia. I must journey to Gorom."

Kira couldn't hide her shock. "Is this because of Jeshua?"

"Yes. The old sage wishes me to intercept someone and return them to Sophia."

"But why you? You are not a common guard. Gorom is dangerous, even deadly. The Warlock has a stronger grip on Gorom than any other city. It's a refuge for all the scum the other cities won't accept!"

"I know. That's why I must go there. The woman I seek will be in grave danger."

"What woman?" Kira paused. "Is this something to do with your past? You said yesterday you would tell me of it."

"It does concern my past. The woman I am to meet is Lena from the Aeon of Dreams."

Kira was stunned. "Your karma is connected with the Summoning?! That is the most important event ever to occur on this plane!"

Cassius sighed. "I know. But I'm not connected specifically with the Summoning, only with the characters who were involved. That is why it must be me who intercepts Lena at Gorom. She won't have any idea what she's stumbling into. She will be vulnerable and defenseless."

"From what I know of the legend, Lena was anything but vulnerable. I think, perhaps, she might surprise you. Knock that sexist philosophy from your thick skull."

"My philosophy has been with me a long time. It has served me well. I'm not about to let go of it now because you disagree with it, Kira. Or even for Lena, whatever importance history ascribes to her."

"Would you have had the guts to step into that circle? To sacrifice yourself to Lilith to save the plane and the one you loved?"

Cassius looked thoughtful for a second. "I leave shortly," he said. "All the preparations are complete. We will continue the discussion about my past when I return. Now is not the right time."

"You give me your word?" Kira knew her father would rather die than break his word.

"Yes."

"Agreed, then. But I want to come with you. Lena is a heroine. I want to meet her."

Cassius scowled. "There are no such things as heroes or heroines. We all do what we must. You can meet Lena when we return. You are not well enough to travel, let alone fight."

"I thought you said you are to find her and return. You are expecting a battle?"

"As you said, it is Gorom. And when I arrive there it will be Dark Moon."

Kira's eyes widened in alarm. "Then you must take an escort for defense!"

"Don't worry, I will take my usual protection."

"And who is that?"

Cassius' lips twisted into a cruel smile; he stroked the hilt of his sword. "This steely friend never lets me down."

Death and transformation are man's unchosen and unchangeable fate. All that he can choose and change is consciousness. But to change this is to change all.

—Doctrine of the White School[3]

4

Tellus
Malkuth of Assiah
City of Prenzlau

Ekanar stumbled wearily through the inner corridors of the cathedral as he followed Thedra, the assistant to the Hierophant of the Order. His limbs were leaden and weary; though he tried to use his staff for support, he still found movement very difficult. He wheezed for air, and was starting to undergo almost imperceptible convulsions. He feared that the journey across the Eastern Ocean and the following one across land had been too much of a drain on his aged constitution.

Thedra noticed his difficulty and stopped. Despite being barely twenty years of age, the girl had an unusual maturity and balance. Her belt sash bore the grade sign of Philosophus, the highest grade of the Outer Order. She was also moderately pretty, Ekanar noticed, with blond hair and a pleasing bone structure.

"Do you require assistance, Frater?" she asked, her tone concerned.

Ekanar almost conceded, but pride gained the upper hand.

"No, thank you. I'm sure I'll manage," he replied.

The slight smile that Thedra showed revealed her understanding of the old man's vanity, and Ekanar immediately felt embarrassed. However, being ill was not a condition that the sage was in any way used to. His optimism, regarded by many as inextinguishable,

3 Rodney Collin

had been sadly lacking of late. Since the death of Tanaka, he'd had very little to celebrate.

In a few minutes the pair reached a large dark mahogany door. Though he was pleased to have reached the destination, Ekanar felt a little trepidation as old memories returned to him. He knew that he was standing before the office of the Order's Hierophant, the man who guided and controlled the school. He reflected upon the man who had been Hierophant many years ago, when he had been an initiate himself. The man had been a wise but stern figure who commanded great respect without effort.

Thedra knocked softly on the large door, which was partially covered in padded red leather. A gold cross was set into the center.

After a moment a voice drifted through the doorway. "Please, enter."

Thedra opened the door and stepped inside. "I have your guest here, Frater Superior. He insists that his business is of the utmost urgency."

She indicated that the sage should step through the door, which he did tentatively. He was conspicuously aware of how much his muscles and limbs ached. He was also extremely cold: a thin sheet of sweat clung to him and it felt like ice.

The office was just as Ekanar remembered it, though it was perhaps larger in his memory. It was strictly functional, even if every piece of furniture breathed antiquity and quality. There were no portraits of past Hierophants or great adepts: the leaders of the Order were chosen due to their ability to lead and organize, not on their popularity or desire for admiration and respect. Most Hierophants had therefore been reluctant to take on the job, but had accepted it as a necessary burden.

A small window admitted the deep red color of the setting sun. Outlined against the window, a yellow-robed figure sat behind a large ornately decorated desk. The agreeable vanilla-like smell of storax permeated the office.

Ekanar balked as he immediately recognized the man; he had been the last person he'd expected to see within the office. Cheiros was at least fifty years of age by now, but looked forty. His hair and beard, though streaked with silver, were still primarily black. His face bore no wrinkles or worries, despite his responsible position.

"Frater Scienta," Thedra said, and then with an easy sweep of the hand, "our Honored Hierophant."

The Hierophant stood up, a slight look of puzzlement on his face.

"Your name seems familiar...." He scrutinized the sage very carefully as he walked around the desk.

Ekanar was suddenly uncertain of how to act. Cheiros had been a fellow neophyte in the order with the sage over twenty years ago, and they had been very good friends. Ekanar didn't know how to greet the man after so many years apart, especially considering his prestigious position. It was even worse that Cheiros hadn't recognized him: would he remember him even if his memory was prodded?

"We...were friends for a...couple of years a long time ago," Ekanar said, feeling very awkward. Subtlety was not his strong point, and he felt very out of place.

Cheiros's eyes suddenly warmed as recognition hit him. He clasped the sage's hand amiably and shook it vigorously.

"Ekanar! How the devil are you? It must be twenty-five years. I didn't think that we'd see you again!"

Ekanar smiled in return, his naturally buoyant character floating to the surface.

"It's been a long time, old friend."

Cheiros nodded appreciatively.

"Please, sit down. You look absolutely terrible!"

He helped the sage to seat himself on one of the formal and rather uncomfortable seats. Ekanar found himself amazed at the transformation that Cheiros had passed through. The man had once been fiery, chaotic, and unstable. He had always been filled with lusts of one sort or another, and yet now he seemed perfectly balanced and focused. His eyes were serene and reflective, showing a spirit very much at home with itself. Ekanar felt hollow at the thought of what he had turned his back on many years ago.

Cheiros seated himself behind the desk.

"So tell me, where have you been, and what have you been doing with yourself these past thirty years or so?"

Ekanar shuffled uncomfortably as the Hierophant's gaze beheld him. It felt as though the old Cheiros he'd known had only been a tiny shadow of the man before him now.

"Well, I traveled a couple of years, until I reached the continent Azia. I eventually settled down in a small village in the Nipponese Empire."

"The island of Hokkaido in the Far East? Isn't that where the famed and fearless samurai warriors live?"

"Aye, but they're not as chivalrous and honorable as their great reputation suggests!"

Cheiros smiled. "I bet they're not....So, what have you been doing with yourself in this village? I didn't think you would ever settle down. After all, that was the reason you gave for leaving us...."

Ekanar frowned. When he was bluntly asked the question, it seemed to him that he had spent the last thirty years on mundane and irrelevant things. It suddenly struck him that he had finally settled down and become like everyone else. As Cheiros said, he had left the Order to gain something, which he later threw away. The last few years felt like the blink of an eye: it almost seemed that he hadn't been away from the Temple.

"I was...err...a wise man for a village, I suppose. There I continued my studies with what materials I had been able to accumulate."

Cheiros raised his eyebrows; he seemed slightly taken aback.

It struck Ekanar that he had changed in Cheiros's eyes as much as Cheiros had changed in his. When younger, he had had a burning desire to see every country in the world. When he had settled down in Kyoto, it had been a temporary arrangement. But the thrill of the culture and the strange society had proved too great an attraction, and eventually inertia had set in.

"I also took my share in the responsibility of bringing up a child, or at least of educating him," Ekanar said.

Cheiros smiled warmly. "Then you married! It's something I never had a choice in, unfortunately."

"No, not exactly. I helped to raise an orphan with a very strange background. In fact, he's the reason that I'm here in Saxony."

"Ah. I wondered. Has this anything to do with the young man who came bound and drugged on a stretcher?"

Ekanar shifted restlessly; his body was demanding more and more of his attention.

"Yes. But I'm afraid that the story I have to relate to you is bizarre and improbable at the least. Shadrack's history is a very strange one."

"Please, go on."

"The boy was found about fifteen years ago in a set of standing stones, built on an ancient holy site. When he was found, he had the appearance of a five-year old...."

Cheiros nodded, genuine interest now showing in his eyes.

"He was adopted by an old friend of mine, a fugitive samurai called Ieyasu Tanaka. Between Ieyasu and myself, we raised the child to manhood, but from his adoption it was obvious that he was no normal child.

"Firstly, Shadrack had an innate knowledge of Hebrew, which as you know, has not been spoken on Tellus for several millennia, not outside of the Mystery schools at any rate. He also possessed a piercing intellect, and an unusual maturity and focus of mind.

"Ieyasu, who had once been captain of the Shogun's Guard, trained him in martial arts, while I provided him with a comprehensive education. But throughout his years at Kyoto village, Shadrack was prone to slipping into strange states of consciousness, lucid nightmares and trances in which he seemed to be possessed. I believe that Ieyasu knew more about these things than did I, but he was always loathe to discuss them."

"Was he prone to violence?" Cheiros asked.

"His martial arts were honed almost to perfection, and he was trained to have the potential to kill with a single technique, yet he always avoided violent behavior, due to the instruction of his father.

"But eventually Shadraack killed three men in what amounted to self-defense, and Ieyasu disowned him. When he returned to the village, he was a samurai in the Shogun's Guard, which had arrived to seize Ieyasu, who had been a fugitive, ronin, for twelve years.

"A complex situation resulted, in which the Shogun ordered Shadrack to kill Ieyasu. The boy underwent an intense emotional struggle, and something seemed to snap within him. When he arose, he was possessed with something...terrible. It was a creature of such evil and malignancy....

"It tore apart almost a score of samurai. Its power was awesome. But it was wounded in the battle, and eventually Shadrack seemed to return. His mind is now shattered, and the demon still comes and goes, even though its full power has never been fully unleashed again."

"And you have brought this Shadrack to our Order for aid?" Cheiros's tone was disapproving.

"You are my only hope. I don't understand the state of the boy's soul, or what his karma is. I still haven't come to terms with the events that happened only a few months ago...."

"We cannot accept a demon into the sanctity of the Temple, you know that. Especially one that is this powerful, and has not been identified."

"But please. I have no other help!"

"I'm sorry, I cannot put the Order at risk."

"Then at least request advice from the Chiefs of the Order, or consult the tarot. Surely it will do no harm to inquire, for something must be done with the demon."

Cheiros considered for a while, and then nodded.

"Agreed. But for now, we must get you to a bed. Your aura is fading, and you look very poor."

He stood up and walked around the desk. He took Ekanar's hand to help him up, but suddenly recoiled as they made contact.

"What is it?" Ekanar asked, suddenly very perturbed.

"Nothing. Forgive me. Let's get you up."

But Ekanar could see the extremely troubled look in his old friend's eyes.

Enya
Yesod of Yetzirah
The Enchanted Forest

A gentle rain fell as Dethen half-stumbled through the golden-barked trees of the Enchanted Forest. His black robe, designed for a peasant rather than a black magician, was ripped and torn, soaked through from the persistent drizzle. His hair was unkempt and disheveled, and several days' stubble covered his jaw.

He had walked for over twenty miles, and his debilitated body was tired and aching. His mind felt distant and unfocused: the blue-green leaves of the trees rustled around him in conspiracy.

Stopping to rest, he leaned against a tree for support. An intense psychological conflict raged within him: after an initial acceptance of Dethen's control, Jaad now fought to regain command of his body. Yet the two personalities were no longer completely separate, and to Dethen it seemed that he battled a fragment of himself. Because Jaad's personality was far more recent, the youngster had a great advantage. Only Dethen's immovable will allowed him to retain control.

He ran his hand over the faded birthmark on his forehead, a blemish that had been with him since birth. He knew exactly how he had received it. Mendaz had tried to kill him at birth in a rage over the death of his mother. His heart pounded quicker, anger coursing through him. He cursed as he sought to control the emotion, but it was impossible to control Jaad's hatred; it had accumulated through too many years of abuse. Dethen knew he had to regain emotional control, and strengthen the untoned muscles of his new body, otherwise he would not survive a week on Enya.

Dark Moon approached, and the minions of Lilith would soon be roaming free; he had to move quickly. Once Mendaz and the others were dead, Dethen knew that integration of Jaad into his psyche would then be possible.

He pushed himself from the tree and continued his advance toward his unsuspecting prey.

What thou seest write in a Book, and send it unto the Seven Abodes that are in Assiah.

—Revelations 1:11

And I saw in the right hand of Him that sat upon the Throne a Book sealed with Seven Seals. And I saw a strong Angel proclaiming with a loud voice, "Who is worthy to open the Books and to loose the seals thereof?"

—Revelations 5:1-2

5

Planet Tellus
Malkuth of Assiah
City of Prenzlau

In his personal meditation chamber, Cheiros held the tip of his lotus wand over the beautifully decorated pack of tarot cards, simultaneously visualizing a brilliant sphere of white light above his head.

He intoned: "In the divine name IAO I invoke thee, thou great Angel HRU, who art set over the operations of this Secret Wisdom. Lay thine hand invisibly on these consecrated cards of art, that thereby I may obtain true knowledge of hidden things, to the glory of the ineffable name. So mote it be."

Shivers of astral energy and apprehension passed through his body as he paused. This confirmed his suspicion: there were potent karmic forces concerning the individual that he attempted to divine. It had been many years since he used the tarot cards for anything other than meditation and ritual use. In the Order, only neophytes used the tarot for divination; this was for the sole purpose of awakening the dormant psychic faculties.

He announced: "I request knowledge of the identity of, and the forces surrounding the demon-man Shadrack."

He stilled his mind, and began to shuffle the seventy-eight cards. He focused his mind upon Shadrack's name, allowing his subconscious to manipulate the cards as it wished. Shortly he received a distinct impression that he should stop. He cut the pack of cards three times and then picked them up in the opposite order.

He took a deep breath and centered himself.

"The Significator," he said as he flicked over the first card and laid it upon the altar.

Though he showed no facial reaction, he stared in surprise at the card before him: the Magician. He knew that this card, as the Significator, was intrinsic to Shadrack's nature. Yet this was extremely perturbing and confusing. It went against everything Ekanar had told him.

"The past," he said, then slowly laid down the next three cards: the Lovers, the Tower, and the Hanged Man inverted.

Cheiros's psychic intuition was triggered by the brightly colored archetypal pictures. He saw a vision of someone he knew was Shadrack, but who was somehow different. With him, more difficult to see, was a beautiful dark-haired woman; the love between the couple was very conspicuous. The scene was suddenly displaced by a huge black tower, which reflected only the light of the moon and stars. Dark things stirred around the tower, and he had an overwhelming feeling that a terrible catastrophe had taken place there. The image was again displaced, superseded by a scene in which a huge wolf devoured a helpless Adept within a dim, dank chamber. Cheiros banished the scene with distaste, dampening the emotional reaction that arose within him. He instinctively knew that he'd witnessed fragments of Shadrack's previous life, rather than his current one.

He studied the four cards in front of him, and realized that all four were major arcana. Potent forces indeed were focused around the man-demon. He breathed deeply, wondering what further distasteful scenes would have to be borne.

"The future," he said.

He watched with fascination as he turned over the next three cards: Death, Strength, and Strife. He immediately knew that Death was a transformation, possibly spiritual, which Shadrack would pass through. It was therefore a symbolic death. The Strength card was what he would gain through the metamorphosis. The Strife card indicated that an intense and closely fought conflict would result. He received no indication of the possible outcome of the battle.

He now had seven cards laid before him, all major arcana except for Strife, which was the five of wands. He knew that such a result was highly improbable. There were seventy-eight cards in the tarot deck; twenty-two of them were major arcana, forty were minor arcana and sixteen were court cards. A majority of major arcana in a reading was extremely rare, and always signified powerful spiritual or diabolical forces at work.

He said, "Related influences."

The first card he turned over was the Princess of Cups. Immediately Cheiros received a vision of an incredibly beautiful woman, with long black hair and alluring deep brown eyes. Her body was very feminine and elegant, her face delicate. Yet he felt her fiery and courageous character, full of beauty and love, but equally capable of vengeance when roused. Cheiros recognized her as the woman from his vision of the Lovers card. If so, he knew that her karma would be intricately connected with Shadrack's.

He turned over the second card, and again it was a court card: the King of Swords. He gasped as he received a vivid impression of a tall, heavily built man with dark hair. The king's eyes were like twin pieces of jet: they were so black that their soulless depths seemed to devour the light. His face was hawk-like, criss-crossed with a paradigm of savage scars. His personality was fierce, possessing a daunting and fearful strength, yet also great subtlety and skill.

Cheiros immediately knew that the man was an Adept of great power. Cheiros grunted and broke the psychic link; he knew that he would never want to antagonize the man he had just seen. The vision of him and the preceding woman, who also seemed to be an Adept, gave a sense of immediacy to the problem of Shadrack. Obviously his karma was an important one, tied in with that of many others.

Wondering what he would encounter next, Cheiros turned over the third card. It was the Moon, a card that at first seemed out of place. Yet he realized that there was a significance behind it that wasn't immediately obvious. Traditionally, the card signified falsity and deception, or referred to hidden enemies. He stared at the surface of the card in puzzlement.

Then he suddenly received a hideous sensation of evil and malignancy. He saw a terrible wolf-like creature stirring within his inner sight. He instantly knew it was demonic, and he closed down the psychic link, breathing hard. Though he had seen little, the card told him a great deal, for he knew it was associated with the demon who possessed Shadrack, which must therefore be lunar in nature.

He shuddered as he realized that the man was possessed with the only female Arch-Demon. It could only be Lilith, Queen of the Night. Despite the Yellow School policy of emotional detachment, sympathy welled out of him for the young man, who now lay chained in darkness within the cathedral's dungeon.

"What will be the final outcome of Shadrack's destiny?" he asked, a barely perceivable tremor in his voice. Already he felt involved with the ronin.

He turned over the final card. It was the Wheel of Fortune. He immediately knew that Shadrack's destiny was firmly planned by his karma, and that fate was keeping the plan close to its chest.

He realized that there was a further question that he must ask, an extremely important one.

"What should be my course of action?"

He turned over the twelfth card; it was the High Priestess. He frowned in bewilderment: the card did not make sense as an answer to his question. The traditional interpretations didn't seem applicable in this instance. The only point about the card that stuck in his mind, for a reason he wasn't aware, was that the Path crossed the Abyss.

Suddenly he felt an intense shock pass through his astral form as it was whipped from his body. He gasped in surprise: the event should not have been possible due to the protective circle around him, unless it had been propagated by a lofty spiritual force.

He automatically shed his astral body as he was dragged higher and higher, his consciousness now in the more refined mental body. He felt as if he were being stretched to a huge height, and still the darkness rushed past him on all sides. He saw fleeting glimmers of various planes, but they passed too quickly to identify; he knew that he was ascending higher than he had the ability to go unaided.

Suddenly he saw a great gap before him, like an area of non-existence in the universe. Here the planes abruptly ended. It was like a vast ocean of nothingness, in which strange and bizarre forms continually appeared, only to be instantly warped or destroyed by the strange currents that flowed through it. With trepidation, Cheiros realized that he was viewing the border that marked the beginning of the Abyss, which no human could attempt to pass, not unless he obtained oneness with God.

His body felt as if it had been stretched to a huge limit: his form was rarefied and barely existent. He felt the beings that had summoned him; though he could not see them, for they had no form, their essences danced and flickered beyond the Abyss.

His vision, rather than being restricted as in a human body, was now omniscient: he could see in every direction. His body was stretched into the shape of a rope, and his "feet" were far below, enveloped by the harmonious yellow glow of Tiphareth. Far below he could see gold globes dancing back and forth around the Sephira. He realized that these were three-dimensional shadows of the beings who dwelt above the Abyss. Their beauty was astounding.

He felt them talk to him, not with words, but by thought forms that vibrated through his body.

"The destiny of Shadrack is momentous…you must protect him…."

They spoke together, their voices passing through his body like a tide of liquid warmth. He wanted to dissolve in the euphonic ecstasy. He knew that these beings were perfect in every way.

"What must I do?" he focused his thoughts toward them.

"You must awaken the man who is almost one of us…."

They read the puzzlement of his mind by the sudden alteration in his vibrations.

"You must awaken the Magister Templi…."

Cheiros was shocked.

"The Master! He has not been within the Temple for five centuries!"

"He must prepare the way for Malak…" the sublime voices whispered; Cheiros allowed himself to be carried away with the sound, throwing him into a heavenly rapture.

"I will awaken the Old One," he affirmed.

Though he felt that it would be wrong to ask a question, he was too awed by the perfection of the beings to resist.

"Who are you?" he asked, fighting the exhilaration to focus himself sufficiently.

"We are the Chayoth ha-Qadesh, the Holy Living Ones."

Cheiros was confused: he knew that the angels belonged to Kether of Yetzirah. They resided far below the Abyss.

"You are receiving communication from Metatron, the Arch-Angel of the Presence, yet you are unable to withstand his words directly. He in turn has received his instruction from above. Yet within the presidency of the Crown, there is no difference between the One and the many. We are all images of one another upon different levels...."

Cheiros's body automatically shifted vibrational rate to express his understanding.

"You must now go..." they whispered to him. "For Malak, time is now short...."

Cheiros felt his mental body contract rapidly, and he felt a great sadness. He hated to leave the presence of the divine beings.

Thedra reached the end of the passage that wound its way through the ancient catacombs. Her flickering torch cast dancing light across a small wooden door, now splintered and rotten. The smell of decay was overpowering.

She wondered once again what she would see within the chamber of the old Master. She expected to see nothing more than an aged and long-dead skeleton. No one had seen the Master for over five hundred years, and she was certain he had died around that time.

Reaching the door, she paused for breath. She knocked gently, urgently wishing she was elsewhere. She hoped there were no rats in the catacombs. It was extremely unfair that Cheiros had sent her, rather than making the journey himself.

She knocked again, this time with more force. Suddenly she cursed and smashed the door with her fist, almost collapsing it. She laughed at her condition; fifty feet below the ground, she waited for a five-hundred-year-old man to appear. It was ludicrous.

A voice suddenly silenced her: "There is something amusing?"

Before her stood a man dressed in yellow robes; they were so grimy and ragged they were hanging from his body, but his face was perfectly clean. The man's eyes penetrated her as if they saw through her body. They were a deep azure, rimmed with an extra circle of blue that seemed to glow.

"I'm sorry, I...I..." she stammered.

Her torch fell to the floor as her body went limp with shock. She tensed as the light extinguished, leaving her in total darkness.

Suddenly, the yellow light reappeared. The old man held the torch in front of himself, apparently having ignited it with his fingers. Thedra stared in a mixture of terror and awe.

"Why have you disturbed me, girl?" Without having any emotion, the voice somehow seemed vexed.

"The Hierophant of the Order bade me do it, Magister Templi. He has a matter of utmost urgency."

The Adept showed no reaction. "Does he indeed? How long have I been in these catacombs?"

"Ah…I don't know…I was told five hundred years, but…."

He looked mildly surprised. "I had no idea." He stared at her. His gaze was ambiguous: incredibly intense, yet somehow not focused on the physical plane. "What do you want of me?"

"I was told to take you to the Hierophant," she said, unsure of herself.

Again, she felt the Adept was unhappy about the situation. He muttered something very fast in a strange language, staring at the ceiling. He nodded his head and muttered again, as if he had received an answer.

"Lead the way, and I will follow," he said.

Thedra nodded. "May I ask your name?"

The Adept seemed confused for a moment; he frowned. "Ah. Of course. Where I have been there is no use for such things." He looked thoughtful. "I don't recall my name in this body, but in most incarnations, I am known as Ghalan."

The angry man will defeat himself in battle as well as in life.

—Samurai Maxim

6

Enya
Yesod of Yetzírah
The Enchanted Forest

Dethen nodded with grim satisfaction as he reached the cascading cerulean waterfall. He remembered it well, even though Jaad's memories were hazy. Within the concealed cavern, he knew he would find Mendaz and his men.

His body felt stronger, and his mind sharper. Though he still was far from the peak of his power, once again he was a force to be reckoned with. Now that his objective was within reach, Jaad had realized his intentions and no longer resisted Dethen's will.

Glancing around, Dethen noticed a sentry sitting beside the waterfall. He immediately recognized the man, though he could put no name to his face. Dethen was sure that the man belonged to Mendaz's band. As he searched more carefully he counted two more guards, semi-concealed amid the blue-green leaves of trees.

He withdrew into cover and crouched down. Looking up, the dirty purple sky slowly darkened. Within half an hour it would be dusk, and then by the cold light of the stars he would begin his hunt. Tonight was Dark Moon. A strange red acrid fog began to form. Hunched next to him, Graymist licked his jowls in eager anticipation, his eyes glowing hungrily.

The sound of crashing water blocked out the cries of the wounded men as Raahd impatiently sharpened his dagger, a task that had occupied him for the last three hours. He glanced around the rocky, dank cavern, frustration causing his hyperactive behavior. The men were discontented; since Mendaz had left there had been two power struggles. Raahd did not have Mendaz's physical authority, and he had clung to power by wounding two of his men.

There were nine able men left. One guarded the cavern entrance and outside were four more guards, but they would retreat into the cavern at the first sign of trouble. The wolf-like demons of Dark Moon were agile and deadly, and experience gave the men good reason to fear them.

"It wasn't like this when Mendaz was here," Lorr said forlornly as he polished his crossbow.

"Mendaz was a drunkard," Raahd snarled. "We're better off without him."

"There were no squabbles when he led us," Lorr continued. "He was strange and moody, and changed like the wind, but at least we were united."

"Hold your tongue, damn you! Or you'll be next to feel the tip of my blade!"

A strange laugh came from the darkness. "It doesn't matter, Raahd. We are all to die. I have seen it."

The cavern became deathly quiet except for the omnipresent waterfall. The bandits shuffled closer to listen.

"What do you know, Fenrin?" Raahd asked, but his voice was uncertain.

"I've told you. I have seen it"

"A dream? Your dreams have been wrong in the past."

"No. A vision."

Raahd fell silent. Fenrin's visions always came true. They happened rarely, but even Raahd could not deny their accuracy. He could not take that risk.

"What have you seen, Fenrin? Tell me everything!"

Fenrin laughed and moved into the light. There was a hint of insanity in his eyes when he spoke.

"He comes for us," he said.

Raahd frowned and glanced at the other men. "Who comes for us? Mendaz? Is he returning to attack us as we sleep? That would be just like him!"

"He comes for us," Fenrin repeated, his voice barely a whisper. "He is half man, half demon. He stands like a giant and moves like the wind. His touch is enough to kill, and he wields a blade of ebony mithril more hungry than death itself."

Raahd's eyes narrowed. "You've been hallucinating, Fenrin. No such being exists, even in this accursed forest."

Fenrin shook his head and giggled strangely. "He comes. The Black One. He comes for us!"

Raahd moved forward and slapped him forcefully across the cheek, throwing him to the ground. Fenrin's crossbow scuttled along the floor.

"Damned fool! You've really lost it!"

Fenrin propped himself up on one elbow, and wiped the blood from the side of his mouth. He laughed.

"And Corwyn is the first to die," he said. "Listen!"

Raahd snarled and moved to land another slap. But he stopped abruptly. From the forest came a soul-shriveling howl. The hairs on his neck prickled in fear; his blood turned to ice. It came from the throat of a man, yet Raahd knew it was an unholy death cry from a victor; Corwyn was indeed dead.

He picked up Fenrin's crossbow and threw it to him.

"Take position in the rear of the cave," he growled. "Whatever it is, we'll be ready for it."

Dethen stalked his prey soundlessly, moving with the grace of a panther. The forest was moderately dense in this region. A thick crimson mist covered the forest floor like an impenetrable blanket. It was four feet deep, with such a distinct demarcation that it almost appeared to be solid. Literally nothing could be seen below a man's waist.

Dethen was submerged under the crimson blanket, moving swiftly. He had memorized the location of every tree in the area, and he followed his route with absolute certainty. His eyes were closed to prevent irritation from the noxious mist: he could see nothing with them anyway. He had ripped off the hood of his cloak, which he used to breathe through. Though the mist still burned his throat and lungs, the cloth at least made the sensation bearable.

He slowed as he approached the target area. He stopped, straining to pick out the slightest sound. In the distance, he heard the baying of a wolf. A few seconds later it was answered, this call from much nearer. Dethen frowned. He knew there would be many creatures prowling the forest at Dark Moon; he wouldn't allow them to cheat him of his quarry.

There was an anxious rustle from barely six yards away, a nervous reaction to the wolves' baying. The sound was faint, almost inaudible, but it was all Dethen needed.

He sprang from his crouched position, breaking through the mist like a wrathful demon. The terrified guard lost the contents of his bowels as he froze in shock. By the light of the red mist, Dethen looked more like an avenging fiend than a man. His *kiai* of rage thundered through the forest, more petrifying than the cry of Lilith's demons. The sound emerged as an unholy howl of rage, mingled with the craze of blood-lust.

The ebony blade of *Widowmaker* glowed eerily as she descended, effortlessly slicing the guard's head from his shoulders. The sword flared scarlet as she stole his life, momentarily illuminating the forest. Dark blood sprayed from the corpse as it hit the ground with a muffled thud; the head spun away into the mist.

Dethen closed his eyes and submerged below the barrier, searching the guard's body with his hands. He found a loaded crossbow, but the bolts had been scattered with the guard's fall. It was therefore good for only one shot. He stripped a keen-pointed dagger from the bandit's body.

He heard the other three guards calling to each other, fear in their voices. He realized they were attempting to join together and retreat to the cavern. But the voices were all that Dethen needed to find them. He made a crouching dash toward his next victim.

A cry of terror told him Graymist had found one of the guards. The slobbering sound of flesh being devoured was the only further sound.

Dethen slowed as he reached the area; the next guard was running and easily tracked. Dethen's acute hearing registered the sound of a second set of footfalls close by. He moved faster; he knew it would be far easier to pick off the men individually. Despite his speed, he moved with absolute silence, using his magick to dampen sounds from within his aura. When he was within a few yards of the nearest mercenary, he let out a guttural growl.

The man stopped and spun around. A crossbow bolt sliced through where Dethen had knelt moments before. The soldier panicked as he struggled to re-cock his weapon. He never had the opportunity. Dethen rose up behind him and grabbed his hair, yanking his head backward. The point of the dagger pierced the soldier's skin between the chin and neck; it penetrated up through the mouth and tongue, passing straight through the brain. The death-thrust stopped only when it struck the underside of the cranium. The man convulsed once before death. Dethen threw the corpse to the ground contemptuously.

"Halt!" the last guard bellowed, charging toward him, leveling his crossbow.

Dethen melted back into the mist and quietly moved away from the dead soldier. He listened carefully, waiting for any sign that might betray his last opponent's position. His ears heard only the natural sounds of the forest, and the baying of the increasingly active wolves. He raised his head above the layer of fog and smiled wryly: it seemed his enemy had also blended into the cover of the fog. It was a timely reminder that he didn't hunt a band of peasants; they were all trained soldiers.

The last bandit crouched low, as motionless as the great oak trees themselves. He knew he could only be tracked by noise, and he intended to make none. His own ears strained to pick up any sign of the man-beast that hunted them. His heart hammered in his ears, so loudly he thought he'd never hear anything above it. It was difficult to breathe in the caustic fog without rasping: it was like breathing in acid fumes.

Suddenly there was a crack to his right: the sound of foliage being crushed. He turned and instantly fired; he was rewarded with a heavy thud as his bolt found its target. There was a cry of pain and something hit the ground.

"Nailed you, you bitch!" he muttered gleefully.

He moved through the red mist, searching for the corpse of his enemy. In a few seconds, he reached the point of the impact. He listened carefully, but there was nothing to be heard. Tentatively, he reached out his hand.

His fingers found the flights of his bolt, and he smiled as he slid them down the shaft. He froze in horror as his fingers encountered the rough bark of a tree. He realized the trap instantly.

"Oh, shit."

Dethen fired his crossbow from barely a foot away. The bolt struck the bandit forcefully in the forehead, just above the eyes. Though still accelerating, the force of the bolt was enough to penetrate his skull. His face contorted in dreadful pain as his trigeminal nerve was pierced. Unconsciousness mercifully took him as the cerebral hemispheres jarred at the rear of his skull. He fell backward to the forest floor, thankfully oblivious of his hemorrhaging brain.

Dethen stood up, looming out of the fog to his full height of seven feet. He smiled grimly. Within him, Jaad rejoiced, in the grip of blood-lust. Dethen's mind now felt focused, his body agile and sharp.

"And now it is time for Mendaz," he said, moving toward the waterfall.

Within a few minutes he reached his destination. He pressed his left index finger to his lip, and his aura glowed blue. Striding into the falling water, not a drop touched him as his aura deflected it. He stepped into the cavern beyond the waterfall.

A warning of his presence echoed through the passage immediately. It took a few seconds before his eyes adjusted to the dim light. He stepped forward to see the vague outline of a man a few yards away.

"It's okay—it's only Mendaz's half-wit son!" the guard shouted.

The fragment of Jaad within Dethen fumed with anger. He recognized the voice; it was a man under whose boot Jaad had suffered many times.

He advanced upon the man, his eyes boring into the guard's in the half-light. The guard suddenly realized how differently the half-wit was behaving. He moved forward, curious.

"So you're back, are you?" he snickered. "Have to say, my boot missed your backside."

He threw a slap at Dethen's face, putting his weight behind it. Dethen caught it easily in a vice-like grip.

"This is for Jaad!" he whispered with venom.

"Wait a minute, you're not…" the guard began, his face ashen.

He screamed as Dethen snapped his wrist. With his other hand Dethen grabbed the guard's throat. His powerful fingers wrapped around the guard's windpipe, penetrating through his skin. With a tearing sound, Dethen ripped the guard's trachea from his throat.

Blood sprayed from the guard's arteries as he stood in shock, staring at the remnants of his throat in Dethen's hand. He tried to breathe, but a loud and painful gurgling resulted. He collapsed, choking in agony.

Dethen stared down at the body in contempt. He bent down to wipe his hand on the writhing man's shirt. Then he stood up and strode purposefully into the cavern. There was no light source, but as he concentrated, *Widowmaker's* garnet flared red at his hip, illuminating the cavern in a small radius.

"Come and get it, cretin," he heard Raahd's voice from deep within the darkness.

Dethen moved forward, but suddenly perceived he had enemies behind him. He turned to see two soldiers pressed up against the walls to the side of the entrance. They both attacked immediately.

The first man jumped forward, thrusting a knife at Dethen's heart. Dethen slipped to the side of the blade and grasped the man's arm with his hand. He crashed a *mawashi-empi* elbow strike into his assailant's face, shattering the assailant's cheekbone. Dethen twisted the man's elbow downward; a moment later his knee smashed through the joint, snapping it.

He allowed the man to fall and turned to face the next soldier. The man lunged with a barbaric iron-tipped spear. Dethen utilized his *tai-sabaki,* slipping to the side of the weapon. With both hands on the weapon and Dethen within striking range, the solider had no chance. Dethen attacked with *nuketé*, thrusting his second and third fingers through his opponent's eyes and into his brain. The soldier's body spasmed once, and then fell to the floor, dead.

A third attacker slid from the dense shadows and landed a hook punch on Dethen's jaw. It sent him crashing to the ground. The black magician cursed with anger. He arched his back and flipped to his feet before his assailant could strike again.

The soldier attacked with another punch; Dethen moved quickly to block it. Too late, he realized the man's palm concealed a black dirk. The weapon sliced into Dethen's left forearm, biting deeply. He grunted in pain and lashed out with a side kick to the soldier's knee cap. His opponent's patella snapped audibly; the man screamed and doubled up. Dethen followed through with an elbow strike to the nape of the neck, severing the spine between the second and third vertebrae. The bandit instantly lost consciousness and fell to the floor, dying slowly from respiratory paralysis.

"Shoot!" Raahd's voice commanded as he backed away from *Widowmaker's* circle of light.

Fenrin slipped from behind a boulder and aimed his crossbow. He fired without giving his enemy a chance to react. The bolt sped through the air, directly for Dethen's heart. Dethen just had time to make the Sign of Harpocrates. His aura glowed an intense blue, and the bolt slowed as it hit his aura, moving as though through viscous liquid. It deflected away from his heart, but skimmed the skin by the floating ribs, drawing blood through his robes.

He closed the distance between himself and Raahd. He stopped a few feet from the terrified leader. Fenrin laid down his crossbow in surrender; he was not eager to attack the black mage.

"Come on, Raahd," Dethen whispered, his voice goading. "How many times did you tell my father I should be put out of my misery? Now's your chance!"

Raahd's hand clenched in fear by his side as he contemplated drawing his sword.

"I will be the death of you, half-wit!" he snarled.

Dethen's smile was cruelly patronizing. "I await your convenience."

Raahd shook with rage but Dethen's gaze rooted him to the spot: he felt paralyzed.

"You are a dead man, anyway," Dethen said. "You may as well try."

Raahd shouted a *kiai* and then moved. The longsword cleared its scabbard and accelerated into a striking position. Dethen watched nonchalantly until the tip of the sword had completely cleared the scabbard. He then moved like lightning, drawing the scarlet blade of *Widowmaker* in a flash. He parried the blow, throwing out a flash of blue sparks as the swords met.

"No, Raahd. Anger is a weakness, not a strength!"

The mercenary's eyes flamed even more. He swung his sword in an arc intended to decapitate his opponent. With incredible speed Dethen brought *Widowmaker* to bear. Raahd's sword was ripped from his hand. Dethen paused before following through.

His eyes met Raahd's. "May your next life be more productive than this one."

Raahd bowed his head, accepting these final words. *Widowmaker* slashed across his abdomen. Raahd was dead before he hit the ground.

Fenrin was the last man alive. In fear, he grabbed his cross bow back up.

"There is no need for such violence," Dethen said. "I have no quarrel with you." He paused. "Unless you wish to create one."

Fenrin dropped the cross bow.

Fenrin watched in apprehension as the Black Adept's sinister figure stepped back into the cavern, his arms loaded with a stack of firewood.

"Can I help you?" he asked nervously.

Dethen remained silent as he dropped the wood.

"Should I collect some tinder?" Fenrin asked.

"No."

Dethen knelt down to the pile and put out his fingers. Quasi-electrical sparks leapt from them, and the wood roared into flames. Fenrin stared in disbelief; it seemed he could see tiny creatures of flame darting in and out of the wood. No smoke rose from the burning mass.

"Who are you?" Fenrin asked. "I saw you in a vision before you arrived."

The black mage seated himself and crossed his legs.

"I am Dethen."

"The Black One of the Second Aeon?"

"Quite probably."

Fenrin licked his lips nervously.

"Have you returned to release the Dark Mistress of the Tower?"

"Perhaps."

Fenrin was suddenly startled as a huge, menacing shape entered the cavern. He gasped as Graymist moved forward; he reached for his crossbow.

"No!" Dethen commanded. Fenrin froze.

The demon growled threateningly, and dropped the much smaller wolf it carried.

"Eat," Dethen said. Graymist lay down next to him.

"Will you not join me?" Fenrin asked as he pulled out his skinning knife.

Dethen shook his head. He didn't eat meat, though it wasn't for ethical reasons.

"You control demons," Fenrin said. "The songs say you are full of evil and darkness."

"No doubt they're true. Have no concerns. You will suffer no harm from me."

"You were Jaad. You know I always treated him right. Never once did I strike the lad!"

Dethen smiled, but there was a vicious edge to it.

"That's why you are alive," he said. "Where is Mendaz? He is the last one I seek. And the most important."

"He has gone to Gorom. He searches for you," said Fenrin. "He seeks information about you at the Yellow School. Waste of time, I say. The Yellow School is weak and stupid."

"You are weak and stupid," Dethen said. "The Yellow School certainly is not. It has always been the strongest of the three schools, and the most organized. If they ever chose sides, no one would stand against them."

Fenrin stared at the ground, reprimanded. "Mendaz thinks you were killed by a Yellow School initiate."

"I almost was. When did my father leave?"

"Last night."

"Then he has a head start on me," Dethen said. He turned to Graymist. "Seek out my father in Gorom." He impressed an image of Mendaz on the demon. "Take him alive and guard him for me. But don't kill him. Mendaz must die by my own hand."

Graymist snarled and loped out of the cavern.

Dethen's black eyes bored into Fenrin. "It seems my first goal lies in Gorom. But my next lies far to the west in the wilderness. Tell me, what do you know of this creature called the Warlock?"

7

Enya
Yesod of Yetzirah
City of Gorom

By Void, I mean that which has no beginning and no end. Attaining this principle means not attaining the principle. The Way of strategy is the Way of nature. When you appreciate the power of nature, knowing the rhythm of any situation, you will be able to hit the enemy naturally and strike naturally. All this is the Way of Void.

—Miyamoto Musashi

If you master the principles of swordfencing, when you freely beat one man, you beat any man in the world. The spirit of defeating a man is the same for ten million men.... In my strategy, one man is the same as ten thousand, so this strategy is the complete warrior's craft.

—Miyamoto Musashi

Cassius stumbled into the dingy room and collapsed into a dilapidated armchair. He rubbed his tired eyes and groaned; he was too exhausted to light the beckoning oil lamp.

For four hours he had scoured Gorom for Lena; he was mentally and physically exhausted. The city was huge, and the sights of degradation and debauchery that thrived here had taken their toll on him; he felt weak with contempt.

He had seen slave markets, open-air brothels, and arenas of battle where the accused were ripped limb from limb by beasts, regardless of innocence or guilt. There were thieves and assassins, rare and exotic narcotics, all available on the city streets. To have an enemy viciously murdered was commonplace in Gorom, and considered perfectly legal, but for a beggar to steal a loaf of bread was rewarded by the arena.

Even more harrowing had been the legion of temples. They were dedicated to a multitude of evil, sinister powers that he didn't recognize. In every one, a huge statue of the Dark Goddess overlooked the proceedings: Lilith. On this night of the month, as daylight succumbed to the blackness of Dark Moon, the temple floors ran deep with the crimson color of blood. Some sacrifices were voluntary, most of them not, but it made no difference to the chanting crowds. They hoped to appease their mistress, to assuage her terrible wrath, which was unleashed at every Dark Moon.

A sick rage had built up inside Cassius. He wanted to raze the entire city to the ground. He knew that the fate of Sophia would become that of Gorom if the Warlock ever gained control.

Pushing himself up, he walked over to the bowl of water he'd prepared earlier. He splashed the cold liquid over himself, washing the dust and grime from his face. He reached blindly for the towel and dried himself. Soon he would have to continue his search.

Where's that damned earth elemental? he thought irritably.

An eerie red light tinged the gloom of the room. He walked over to the window. Gorom spread itself before him like a contagious disease. Poorly constructed from cheap wood, the buildings were decrepit and scorched; narrow and thin, they reached three to four stories into the air.

The streets—narrow and claustrophobic, an architect's nightmare—formed a mishmash pattern that offended the eye. Many of the buildings slouched against each other, leaning across the street to form dark, foreboding passages. It seemed that if one building was pushed, the whole city would collapse like ten thousand dominoes.

The sky, which had gradually shifted from dark purple to midnight black, was now a vivid scarlet. Below, red mist formed in the city streets. Cassius tensed: he knew the nightmare was about to begin. People rushed for the cover of their homes. The black-uniformed guards grudgingly took up defensive positions to protect the rich.

Cassius looked down as he felt a tug on his leggings. He scowled as he saw Squint's miniature frame standing behind him.

"Where the hell have you been?!" he demanded angrily. "I've been searching for hours!"

The gnome jumped up and down excitedly, squeaking in a strange language.

"You've found Lena?"

Squint winked and started running towards the door, his little legs pumping rapidly back and forth and his belly wobbling; in a second he passed straight though it. Cassius muttered to himself, then followed him.

A minute later he was galloping through the dark, dangerous streets of Gorom. The red mist thickened as he rode. Half-formed creatures lurked within it, but the Dark Moon had not yet fully risen and Cassius remained unchallenged.

Squint clung to the steed's mane, his obese body bouncing up and down. As they approached the end of the street he released his grasp to point; he gave a strangled cry as a bump catapulted him from the horse's neck and over Cassius' head.

Cassius swore. "Damned elemental!"

He swerved right into the next street. A moment later, Squint appeared on the top of a building in front of him. The elemental sulkily rubbed his rear but stopped when he saw Cassius tearing toward him. He pointed into a dark alley and started to jump up and down, more urgency in his manner.

Cassius spurred his mount on, praying he wasn't too late.

Lena paused as she approached the huge, rusty iron gates of Gorom. Looking up, she was overawed by the colossal hexagonal wall that surrounded the once-peaceful city. The battlements were fortified with vicious-looking spikes that pointed outward to repel scaling attempts.

Lena was within a steady flow of people who sought to enter the relative sanctity of the city, on this most dangerous of nights. The odors of stale sweat and pungent spices mingled in the crowd, producing an overpowering stench.

Soon Lena realized she was attracting unwelcome attention from the men. Bast sat balanced on her shoulder, hissing at anyone who looked at her. The familiar was no bigger than a house cat at present, but her muscular body and alien green eyes were enough to intimidate even the most lecherous. Lena tucked in her long black hair and pulled her hood over her head. She stroked Bast soothingly, and in a few moments the familiar stopped threatening the crowd and purred contentedly

Lena wondered where Squint was. She hadn't seen the gnome for several days, though this wasn't unusual. Sometimes he would disappear for weeks at a time, playing with other elementals on his native plane. He usually turned up when he was bored, or to antagonize Bast.

Probably best he's not here, Lena thought.

Scuffles broke out in the crowd around her as the people became impatient. To be caught outside with no protection would mean certain death at Dark Moon. Lena palmed her dagger, just in case it was needed. She held her ebony quarter-staff in her left hand, but it was always useful to have a backup. She ran her fingers gently over the inscribed marks on the dagger's hilt. It had once been her mother's dagger. Yhana had tried to kill her with it the night she left the Yellow School sanctuary. Once, many years ago, Yhana had killed a young woman with the weapon after delivering her baby. Lena remembered her mother telling her the story, knowing it would frighten her.

She wondered whether Yhana was alive. It was two weeks since her mother had attacked her. Bast had interceded, pouncing on Yhana and maiming her, but Lena had no idea whether Bast had killed her mother or left her wounded. She looked at the familiar quizzically. Bast's jade eyes glittered with an incomprehensible intelligence.

"So did you kill her?" Lena asked.

She knew Bast was aware of what she was thinking; the familiar had a strange telepathic ability that she could use on her master and mistress. Very little was known about Bast; though the familiar was at least as intelligent as a human, she rarely communicated in any way. Even Malak had known little about his familiar's abilities after three lifetimes with her. The only thing that was certain was Bast's absolute loyalty to both her master and mistress.

"Well? Did you?"

Bast tilted her head and licked Lena's face with a sandpaper tongue.

"You're not going to tell me, are you?"

Bast swatted her face playfully and made a peculiar coughing sound, which Lena had long ago presumed to be a laugh; it was a strange sound to come from a cat. People in the crowd stared at Lena now, wondering why she was talking to her cat.

"We'll continue this interrogation later," she whispered.

Bast made the coughing sound again and nuzzled her cheek.

Within a few minutes she reached the enormous gates. She was thankful: the proximity of the crowd made her claustrophobic.

There were several guards at the gates, assigned to check incoming travelers. The one who approached Lena was a small, greasy man, his body too small for the chain mail armor that hung from him.

He pulled back her hood, and leered menacingly.

"What's ya business, wench?"

Lena fought her strong repugnance.

"I need to rest for two nights."

"Sure you're not a new recruit for one o' the brothels?"

Lena's eyes flared with fury; her hands flexed on her staff as she considered ramming it into his groin. Bast snarled viciously, a chilling sound. The guard stepped back, uncertain which creature was more dangerous—the woman or the cat.

"No offense meant, madam," he said uncertainly, taken aback by the intensity of her stare. "Well, it's two coins to enter, and maybe I'll waver the coin for that staff there you're carrying."

Lena frowned and pulled three copper coins from her belt purse.

"Don't do me any favors," she said icily.

The guard tentatively took the coins, tipping his helmet courteously.

Lena stepped forward into Gorom. It was the first city she'd seen in her present life, and she was shocked by what she saw. The city spread out before her like a terminal infection, its buildings an amalgam of cheap wood and crude bricks, many of them derelict or fire-damaged. Idols of bizarre gods and demons, some stained with blood, stood like sentinels on every street corner.

Even from the outer edge of the city, the smell was overwhelming; such a bizarre mixture, it was difficult to identify exactly what formed it, but the main ingredient was obvious—filth and squalor. There were no sanitary facilities in Gorom, except for the River Wye, which was thick with brown sludge and waste.

As she made her way into the town proper, Lena felt conspicuous; though her yellow robes were travel-stained, they were fresh and clean compared to the general populace. Already she attracted glances of attention. The city's inhabitants were rugged and tough, all of them armed. The true mercenaries and soldiers, intolerant and haughty professionals, were easily recognizable by their chain-mail vestments.

Dusk broke on the city; the purple sky began to darken. Lena knew she had to find shelter for the night. She had a suspicion that the city would sleep little tonight—armed guards prowled everywhere, waiting for the horror that the night would bring.

She walked for some distance, searching for an inn with space available. She soon realized the futility of the situation—every inn had a queue reaching halfway down the street. It was obvious that even those near the front of the queue would be turned away. Her plan had been to find the Yellow School temple and seek shelter there. Technically, she was still a Yellow School initiate and there was no reason why she shouldn't be welcomed, since she knew the necessary password, but the Yellow School temple was somewhere in the north of the city, and it would take half an hour to cross Gorom. She looked up at the rapidly darkening sky and realized she had nowhere near that much time.

She cast her gaze around.

Think, Lena! Think!

People dashed past her on all sides, seeking the safety of their homes. Those not native to Gorom stood haplessly in the queues, uncertain what to do. They had entered Gorom seeking haven, and unless they were loaded with coin, they found none. Lena was determined not to become another naive victim. She wouldn't allow it to happen.

Her eyes settled on two men who stood watching her from across the street, casually leaning against a door. One was tall, the other rather short. They joked about something as they watched her; she didn't care to know what, but she was willing to risk anything in order to find shelter. She fought her way through the crowd to them.

"Excuse me, are you two native to the city?" It seemed a stupid question but she had to start with something.

"That we are, sweetheart. But you're not," said the tall man. He looked to his friend and they chuckled like school boys.

"I'm looking for shelter. Can you tell me where I can go? I can pay well for it."

"Unless your coin is gold, you won't buy shelter tonight," said the short one. "Unless you have other wares to sell." His eyes flashed down her body, her developed figure conspicuous even through her robes.

Lena scowled. "I'm a Yellow Adept," she lied. "I would never sink to such a level."

"Pity."

"Pity," agreed the tall man. "Looks like you'll have to take your chances outside."

"Are you sure?" she asked, her eyes intense. Bast leaned forward on her shoulder and growled. The sound would have fitted a tiger rather than a cat. The two men suddenly became attentive.

"You could try the *Murky Chasm*," said the short man quickly. "It's about five minutes down the street. That's the only place you'll find with room to spare. But the patrons in there can be more dangerous than Lilith's minions."

The tall man chuckled, nervously eyeing Bast. "It draws the scum of the city like a magnet. Thieves, assassins, bandits. They're the only ones who dare enter. They keep company with their own sort."

"Highest body count in Gorom," said his friend.

"Body count?"

The short man grinned, showing blackened teeth. "Number of kills a night. They all end up in the Wye, floating away downstream. The back door opens onto the river, see."

"But if you're a Yellow Adept, you might be safe," said the tall man. "Of course a pretty woman like you will get noticed real quick. The only pretty girls in there are working, and most often they get no money for it. Slaves you see."

Lena's eyes narrowed in disgust. "Thank you," she said coldly.

"Sure you don't want to stay with us?" asked the short man. He reached out to brush back her hood. "Course, you'd have to play with us, but it'd be a fair sight safer."

Bast's claw lashed out, gouging a deep wound in his hand. She jumped down from Lena's shoulder and pinned the man against the door, snarling.

"Ahhhh! That's not a cat, it's a demon!" the wounded man shouted. The taller man backed away quickly, just in case his friend further aggravated the familiar.

Lena smiled with satisfaction. "Come, Bast. We have an inn to find."

She turned and continued her walk down the street. Bast glared at the cornered man and then retracted her claws. She loped after her mistress.

The sky was scarlet now. Lena knew she had only minutes before the horror of Dark Moon was released. Others around her panicked, running in any direction. Those native to Gorom had already retired to their homes.

A sign creaked irritatingly in the wind. Lena looked up and smiled grimly. It was the *Murky Chasm*. Several travelers tried to force their way through the door as she approached. There was a scream, and suddenly they fell back, running for shelter elsewhere. Lena realized why: two men lay dying on the doorstep, brutally repelled by the huge bouncer.

She tightened her grip on her staff and strode toward the door. The bouncer loomed in front of her, amused by her audacity.

"This here building's off limits, missy," he said. "Move on."

Lena felt physically exhausted after walking all day, but she focused her mind to unleash her magical energy. She had barely a trickle to spare; the Dark Moon worked against her. A more subtle approach was necessary, she realized.

The bouncer paused as she reached out to touch his mind, gently manipulating his perceptions. His will was surprisingly strong, but his resistance lasted only a second. He looked confused, as if unsure what he was doing. Lena stepped over the bodies and quickly slipped past his bulk and into the tavern.

The tavern's main room was dingy, the corners so full of shadows it was impossible to guess what lurked in them. The smell of tobacco and marijuana melded with the bitter odor of opium. Lena blinked her eyes, irritated by the thick smoke.

She walked over to the bar, feeling the attention of many eyes on her body. The atmosphere was tense and expectant. Few people talked; most of the patrons sat by themselves, losing themselves in the forgetfulness of narcotics. The room was quite empty considering the mad rush outside. Lena couldn't help noticing two bodies, one slumped over a table, another lying on the floor, staring lifelessly at the ceiling.

The barman walked over to her. He was a small but very broad man with a bald head. He ran his eyes up and down her, but the smug attitude of those outside didn't materialize. She realized it was because she'd passed his bouncer unharmed; it gave her the right to enter his tavern.

"What you want?" he growled, pulling his pipe from his mouth to speak.

"A room," she said, "for two nights. Until the moon phase has ended."

He scoffed. "You think I have rooms at this time of the month? They're full. Packed twenty a room. But you can stay in here if you want." He gestured with his hand to indicate the main room.

"How much?"

He shrugged. "To a pretty lady like you, nothing."

"Spare your charity," Lena said icily, leaving a silver piece on the bar. "And give me a cup of water."

The barman raised an eyebrow, surprised. "You have backbone, miss." He smiled, somewhat callously. "But there again, you might need it in here if they act up."

Lena took the mug of water and retired to a vacant table close to the exit, her back against the wall. Bast settled in the middle of the table, eyes closed but ears tracking the room as she dozed. The gaze of some of the patrons lingered on Lena for some minutes, but eventually their attention died away. Despite what the two men had told her, there were no women in the tavern. It seemed the men had no drive for such activities on this night. They simply sought to lose themselves in drugs or spirits. She smiled wryly; it was probably the safest night of the month, since no one had the desire for violence, either.

She took a sip from her water. It tasted bitter, and the mug was dirty, but she was too thirsty to care.

"Close the door!" bellowed the barman. The bouncer stepped back inside the tavern and slammed the door shut, dropping a heavy wooden bar to reinforce it. The wind whistled apprehensively.

Lena's attention was drawn to a group of men across the other side of the room. There were at least a dozen of them, perhaps soldiers or bandits. One of them seemed to be staring at her, though it was difficult to tell in the gloom. The stare wasn't the usual lecherous glance she received. It was a stare of hatred. She pulled her hood over her head and looked away.

She sipped the water, brooding upon her situation. Her plan was to reach the Celestial Tower. She was bound to find some answers to her questions there. Her objective was simple: to find Malak. The Celestial Tower was the only place she could think to search for him. She yearned to be reunited with her husband; without him she felt empty. They had been separated in time for a thousand years, but the real length of time seemed much greater than this.

Adjusting to the new Enya was difficult for Lena. In her previous life, her natural personality had been one of joy, admiring beauty and nature, but her experiences as Fiona had changed her. She had never been weak in spirit: even when brought up with the White Adepts, who were almost pacifists, she had had no lack of courage. However, through Fiona's experiences with Yhana she now had a far deeper strength.

Her self-sacrifice to Lilith had also greatly strengthened her. The pain and suffering she had experienced in that immeasurable time in the Qlippoth made physical anguish appear transient and unreal. Yet in another way, the experience had weakened her, because the mere mention of Lilith was enough to send icy pains through her body. She feared the Arch-Demon with every fiber of her essence.

Outside, the wind shrieked as Lilith's essence crept over Enya, covering it like a quilt. Wolves bayed in the distance as they gathered into hunting packs. Lena shuddered violently.

A deep guttural growl suddenly infiltrated the room. Bast's eyes flicked open, her black pupils in narrowed alarm. She hissed to her mistress; Lena immediately knew there was danger present. The room fell silent as the patrons realized the sound came from just outside the door. Several laid their hands on their weapons. The sound was unusual even for Dark Moon.

The door rattled gently, and then more violently. A growl of frustration filtered through.

"Move on," muttered the bouncer. "Nothing interesting in here. Move on." He gripped a vicious looking battle hammer in his hand.

But the creature outside had obviously chosen the *Murky Chasm* for a purpose.

"It's after us, Mendaz!" said one the group of bandits. "Remember what Fenrin said! He said we'd die in Gorom!"

"Quiet!" hissed the leader. His hostile gaze still studied Lena.

The door rattled again, this time so violently the wood bent under the strain. Then it fell quiet.

The bouncer grinned. "Can't get in."

Mist exuded through the gap under the door, feeling its way into the tavern. The bouncer stepped back, confused. The mist coagulated into a form, steadily growing as the mist fed it.

"It's a wolf," said the barman.

The bouncer shook his head. "That's not one of Lilith's beasts."

The wolf was huge, standing well above waist level. As the last of the mist entered it, it opened its eyes. They were red, loaded with hatred. Lena gasped as she recognized the creature she had unwittingly created only two weeks before. It had pursued Jaad, intent on killing him.

Bast reacted first. She leapt at the demon, her claws ready to strike. The wolf swatted her away with tremendous power, unperturbed with her small size. Bast crashed into the wall, landing heavily. She didn't move from where she landed.

"So you like to bully pussy cats, do you?" the bouncer said. "Try some of this!"

He stepped forward and brought the battle hammer forcefully down on the demon's skull. The weapon passed straight through the beast's head, and the bouncer stumbled forward, his balance toppled by the lack of impact. The wolf pounced, ripping the bouncer's throat out with stained yellow canines. The blood sprayed across the demon's rippling, incorporeal gray coat.

"Harpocrates help us," muttered the barman, backing away.

For a moment there was silence. The wolf scanned the tavern as if searching. The patrons didn't dare move. Then the beast leaped forward, running for the group of bandits. Chaos gripped the room. Tables and drinks were scattered as the men reached for their weapons or dashed for the back exit. One of the bandits stabbed at the wolf with a long sword. The blade slipped through the wolf's body, meeting no resistance. The beast smashed him out of the way, intent on one goal. Mendaz slowly backed away, realizing he was the prey.

The wolf pounced, knocking him to the floor. Mendaz kicked and punched, but none of the blows had any effect. Fear paralyzed him as the red eyes bored into him, seeking to quench his will. The other bandits attacked with swords, fists, and chairs but none of these had any effect. The beast didn't even notice their feeble assault.

Momentarily in the grip of shock, Lena realized she couldn't stand by and watch the beast kill. She had created the creature, and her conscience felt responsible for its actions.

She kicked her table out the way and pulled out her dagger. Moving closer, she hurled the weapon with all her strength. It was perfectly aimed, piercing the wolf through the throat. She cursed as it emerged out the other side, the demon unscathed.

Mendaz fought like a wild animal, trying to protect his throat. But the demon didn't seem interested in killing him. It pinned him to the floor, slowly hypnotizing him with its awful stare.

Lena closed within a few paces.

"Get out of the way!" she shouted to the attacking bandits.

One of them obeyed her, eager to escape the creature. The others ignored her, intent on saving their leader.

"Move!" she demanded.

The men ignored her, and she swore. "You were warned!"

She formed the Sign of Horus, focusing every ounce of power into a single blast. The blast wave struck the skirmishing group. The men reeled away, smashing into tables and walls. The wolf was knocked from Mendaz to land a few feet away.

The demon turned around to stare at her, its scarlet eyes furious. Lena realized her mistake. She had only managed to annoy the creature; due to the Dark Moon her blast had caused it no injury at all. She was physically and psychically exhausted, but she held its terrible gaze as it prepared to pounce on her.

Suddenly the beast paused, uncertain. It recognized its creator. It snarled and moved forward to seize Mendaz, intent on carrying him away.

"No!" Lena commanded. She stepped forward to block its path.

The beast snarled viciously, and the tavern fell silent again. The patrons held their breath as the demon stared at Lena, unsure what to do.

Then the beast snarled and ran toward the exit. It disappeared under the door in a cloud of mist.

Lena's legs suddenly gave way, and she staggered forward to catch her balance with a table. A moment later she felt a gentle hand on her shoulder. It was the man she had saved.

He smiled at her. "I am Mendaz. At your service. Let me help you sit."

"I'm all right. I can sit myself," Lena said, but he didn't remove his hand until he had guided her to a chair.

He sat opposite her. "Let me replace your drink. It seems yours was spilled in the melee. What were you drinking?"

"Water," she said, too tired to resist his forced hospitality. She could barely keep her eyes open: the blast of energy she had released had utterly exhausted her.

Mendaz raised an eyebrow. "Very exotic. Barman! Fetch me a mug of water. And make it clean!"

"Yes, Mendaz."

The tavern gradually returned to normal as the patrons relaxed.

"Set the tables and chairs straight," Mendaz ordered his men. "And bring the lady's dagger here." He looked at Lena. "May I ask your name? I don't normally associate with my enemies from the Yellow School, but I think I can make an exception here."

"I am..." Lena paused; even in her sheltered upbringing in the Enchanted Forest she'd been told about the Summoning. To use her real name was inviting trouble. "I am Fiona."

The barman placed a cup of water down for her and a mug of ale for Mendaz. "Well done, miss," he said, his voice gruff. "I thought that beast would take us all."

"Leave us," Mendaz ordered, dismissing him with a shake of the hand.

"Yes, Mendaz."

Lena realized that Mendaz commanded a great deal of respect; it seemed likely he was a very skilled warrior. Some of his men stood almost in awe of him.

One of the men handed Lena's dagger to him. Despite her fatigue, she noticed the instant change in his expression. She tried to force herself back to alertness. She sensed more danger here.

Mendaz smiled, a predatory gesture. Lena noticed how changeable his eyes were; she sensed the same unpredictability in his aura.

He laid the dagger on the table before him and took out his own, placing the two weapons side by side. Lena's eyes widened. The inscriptions on the daggers were the same.

"The mark of my band," Mendaz said, almost conversationally, but his eyes were dangerous. "Tell me, where did you get this dagger?"

Lena looked at him groggily. It dawned on her that he had called the Yellow School his enemy, but still she had no idea what was going on.

"It was my mother's," she said carefully.

Mendaz nodded. "And was your mother a Yellow Adept too?"

Lena nodded but volunteered no more information.

"You mother was short, with blonde hair. Quite ugly?"

Lena hesitated, unsure whether lying would plunge her into deeper trouble.

"My mother was blonde. And, yes, she was unattractive."

Mendaz picked up Lena's dagger, studying it carefully. "This belonged to a man under my command who died over twenty years ago." Lena became anxious; the tone of his voice was like the subtle building of a storm. "It was your mother who took this from him. And it was your mother who killed my wife."

He looked at her, and there was more hatred in his eyes than Lena had seen in the wolf that attacked him. The intensity of the stare made her shudder.

"I have waited a long time for this," he said quietly.

Suddenly he was upon Lena. She barely saw him move before the dagger was poised at her throat. He held her roughly by the hair, restraining her movement. Lena felt fear, but was too tired to resist. She was almost ready to give in simply to gain some rest.

"We've met before," he whispered in her ear. "Your mother was pregnant with you when she entered my cavern all those years ago."

He twisted the fistful of hair.

"Strange how you should walk straight into my arms," Mendaz said. "I knew there was something to find in Gorom. I don't have the second sight like Fenrin, but I know when something feels right. We were fated to meet like this, you and me."

Lena struggled feebly in his grip. "I have done you no harm."

"No harm?" Mendaz laughed, then his grip became vicious. "Janus! Get yourself over here, boy!"

A young man detached himself from the bandit group and quickly walked over.

"Is this her?" Mendaz asked. "Is this the one who attacked you?"

Lena groaned. It was the guard she had stunned two weeks ago when searching for Jaad.

Janus' eyes widened in recognition. "That's her, Mendaz! I'd never forget a face like that. She's a looker!"

Mendaz smiled maliciously. "You see, my pretty. You have done a great deal of harm to me. You were the one who attacked my son."

He pressed his rough cheek against Lena's; she shuddered at the intimacy of the position, but didn't dare to move. The other patrons of the tavern watched with interest. None of them were likely to interfere.

Suddenly a growl came from the table. Lena looked down to see Bast, the familiar's eyes focused intently on Mendaz. She clawed a deep gash in the table.

"One move and I'll slit her throat!" Mendaz shouted.

Bast hissed.

"If you think I'm not quick enough, just try it," Mendaz challenged. "Let's go for it!"

Bast glared at him, body tensed like a spring about to be released. But her eyes dropped to the dagger at Lena's throat and she stayed still.

Mendaz laughed. "I thought not. You're a clever pussy, aren't you?"

Again, Bast seemed ready to tear out his throat.

"What happened to my son?" he asked. "Where is Jaad?"

"I don't know," Lena said. "I haven't seen him since that night."

Mendaz pushed the dagger against her throat with more force, drawing a line of blood on her slender neck. She didn't give him the satisfaction of showing the pain.

"Is he alive?"

"I don't know, but I didn't kill him. He ran from me. The wolf demon that just attacked you was chasing him."

Mendaz looked thoughtful.

"If he lives, then you might find your son to be quite different," Lena said. She couldn't think of two people more different than Jaad and Dethen.

Bast snarled again, barely able to resist attacking.

"I will kill her no matter what you do," Mendaz said. "I've waited half my life to avenge my wife. Now it seems I avenge my wife and son at the same time." He smiled. "Goodbye, Fiona."

Suddenly the door rattled. Mendaz paused. The room fell silent.

"That damned wolf," said the barman, backing away.

"Open the door!" shouted a voice from outside.

"Who the hell would be out in that?!" Mendaz asked. The wind shrieked in agony outside, and wolves howled as they hunted those without shelter.

Bast leaped down from the table and ran over to the door. She jumped as she reached it, dislodging the wooden bar that held the door shut. The door swung open and a warrior with silver-gray hair and mustache stepped inside. His pale blue eyes narrowed in anger as he saw Lena's predicament.

"Release her!" he ordered.

"Who the hell are you?" Mendaz demanded.

"Cassius Hawkin of Sophia. Release her or I'll take her by force!"

"Prince Cassius Hawkin? Right. And I'm the Warlock. Take care of him." Mendaz waved his men over.

Cassius held his ground as the eight men advanced on him in a line, their swords drawn and raised. The anger disappeared from his eyes as they approached. A calm sense of detachment washed over him. Mendaz and Lena were the only ones to notice his relaxed, confident stance.

The line suddenly rushed him. Cassius drew his katana with breathtaking speed, slicing the first man before he could react. He spun counter-clockwise into the next, stabbing the sword under his armpit to attack behind. Without pausing, he reversed his spin to whirl away. He now stood on the other side of their line.

The bandits turned in disbelief. Their enemy's attack had been far too quick and fluid for them to react.

"Run him through!" Mendaz bellowed.

Cassius changed the grip on his katana to one-handed, and drew his wakizashi with his left hand. He span both swords in a whirling barrier of steel, forming a defensive shield through which no blade could penetrate. The bandits found their attacks forcefully parried as Cassius moved around the tavern, using tables and supporting pillars for cover. No more than three opponents could reach him at any time.

He used his wakizashi for close range parrying while his katana sliced in tremendous arcs, whistling through the air with a vengeance. He slashed two more opponents, his fine sword biting through their cheap armor. The other bandits stabbed crudely at him, their sword skills pitiful next to his own.

Lena watched in amazement as Cassius moved from side to side, hypnotically weaving like a deadly snake. His movements were as fluid as water, his techniques clinical and precise. He varied the speed of his maneuvers, sometimes moving slowly, other times fast; he even altered the speed of individual attacks when halfway through them, in order to avoid his opponents' parry and to pierce their guard.

He feinted at one opponent with his sword, and threw in a deadly front kick as the guard tried to parry the deceptive sword strike. The ball of his foot impacted forcefully with the soldier's xiphoid, severing it from his ribcage even through his armor. The xiphoid was blasted upward at forty-five degrees, piercing the soldier's heart and killing him instantly. The technique took a fraction of a second, and Cassius immediately spun into his next opponent, clinically decapitating him with his katana.

There were now only two guards standing, and Cassius pushed them back easily. He attacked with speed and strength, yet his mind remained detached. The last two bandits backed off rapidly, heading for the door. Cassius ceased his attack. They immediately bolted from the tavern, more willing to risk the horrors outside than the sword-wielding warrior inside.

Cassius wiped the blade of his wakizashi and slid it back into its scabbard. He turned to Mendaz. The leader's eyes were shocked: he had never seen such a demonstration of iai-jitsu.

"One step and I'll kill her!" he shouted.

Bast jumped onto the table and growled threateningly.

"Really?" said Cassius, advancing menacingly.

"Her mother killed my wife," Mendaz said. "I'll take my vengeance for it, whether you kill me or not!"

"Mendaz, my mother is dead," Lena said, bracing herself as the dagger bit deeper into her throat.

"Dead? By what?"

"By the cat," Lena said. "She was killed two weeks ago. The same time Jaad ran away."

Mendaz's eyes narrowed in suspicion.

"Mendaz, my mother and I are enemies. If you kill me you will be doing her a favor. And take my word for it, Jaad is still alive."

Cassius waited a few feet away, his katana ready to strike.

"How do you know this?" Mendaz asked. "You said you didn't know."

"It would take more than that demon to kill Dethen," Lena said. "Your son is still alive, believe me. Surely you want to live to reconcile your differences with him?"

"Dethen? I do not know that name. Of course I want to reconcile my differences with Jaad. I made his life hell."

Lena grimaced. "If you made his life that bad, then very soon you will understand who Dethen is, because your son will seek you out."

Mendaz shrugged. "You may be lying, but I can't take this risk. If my son is alive, then I must see him."

He released his hold on Lena and gently pushed her away. Bast retracted her claws, but Cassius still held his katana ready.

"I would keep this," Mendaz said, holding up the dagger Lena had owned.

She nodded. "Consider it returned to its owner." She paused. "Seek peace with yourself before Jaad comes to you. There is a Yellow School temple in the city. Speak the password 'Maat' and they will allow you to enter."

"My thanks, Fiona. Perhaps our paths will cross again."

Lena thought of Dethen pursuing him. "I doubt it, Mendaz. I doubt it."

"Are you injured, Lena?" Cassius asked.

"No. Thanks for your help." Lena's eyes suddenly clouded with suspicion. "How do you know who I am?"

8

Planet Tellus
Malkuth of Assiah
Saxon mid-lands

A ship sails and I stand watching 'til she fades on the horizon and someone at my side says, "She is gone." Gone where? Gone from my sight, that is all; she is just as large as when I saw her. The diminished size, the total loss of sight is in me, not in her, and just at that moment when someone at my side says "She is gone," there are others watching her coming, and other voices take up a glad shout "There she comes!" And that is dying.

—Bishop Brent

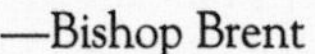

Cheiros entered the dimly lit bed chamber where Ekanar lay resting. He dismissed Thedra with a nod; she rose from the chair and silently slipped from the room.

"Ah, Cheiros," Ekanar said weakly. "You know, the trip from Nippon must've taken more out of me than I thought."

Cheiros smiled sadly and crossed the room to stand beside the bed. He could see that Ekanar's aura had contracted to within a couple of inches of his body; the colors were dark and unwholesome. His face was pale and drawn, and his body shivered in spasms.

Cheiros seated himself. "You must try to rest yourself, old friend."

There was a poignant sadness in his voice that Ekanar immediately recognized.

"What is it? Have you made a decision regarding Shadrack?"

"Yes. But don't worry. He is to be looked after by the Order, though he certainly won't be initiated into it. I was instructed to awaken the Master of the Order."

"Thank the gods. But I thought the Master was just a myth."

"No. All Hierophants are educated in his history. Don't worry, Ghalan will look after him."

Ekanar's strained face relaxed, but Cheiros noticed his aura dim slightly too. For a minute there was silence between the two men. It was broken by the sage.

"Cheiros, what did you find in this Order? What was it that I turned my back on?"

Cheiros smiled to himself in reminiscence.

"When I was initiated into the Inner Order, something beautiful beyond description touched me. It was the most incredible experience: it touched me so deeply that everything else in life came sharply into focus."

"What was it?" Ekanar asked, his eyes full of longing.

"The higher self, or Holy Guardian Angel. And once it has descended, it never quite leaves you. Its support is always there. You retain a sense of calm detachment, and a sense of wholeness. One has a certain...independence from external factors."

"When I last knew you, you were fiery and full of nervous vitality."

"Ah. That gradually changed in the Outer Order, as the elements became balanced in my Sphere of Sensation. By the time I reached the Portal Grade, the balancing was complete."

Ekanar nodded in understanding. "I was wrong to leave. It was the biggest mistake of my life."

He grasped Cheiros by the arm, exhibiting surprising strength.

"It's not too late, is it? Isn't it written that once initiated, a man will always return? I'm committed to the Path. Is that not true?"

Ekanar's eyes were pleading; Cheiros closed his eyes in pain.

"What is it, Cheiros?"

"Ekanar, when I touched your hand earlier, I...I received an impression."

"Impression?"

"Ekanar..." Cheiros's eyes were deep and sorrowful. "You will not live through the night."

The sage panicked. "But...but it's only influenza or pneumonia or something. Surely it can't be that...."

"Ekanar!" Cheiros said gently but firmly. "Please calm yourself. You cannot fight karma."

"What do you mean?" His eyes contained terrible fear.

"You were meant to bring the demon-man Shadrack here, and deliver him to Ghalan."

"But what of my own life and plans? I wish to tread the Path of Return more than anything else: I now know my mistake. How cruel can fate be to end my life now! I will fight this!"

Cheiros took his weak hand and shook his head. "Oh, old friend. Do you not understand? It was just that realization that you were meant to make. By returning here, you have completed the cycle of your life, and recognized your mistake."

"But to what end! Tomorrow I will be dead, and I will not gain that which I now fervently desire!"

"Your soul has now been educated, and what you have learned in this life will stick like a thorn. Bitter lessons are the ones we learn best. If you had stayed at the Order many years ago, you might have become an Adept of average ability. Now you will be something very special in your next life."

"What do you mean?"

"You will carry the lesson you have learned with you. And in the next life, I'm sure you will be the most motivated initiate of whichever Order you join. If this is so, I'm sure you will soar beyond the spiritual level that I have attained."

Ekanar looked shocked for a moment, and then his face slowly broke into a smile.

"You are very wise, Cheiros. I think I understand...."

Cheiros returned his smile. "If you do, then already you have begun your spiritual transformation. Things often appear cruel from our limited perspective. To truly understand, that perspective must be expanded mightily."

Ekanar nodded, and was silent for a while, before saying, "Will my death be painful?"

"No. I believe that you will die peacefully in your sleep. There is nothing to fear."

"What will happen? I mean...when my soul leaves my body."

"For a few days, your astral form will continue to sleep and dream on the astral plane. The astral body will slowly disintegrate, and once this is accomplished, you will be able to ascend the planes. There you may rest, before once again reincarnating."

"I wonder who I'll come back as. It seems an exciting adventure..." the sage mused.

"I will stay here until morning, if you wish."

"That's very kind of you, I'd like that. I think I'll just get some sleep now...."

Cheiros watched his friend with sadness: he knew that Ekanar would never open his eyes again in this life.

Cheiros followed Ghalan down the steps that led to the cathedral's single dungeon. The stairs were narrow and crumbling, covered in fine dust from hundreds of years of disuse; the two men left distinct footprints as they descended. The air was damp and the stale, musty smell was overpowering.

The stairs led down into a cramped chamber, lit by two half-spent flickering torches. The chamber walls, buckled and cracked, produced a myriad of insect-infested fissures and rifts. Thick, silver-gray spider webs cloaked the entire chamber like a delicate fleece. Within them, corpulent arachnids basked lazily, the torch light glittering off their legion of eyes.

The bars of the single cell formed the far wall of the chamber. Posted outside it were two neophytes, a male and a female, who acted as both guards and guardians. They looked anxious, their skin crawling with the proximity of the seething insects and spiders. Relief flooded their faces as the two figures descended the stairs.

Ghalan's intense gaze fell on them. "Leave and refresh yourselves. This tomb is no place for the living. The creatures of earth claimed this place long ago."

The pair quickly exited the claustrophobic passage.

The dense webs had been slashed away from the cell bars, though wisps of gray still clung here and there, quivering in the air currents. Ghalan saw Shadrack lying behind the rusty iron lattice, still bound with iron chains; he murmured incoherently to himself. The two Adepts advanced to within inches of the bars. Shadrack raised his head.

The demon immediately singled out Ghalan as a threat. A low, threatening growl came from its throat, a guttural snarl that no man could possibly make. Its dull red eyes glowed as it roused itself from apathy. Here was a threat to its well-being.

"Magister Templi, I was told by Ekanar that the power of the demon was unleashed fully only once," Cheiros said. "Since then, the possession has been only partial. Ekanar said the chains would not be sufficient to stop the full might of the creature."

Ghalan nodded absently, as if preoccupied. Cheiros realized he was involved in a mental battle with the demon, whose eyes now glowed with frightening intensity. Without breaking eye contact, it shuffled to its feet, leering forward.

Ghalan's gaze became even more focused. It may have been imagination, but to Cheiros he seemed to have grown immensely, as if he had cast away the bounds of his physical body. Cheiros moved back a step as he perceived a scarlet glow in the old man's aura.

He realized that as a Magister Templi, Ghalan had risen above the Sephira of Geburah; he therefore commanded its power. From him flowed the divine wrath of God, the power of Geburah that destroyed evil and iniquity.

The demon looked very dangerous now. The chains creaked and strained as it flexed its body. Yet its stare deflected off Ghalan as if it was insubstantial.

Ghalan's aura flared brighter as he vibrated the divine names of Geburah through it. He used the attacking sign of Horus: he raised his hands to either side of his head and thrust them forward toward the demon, simultaneously stepping forward with his left foot. With his second sight, Cheiros saw the crimson energy burst from Ghalan's aura.

A cry of agony escaped the demon as it staggered back to slump against the rear wall of the cell. The air around Shadrack's body darkened and distorted, as if something sought to escape from him.

Ghalan gave the creature no reprieve. He pulled back his left foot and pressed his left index finger to his lips, forming the sign of Harpocrates. He framed his third-eye chakra in his forehead, touching the tips of his thumbs and index fingers to form a triangle. Visualizing a bright blue pentagram within the triangle, he threw his hands forward, hurling the pentagram at the creature.

The pentagram sped through the cell bars, rapidly growing in size. It was the height of a man when it hit the demon a moment later. The demon roared in anger and pain. Knocked from Shadrack's aura, small black entities writhed in the air before speeding away through the walls, ceiling, and floor.

Shadrack fell forward to smash against the floor.

Without taking his eyes from the demon, Ghalan said: "Open the door, Cheiros."

Staggered by the power Ghalan had just released, Cheiros hesitated for a moment. He remembered himself and moved forward to unlock the cell door; the key turned stiffly in the ancient lock. He watched in fascination as Ghalan entered the cell and advanced upon the demon, which now lay on its back. It had been severely weakened, and it stared up in nefarious hatred at its opponent.

Ghalan stood above the creature, tracing a banishing pentagram from his left hip. Cheiros watched in amazement. The symbol pulsed a brilliant blue with gold sparkles. Its intensity almost blinded his astral vision.

When Ghalan spoke, his voice seemed utterly different. It contained a strength and authority that nothing would dare to defy:

"By the power and might of SHADDAI EL CHAI, God the Omnipotent, I command thou creature of the shells to immediately, and without retribution, leave the body of this child of earth. Seek not to return while he lives within the protection of this Order, or thou shalt be cursed by the divine name of SHADDAI EL CHAI! So mote it be!"

There was a distinct hissing noise like a release of pressure; a black gaseous shadow flowed from Shadrack's body. It streamed across the stone floor towards the two Adepts. Cheiros felt his legs gripped with an icy chill as it passed, but the shadow rolled around Ghalan like a wave passing an island: it didn't have the power or desire to enter his aura.

"Is it exorcised?" Cheiros asked in a choked voice.

Ghalan turned to him; his eyes reverted to a more passive state, as if once again his attention was not entirely focused on the physical plane.

"I have externalized the demon. It will no longer be able to possess him, but it will be able to return to taunt him. However, I suspect that it will only be perceived by Shadrack, since the other Order members are protected."

Shadrack sat with his legs before him, blankly staring at the wall opposite.

"Shadrack," Ghalan said, but he received no answer.

He looked closely, noticing that Shadrack's eyes, once blue, were now a watery gray. They were almost colorless, as if they had been bleached.

Ghalan said: "Remove the chains from his body, Cheiros. We're safe now."

He stepped back a pace as the Adeptus Minor unraveled the chains from the ronin's body. Shadrack didn't even register the

Adept's presence when Cheiros knelt directly in front of him. Neither did he react when Cheiros called his name several times: he seemed oblivious to the two men.

"I think his mind has gone, Magister Templi."

"It has been shattered, but perhaps we can draw the fragments back together."

Ghalan knelt in front of Shadrack, putting his face at the ronin's head level. The facial similarity between the two men suddenly struck Cheiros: they both had a hawk-like, predatory look to them. It was a bizarre coincidence: they could have been mistaken for close relatives.

"Shadrack, can you hear me?" Ghalan asked.

"Ghalan, I do not believe he speaks any of the western tongues," Cheiros said.

Ghalan nodded, and took Shadrack's head between the palms of his hands. He slowly twisted the ronin's head until he stared into his face. Shadrack's eyes suddenly snapped into focus, his expression incredulous.

"Ghalan?" His voice was cracked and hoarse, but the word was unmistakable.

Ghalan and Cheiros exchanged an astonished glance.

"How do you know me, child?" the Magister Templi asked in Hebrew.

"Are you not the..." his eyes became clouded, "Magus?"

"I do not yet have the honor of that grade. What is your name, child?"

"I am Ma...Mal...." He looked confused. "I am Shadrack, the strange one."

Ghalan exchanged another bewildered glance with Cheiros.

"Are you a warrior of some kind, Shadrack?"

"I am sam...I am ronin." He hung his head, and then looked up in puzzlement, the recognition gone from his eyes. "But who are you?"

The Magister Templi stretched out his hand. "I'm Ghalan. I have been chosen to help you. Will you trust me?"

A glimmer of recognition showed in Shadrack's face again.

"Yes...trust."

He grasped Ghalan's hand and weakly fell forward to hug him. "Need help...father...please...help...."

Every man must overcome his own obstacles, expose his own illusions. Yet others may assist him to do both, and they may enable him altogether to avoid many of the false paths, leading no whither, which tempt the weary feet of the uninitiated pilgrim.

—Aleister Crowley

9

Planet Tellus
City of Prenzlau

Ghalan removed the astral seal from Shadrack's quarters and opened the heavy mahogany door. He closed it behind him and scanned the room.

As with all of the cathedral's chambers, the room had once been occupied by monks, though recently renovated. The design was very simple. There was a crude, uncomfortable bed set against the right wall and a rather old, battered set of drawers next to it for personal items. Upon the drawers rested a grimy brass oil lamp that hadn't kindled a flame for decades.

Set against the opposite wall was a respectable library of scientific and occult subjects, most of them incredibly old, and some of them handwritten. The pages were musty and discolored yellow with age, but within them lay the keys to the secrets of the universe.

Next to the sizeable bookcase stood a small pine table and a rickety wooden chair. The final piece of furniture was a black altar, formed of two bonded cubes. Within it was a host of equipment for ritual magick, left behind some years ago by the previous occupant of the room.

Every item in the room was pressed up against the walls, leaving the spacious wooden floor free and uncluttered. It was decorated by a thin rug, once a colorful and priceless gift from Azia, but now worn and faded. A narrow, arched window allowed daylight to seep reluctantly into the room.

Shadrack sat cross-legged in the center of the chamber, head bowed and oblivious to everything about him. His chains had been removed, and he had been dressed in a gray robe, revealing his status as a non-initiate.

His black hair had grown long, and his full beard almost matched Ghalan's unruly specimen. His skin was pale, even for one from the icy land of Nippon. Ghalan found himself amazed at his own physical resemblance to Shadrack. The karmic link between himself and the ronin still had great strength.

And the twin brother, Ghalan reminded himself.

He crossed over to Shadrack and knelt before him. He opened his second sight and studied the ronin's aura. Since the demon had been banished from him, Shadrack had remained quite incoherent. Though he could talk rationally, he was forgetful, and often repeated himself when speaking. He would not suffer anyone other than Ghalan to approach him; besides, no one in the Temple spoke Hebrew or Nipponese fluently enough to communicate with him.

Ghalan was not surprised to see Shadrack's chakras were still disaligned; several of them were wrongly colored as if dysfunctioning. The possession of the demon had taken a terrible toll on his physical, astral, and mental bodies. Ghalan knew that Shadrack had no link to his spiritual body.

In silence, Ghalan restarted the laborious task that he'd undertaken several weeks before. Taking one chakra at a time, he induced the correct function by using his own chakras to induce a sympathetic energy current. The task had to be performed several times a day: Shadrack's etheral body had been severely damaged, and many of the energy flows had been altered. Once the chakras were restored, however, Ghalan knew they would sweep away the blocks like a river collapsing a dam.

After several minutes' work, Shadrack raised his head lethargically. Ghalan knew he had been aware of his presence all along; unfortunately, Shadrack's main character attribute was now apathy. Purely and simply, he cared about nothing.

"There is a yellow glow in my chest," he said.

Ghalan nodded. "That is good. It means your chakras are beginning to respond. Is it an agreeable sensation?"

"It is pleasant."

The Magister Templi continued his work, shifting his attention to the next center of power.

"How do I know you, Ghalan?" Shadrack asked. "Sometimes you are in my thoughts, and I remember. But usually I forget."

"I am an echo from your previous life. Do you know of reincarnation?"

"Yes. But I didn't think it was real. I remember a pink-skied plane, and a tall man who is powerful and full of evil. Most of all, there is a dark-haired woman, who I once thought was very beautiful."

Ghalan paused in his task, his interest aroused: it was the first time that Shadrack had talked about his memories, or attempted to communicate without being asked a question.

"Have you always had these memories?"

"In fragments. But I feel little for them now. My emotions have left me; they are dead. What happened to me in my past life? You must know, if you were a part of it."

Ghalan shook his head. "The situation is more complex than that. To explain it simply, you have incarnated in the past on the plane below Enya. Thus, I was indeed a part of your last life, though only fleetingly. For me, however, that occurrence lies in the future. In my next life, I will be your genetic father. For you, however, that was three lifetimes ago. We are out of time, relative to each other."

"So I may know your future, but you do not know anything of me. If so, where did you gain this knowledge?"

"Strange as it may seem, once my memory is jogged, I can 'remember' fragments of my future as if it were my past. Time for me is quite illusory."

Ghalan resumed his work.

Shadrack watched him with detachment. "What are you doing?"

"Do you really care?"

Shadrack shrugged. "It matters little."

"That's what I thought," Ghalan said disapprovingly. "I'm trying to realign the chakras in your body, which receive various powers from the astral plane, from food and the air you breathe. They then distribute the energy through a network, which sustains you astrally and therefore keeps your physical body alive."

"The astral body is a finer version of the physical?"

"Yes. Yes, that's correct."

"I think I read that in a book, but I don't know where...." His face became clouded, then he suddenly asked, "Is Ekanar all right?"

"Ekanar is dead," Ghalan said bluntly, carefully watching for any emotional reaction.

"Oh," Shadrack said, his face contorting. "He was old anyway, I suppose."

Ghalan frowned: the reaction was not a healthy one. He finished working on the chakras around Shadrack's feet, and straightened himself up.

"That's it for today. Do you feel more balanced?"

Shadrack shrugged. "More balanced, I suppose. And dead."

Ghalan nodded. "You have an unusual form of schizophrenia. Your intellect is recovering, but is utterly cut off from your emotions. It may be fear—it was through emotions that Lilith possessed you in the first place."

Shadrack recoiled backwards, insanity in his eyes. It was the first time Ghalan had seen a strong reaction from him.

"Please..." Shadrack whispered, "don't say her name."

Ghalan realized his theory was correct. Other than his dreadful physical and astral conditions, it was fear that produced Shadrack's apathy. Ghalan knew that if this apathy wasn't broken, the demon's hold would never be loosened. When Shadrack left the Order, as eventually he must, Lilith would be waiting for him.

Shadrack awakened and struggled to open his eyes. The dimly lit room was unfamiliar, but he somehow knew he should recognize it. The world shifted and swam before him; the objects in the room seemed to vibrate. Sparkles of light flickered in and out of existence around him, and comet-like streaks of brilliant white glistened in the air.

He knew his mind had been damaged, perhaps irreversibly, but his awareness was a hundred times better than when She had possessed him. He shuddered violently at the thought.

He had great difficulty keeping his mind focused. He wondered where Tanaka was; or was Ghalan his name? One of them was his father, or had been. It didn't matter which; everyone who knew him eventually died.

He tried to stand. After several attempts he succeeded. His body buzzed, especially his chest, legs, and hands. There was also pain in his forehead, in his third-eye chakra.

He wondered where his sword was. It was deeply rooted within him that a samurai must always keep his katana with him at all times. Even more, he wanted his wakizashi. He should end his life now, before he caused more pain to himself and others.

Why couldn't I be normal? he wondered bitterly. Even his childhood had not been natural.

He saw a double cubical altar across the room. He started to move toward it. As he walked, his legs dragged behind his body, yet they felt as if they were ahead of it.

The altar would open up to reveal instruments inside; he felt sure of this without knowing why. He was conscious of having memories which, though they were his own, seemed to have occurred to a different personality. They were chaotic, and easily forgotten. He could discern very little from the muddle in his head; the memories were mixed with those of his present life, creating a confusing torrent of knowledge.

He hadn't reached the altar yet. It was taking a long time to get there. Or was he suffering from time distortion? His legs fell farther and farther behind and his body felt stretched. He felt a dull pain across his face. Somehow he had fallen over. He started to crawl across the rug.

Now he could see inside the double cubical altar, though he couldn't remember opening it. There were several items within it, but it was the yellow-painted dagger that immediately drew his attention. Its captivating purple sigils seemed to flash and change color. He grasped the dagger.

Before his mind's eye, two people plagued him. One was a dark, powerful man with a haunting gaze. He was an enemy who must be destroyed, yet who was far too powerful to confront. Better to run and hide. There was hatred for this man, but it belonged to another; it was no longer his own. He cared little now.

There was also an exquisitely beautiful woman, with deep alluring brown eyes that yearned for his help. He was stirred greatly by the woman, and he felt a powerful tide of love breaking through his apathy. The emotion felt distant, as though it were someone else's, but this time he couldn't pretend it didn't move him.

He yearned to be with the woman more than anything else. But he feared the Arch-Demon; she would return and reclaim him. He began to shake uncontrollably in fear. Lilith's tortures were terrible: he couldn't survive them again.

The room swayed back and forth in his vision, and he realized he was rocking on his knees. He placed the point of the dagger against the pit of his stomach. The eyes of the dark-haired woman haunted him. To commit suicide would be to betray her, which he couldn't do, but he knew he must. The black oblivion of death was his only chance of peace. He could not accept the responsibility that had been thrust upon him, nor could he take any more pain. If he found the woman, he would be likely to destroy her anyway. He had destroyed everything else in his life.

With his decision made, he thrust the dagger into his stomach. He gritted his teeth and waited for the pain. But there was none. Tanaka had grabbed the dagger; or was his name Ghalan?

He heard a voice whispering in his ear: "Don't do this, Shadrack. If you don't free yourself of Lilith in this life, you will not incarnate again, and she will possess you even in death. There is no peace for you there."

Shadrack released his grip on the dagger and started to tremble, tears rolling down his red face.

"Then I am utterly lost...there is no escape," he said.

"Only one," said Ghalan. "You must regain the strength you once had, and then you must defeat Her. Ahead of you lies a challenge that no normal man would attempt. But I will teach you now, as I taught you in your past, and I will in my future."

Shadrack looked at the old man, his colorless eyes tearful. Profound confusion filled them.

"Then teach me, father, and I will learn," he said, his words suddenly emphatic.

In life, we move through a complex karmic web, leaving an impression on every individual we come into contact with. Be warned, nothing is ever truly forgotten, even after many incarnations. But though enemies may be assuaged and even befriended, true allies are eternal.

—Doctrine of the White School

Enya
Yesod of Yetzirah
City of Gorom

The *Murky Chasm* rattled as shrieking winds buffeted it. Lena stared through the gaps in the shuttered window. Crimson mist flowed through the streets like a turbulent river. Dark, ominous shapes lurked within it, ready to seize their prey. Green whirlwinds rose up from the mist, their eerie light casting a ghastly glow over the city. The whirlwinds howled with primeval hunger.

Lena shuddered violently and pulled back from the window. She felt Lilith's essence everywhere, and she was on edge.

"You should try to relax, Lena," Cassius said as she sat opposite him. "It will be dawn in a few hours."

He stroked his horse, which he had led into the tavern after the battle.

"You are really Cassius Hawkin?"

"At your service."

Lena studied him, her eyes suspicious. "I owe you my thanks, it seems. But tell me how you know my name. You were obviously searching for me."

"You don't trust me?"

Lena smiled sardonically. "Trust has to be earned. Unfortunately distrust comes to me first these days. A gift from my beloved mother."

Cassius scrutinized her carefully. Lena's physical appearance was much as he had expected. Her skin was flawless and lightly tanned, her features feminine but strong. Reaching halfway down her back, her hair was a lustrous black. Her eyes were dark brown, deep and alluring, flecked with gold.

"You are as beautiful as history remembers," he said. "But I think it is a sad, poignant beauty. I had expected an idealistic girl, not a cynical woman."

"Expectations are dangerous things," Lena said. "Once I was an innocent, but I've suffered too much to ever go back to that. And until I find my husband, I can find no joy in anything."

"Ah, to escape the past," Cassius said, his eyes clouded. "If only. . . ."

"Barman! Bring me some wine!" Lena ordered.

She cast her gaze around the tavern. Almost all the patrons were asleep by now, either through drink or drugs. One group of men played cards, but even this wasn't rowdy. It was as if Dark Moon had brought a truce to the tavern. In the corner, Mendaz sat alone, holding his head in his hands.

"I thought alcohol was restricted for White Adepts," Cassius said, shocked.

"It is. But I need a drink."

"But the rules. . ."

"Damn the rules!" Lena interrupted. "I'm tired and I can't be bothered with them. I had enough of rules in the Yellow School."

"Rules and laws are not meant to be broken," Cassius said, disapproving.

"That's a matter of opinion," Lena said, taking the cup from the barman.

There was an uncomfortable silence as she drank her wine. It was broken by a quiet click, a sound Lena instantly recognized. A moment later, Squint materialized on the table.

"Hello, Squint," Lena said, too tired to greet him properly. The elemental winked and walked over the table to sit on her lap.

"That's how I found you," Cassius said, pointing to Squint. "The elemental led me to you."

Lena raised an eyebrow. "So how is it you were looking for me?"

"I was sent by Jeshua of the White School."

"Jeshua?" Lena frowned.

"Yes, the same man you knew in your last life."

"That was over a thousand years ago," Lena said dismissively.

Cassius shrugged. "Many things are possible on Enya now. Jeshua sleeps nearly all the time, and he has to use every scrap of his willpower and magick just to cling to life. He has been waiting for you to return."

"Why me?"

"The events surrounding the Summoning in the Second Aeon are the direct cause of current events on Enya. The karma surrounding all involved in the event is extremely strong, and you will all be drawn to this time. Battle must recommence, and the intimate karmic web must be resolved."

Lena sipped her wine thoughtfully. A voice interrupted the conversation.

"Mendaz, what shall I do with your men?" the barman asked.

Mendaz didn't even register the barman's presence. At his feet he had piled up the dead guards.

"Mendaz, I'm going to have to throw them in the river. The smell will attract Lilith's demons if I leave them here. Mendaz?"

The bandit leader looked up, his expression glazed. "Take them," he said, his voice emotionless.

Lena and Cassius watched as the barman and a helper started to haul the bodies away.

"He is without honor," Cassius said. "It is dishonorable to allow your men to be treated in such a way."

Lena twisted her head to look at Mendaz. "He has some things to come to terms with. Besides, honor is a personal thing. What is honorable for one person is meaningless to the next. We must be true to ourselves."

Cassius scowled. "I wouldn't expect you to understand. You're a woman. You know nothing of honor."

Lena leaned forward. "It seems you know nothing about women."

Cassius tensed and seemed about to angrily retort, but he regained his composure in time.

"I see that one was close to the truth," Lena said. "You have trouble with your wife or concubine? Or your daughter maybe? With that kind of talk, I'm not surprised."

Cassius stared at the table, unsure whether he was angry or embarrassed.

"Tell me, Cassius. You seem to know a great deal about me. What do you know of my husband?" Lena asked. "I journey to the Celestial Tower to find him."

Cassius sighed. "You are aware that it was Malak that pulled you from the clutches of Lilith. After your voluntary sacrifice, he bargained for your soul and retrieved it."

Lena nodded. "I guessed this much."

Deep sadness showed in the warrior's eyes. "Lena, in the process, Malak lost his own soul."

Lena stared at him in absolute shock. "No, that can't be right…he wouldn't do something so stupid."

"Lena, Malak belongs to Lilith now. His soul is one with hers. He is her puppet. I know this better than anyone."

"No," she shook her head, "it can't be true!" Her eyes watered as her emotional control began to slip. Cassius noticed the tremor in her hand as she lifted her cup to drink.

"Where is he now?" she asked, her voice barely a whisper. "I must find him! He needs me!"

Cassius sighed. "He is not on this plane. At present he is in Malkuth. But he will return very soon. It is his destiny. In the meantime, Jeshua wants you to return with me to Sophia. It is there that we will gather our forces against the Warlock. But Malak will be the focus of the battle. He will be either our salvation, or our destruction."

"What do you mean? Malak would never jeopardize us!"

"Lena," Cassius said gently, "Malak's soul belongs to Lilith. He cannot resist her will. No human can. I have seen her power."

Lena's eyes flamed. "I have seen her power closer than anyone! But I will not forsake my husband! He will never betray me, no matter what his condition! And even if I have to confront Lilith face to face again, I won't back away!"

Cassius nodded. "I can't doubt your spirit after seeing the conviction in your eyes. I know Lilith is your greatest fear after what happened to you."

"She would be yours too, if you'd experienced what I have," Lena said. Somehow the tone of her voice disturbed Cassius; it sent a shudder down his spine.

"Perhaps you are right. But no one is talking about forsaking Malak here, Lena. Besides yourself, I am the last person who would do so."

Lena frowned. "What is your connection to Malak? How is it you know so much information about him?"

Cassius' lips twisted, and Lena realized he was trying to smile. "I have an interest more personal than you can know. You see, in my last life I knew Malak as a son."

Lena shook her head. "I'm lost…I don't understand. Then surely I would know you too. What was your name?"

"No, my previous name means nothing to you, Lena." He took a deep breath. "But to Malak, to Shadrack, the name of Ieyasu Tanaka is very dear."

If we could read the secret history of our enemies, we would find in each man's life a sorrow and a suffering enough to disarm all hostility.

—Doctrine of the White School[4]

11

Enya
Yesod of Yetzirah
City of Gorom

Dethen stood within the huge iron gates of Gorom as people bustled past him on either side. Despite his ragged robes, no one approached his dark, ominous frame.

The sun dipped behind the sprawling city, and darkness seeped through the streets. After a hot day, the smell of sewage from the River Wye filled the air; it formed a strange contrast against the scent of aromatic spices. Heavy rain poured from the sky, but no more than a few drops touched Dethen. The black clouds promised a thunder storm. Dethen's eyes narrowed. He hated thunder; it brought back gruesome memories of a life he sought to bury.

He closed his eyes, seeking his prey with his inner vision. Gorom was huge, but he knew Mendaz's signature as well as his own.

The minds of the people he touched sickened him. Gorom was diseased. The populace were bloodthirsty and merciless, gluttonous and greedy. He felt barely a single healthy mind in the heaving city. There was no balance, no harmony. He felt the dark temples of blood sacrifice, the open-air brothels and fighting arenas.

His Purpose was to end the kind of sickness he now sensed: to end the eternal suffering of the human race. Though he himself could be cruel and merciless, it was always for the Purpose. He didn't enjoy lowering himself to such a level, but it was a sacrifice that had to be made. To destroy the Tree of Life he would sacrifice

4 Henry Wadsworth Longfellow

anything. He dedicated his entire existence to the moment when he would hurl the Arch-Demon Chronzon from the Abyss and into the depths of the Qlippoth.

With a start he recognized Mendaz's psychic signature. Instantly, a terrible rage exploded within him. The emotion was from Jaad, and impossible to suppress. Dethen knew that if he suppressed it, it would eventually return ten-fold.

Mendaz was the only living man Jaad desired vengeance against, but it was a passionate desire. And with Mendaz's death, Dethen's full power would return.

With a determined stride, he set off in the direction of his quarry.

Mendaz knelt before the statue of Maat, his face bloated from a constant flow of tears. He studied the dark-eyed goddess of balance. She was tall and slender, her hair long and black; a black and white nemyss almost concealed it. Her skin was golden and in her hands she held an ankh and a feather.

From the entrance to the hall two Yellow Adepts watched him impassively. He twisted his head to glare at them. He hated their kind with a vengeance, and found it ironic he was within a Yellow School sanctuary. Yet he had much thinking to do, and the temple had a peacefulness the rest of Gorom lacked. It was the only place he could think without being disturbed.

Seek peace with yourself, because if you treated him so badly, your son will seek you out. He remembered Fiona's words. Though he craved to see his son again, somehow the words caused the nape of his neck to prickle in fear.

Mendaz was wracked by guilt. Jaad had never had any life to speak of. He had been bullied and ridiculed for all of his twenty-five years, yet never once struck out in revenge despite his huge size. Mendaz felt ashamed; he knew he had tormented the boy more than anyone.

Poor sod.

Jaad had been a half-wit; instead of protecting him, his father had constantly beaten and humiliated him. His mother had died in childbirth, and for that Mendaz had blamed him too. He remembered how he had brought the hilt of his dagger down on the infant's head in rage.

Gods protect me! What have I done?

He stared at the bottle of liquor he held. He swilled the brown liquid around, staring at the poison he ingested every hour without fail. Since the death of his wife he could barely remember an occasion when he had been sober. He was sober now, and reality was worse than he remembered.

Slowly he unscrewed the top from the bottle. Only the elixir of forgetfulness could ease his pain. He lifted the bottle to his lips.

Suddenly he hurled it at the statue of Maat. It shattered, scattering glass and liquor everywhere. The goddess stared at him with the same tranquil expression.

He turned to look at the Yellow Adepts. They watched him carefully, but neither of them moved towards him.

Mendaz looked at the figure of Maat. He knew she represented balance, among other things. That was what he had always lacked in his life, and perhaps that added to his hatred of the Yellow School. He moved from one emotional extreme to another, lashing out at his men on a whim. He closed his eyes for a moment in sadness as he remembered he no longer had any men.

His lack of balance had been worsened by the death of his wife. She had meant everything to him. Yet he knew he had been without balance even before this, a victim of a childhood that made even Jaad's seem leisurely.

He licked his lips as the horrific memories returned. He needed a drink.

"Death strike me down!" he shouted, furious with himself.

"He is here, Father," said a deep, bass voice. "And he intends to."

Mendaz turned slowly. Dethen stood at the temple entrance, his black eyes simmering with the most intense hatred.

"Jaad." The word choked in Mendaz's throat.

Dethen stepped into the sanctuary. The Yellow Adepts immediately moved forward to intercept him.

"Password?" one of them demanded.

Dethen continued walking as if unaware of their presence: his attention was focused solely on Mendaz. The first Adept formed the Sign of Horus, hurling astral energy at him. The Adept collapsed as the energy reflected off Dethen's aura.

The second Adept laid a hand on his shoulder.

"Stop or I'll be forced to…ah!"

He screamed as Dethen grabbed his hand, twisted the wrist and broke it in one fluid movement. His other hand locked around the Adept's throat in a vice-like grip. He continued walking, dragging the Adept along with him as the man struggled to pry his fingers away. In a few moments the Adept stopped struggling and Dethen allowed him to fall into an undignified heap.

Mendaz stood as his son reached him. "You're not Jaad…" he said uncertainly.

"I am exactly who you think, father. Only I am now known as Dethen. I have grown. I am my true self now."

Mendaz looked carefully. His son had been gentle and stupid, but this man was incredibly dangerous. His gaze sent shudders through the soul. Yet he knew that the man before him was still his son.

"Fiona said you would come for me," Mendaz said. "She even knew your name: Dethen."

Dethen rested his hand on *Widowmaker's* hilt. "I found your men at the cavern."

"Do any of them live?"

"Only Nehmoth."

Mendaz cast his eyes to the floor. "He was the one who never mistreated you. The rest deserved no better."

"As you deserve no better." Dethen said, his voice menacing. "Draw your sword."

Mendaz swallowed hard. His fingers wrapped around the hilt of his sword. Tears appeared in his eyes as he slowly drew the blade. Dethen watched him like a bird of prey, his eyes pinpoints of fury.

The tip of Mendaz's blade cleared its scabbard. The sword remained suspended in mid-air as neither man moved; Dethen wanted to prolong his suffering.

Mendaz released his grip, and the sword clattered to the floor. "Please…just do it. I cannot live with myself as I am. And I certainly can't kill my only son."

"Jaad desires revenge."

Mendaz bowed his head. "So be it. He has the right, after all his suffering."

Widowmaker's fist-sized garnet glowed hungrily.

"Before you do it, I just want you to know one thing. I know it's pathetic that I waited so long to tell you, Jaad, but I love you. I always have and I always will. If I could have admitted it to myself, then maybe I could have admitted it to you."

Dethen's eyes seemed hesitant.

"I may have been a bad father, Jaad, even a terrible one. But at least I wasn't as much of a bastard as my father was."

Dethen drew *Widowmaker*.

"You think it vindicates you because your father mistreated you. You think that gave you the right to do that to me?" The hatred had returned to Dethen's eyes, though the intensity had dimmed.

Mendaz laughed, a sound that choked in his throat. "Gods, no. But perhaps things would have been different if someone had killed him before I did."

"You killed your own father?"

Mendaz smiled bitterly. "Funny, isn't it? You're about to do what I did all those years ago. I was fourteen when I killed my father, and I've done nothing decent since that day. I learned how to kill that day, and I've been robbing, plundering and killing ever since."

Dethen stared at his father. There was more hatred in Mendaz's eyes than Dethen's as he described his father.

"Why did you kill him?" Dethen asked. He shifted his grip on *Widowmaker* as the sword vibrated impatiently.

"Why? Why did I do it?" Mendaz's voice was dangerously quiet. "Do you know what it's like to be raped night after night? To be abused every day before you have reached your tenth birthday? No. I may have beaten you, but I never subjected you to *that*."

Mendaz's face twisted into a mask of agony, as if he relived what he told. Dethen couldn't doubt his word.

"You killed him for *that?*"

"No. Even for that I might have forgiven him. Eventually. But to hear my little sister abused night after night, to never be able to do anything about it. *That* was why I killed him. I killed him and I enjoyed it. Just as he killed her."

Dethen studied him, shocked. He had seen so much pain in a face only once: when looking in a mirror.

"You must release your hatred, father. If you don't, it will burn you up. It will consume you until there is nothing left for you but hatred."

Mendaz looked up. "And what about you, Jaad? Should you not release your hatred too? I see terrible blackness within you."

Dethen smiled grimly. "It is too late for me, father. Perhaps once I could have turned back, but no longer. The pain and hatred are all I have."

"Too much pain, Jaad," Mendaz sobbed. "There is too much pain."

He leaned forward to hug his son. Dethen tensed, uncertain. Then he resheathed *Widowmaker* and put his arm around his father. A single tear formed in his eye. He reached up and touched it, amazed.

"You look like you've never seen a tear before," said Mendaz.

Dethen frowned. "Jaad cries, Dethen does not. Not for three lifetimes."

He released Mendaz to stare at him intently. "Tell me, father. Would you like to put an end to the pain? All of it? To end the pain of the entire universe?"

Mendaz looked puzzled. "Is that possible?"

"It is the Purpose." He laid a hand on Mendaz's shoulder. "Come, father. We have much work to do."

"Where are we going?"

"To the lair of the Black School. It is time for me to reclaim my throne. . . ."

Bal sat within the pentagonal throne room of the Warlock, his movement restricted by the magical chains that bound him. The chamber was moderately small, with little decoration. The huge throne was chiseled from solid jet, without a join or blemish to be seen. Studded with rubies and sapphires, the harsh edges were trimmed with gold and platinum.

The walls were decorated with tapestries of the finest quality, blended with colors of breathaking beauty. Each tapestry portrayed one of the Warlock's many triumphant victories. The walls themselves were luminescent with a soft blue-gray light. They were enchanted with a protective field through which no magic inferior to the Warlock's could penetrate, rendering them utterly impregnable.

Suddenly the door flew open and the Warlock strode in, the chamber vibrating under his heavy tread. The bottom of his staff cracked off the floor with every step. Bal had noticed that the staff never left the Warlock's side. More than anything, the Demon valued this possession.

The Warlock's eyes seemed brighter than usual. It was difficult to imagine that eyes of such an enchanting color could exist within a being so evil.

"You are still here?" the Warlock asked, his tone heavy with sarcasm.

"I have nothing better to do," Bal said coldly.

The Warlock seated himself and stared at Bal, his eyes piercing. Bal felt himself being probed and suddenly couldn't break eye contact. It was the first time the Warlock had paid attention to him since his capture, and it boded ill.

"You have conflict within you, Bal. I wonder how you will resolve it."

"You are mistaken. There is no conflict within me. I live only to serve my Master."

"Really?" The Warlock's black skeletal face leered closer. "Yes, I see your loyalty. Tremendous loyalty. If only my adepts were as loyal as you."

"Then you realize I could never betray my Master."

"Perhaps. But do not underestimate the other dominating factor of your personality."

"And what might that be, Oh Great Wise One?" Bal said, returning the sarcasm.

For a moment it seemed the Warlock would lash out with his staff, but the moment passed.

"Your ambition, of course. And believe me, it is as strong as your loyalty!"

"Never," Bal said, but there was shame on his face, as if a great secret had been drawn from him.

"I wonder which will prevail. Tell me, do you wish to rule the Black School in place of your Master?"

Bal remained silent. The Warlock seemed amused.

"Let us see. I will look into your soul to read your future. We will see how great a man you will become."

Bal struggled as he felt his mind scrutinized. With every scrap of will he could still not break the Warlock's gaze.

"What is this?" The Warlock's voice became serious. "It seems your future will be greater than I thought."

"What is it you see?" Bal asked, trying not to betray his interest.

The Warlock's skeletal features melded into a frown. "It seems that you will rule one of the Schools of magick after all."

"That is not possible," Bal said. "You have seen false."

"I do not see untruth," the Warlock said. "It may be as well that I kill you now. I spared you to see Dethen kneel before me, but perhaps I should be wary of the student, rather than the Master."

Bal smiled thinly. "It is Dethen who will cast you down. Have no doubt about that."

"That is not possible. But as a precaution, I should deal with both of you quickly."

Bal swallowed hard as the Warlock's staff began to glow.

Suddenly a Black Guard captain entered the room. He looked panicked as he saw the glowing staff, but quickly regained his composure and knelt.

"Master, I have news for you."

The Warlock seemed undecided what to do. He paused, and the staff obfuscated.

"What news do you bear? The death of Cassius Hawkin, I hope?"

The captain's eyes betrayed his nervousness. "No, Master. It seems Hawkin survived the attack, and Greshwin was captured by the enemy. Hawkin was seen in Gorom yesterday."

"He still lives!" The Demon's voice shook the chamber. "It seems I will have to deal with this man myself, even if I have to journey to Sophia." He stopped for a moment, deep in thought. "What were you doing in Gorom, Hawkin?"

"Master, something else happened in Gorom. It may be nothing, but we were instructed to report everything...."

The Warlock gestured impatiently for the captain to continue.

"There was an incident at the Yellow School temple. It seems a large man forced his way into the temple and then left a few minutes later."

The Warlock's brow furrowed. "The Yellow School are not weak. Such a task would not be easy. The entrance would be guarded by powerful Adepts."

The soldier nodded. "Master, the intruder wore black robes."

Bal chuckled. "He is coming, Warlock. My Master is coming for you next."

The Demon stared at his prisoner. "Then let him come. I have waited centuries for this confrontation, preparing my defenses. No human can possibly challenge me now." He stroked the gem of his staff. "Isn't that right, my pretty?"

The gem vibrated angrily.

Planet Tellus
Malkuth of Assiah
City of Prenzlau

This Order has often been criticized for its involvement in the martial arts. But I say unto you: If a man never has an opportunity for evil, how can he take credit for following the Light? Likewise, if a man knows not how to injure and destroy, how can he assume credit for not doing these?

Beware that pacifism does not become an excuse for cowardice. To rise above fighting, one must first become a warrior."

—Magus of the Yellow School

Shadrack stood in the center of his chamber, his mind mulling over his situation. He had been at the Order for six weeks now, and his mind was much more focused. Though there was still great internal confusion, he felt his previous life as a part of him now—he knew that he and the White Adept of his dreams were the same person. The connection was extremely tenuous, however.

Shadrack focused his concentration and crossed his arms in front of himself, slipping into *yoi*. His body was beginning to recover from the demonic possession, but it was still weak. His ethereal body was now properly bound to the physical and he had not felt the sensation of his legs dragging in a fortnight.

He stepped forward into *gedan-barai,* blocking his lower body with a sweep of his left arm. He grimaced in disgust; the technique lacked any speed or power. He realized he would have to reconstruct his *budo-kai* from scratch. First he would have to regain his fitness, balance, and technique. Then he could begin work on speed and power.

He started to practice basic techniques, moving up and down the chamber. He performed each attack slowly, constantly monitoring the position of each body part. In this way he determined any deviations from the optimum line of power.

This time he would have to rely on himself. No longer did he have his father, Ieyasu, to correct his techniques and mental attitude.

Very quickly he began to tire. He pushed on, forcing his body to feel the discipline it had lacked for so long. His mind attempted to wander, and each time he had to gently push it back to focus on his body.

He found the condition of his *budo-kai* extremely discouraging, but he knew an important truism, which his father had taught him when young: practice for the sake of the practice, not for lust of results. Because people lusted for results, they repeated what they were already proficient at; they therefore neglected their weaknesses. In reality, weaknesses were the Achilles heels to be eliminated.

Shadrack turned to face the opposite direction. Suddenly the ambience of the room shifted. He thought that perhaps it was a trick of his subconscious, trying to grab his attention and avoid the discipline he imposed, so he continued his work. However, two punches later he heard the malevolent whispers circling about him in ever-decreasing circles.

He stopped, fear rising within him. He saw the outlines of the black shadow-like entities that whirled around him. A deep, threatening growl shook the foundations of the chamber. He sank to the floor, his eyes wide with terror. He knew that She was returning.

Colors akin to the aurora borealis flickered around him; the chamber gained a surreal quality. For the first time in many months, he felt the kick of his libido.

He scrambled quickly across the floor, passing under the ring of circling entities. Reaching the opposite wall, he tugged hard on the doorknob. It refused to move. He turned to stare back into the room, his back pressed tight against the door.

The black demons whirled in the center of the room, accelerating faster in ever-decreasing circles. Shadrack watched in horror as they flowed together to form a single spinning black mass. It glowed a beautiful green, slowly elongating into a vertical bar six feet tall.

A blast of wind extinguished the oil lamp. Shadrack shook as he was left in pitch blackness; he could only see the green light, but despite its brightness it cast no illumination into the room. He felt an intense sensation of déjà vu.

Slowly, the bar broadened to form a glowing human figure. Then the light died, leaving Shadrack alone in impenetrable darkness.

His heart pounded painfully, and his breathing rasped as he hyperventilated. She had returned for him; she was here. He felt her laughing within the depths of his soul, the soul that she owned.

A tiny spark of anger lit within him. The memories of his past self had strengthened him to some degree; he could now draw fortitude from both identities. The lamp flickered back into life, and he saw her. Her face was barely an inch from his own, and his anger instantly evaporated.

For the first time in his present life, Shadrack saw the seductive aspect of Lilith. Her lips were a vivid red, pure and untouched by man. Her perfect bone structure and elegant eyebrows were well balanced with her elfin ears and nose. Her skin was flawless, perfectly white and unblemished. Her shining, black hair cascaded over delicate shoulders, almost reaching down to her naked breasts.

Yet it was her eyes that drew him into them, snaring him like a helpless insect in a web of steel. They were a deep, exquisite purple; yet it was the color of another world that could never quite manifest on earth. The color had a life and vibrancy of its own, containing an untouchable quintessence. He knew he belonged within those eyes, within the reflected otherworldly domain; and he knew that his mind and soul formed an insignificant dot within that world. For the first time he realized that though she was an Arch-Demon, Lilith was more akin to a Goddess than a woman. Her power daunted him.

"Do you recognize me, Shadrack? Or should I say…Malak?" she purred; her voice sent shivers of sexual desire through his body, rapidly causing an erection.

"I am Shadrack…" he whispered.

He could barely control himself as her eyes sucked the life force from his body. She was both the creature he desired most in the universe, and the creature he feared most. The desire was an obsessive craving, impossible to deny except for the terrible dread. Though she was before him in her seductive, sexual form, she had possessed him for several months in her vicious and brutal demonic form. It was something he could never forget, not for one minute of his life.

"Do you know who you belong to, Shadrack?" she asked.

He tried to close his eyes and break eye contact with her, but his body refused. He gasped in agony as hormones of incredible potency were pumped into his system.

"You belong to me, my plaything...." She ran a finger down his chest. He choked out a cry as his skin blackened under her touch, leaving an ebony, smoking trail of pain; at the same time, orgasms of ecstasy swept through his body.

He had no willpower; his existence was a mockery. He nodded his head in agreement.

"I...belong to you."

"Remember always that your soul is mine, and that you were born upon this world because I decreed it. Soon, you will be drawn back to your home-world, in Yesod. There you must fulfill your given task."

"Anything, mistress...." Despite the agony, he would do anything to feel her touch again.

"When you are drawn back into Enya, you must seek out your brother, Dethen. With his help, I can use your body as a gateway back into the plane. You will do this thing for me, and this time there will be no boundaries to limit me. There will no limitations this time."

Shadrack frowned in puzzlement as a thought struck his drunken mind.

"What of Enya, it will be destroyed...."

Lilith's eyes darkened in fury, a glittering blackness beyond description. She pressed her index finger against his lips.

"Shhhhh! Remember!"

Shadrack tried to scream at the touch as the flames flickered around his mouth, but his lips had been sealed together. Around him, the room started to lose its reality. He felt a painful stinging sensation on his face, and everything turned black.

Then he was staring into the blurred face of Ghalan; the pain slowly fading.

"What...what...."

"Relax, child, you have had a fearful experience," Ghalan said.

"She was here...."

Ghalan shook his head. "She drew you into your own mind. She has no power to possess you now, or cause effects on the physical plane, which is not in harmony with her own. That she can only do through you."

There were tears in Shadrack's eyes. "I cannot fight her, Ghalan....She is too strong!"

"You must, or we will all be lost..." Ghalan said. "I may aid you, but the battle is yours alone."

Shadrack hung his head in defeat, once again feeling his psyche begin to rupture.

A few minutes before dawn Shadrack sat on his bed, staring nonchalantly across the room. His posture was slumped, his head angled downward. His skin was pale and unhealthy, his eyes sunken and colorless. There was no will to live left within them.

He saw the first rays of morning filtering through the arched window, and heard the singing of the birds as they heralded a new day. Yet these things only irritated him, though he was dimly aware of them at best. The oppressive heat of the chamber was uncomfortable; in Nippon, midsummer had never been as warm, even at noon.

As he lifted his head, comet-like streaks of brilliant white flowed past him and blue sparkles glittered in the air. Yet these were just more phenomena he was unable to control, and worse still, the astral spectacles reminded him of Lilith. A shudder of fear passed down his spine at the mere thought of her name; he cringed, expecting the Arch-Demon to lash out at him for his audacity.

His mind wandered lazily from subject to subject. One subject he returned to continually was the question of his identity. Within him existed two sets of memories, once distinct and defined, but now intermingled and tangled. Neither set of memories was complete, and he constantly confused them with each other. He could feel two distinct personalities and lifetimes, yet he was neither Malak nor Shadrack, not even a peculiar hybrid. He drifted in a limitless void, an unchanging limbo from which there was no escape.

His emotions cycled through apathy, confusion, and fear, each always present—they simply varied in intensity as their dominance fluxed. He knew that Lilith's reappearance had triggered his cowardly impassiveness: he feared the demon with every fiber of his being.

His mind was unable to differentiate between illusion and reality. A small red devil with black horns and iniquitous ebony eyes sat next to him on the bed. It sat as he did, mimicking his every movement, and sailing tranquilly across the room was a tiny, slim female figure. The creature was incredibly beautiful, with large transparent wings that flapped gracefully. Yet Shadrack was utterly blind to the beauty: he was wrapped in a cocoon through which sensations and feelings barely penetrated.

A strange noise disturbed his mechanical thought processes, and for a moment he felt a glimmer of interest. He turned his head toward the door.

"Meeoow!" He was startled by the sound once more. A noise he had never heard before, yet something deep within him reacted to it.

The kitten padded into the room and looked up at him with playful curiosity. Barely a few weeks old, its wide green eyes watched everything with enthusiasm. Its coat was black, shining with health and its ears twitched continually.

Shadrack stared at the creature in fascination, feeling it call to something deep within him. The kitten seemed the most real thing he'd ever seen: next to it, everything else seemed two-dimensional. He realized with a start that this was how he'd begun to see the world: for him, it had lost all depth.

Yet this kitten was a wonder, more adorable than anything he could have imagined. It scrunched its face up and closed its eyes as it yawned, opening its mouth wide. Shadrack smiled as he noticed the needle-like teeth, and the small pink tongue. The kitten's whiskers were almost as wide as the body was long, and its belly hung near the floor, showing it had recently been fed.

It now stood before him, its head tilted in curiosity as it watched him. The green of its eyes seemed incredibly vivid to Shadrack. There was a peculiar vibrancy to them that was almost surreal. Yet he knew the eyes were not unusual: he was simply seeing things very differently, much more clearly than before.

The kitten set itself playfully and raked his leg with its paw.

Shadrack gasped as memories of another cat came flooding back to him. He saw the creature before his mind's eye: a jet-black coat with eyes like twin pieces of jade. Yet this beast was no kitten: she had the sleek body of a panther, with fluid, rippling muscles. And suddenly he knew her name: Bast.

Now he felt a great longing for his familiar. He remembered the alien gaze of the creature, and her loyalty through several lifetimes.

He remembered their last moment together, when she had deserted him at the Celestial Tower before his evocation of Lilith. He didn't blame Bast for this, for it was he who had betrayed her, along with the rest of the White School. He wondered whether Bast would ever return to him.

Triggered by his memories of Bast, other images sprang up before his mind's eye. Slowly, the world about him faded from consciousness as he sank into himself. He saw a vision of a unicorn beside a waterfall and an image of a wounded hawk he had once healed. Then he could actually feel and smell the body of his old horse as he galloped through the golden-barked trees of the Enchanted Forest, brushing through the playful blue-green leaves.

He realized with a start that they were all Malak's memories. For a moment he struggled against them, fearful of losing his identity. Yet he knew beyond all doubt that they were his own memories, also, that he and Malak were one and the same essence, separated only by time and experience.

The visions expanded and intensified, becoming more tangible and distressing. He lived through scene after scene, passing through old experiences in an instant, yet feeling their totality. The visions penetrated from all angles, and his vision suddenly became omniscient, perceiving all directions.

The visions were from previous lives before Malak's now, and they came with breathtaking speed, like moving through a limitless cone. He struggled to retain his identity, to remember he still lived, but the sensations carried him away like a tidal wave.

He panicked as he fought to breathe, feeling he was drowning. The visions produced an enormous pressure, crushing him from all directions, even while he lived through them. They flickered and changed continually, showing alien landscapes and creatures beyond his imagination. He tried to scream as he moved faster, accelerating toward some unknown, mystical point.

And then the images were gone. He drifted in blackness that pulsed with serenity and radiated a feeling of safety. It was a warm, comforting darkness, like the long-forgotten womb. His mind felt free, hovering like an eagle over his many incarnations, and accepting them easily. For a moment, he felt the eternal truth. He realized the irrelevancy of his name, whether he called himself Malak or Shadrack. His essence was eternal, passing from life to life in its quest for experience. And though a new name and personality was assumed in each incarnation, the essence itself was unchanging and permanent—he was immortal.

The cognition lasted only a brief second, though he longed to hold onto it. And then he felt himself falling, falling. With a jolt he felt his body once more and he opened his eyes. Gradually, the physical world came back into focus and he breathed deeply, astounded at the journey he had undertaken.

Seated on the floor in front of him was Ghalan, holding the black kitten, which purred contentedly.

"You caused that on purpose," he said.

"I knew there would be a strong reaction to a kitten with this likeness."

Shadrack shook his head. "You know me too well, Ghalan."

As he looked around the room, he realized the incredible mental change that had occurred to him. His apathy had been smashed; everything was new and fresh, like his perception of the kitten when it first arrived. The golden rays of the early morning sun shone through the window, and the sound of birdsong drifted into the chamber. He felt reborn.

"How do you feel?" Ghalan asked, as if reading his mind.

"Almost complete," he said, and realized that he meant it.

Ghalan nodded. "The feeling will gradually wear off as the experience fades in your memory, but you will not sink back into your previous emotional state. You will now make significant progress."

Shadrack sobered a little and nodded.

"Anyway," continued Ghalan, "to encourage you further, I have some gifts for you."

"Gifts?"

Ghalan gestured with his hand, drawing Shadrack's attention to the two bundles that lay next to him on the bed. One was a square box, the other long and thin.

"What are they?"

"Only one way to find out."

Shadrack opened the box carefully. He gasped when he saw the contents: a canvas training gi, the traditional karate uniform since ancient times. Even with Ieyasu Tanaka, he hadn't possessed one of these.

"I thought it appropriate," Ghalan said. "Now open the second."

Shadrack unwrapped the black silk from the longer parcel and stared in shock. Ghalan had returned his katana and wakizashi to him.

He drew the blade of his katana respectfully, noticing the blade had been sharpened after the battle at Kyoto village. He slashed his finger on the edge and resheathed the weapon.

"Now you are samurai once again," Ghalan said. "And you can draw upon the immense strength that Ieyasu Tanaka drilled into you."

Shadrack held the swords tightly to him and closed his eyes.

"Yes, I am samurai."

Ghalan nodded in satisfaction as he heard the strength and resolve in the ronin's voice.

The most incomprehensible thing about the universe is that it is comprehensible.

—Albert Einstein

13

Planet Tellus
Malkuth of Assiah
City of Prenzlau

Shadrack lowered his hands to his sides as he finished his banishing pentagram ritual. He breathed deeply, enjoying the sense of calm detachment the ritual bestowed upon him.

For three months he had followed the program of ritual magick advised by Ghalan. Each morning he rose with the sun, and at night he retired as it set. He performed the banishing pentagram ritual several times a day to dismiss negative psychic forces, and the Rousing of the Citadels, in which he stimulated his major chakras by visualization.

The program had had a beneficial effect on him. He felt much more balanced now, and though he was often cynical, he was no longer locked in the apathy that earlier characterized him. Neither had he received any further visitations from Lilith. He knew that the plane of Malkuth was alien to her and that she had difficulty in flexing her power here. She was also very wary of Ghalan's power, knowing he had considerably more strength than his quiet personality suggested.

As if he knew he was in the ronin's thoughts, a knock sounded at the door.

"Come in," Shadrack called.

Ghalan stepped through, and looked at Shadrack quizzically.

"You have just completed your rituals," he said.

"How do you know?"

"I can see the pentagrams. They are dim: you should try to visualize them stronger."

"Yes, father."

Ghalan crossed the room and sat in the middle of the floor. Shadrack knelt down to join him.

"I think that perhaps it is time for your diet to change," Ghalan said.

"Change?"

"We will exclude meat, fish, and eggs."

"Why? Surely my diet is irrelevant?"

"The new diet will open up your chakras further, and refine your astral body. Dense foods are not good for your astral form, or for your physical body for that matter. Although man has the teeth of an omnivore, he has the intestines of a vegetarian; meat is never fully digested. I think that your progress in ritual should shield you against being psychically opened too much."

"But why not eggs?"

"With meat and fish, a karmic debt is gained that is in proportion to the evolved state of the creature that is eaten. By eating it you are partly responsible for its death. But eggs have quite a different effect upon the gross astral form. The dense proteins contained in eggs cause animalistic behavior in humans. There is an old maxim that states that one is what one eats, and this is absolutely true. You have been fed on such foods thus far in order to heal your once-shattered body."

Shadrack smiled. "Does this mean I am a vegetable?"

Ghalan didn't respond. Shadrack had noticed that he only spoke when there was something meaningful to convey. It was as if he resented every moment he spent on the physical plane; he never seemed totally focused within it.

"Ghalan, you are wise. Will you answer a question for me?"

"A wise man simply knows the extent of his own ignorance. But I will try to answer."

"Why are we here? I don't mean on Tellus—I mean why do we exist. We suffer continuously, yet death seems to be the only goal. And then we repeat the cycle of suffering by incarnating again."

"You almost sound like a Black School initiate."

"Their doctrine as you explained it makes sense to me. Would it bother you if I embraced the philosophy of the Black School?"

Ghalan frowned. "Personally, no. All paths lead to the same destination. The art is in choosing the right path at the right time in order to grow. That path would not aid your growth. But it is your choice. It does not affect me."

Shadrack looked at the floor. "Sometimes you sound so callous, as if you care about nothing."

Ghalan stared at him, and for a brief moment his attention was completely focused. Shadrack shuddered; the intensity of the gaze reminded him of Dethen.

"You have to realize, Shadrack, that I have grown beyond anything you can imagine. Nothing can ever prepare you for the bitter experience of Binah. I have crossed the Abyss, cast away my mortal limitations in ways you cannot comprehend. I see the Divine Light in everything, sense its reality in every cell of my being. Yet despite this, I am still apart from the Light."

"You desire to be joined with it?"

Ghalan's eyes became so intense, Shadrack thought they would incinerate him.

"Yes! It is all I desire! Nothing else matters to me. This planet is a mere speck in an almost infinite universe, which is itself a mere speck in the Divine. Any events that occur here merely postpone my unity with the Light."

"You have a darkness about you, father. Yet I know that once you obtain your goal, you will not be like this at all. As Magus you cared for everyone and everything: no creature was below your attention."

Ghalan smiled; suddenly there was so much compassion in his eyes it pierced Shadrack to the core.

"No creature will be below my attention. Remember that for me these events are yet to happen." He paused. "I may seem callous to you now, and perhaps I am. But unless I focus purely on my goal, I will not obtain it. You must realize that my awareness is not at all like yours. As I sit here, I am aware of planes you do not even know exist. On some of them I am working, teaching, or communicating with others that need help. This is required of me by the Light. It is difficult to distribute my attention evenly. If I seem lacking in emotion it is because I am preoccupied with many others' problems. I may have taken the first step across the Abyss, but I am still a man.

When I become one with All That Is, then my resources will be unlimited."

"Is it worth it? All the pain we go through?"

"You have suffered greatly in this life, and in your last. But you should ask always for the reason behind it all."

"I don't want to know. I desire only peace, and an end to pain. And perhaps also to be reunited one day with Lena."

Ghalan raised an eyebrow: it was the first time Shadrack had intimated the latter desire.

"Life is difficult: it is the most impossible task. Yet remember that it is a continuously assessed test. We are presented with goals that we can achieve, if only we dig deeply enough. And eventually, man achieves a prize far greater than the peace that you desire.

"Once a man can stare into the deepest darkness without flinching, then there is hope that he can approach the brilliance of God without being burned." He sighed. "And I am presently within the deepest darkness—that last, most severe test before my graduation."

"There is no God where I exist," Shadrack said.

"He is everywhere, yet impossible for a normal man to perceive."

"Because he is separated in his self-proclaimed holiness by the Abyss!"

"The Abyss does indeed exist, and it does separate us from God. But that is due to our own smallness. To appreciate God, man's puny nature must make the transition from the finite to the infinite, from mortality to immortality.

"A man must expand his consciousness from being locked in one place and time, with petty selfish desires, to being omniscient, omnipotent, and universal. God created the male and female, the dimensions of space and time. To describe him in these terms is more ludicrous than explaining the nature of the sun in such human terms as anger and jealousy. Remember: 'Light is the shadow of God.' His nature transcends all description, and he can only be known by experiencing his presence."

"Which we are committed to doing."

"Every man and being will eventually fuse back into him, but this will all occur by free will. Every being must make its own choice of its own volition."

"Why do you refer to God as 'him'?"

"Limitations of the language. God has masculine and feminine aspects, and yet transcends both."

Shadrack mused thoughtfully. "Then how de we reach him? How do we develop?"

"There are many ways, and it is wise never to criticize another man's path. But in the main, it is life itself that leads us through the experiences we need to grow. There are quicker methods, but often these are more dangerous. Your twin brother found this out. He once attempted to use ritual magick."

Shadrack nodded. "My own rituals seem to be gradually increasing in power. I sometimes see flashes in the air as I perform them."

"That's good: you are beginning to develop astral sight. I've noticed that your fighting arts are rapidly improving now that your physical health is better."

"Yes, my *budo-kai* is much better."

Ghalan's eyes showed rare humor.

"Then perhaps we can make an exchange: I help you with your magical studies, and you teach me martial arts."

"Don't you think five hundred years is a little too old to start?"

"It is pre-ordained that you will teach me. Otherwise, how would you have known *budo-kai* as Malak? As you know, my future life lies in your past, and you're the only man capable of teaching me so that I can teach Malak and Dethen in my next life as Magus on Enya."

Shadrack frowned, confused. "So…you want me to teach you, so that you can then teach me in your next life?"

Ghalan nodded, his strange eyes glittering. "An interesting paradox."

Whatsoever a man soeth, that shall he also reap.

—Galatians 6:17

And if any mischief follows, then thou shalt give life for life,
Eye for eye, tooth for tooth, hand for hand, foot for foot.

—Exodus 21:23-25

14

Enya
Yesod of Yetzirah
Black School
subterranean lair

Murky black and purple clouds coalesced in the evening sky as night crept across the wilderness of eastern Enya. Two mounted figures sat silhouetted against the gently glowing skyline.

Dethen knew he was close to his goal. Around him lay the broken and arid ground of the huge wasteland, known only as the Wilderness Region. No one had ever lived within it in Dethen's last life, and even now it was populated only by hermits, snakes, and scorpions. But Dethen knew that the underground labyrinth he had once constructed lay less than a mile ahead, its multitude of entrances hidden from even the most persistent prier.

"We are here," he said. "It is best that you wait here."

Mendaz frowned. "I would fight by your side, Jaad."

Dethen nodded. "I know, but your skill with a blade will offer you no protection here."

He turned to Graymist. "Guard him," he ordered. He paused a moment, surprised at himself.

He urged his anemic mount forward. Within the Black School he knew he would find the Warlock, a being of tremendous power. Yet his own power had now fully returned. He knew the battle would be fierce; there could be only one victor.

Dethen pushed his way through the tight passageway, brushing away the enormous, dense spider webs that blocked his path. He knew the entrance would be unknown to the Warlock. Previously, only Dethen had known of its existence and the webs indicated this was still the case.

He had scried the labyrinth-like passageways of the underground lair, checking for new defenses since his last occupation. Very little had changed, though parts of the structure had been extended. He had found a magical seal near the center of the labyrinth. He had been unable to penetrate it by clairvoyance, but he knew his goal resided within the sealed chamber, which had once been the Black Guard initiation room.

He pushed on, ignoring the giant insects trapped within the webs. *Widowmaker* cast an unholy red light in a small radius around him, but beyond this limit he was blind.

In places the passage closed so tightly he thought he wouldn't be able to continue. His already bedraggled robes became filthy and torn, covered in web fragments and dead spiders. Even his hair wasn't safe from the grime.

After forcing his way for several minutes, the passage widened and the webs died away. He knew he approached the inhabited sections of the hideout. Whispers in the air informed him that he neared the first ring of etheral defenses.

When he had commanded the Black School, the defenses had been severe indeed. He expected they would be even stronger now, since magical effects were far more dangerous.

He gained only a few more yards before his expectations were fulfilled. Ahead of him, sections of the rock passage broke smoothly away from the walls. The boulders fell to the floor, glowing red-hot as they became molten pools of liquid. They took form as they cooled, gradually metamorphosing before Dethen's eyes. They slowly rose up, white putrid skin pulsating across their deformed, ghoulish bodies. The skin moved as if turning itself inside out; thick black veins erupted to form quivering networks, rippling with an intelligence of their own. The accompanying stench caused Dethen's gut to wrench.

He grimaced and controlled himself before moving forward. The white ghouls sprouted armor composed of fine black spikes, and the nearest started to develop tentacles. Dethen continued to advance, burying his disgust for the abominations.

"Who is it that dares to challenge the might of the Warlock?" the nearest creature asked, its hoarse growl sounding without a mouth.

Dethen stopped and held the gaze of the leader's pink albino eyes.

"His Nemesis," Dethen said, raising his arms to point splayed fingers at the ghouls.

The creatures staggered forward, but they advanced no farther. Purple lightning lanced from Dethen's fingers, searing the creatures. With high-pitched squeals, they exploded in a mass of foul-smelling blubber. Dethen protected his hands and face as the material rained down on him. He cursed as it burned through his robe like mineral acid, but it didn't damage his skin.

He took several breaths to control himself, weakened by the intense blast of energy he had released. He knew he couldn't release many bursts of power before his astral body was completely drained of energy.

With his composure regained, he recommenced his march toward the heart of the subterranean complex. He eyed the bodies of the dead creatures warily as he stepped over their corpses.

Nothing else challenged him for some time. Dethen was pleased: once through the outer ring of defenses, he knew he would be safe. However, this thought came to him too soon.

A specter materialized in the air before him, its insubstantial form levitating effortlessly. Its body rotated through the colors of the spectrum like a kaleidoscope, creating beautiful and bizarre images. Its eyes were like pieces of jet, blacker than the night sky, yet it was a darkness that seemed luminous.

Dethen saw several more beings hovering behind the first; he didn't have to turn to feel the icy chill of more spectres behind.

When the first spectre spoke, Dethen realized the entity was sentient.

"You should have turned back long ago, intruder. For now you must face our wrath, and a death more painful than you imagine. . . ." The words vibrated down Dethen's spine without crossing the air in between.

For the first time, Dethen became anxious. There were at least six entities crammed into the passageway, and he was unsure whether he had enough strength to defeat them all. If he did, it would surely mortally weaken him for his confrontation with the Warlock.

The phantoms advanced on him, their ebony eyes intent on his life-giving aura.

Dethen stood his ground.

"I am Frater Dethen of the Black School of Magick, Adeptus Major of the mighty Sephirah of Geburah! Harm me not, for there is no animosity between me and thee!"

The phantoms didn't slow their pace. Dethen paused for a moment, then drew the midnight blade of *Widowmaker*. She hummed voraciously at the sight of the spectres, her vibrations attuned to those of her master.

Dethen held the sword at eye level, his arm outstretched with the gently curved blade pointing downwards. The deep, blood-red garnet began to pulsate with light, searing along the passage in both directions. It intensified until its strength was almost blinding.

Now within a few yards of Dethen, the specters gasped in pain.

"The light! It is agony!" Dethen felt the exclamation down his spine.

"What you feel is my essence, creature of shadow. For the soul of this sword is joined intricately with mine own."

The light brightened further. The phantoms hissed, obviously in great pain.

"Frater Dethen of the Black School, mighty Adeptus Major of Geburah, there is no animosity between we and thee. Pass on unhindered, for thou art truly a Master."

Dethen bowed his head in acknowledgment and lowered *Widowmaker*. The specters dematerialized and *Widowmaker* dimmed in disappointment as he sheathed her.

Dethen continued his trek forward, satisfied in the knowledge he had left behind the last of the ethereal defenses.

The Warlock's skeletal hand tightly grasped his ivory staff; its gem glowed urgently in the dim light. Shouts of panic and screams of terror echoed through the passageway outside the throne room.

Within the chamber stood six armed Adepts. Bal sat beside the throne, still bound by the Warlock's magick.

"He should not have been able to penetrate the outer defenses, Master," said one of the Adepts, concern in his voice.

"Worry not, children. I expect nothing less from Dethen. Only the full unleashing of my power will stop this man."

A particularly bloodcurdling scream came from beyond the huge oaken door. The six Adepts visibly paled.

Bal smiled maliciously. "My Master comes," he said, unable to hide his glee.

The Warlock snarled. "I allow you to live only to see the downfall of your so-called master. You will see him kneel before me!"

All eyes turned to the chamber's entrance, which like the rest of the chamber, was immune to magickal attacks. The door imploded as Dethen's *yoko-geri* side kick shattered the structure. He strode into the chamber, *Widowmaker* humming eagerly in his hand.

He paused inside the door, his gaze locking with the Warlock's. The Demon's exquisite blue eyes battled fiercely with Dethen's austere black gaze. Neither flinched for several long seconds as a stalemate was reached.

Dethen was shocked by the demon's appearance, with its burning eyes, skeletal face, and protruding horns. He was even more shocked by its size: it stood over eight feet tall.

"So, this is the great Dethen of legend?" the Warlock mocked.

He laughed, and the group of Adepts joined in nervously. Dethen's robes were ripped and burned through, hanging from his body. Fragments of web clung to his hair, mixed with white ooze from the destroyed ghouls. The sight contrasted radically with his grim expression.

"You will kneel before me, Dethen of Enya."

"I think not," Dethen said; he started to advance.

The Warlock motioned to the group of Adepts. After slight hesitation, two of them rushed in to attack. Dethen slid to the side of the first attacker's sword and slashed him across the torso. The man fell with a choked cry. He sliced through the blade of the second attacker with *Widowmaker*, reversing the direction of the slash to decapitate his opponent. He turned to continue his ominous advance.

The Warlock's eyes burned even more ferociously.

"It seems I must destroy you myself, Dethen."

He raised a skeletal hand. A blast of violet flame sprang from it. Caught by surprise, the force threw Dethen to land heavily on his back. *Widowmaker* bounced from his grip as he hit the floor. He lay still, the wind knocked from his body. The force of the blast shocked him. He felt scorch marks across his face, and his hair smoldered.

The Warlock walked over to his prone prey.

"You were unwise, Dethen. Against any other opponent, you would have been victorious. But to challenge the warlock is foolishness itself."

He turned to face the four Black Adepts.

"Pick him up!"

Two of the men rushed over to drag Dethen to his feet, then quickly retreated.

Dethen stared at the Warlock with an unfocused gaze. The impact had dazed him. The demon stared into his eyes, amazed to see there was no trace of anger or embarrassment.

Again, he raised his hand; suddenly a glowing circle of brilliant light surrounded Dethen. It faded, leaving Dethen's upper body heavily chained and restricted. The Black Adept struggled for a second, then gave up: it was obvious he would never escape the trap.

"Now, Dethen of Enya. you will kneel before me and serve me, or suffer agonizing torture for the rest of your life on this plane."

"No."

Dethen's body spasmed; a cry of agony escaped his lips as unspeakable pain racked through his body.

"You will kneel, human!"

"No."

Dethen screamed as his essence was violated by unbearable torment; he felt his soul being torn apart.

The Warlock's eyes locked with his.

"OBEY ME!" the demon commanded, his voice ripping through the chamber.

Dethen bowed his head in defeat, streams of sweat dripping from his forehead. With a pitiful sigh, he sank onto one knee. The Warlock's eyes flamed with triumph.

"You were a fool to challenge me."

"I was a fool," Dethen agreed.

"And you will now address me as Master, slave!" The Warlock wielded his staff as one would to a disobedient dog.

"Does this please you, Master?" Dethen asked, the resistance stripped from him.

"Oh, yes," the Warlock said, his demonic grin now a leer. "Oh, yes!"

Dethen lifted his head to hold the Demon's gaze.

"Good. And now I will destroy you."

The Warlock stepped back a pace at the terrible intensity of rage in the Black Adept's eyes. Dethen stood up, his aura glowing scarlet. It expanded and strengthened with the awesome vigor of his rage.

His shackles melted, the molten iron flowing from his body. He took a step forward. The Warlock, fear evident in his eyes, lifted his hand. A burst of violet flame erupted, even more powerful than the last. Dethen made the Sign of Harpocrates. The energy deflected off his aura and hit the four Adepts, incinerating them instantly.

The Warlock panicked, his hands shaking. Yet he still had the advantage of physical size. He lunged forward, raising his staff to strike.

Dethen ducked under the powerful blow and put out his hand. *Widowmaker* leapt across the room and into his palm, just as the second swing bore down on him. Dethen's parry was so forceful, the ivory staff snapped with the impact. The Warlock stumbled backwards, his face horrified.

Dethen looked at the pieces of staff at his feet and picked up the glowing blue gem. He frowned as he studied it.

"Please, be careful!" the Warlock gasped, desperate to retain his property.

Dethen smiled malignantly as he lowered the gem. The Demon froze as he realized his secret was known.

"Perhaps you would like to battle me without the aid of this gem?" Dethen asked, the anger dying in his eyes.

The Warlock shook his head emphatically. "Perhaps a truce, we are both reasonable men...."

Dethen threw his head back and laughed, a sound made sinister by its lack of humor. "You are right, we are both *men*."

A look of concentration crossed his face, and the Warlock's fearsome appearance began to change. The horns retracted, the skull becoming more human as the massive frame began to shrink. Within a few seconds, the Warlock was gone. In his place was a dark-haired woman in chain mail, perhaps forty years old.

"And you are?" Dethen asked.

"Kalinda." There was fear in the woman's eyes, yet she didn't cower.

Dethen's black gaze dissected her. "You may call yourself Kalinda in this life, but I think I know you by an older name."

The woman nodded. "A different body, but the same soul."

"Yes, I remember you, apprentice. The gender may be different, but you are still Felmarr." He fingered the gem thoughtfully. "Do you realize the crime you have committed in imprisoning this creature?"

Kalinda shuddered. "Please, Dethen. Do not…"

"…break the gem," Dethen finished.

Kalinda's bottom lip quivered. "I would face even your wrath before hers."

Dethen smiled maliciously. "We shall see."

He let go of the gem; it hovered in the air. As he stared at it, flickers of green electricity sparked across its surface. Suddenly it accelerated towards the ground with tremendous speed. Kalinda screamed in horror, but knew she was helpless.

The gem shattered in an explosion of azure light, releasing a tremendous blast of wind. The room's temperature plummeted, thick ice forming on the walls and floor. A frozen mist hung suspended in the air as the wind died. Absolute silence reigned as their breath crystalized in the air. Despite the silence, great anticipation lay in the air.

Dethen sheathed *Widowmaker*.

"I am Frater Dethen, Adeptus Major of Geburah. It was I who released you, spirit of the gem."

The air luminesced with a warm golden light. The voice that replied was soft and feminine, with the quality of velvet; at the same time it seemed strong and forceful.

"You have my eternal gratitude, Dethen of Enya."

The air shimmered and a Chinese dragon appeared, its emerald scales glittering. Its immense body wrapped around the perimeter of the room several times. The dragon's eyes were captivating, the same supernatural blue as the Warlock's but even more intense.

"I am Tien Lung, protector of the celestial spheres. Ask me a favor, and it shall be granted."

"I ask only that you spare the life of this woman," Dethen said.

The dragon's lips pulled back into a smile, revealing an array of fearsome diamond canines. "This human has wronged me, imprisoned me for a thousand years. I cannot grant this as your favor, but I will repect your wish for now. My revenge will descend when she least expects it."

Kalinda stared at the dragon, rooted to the floor with fear.

"Get it away from me, Dethen. You don't know what it's capable of!"

The dragon leaned forward, its hypnotic eyes inches from Kalinda's. "Don't worry, little one. We will have plenty of time to play later."

Kalinda shivered violently; her knees gave way and she collapsed to the floor, still transfixed by the exquisite stare.

The dragon's body began to spin, twisting into a whirlwind of mist.

"Dethen of Enya, know this. Tien Lung repays her favors. You have saved me this day by freeing me. I leave you with this prophecy: I will save you in the future by entrapping you. Until then, our paths will not cross."

The whirlwind spun faster and faster, shearing through the chamber. Then suddenly it was gone.

Kalinda looked around her suspiciously, the tears already drying on her face. Out of immediate danger, the arrogance had already returned to her eyes.

Dethen felt incredibly tired. His eyes strayed over to the only seat—the Warlock's throne. Sitting next to it was a Black Adept. Though his face was different, Dethen immediately recognized him.

"You have not dwindled in power, Master," Bal said, his eyes sparkling with pleasure.

Dethen smiled, and for once it was a good-natured gesture. He walked over to embrace his old disciple.

"Well met, Bal," he said. "Well met."

Perhaps what is not intelligible to me is therefore not unreasonable. There may be a realm of wisdom from which the logician is banished.

—Socrates

Enya
City of Sophia

Amethyst light glittered in the eastern sky as the two riders approached the pentagon-walled city of Sophia. The air was fresh and damp, becoming more vibrant as the dawn rays massaged it from lethargy. The walls of Sophia coruscated as they fractured the morning light into a million shards of blue.

Lena rode the last half mile in silence with Cassius, as most of the journey had been spent. They had crossed many miles over two days, with little rest and no sleep. The wilderness was simply too dangerous to relax in, and Cassius had taken no chances, especially when the waxing moon was still weak. There had been little opportunity for conversation and the journey had been tense.

Lena was surprised by the size of the city. Though it was large compared to the cities of old, it was dwarfed by Gorom. There seemed to be nothing in common between the two cities. Gorom was a disgusting cesspit, crawling with vermin, disease, and corruption. Sophia was immediately noticeable for its cleanliness and the stout, square Egyptian-style buildings. Though perhaps over-proud, the few people around carried themselves with dignity and grace. Unlike Gorom, not all citizens were armed, and the women and children were obviously held in far higher regard.

The contingent of guards at the gate saluted formally as Cassius passed through.

"Hail, prince of Sophia!"

Cassius nodded and waved them away, too tired for formalities.

Lena noticed the guards took pride in their appearance. They wore polished chain mail and carried longswords of fine steel. Dark blue capes flowed from their shoulders, a silver pentagon embroidered on the back.

There were few people about at such an early hour, but Cassius was still recognized several times. Lena noticed that he was received very coolly by the people, but greeted with warmth by the soldiers. It struck her that after several days she still knew very little about her riding companion. She realized that there were some things she needed to know.

"Cassius?" she asked.

The warrior's attention was fixed on the city walls as he brooded on matters of defense. He seemed startled by her voice, as if he'd forgotten her presence.

"What is it, Lena?" His voice was neutral but tired.

"Will you tell me more of this…Shadrack?" The name was strange to Lena, but she would seek out her precious Malak in whatever form he now took. "Did he have memories of his lives on Enya?"

Cassius turned his face to her, and instead of the offended look she'd half-expected, his pale blue eyes held slight affection.

"He had no direct memories, yet he did speak our language, which on Tellus is known as Hebrew. And he was constantly haunted by his previous identity, which he had no understanding of. Yet, he would often dream of you, and he recalled your name to me on occasion."

Cassius saw hope and relief appear in Lena's eyes. It was poignant to him, for only he had experienced the true horror of Shadrack's soul.

"What was he like? Did he resemble Malak in many ways?" Lena asked.

He shrugged. "A difficult question to ask any father, and besides, I never knew Malak. But Shadrack's name came from his character, and meant 'strange one.' Ekanar gave the name to him as I recall. But everything that he was came from his life as Malak, and from his possession by Lilith."

"His life must have been hell."

The smell of freshly baked bread greeted their nostrils as they passed a small bakery; the lights within the building were being extinguished as the baker completed the preparation of his wares.

Cassius inhaled the aroma, suddenly feeling very hungry. It caused his mind to dwell on Nippon, where luxuries such as bread had not existed. For the villages of the Empire, each day had been a struggle for survival against the bitter cold and lack of food and resources. The more Cassius dwelt upon Nippon, the closer his mind moved to the great shame that haunted him.

"Shadrack was an outsider," he affirmed. "He was forever separated from others by something he was unable to understand. As a child, he was strong and intelligent, and powerfully motivated. He almost seemed to know that a great task lay ahead of him.

"But later my teachings had a greater effect upon him. He desperately wanted to become samurai, an elite warrior class of the Nipponese Empire. Eventually he did become samurai, after I made a grave and unforgivable mistake."

He hung his head in guilt. Lena saw the weight of shame upon him. She perceived that few others had witnessed Prince Cassius Hawkin in this state.

"Something haunts you from your past," she said.

Cassius sighed. "As Ieyasu Tanaka, I bounced between two extremes without realizing what I now know to be true. I was born to a western father, which in the harsh land of Nippon made me a despicable half-breed. Yet I was proud, and extremely ambitious. My low birth status, humiliation, and lack of honor in the eyes of others drove me to seek recognition.

"In Nippon, samurai are like lords, and all others are peasants, even the rich merchants. Yet I worked my way up from being a lowly half-breed warrior, little better than a ronin."

"A ronin?" Lena mouthed the strange, foreign word.

"A masterless samurai. To the Nipponese, everything has its place in the world, fitting perfectly into a strict hierarchy. Samurai are warrior aristocrats, the elite of humanity. But a ronin is an outsider, one who has lost or betrayed his lord. The ronin is considered purposeless in the world, isolated and severed from his roots. Any honorable samurai would commit *seppuku*, the hara-kiri death ritual, before accepting such a fate.

"And my beginnings were little better than this. But eventually I clawed my way up to captain of the Shogun's Royal Guard, a position of great honor and prestige. And in my climb to glory, I was brutal and completely merciless. I was utterly without the honor that I sought to have in the eyes of others. I was, in truth, a monster.

"But what seemed to be a chance encounter with a wise old man triggered a change within me. It finally manifested dramatically many years later, when I refused to perform my duty for the Shogun."

"Which was?"

Cassius' voice was bitter: "To kill the leader of an opposing sect. And to murder his only child."

Lena saw the anguish in his eyes, and she knew the memories still held great emotion. Though he bore a different name, the man before her was still Ieyasu Tanaka.

"It is no secret that life is often circular," he continued, "and after my disgrace, I returned to the bottom of the social hierarchy. But this time I was a fugitive, a true ronin. I was an outcast, drifting alone through a barren world. My attitude to life had changed completely. Though I still practiced *budo-kai,* I abhorred violence, and considered it to be inexcusable under any conditions. This philosophy I drilled into Shadrack, night and day, until it was second nature to him."

"He killed someone, didn't he?"

Cassius looked up, surprised by her perceptiveness.

"He killed three men. And though he did it to save my life, I disowned him." He hung his head low in shame. "I ordered him to leave the village."

Lena's eyes became hard, her voice cold. "Was that the last time you saw him?"

Cassius shook his head, and gave a smile that resembled a snarl.

"I failed him utterly. He returned to Kyoto village two years later, as part of a contingent of the Shogun's Royal Guard. Ironic, really. He was ordered to kill me, since I was a fugitive. When he refused, his life was made forfeit."

"Was he killed?" Lena asked, her tone guarded.

Cassius shook his head. "That might have been easier for him than the horror that unfolded. The pain and pressure of all his years suddenly exploded, and Lilith possessed his body. Samurai are elite fighters, unrivaled anywhere, yet he tore a score of them limb from limb. He eventually murdered the Shogun, hoisting him up like a rag doll and snapping his neck like a twig."

Tears formed in Lena's eyes as she listened: she couldn't begin to imagine the pain her husband had been through.

"Was Shadrack killed?"

Cassius looked at her, his eyes red. "I don't know. He was mortally wounded in the battle, but I died before he did." His voice became a whisper. "I thought I followed the honorable path, but I committed perhaps my greatest crime. I selfishly took my own life when Shadrack needed me most."

"You abandoned him?" Lena's voice was accusing.

Cassius closed his eyes, the accusation cutting him to the heart. "I think he may have survived, but as to the state of his mind.... I think his humanity was all but destroyed."

Lena blinked away her tears. "I can't accept that. Whatever his condition, I will be here for him. It seems that no one else has stood beside him."

Cassius winced at the pain in her voice. "Lena, I know you must feel I betrayed him. But that was not my intention. At the time, I followed what I thought was the only honorable path. I hope you find it within you to forgive me." His eyes were pleading.

"It is not me that has to forgive you Cassius," Lena said icily. She leaned forward in the saddle. "But if I discover Malak has suffered because of your betrayal, I'll make sure you pay for it."

She urged her mount forward, leaving Cassius behind.

Cassius frowned. Normally he would have laughed off a threat from a woman, but something about the look in Lena's eyes disturbed him. He shuddered and trotted after her.

As a man thinks, so does he become. Every man is the son of his own works.

—Cervantes

16

Enya Black School subterranean lair

Dethen sat in lotus posture within the room that had once been his personal chamber, and had now been reclaimed. Little had been disturbed since he last occupied it and the room had been thoroughly cleaned of dust. The room still bore magnetism from Dethen's previous incarnation, and this had somehow dissuaded spiders and insects from inhabiting the room.

Bal sat in front of Dethen, ecstatic at the return of his Master. Though it pleased Dethen to recover one of his faithful disciples, his attitude was cooler.

"This is your first return to Enya since the Summoning?" Dethen asked him.

"Yes, Master."

Bal studied the Black Master. He saw that Dethen's face had changed slightly, the unavoidable consequence of taking a new incarnation. The harsh, cruel scars were still present, as were the deep black bags below the eyes. The bags now extended upward, however, to form black rings around his eyes, which seemed even more haunted.

"You have been alive how long?"

"Forty-five years, Master."

"And how have you spent this time?"

"My early years were spent regaining my identity and memories." He paused, uncertain. He didn't want to reveal the years of debauchery he'd wasted on prostitutes and drugs of decadence.

Dethen would never understand such a waste of time. "I have been determining the political structure of Enya as I awaited your return."

"Indeed? And tell me, Bal, what have you discovered?"

"The Black School totally dominates the plane through the campaigns of the Warlock. We have more troops and better organization than anything else on the plane, which is why nothing stands against us. Only Sophia managed to resist the Warlock."

"And what makes Sophia different?"

Bal shrugged. "The leader is unusual. His name is Cassius Hawkin, and he is a seasoned warrior. There are also rumors that he is resistant to magick."

Dethen raised an eyebrow. "He is a great Adept?"

"No. He has no magical training whatsoever."

"Interesting. And what of the Yellow School?"

"If they decided to interfere, they would be an irresistible force on the plane. There is little information regarding their numbers, but no one ever doubts their strength. Even the Warlock was careful not to antagonize them. But, as ever, they seek non-interference. They are nothing to worry about."

"Do not make assumptions, Bal. Especially dangerous ones like that."

"Yes, Master," Bal said, chastised.

"Now, you mentioned the Warlock, and I believe Kalinda is waiting for an audience."

Bal frowned. "Master, you said that Kalinda was once Felmarr?"

"That is correct."

"How could he betray you? He was once as loyal as myself!"

Dethen smiled cynically. "Don't be bitter, Bal. Don't even be disappointed. His betrayal of me is nothing, but his betrayal of the Purpose is poignant. However, it simply reveals once again the squalid condition of human nature, and Kalinda strengthens our resolve for the Purpose, even as she denies it herself."

Bal nodded, feeling more relaxed. He had been reunited with his master's wisdom, and all was well.

"What was the creature that you released from Kalinda's gem, Master?"

"A Celestial Dragon called Tien Lung. Probably summoned by Kalinda, and imprisoned via a ritual. She may know its true name. They are beings of great power and wisdom, and they properly dwell on the higher astral, in the upper realms of Yetzirah. After imprisoning the creature, Kalinda forced it to channel its power into her."

"Why did you aid the creature, Master? It is a being of light, surely not an ally of ours?"

Dethen looked at his disciple with impatience. "My quarrel is with Chronzon only. He rules and dictates everything that exists below the Abyss, and therefore I will destroy all that exists below the Abyss. And once the mighty Chronzon is defeated, God shall answer to me for the abomination of the Tree. Yet, I have no quarrel with individual creatures, unless they seek to interfere with my plans."

"I understand, Master. We are to focus solely on the Purpose."

A knock on the door suddenly interrupted the conversation.

"I have asked someone to join us, Bal. It is someone I particularly want you to meet." Dethen raised his voice: "Enter!"

The door opened and Mendaz stepped in. "You wanted to see me, Jaad?"

"Yes, Mendaz. I want you to meet Bal, who was my father in my last life."

Mendaz nodded and stepped forward. Bal stood up and turned to face him.

"You!" he said, stunned; Mendaz had changed little in twenty-five years and Bal remembered well the event in the cavern.

Mendaz frowned. "Have we met?" He studied the bald, dark-skinned Adept. Somehow the Adept seemed familiar.

"That night!" Mendaz hissed. "Dark Moon, all those years ago. You bewitched my wife!"

Dethen stood up. "What is going on here?" he demanded.

Mendaz leapt forward, drawing his dagger. Bal was caught off guard, shocked by his attacker's speed. He managed to slip aside, barely escaping with his life. Mendaz turned and attacked again, a death thrust to the heart. Bal dodged and prepared to release an astral blast intense enough to kill the warrior.

Suddenly Dethen's body was between them. The dagger glanced off him as if he were stone and the blast of energy deflected away, shaking the room as it collided with the wall.

"There will be no fighting here!" Dethen commanded. "What in the ten hells is going on here?"

Mendaz glowered, and seemed about to disobey. "This scum was responsible for the death of my wife, your mother. He used magick on her to complicate the birth."

"What do you mean, his mother?" Bal asked, angry yet confused. "I am Dethen's father. I used magick on your wife because I was defending Yhana, my mate. Yhana was pregnant with Dethen."

Dethen raised an eyebrow. "No, Bal. Mendaz is my father. I do not know this Yhana you speak of."

"But surely. . . ." Bal stopped, uncertain.

"Dethen was the baby you worked your magick on, cretin!" Mendaz shouted. His eyes glittered dangerously but Dethen's stare silenced him.

"Then by the gods, who did Yhana give birth to?" Bal asked, his eyes shell-shocked.

Mendaz sneered. "It seems you had a daughter and didn't even know it. I met her a few days ago in Gorom. Her name is Fiona, and she's far prettier than you are!"

"Enough!" Dethen said. "You two will settle your differences now."

"He is responsible for your mother's death!" Mendaz hissed. "His mate sliced her throat!"

Bal shook his head. "I only caused the baby to be born. I wouldn't have wasted magick on anything more. And whatever Yhana did in my absence is hardly my responsibility. I am sorry for your loss."

Mendaz hesitated, unsure. Dethen scrutinized Bal.

"He speaks truth," he said after a moment. "About the magick, anyway."

"And about being sorry?" Mendaz asked.

Dethen remained silent.

"Doesn't it bother you that he had a part in your mother's death?" Mendaz said, his eyes still dangerous.

Dethen shrugged. "People die. That is life. That is why we seek to achieve the Purpose. Leave us awhile. Bal and I must talk."

Mendaz lifted the dagger higher, uncertain.

"Leave us," Dethen said. "And I don't want to have this conversation again. You seek to be more than you are. Well, that evolution begins here."

Mendaz sighed and sheathed his dagger. "Yes, Jaad. I will leave because it is your bidding." He glared at Bal, a look of pure hatred, and left the room.

"I want you to do something for me," Dethen said once he had gone.

"Anything, Master," Bal said immediately.

"I want you to appoint him captain of the Black Guard."

Bal smiled viciously. "That will end his life quicker than anything I can do."

"He is far tougher than you think," Dethen said, then looked thoughtful. "Just in case, I want you to keep an eye on him. Make sure no one harms him."

Bal was incredulous. "Surely he should look out for himself! Only the strong survive! That is the rule! That is *your* rule!"

"Just do this one thing for me!" Dethen shouted, his voice uncharacteristically emotional.

"Yes, Master," Bal said quietly.

"Leave now," Dethen said. "I have much to think about."

Bal stood up and bowed; when he left his eyes were still angry.

Dethen pulled the hood of his robe across his head and closed his eyes. He felt fatigued from his battle with Kalinda, and he had much to consider. Now that Enya was without a Magus, he had to reconsider how to achieve the Purpose. His first attempt had failed with the summoning of Lilith.

There were three factors of significance. The first was the potency of magick on Enya, which would be an important factor in his plans. Second was the fact that the Celestial Tower was now an extension of Lilith's domain, and that the Tower's dimension was almost synchronous with Enya. It might be possible to create a bridge for Lilith to cross. The third factor of importance was Malak. With his soul now joined with Lilith's, he could present unforseeable consequences.

Dethen wondered whether his brother had returned to Enya. It seemed likely he had incarnated, since Dethen knew that himself, Felmarr, Bal, and Lena had reincarnated. It was all too coincidental: it seemed that those who played a part at the time of the Summoning were returning to resolve the problems created. Between them existed a complex karmic web that demanded resolution.

However, if Malak was on Enya, Dethen felt he would have sensed him. It was a puzzle, because Malak would obviously have a large part to play in the battle ahead. If he was under Lilith's control, the Arch-Demon could have anything planned.

Dethen suddenly raised his head and opened his eyes. He felt a presence within the chamber, gradually intensifying. The force emanated from behind him: the hair on the nape of his neck prickled in anticipation. He looked at the dark purple altar a few feet in front of him. *Widowmaker* lay across it, slowly pulsing with an anxious blood-red light. He felt a twinge of concern as he realized *Widowmaker* was nervous. His solar plexus tightened with the tension.

He sat perfectly still, watching the air behind his head through the scrying crystal on the altar. His psychic hearing became imperceptibly high; there was no doubt something materialized behind him. The sickly smell of jasmine drifted through the chamber as a soft blue-green light expanded behind him. Its surface rippled like water as it slowly took form.

Within a few seconds, the light resolved into a human shape. When it faded, Dethen saw the vague image of a blonde-haired woman within the crystal. Even without the face being focused, he immediately knew who stood behind him. His throat constricted with emotion.

The woman walked seductively over to him, wrapping her arms around his neck. Dethen trembled at her touch, his mind losing its sharpness. She gently turned his head to look into her face; his heart almost stopped.

Her eyes were deep and brown, just as he remembered them. Her hair was soft and blonde, reaching down to her bare shoulders. He reached out and touched the smooth, lightly tanned skin of her face. Even the mole that had graced her left cheek was present, and the smell—the soft, caressing smell of her hair aroused memories of lovemaking that had been buried for four lifetimes.

"Anya!" the word choked in his throat.

Had she returned to finally forgive him, to end the burning hatred he had of himself? Deep down he knew the intense hatred he held for himself, for Chronzon, and the whole universe consumed him utterly. Though he controlled it with an iron grip, there was nothing else left in him.

She leaned forward to kiss him, her eyes locking with his. His sluggish mind fought for lucidity; he knew something was wrong, even as his body yearned for the touch of her tender lips.

"No!" he said, slowly pulling back. "You can't be! Anya is dead!"

Yet as he backed into the wall, he didn't believe his own words. He didn't want to believe them. She smiled disarmingly, showing the perfectly white teeth he remembered so well. He stood with his back against the wall, unable to retreat any further.

His libido raged out of control. After being forcefully subdued for so many lifetimes, the suppressed energy returned in a single, engulfing wave. Dethen's breath rasped with a passion even he couldn't control.

"Come, Michael!" she purred. "Is this your welcome to me after so long? Come, and we will make gentle love as we used to...."

Dethen winced involuntarily at the mention of his previous name. It was a name he had sought ruthlessly to forget.

As she reached him, he found himself pressed against the wall, unable to retreat any farther. He knew his mind was being influenced; his thoughts were unclear. Yet he desperately wanted the fantasy to be real.

She pressed her body against him, holding her face less than an inch from his own. She moved to kiss him, and he moved forward to accept her embrace, their arms wrapping around each other. Her tongue slipped into his mouth, searching for his, and his head swam dizzily. His heart soared among the stars.

Suddenly she screamed and pushed herself away. Dethen opened his eyes, his mind reeling in horror. He had thrust his longsword into his love, the blade biting deeply through her flesh. The blood flowed in merciless quantities, staining the white nightdress a violent red.

Dethen shook his head, tears flowing down his face. In her eyes he could see terrible pain, and the unfathomable love had become abysmal hatred. The look of betrayal pierced him to the heart.

"Why? I loved you more than my life!" she gasped as the last breath slipped from her lips.

Dethen fell to his knees, screaming in agony and torment. Each time he relived the torment he found it more difficult to live with himself, and his hatred of Chronzon increased ten fold. He collapsed into a fit of sobbing.

The sound of girlish laughter gradually penetrated through his shell. He looked up, his face tear-streaked. In the center of the room stood an incredibly beautiful naked woman, with lustrous black hair and purple, alien eyes.

Lilith giggled. "I didn't think I'd ever see the great Dethen cry at the sight of such an illusion! And you are the arch-enemy of Lord Chronzon! How amusing! And how pathetic!"

"You!" Dethen gasped, the rage mounting within him.

Lilith gave a flamboyant bow, oblivious to the look in Dethen's eyes, which gained a depth even her own demonic gaze didn't match. Fury coursed through him, bursting like a tidal wave from the pit of his soul. He stood up. Lilith gained only a momentary warning and as his aura flared such an intense scarlet, the room was blinded.

With a scream of rage, Dethen projected his astral body. It accelerated at tremendous speed, impacting with Lilith's unprepared astral form. The two bodies merged into one as they were carried beyond the confines of the chamber, their speed carrying them through several sub-planes.

Dethen's cry wailed through the astral plane. His body mingled with Lilith's to form a shooting star. Every part of him burned agonizingly as the Demon's essence penetrated into him. It was an unbearable pain that no normal man could endure, yet Dethen clung to the Demon dearly. Pain was his closest friend, more familiar then breathing.

He forced Lilith higher up the astral, away from the vibrational rate of her own domain. Yet the Demon had recovered from her shock now; she slowly suffocated the life from him. She wrapped around his astral form, squeezing with incredible pressure. Dethen battled fiercely just to retain consciousness. The memory of Chronzon's crushing hand came rushing back to him, along with the feeling of helplessness he had suffered.

With the memory came the remembrance of his escape, and he fought back viciously. He caught Lilith off guard, almost reversing positions with her. But she held fast, preparing the final crush that would shatter his body and wipe him from existence.

"No, Dethen!" he felt her words vibrate through him. "You won't pierce the heart of this woman with your sword!"

Dethen's rage surged and augmented beyond his control, until he thought he would drown within it. He hurled every atom of his being at the demon. With it went all his torment and hatred, his frustrations and experiences of battle with Chronzon.

For the first time in eternity, Lilith screamed.

A moment later, Dethen was hurled back into his body. As his astral form reintegrated itself, he stumbled backwards into the wall.

His blurred vision came into focus, and he saw Lilith seated in the middle of the chamber. His eyes hardened and he moved toward *Widowmaker*.

"There'll be no need for that," Lilith said. "I didn't come here for a battle, Dethen."

He stopped and turned to face her.

"Really? Then, pray tell, why did you come, Demon?" he asked, his tone bitter.

Lilith smiled, yet a little of the arrogance had disappeared from the gesture.

"I came to discuss matters with you. The illusion I forced upon you was a weakness I couldn't resist. However, you paid me back in kind. You are a powerful man, Dethen. As powerful as your reputation, even. And you have such rage inside you.

"You do realize, however, that I am only at a fraction of my power on Enya, otherwise I would have crushed you instantly when you attacked."

Dethen didn't react, but he knew she wasn't lying. If she had been present in all her power, the manifestation would have split the entire plane. Though minor entities could squeeze through the weakened Boundary, only a fraction of Lilith's essence could.

"What is it you want, Demon?"

"I still want this plane," she said. "For by entering it from my domain in the Qlippoth, I can break through into Yesod. And there I can achieve exactly what you desire."

Dethen sat down tiredly. "And how do you suggest this is achieved?"

Lilith smiled insidiously. "There is only one way, and I have already begun preparations. To summon my full essence requires a proper gateway, and the Rose Circle has already proven unsuitable."

Dethen nodded, casting his memory back to the awesome explosion that had killed him in his previous life. The contrast between the being he had summoned there and the incredibly beautiful woman before him was unbelievable, but he knew they were the same entity.

"What gateway do you propose?" he asked. "The Rose Circle is the only one gateway Enya possesses."

"It is the only permanent gateway. But I have a plaything that will perform the task admirably. It is your dear brother."

"Malak? He is on Enya?"

"He was Malak. He is now Shadrack, and he has incarnated in the world of Assiah, on a planet known as Tellus."

"I know it. I spent an incarnation on Tellus, what was then Earth."

"All you have to do is wait for him to return. And then you can use him as a focus for your second ritual, because his soul and mine are one."

"And what makes you certain he will return?"

Lilith laughed. "Worry not, dear Dethen. I will push him myself, and I think sufficient impetus will come from his lovely wife on this plane...."

Dethen nodded. "Do we have anything else to discuss, Demon?"

Lilith could see that he had still not recovered from the illusion she had forced upon him. She didn't tell him that it had simply been a fantasy in his own mind, which she had made reality. She took no pleasure in the emotional wound she had inflicted upon him, for she still felt the repercussions of his attack on her.

"One thing I will tell you, Dethen. And take good notice of this, for I would swear it by my own name."

"Go on."

"There will be a great battle in the end between you and your brother, and only one of you will cross the Abyss to become Magus of Enya, should Enya survive our current plan."

"That I already know."

Lilith smiled. "It is already written who that will be."

"And that is?"

"It is you, of course. If your ritual fails, then ultimately you will still be triumphant!"

She laughed and faded away in a burst of blue-green light, leaving Dethen perplexed. For some strange reason, he felt sure she spoke the truth.

This above all: to thine own self be true,
And it must follow, as the night the day,
Thou canst not then be false to any man.

—*Hamlet*, William Shakespeare

17

Planet Tellus
Malkuth of Assiah
Saxon mid-lands

"Enough!" Ghalan shouted, falling to the ground in defeat. Shadrack tilted his head in surprise.

"There are limits to a five hundred-year-old man's fitness," Ghalan said.

Shadrack sat next to him. Over the past months Ghalan's fitness had shocked him, along with his incredible ability to learn *budokai*. The old man always seemed in perfect control of his body, and though the movements weren't breathtakingly sharp, they were fluid and precise. Shadrack could only suppose that Ghalan's sublime spiritual level, and his ability to focus his consciousness contributed to his unnatural ability.

Even though Ghalan wouldn't be the greatest warrior in this life, it was the mental understanding he gained that was important. When he recalled his skills in his next life, supposedly as Malak's father, his body would be able to put to use what his spirit had learned. Shadrack still found the paradox disturbing, but he avoided thinking about the subject.

Ghalan now lay flat on his back, arms by his sides. His eyes were closed, and sweat covered his face. Shadrack watched him sadly. He loved the old man dearly, but it was rare that Ghalan showed any emotion in return. He seemed to resent every moment spent on the physical plane.

In a few minutes Ghalan pushed himself up, his lungs recovered.

"Come," he said, "there is something I must show you before you leave."

Shadrack stood up to follow him, then realized what the old man had said.

"Leave?"

Ghalan stopped and looked at him quizzically.

"You must realize you are near full health. Your destiny will not await you for much longer."

There was silence between the two men as Ghalan led his student through a part of the cathedral he hadn't passed through before. In truth, Shadrack had left his chamber rarely in the last few months.

Eventually the pair reached a little-used door that led to the bottom of a spiral staircase.

"I hope you appreciate the strain you're putting an old man's joints under," Ghalan muttered as he ascended, his student behind him.

The staircase was narrow, and seemed to stretch up without end. Shadrack became lost in a light trance, as he counted each step he passed. He had counted 325 before he almost bumped into Ghalan.

"We're here," the old man said.

Shadrack followed him out onto the top of the last surviving spire. They walked over to the battlements.

The late autumn air brushed coolly against their skin as a light rain gently fell. Below them, the cathedral gardens were tiny, like a picture painted by some talented artist. The wreckage of Prenzlau spread out for miles in every direction.

"Amazing..." Shadrack said under his breath. "I've never been this high up before."

"This is not what I wanted to show you," Ghalan said, indicating the scene before him with a sweep of his arm. "Look over there."

Shadrack followed the direction of his finger, but the distant countryside was masked by the thin mist that hung in the morning air.

"Let me show you," Ghalan said.

He touched his fingers to Shadrack's temples. Immediately the ronin's vision swam, and he seemed to hover over the land like an eagle. He swooped over a green hilltop, where there stood eight stone sentries.

Within seconds he swooped back, diving down into the stone circle of megaliths. He drew in his breath sharply, vaguely remembering the day Tanaka had found him inside a stone circle in Nippon.

"What is it?" he asked, a tremor in his voice.

"They are the witch stones. They lie several miles to the north, and they form a powerful gateway between worlds."

"I am to return to Enya through the circle?"

"Yes," Ghalan said, removing his fingers. Shadrack's vision blurred and returned to normal.

"I'm not ready to return yet," Shadrack said as he stared off into the mist. "I am still preparing."

"You are near completion. Your skills in *budo-kai* have returned to a formidable level, and your body is once again strong."

"And my mind?"

Ghalan stared at him with his dark, poignant gaze. "There is a great deal of strength within you, inherited from Ieyasu Tanaka. And though Malak had only developed a fraction of his strength when he died, you can draw from his power, also."

"I can feel the spark within me that is Malak, and it perturbs me. What if he takes over my mind?"

"It is destined to occur that Malak will again live through your body, but do not fear this. For he is you, and you are him. When Shadrack and Malak merge, you will be far closer to your true self, regardless of what name you call yourself. You will then have the strength of both personalities, and perhaps memories of incarnations even before Malak."

Shadrack nodded, accepting this, but he was still perturbed.

"Ghalan, you are right. I do have great strength. Ieyasu once told me that I needn't fear any man. Yet I cannot fight."

Ghalan sighed. "I know. I know you better than you think, Shadrack. The teachings of Tanaka, though martial, were of absolute pacifism. Yet consider whether he was right. For he died a pointless death. It is almost always inexcusable to take one's life."

"He was a man of honor!"

"Undoubtedly, yet he committed *hari-kari* for breaking an outdated, inappropriate, and spiritually corrupt code of conduct. Much of the samurai code was concerned with petty egoism rather than honor, and Tanaka himself realized this in later years."

Shadrack's eyes clouded: though he felt Ghalan was right, it was an attack on the fundamentals of his beliefs that he could not accept.

"Remember this always," Ghalan said, fixing him with a somber gaze. "Malak's greatest mistake was in not realizing the need for strength to survive. He was content to live in the paradise that Enya once was. But life is a continuous battle. It would be pointless to incarnate if God was to mollycoddle us through life. He is always with us, as he is everywhere, but the mistakes are our own to make. In life, we must forge our own world, or be crushed by the worlds forged by others."

Shadrack shook his head sadly. "I hear you, Ghalan. But I cannot escape the ghost of Ieyasu."

"You must escape his spectre. You must, because neither Dethen nor Lilith will hesitate to crush you."

Shadrack closed his eyes and sighed mournfully. "So be it."

Ghalan watched him as the ronin stared at the countryside with a subdued expression.

"Shadrack, are you familiar with the doctrine of Christianity?"

Shadrack frowned, surprised by the conversation's change of direction.

"There was a woman who lived outside of Kyoto," he answered after some thought. "People thought of her as a witch, but I realize now she was just a strong psychic. She was a Christian, and when I asked Ekanar, he explained the basis of the mythology. Did Christ actually exist?"

"Of that there is no doubt: the records are clear. Historians and theologians argue over the events of his life. I have no doubt that Christ was a great prophet, an Adept who had crossed the Abyss. But his historical reality is not what is important. It is his relevance, which has been mistaken by so many."

"Which is?"

"The story of his rise from death is intimately connected with other mythologies, such as that of Osiris or the Phoenix. It is a story of rebirth. Whether it occurred or not has no importance; the story has a power of its own, like all archetypal patterns. Christ was taunted and tempted in many ways as he hung from the Cross, but he did not stray from the path. He did what he knew to be right."

"Why are you telling me this?"

"When you return to Enya, you know you must face Lilith. You must confront her before Dark Moon or all will be lost. Her essence will smash through your mind, destroying Enya and the Tree of Life. The future holds either your destruction or rebirth. The rebirth is Adepthood, symbolized in Christian mythology by Christ rising from the dead."

"I think I understand."

"You must not submit, Shadrack. You will be taunted and tempted just as he was, as every man is. But if your resolve does not weaken, you will regain your Adepthood and your soul. You must reach the underground chamber where you lost your soul. And above all, remember that on the third day, Christ was risen."

Shadrack frowned. "What's the relevance?"

"The third day!" Ghalan said, his eyes so intense they burned. "When the time is right, you must remember!"

Shadrack stared at him, shocked by the conviction in his voice. "Yes, father. The third day. I will remember."

Whenever two people meet there are really six people present. There is each man as he sees himself, each man as the other person sees him, and each man as he really is.

—William James

18

Enya
Yesod of Yetzirah
City of Sophia

Lena stirred from deep, dreamless sleep to the sound of knocking on the door. She opened her eyes, momentarily blinded by the light of mid-afternoon.

She was in a guest bedroom of the Sophian palace, sprawled on a four-poster bed with expensive silk sheets and a luxurious mattress. She loathed to move from the warmth and solace, but she was disturbed by another knock from the door.

"I'm coming," she said, trying to hide her irritation.

She slid from the sheets and onto the deep, intricately decorated carpet, so thick it molded itself around her feet in a sensual embrace. The carpet's pattern depicted a huge flight of dragons in deep exotic hues, yet their bodies blended into each other so that each dragon was joined to every other dragon.

Throwing a midnight-blue robe around her negligee, she realized she had slept nearly twenty hours. Lack of sleep and the comfort of a real bed had enticed her exhausted body.

She walked over to the door and opened it. Cassius stood there, looking tired. It seemed that affairs of state had allowed him little rest since his return.

Lena stretched like a feline, her breasts heaving under the thin fabric of the satin robe. Cassius cast his gaze to the floor, embarrassed.

"I didn't mean to intrude," he said awkwardly. "But Jeshua asked me to give this to you." He handed over a small flat object wrapped in dark blue silk.

Lena frowned. "What's this?"

Cassius shrugged. "Jeshua said you would understand. He said it will draw Malak to you."

Lena unwrapped the object. In her hand she held a flat fire opal, about four inches square. The gem was flawless and perfectly flat, its color a vivid orange. Her brow furrowed as she wondered what Jeshua was up to.

"Lena," Cassius said, "I know that what I told you yesterday must have shocked and hurt you, but it would mean a great deal to me if we were friends. I'm sure Malak will want it that way."

Lena wrapped the fire opal and sighed. "Cassius, at the moment I have no friends. I can rely only on Bast and Squint. There is too much pain to reach out to anyone else. All I care about is being reunited with Malak. It is my obsession. Until that happens, I can feel no joy."

Cassius nodded. "Perhaps when he returns, we will both be healed."

"Perhaps," Lena said, but Cassius still saw accusation in her eyes. The expression pierced him.

"I will leave you," he said. "I hope you figure out what it is Jeshua has sent you."

He turned and strode away, not waiting for a reply. Lena watched him go, undecided whether she hated him or felt sorry for him. She knew that hate came all too easily to her now, another gift from her mother. She remembered a time, in her last incarnation, when she had hated only two things: Dethen and swords. She smiled grimly.

Some things don't change.

Lena sat on the bed, idly turning the fire opal in her hands. The gem was a piece of art, and she was sure it hadn't been cut by natural means. Yet she had no idea why Jeshua had sent it to her.

It will draw Malak to you.

Surely magick was the only way she could accomplish that objective? In magick, gem stones were generally used as Talismans or Amulets. Realization suddenly struck her. The purpose of a Talisman was to draw something to you. And she wanted to draw Malak back into Enya.

Why fire opal? she wondered.

Qabalistic knowledge told her that opals were associated with the Sephira Hod. Likewise, the vivid orange color of the gem alluded to Hod. Yet this was puzzling, because Hod was related to intellect, learning, and wisdom. She didn't grasp the connection.

But it occurred to her that the Greek god Mercury was associated with Hod, and despite being god of learning, he was also the wing-footed messenger, who could cover vast distances. And more importantly, the Egyptian god Thoth was connected with Hod. Like Mercury, Thoth was the great teacher of academia and occult wisdom, but he was also the Lord of Space and Time.

She suddenly realized that Jeshua intended her to make a Talisman of Hod, and to use it to draw Malak to her. She had never attempted such a magical operation before; in past lives the effect of the Boundary had rendered such acts ineffective. Yet she was well acquainted with the theory, and she was sure her skills would be adequate.

For the next eight days, Lena worked studiously. She extracted from Jeshua's grimoires the necessary names and sigils that she required for charging the Hod Talisman. As an Adept, she had most of the information memorized, yet everything had to be double checked. A corruption in one of the names, and the Talisman itself could be corrupted. Likewise, all sigils had to be perfectly transcribed, and she worked out their shape herself to ensure the grimoires made no mistake.

It was dangerous to work with the names and sigils on Enya, for despite the Boundary, the plane was still a part of the astral. This gave the sigils a life and vibrancy, as if the sole act of scribing them would evoke the mighty power they represented.

Care had to be taken that the names were not said aloud, lest some demonic splinter of the holy forces attempted to manifest. Each and every force in the universe, save for the Godhead itself, had both an opposite and an extreme. When evoking the beneficial aspect of any force or essence, it was paramount that precautions were taken to ensure that it was harmonious. Otherwise the force might be evoked in an extreme form, and it was well known that anything taken to an extreme was in essence evil.

If spirits were evoked to promote courage and fearlessness in battle, one might call forth bloodthirsty and merciless demons if done improperly. These unbalanced spirits were known as the Qlippoth, and were a major danger in magick. This was why the untrained magician sometimes had frightful experiences, and the common people regarded magick with fear and suspicion. Just as heat could keep one alive and cook one's meals, it could also inflict terrible burns. Likewise magick was a potent occult science, with results dependent entirely on the magician's training and intentions.

Lena used Jeshua's ritual chamber, which lay underneath his tower. Once inside, she reawakened the powerful astral seals to exclude any unwanted entities—in this way, only beings that she specifically called on could enter her sphere of sensation. No one witnessed her work other than Squint, but even he was forced to depart once the chamber was banished.

Apart from the grimoire research, she also constructed the implements necessary for the coming ritual. She created a ceremonial robe for herself, to be used purely for magical work. To perform a ritual in everyday clothes could be problematic, because the clothing would be riddled with impure magnetism and impressions. This could spoil the sanctity of the chamber, where all rogue forces had to be banished.

Other than the robe, she constructed the four elemental weapons: the pantacle, the dagger, the cup and the wand. These represented the four elements, and could be used to control and direct their energies. The final implement she required was the magical sword, which represented the magician's will and could be used for many tasks, including invoking and banishing. Yet for practical and psychological reasons, she decided to make use of a long-bladed stiletto for this purpose.

She was able to carve the wooden pantacle and wand herself, but she allowed Kira to furnish her with the dagger, cup, and stiletto. Lena impressed on her that the items would have to be virgin, unused since their manufacture. Even so, she purified them once received. With due solemnity, she flexed her ritual muscles by consecrating each of the magical items in turn at the correct hour, and when the correct elemental currents flowed in the astral.

She decided to charge the Talisman at Full Moon, when the maximum amount of astral energy was available and the protective forces were at their strongest. It amused her to think that in some cultures, the Full Moon was regarded with suspicion. In actual fact it was benign; the Dark Moon was much more sinister.

Two days before Full Moon, she began to correlate all the data she had gathered. She then started rough sketches of the form the Talisman would take. Included in the design, written in their Hebrew form, were the Names that she had painstakingly researched. With them were drawn the corresponding sigils and geometrical shapes associated with the number eight (since Hod was the eighth Sephira). In occultism, numbers were considered extremely important. Each number was an individual essence, almost alive, and completely unique.

She created two designs: one for each side of the fire opal that Jeshua had given her. She used paper for her sketches, and she eventually arrived at two designs she felt were right. Into the designs were woven her husband's name and sigil, both as Malak and as Shadrack. Also included was the sigil of Enya, since this was the plane she wished to draw him to.

The day before Full Moon, everything was complete. She carefully burned all the Talisman sketches, committing the ones she required to memory. Now she had only to work out the astral currents, and to select the hour in which the planet Mercury ruled. This done, she could only sit back and await the hour.

19

Enya
City of Sophia

A talisman is a storehouse of some particular kind of energy, the kind that is needed to accomplish the task for which you have constructed it.

—Aleister Crowley

I cannot now think symbols less than the greatest of all powers whether they are used consciously by the masters of magic, or half-consciously by their successors, the poet, the musician, and the artist.

—W. B. Yeats (Frater D.E.D.I.)

Lena stood in the center of Jeshua's ritual chamber, her eyes closed as she sought to balance herself.

The chamber was perfectly square, with smooth walls like black onyx. There were no blemishes in the chamber's structure, and the only furniture present was the centrally placed black altar. The altar was formed of two cubes, stacked one on top of the other. This produced a total of ten sides, symbolic of the tenth Sephira Malkuth, where the effects of the ritual were to take place.

Lena's long black hair was loose, cascading down her back to reach her waist. She wore two robes: the outer one black, the inner white. The inner robe symbolized her true self, which would remain forever untainted by the world about her, its spirit gliding above material concerns. The outer robe was a shroud, to hide her true self from the prying eyes of others. It also signified secrecy; nothing she was about to perform would be discussed outside the chamber.

Arranged before her on the altar lay the elemental weapons: the pantacle, cup, wand, and dagger. Arranged to form a cross, they signified the balance and harmony of the elements within her aura. Set at the center of the cross was the square fire opal, wrapped in black silk and bound thrice.

Below the Talisman was a tarot card: the Universe, representing the thirty-second path of the Tree of Life. The card reflected the dark, heavy nature of the path that formed a bridge between Yesod and Malkuth. In order to draw Malak back to Enya, Lena knew her husband would have to first traverse the thirty-second path.

Eight orange candles burned around the edges of the temple, spaced equidistant apart. Beside each of them was an incense burner, and the pleasant vanilla-like smell of storax filled the atmosphere.

Lena took a deep breath and opened her eyes. She was ready to purify her aura and formally cleanse the chamber.

She moved to the east of the chamber and drew a large pentagram before her. Using the stiletto, she started from a point before her left hip. The pentagram was a vivid blue, flickering with gold like a gas flame. When the figure was complete, she charged it and drew a horizontal white line of astral energy. She drew the line at waist height, moving in a circle until she faced south. There she repeated the procedure, before passing to the west and north. Finally she returned to the east, now surrounded by four pentagrams linked by an unbroken circle of astral energy.

She returned to the center of the circle and invoked the four archangels of the elements.

"Before me stands RAPHAEL!" she declared, vibrating the name of the angel forcefully through her aura.

As she vibrated Raphael's name, he appeared before her to the east. He wore yellow robes with purple highlights. In his right hand was a Caduceus Wand, and though he appeared human, his aura glowed with incredible power. A strong wind blew all around him, causing his robes to flail about.

"Behind me stands GABRIEL!" she affirmed, again vibrating the archangel's name.

With her mind's eye she saw the angel behind her. He wore blue robes with orange highlights, and held a chalice in his hands. He stood within a gently rippling pool of water, and the sound of a crashing waterfall could be heard behind him.

"To my right stands MICHAEL!" she intoned.

Immediately, she felt heat from the south as the red-robed figure of the archangel materialized. She felt Michael more strongly than the other elements, since he identified well with her fiery personality. His robes were tinged with a vivid green, and he held aloft a sword with a flaming blade.

"To my left stands AURIEL!" she said, feeling the archangel's presence solidify to the north.

Auriel's robes were green and brown like the fertile earth, and within her hands she held a golden bundle of wheat. Though feminine, she was strong and steadfast: a representative of the mighty element earth.

Lena held her arms out so that her body formed a cross.

"Holy art Thou, Lord of the Universe! Holy art Thou whom nature hath not formed! Holy art Thou, the vast and mighty One! Lord of the Light and the Darkness!"

As she declared her adoration of the Godhead, the angels bowed their heads in respect and humility.

She said: "I invoke ye, ye mighty Angels of the celestial spheres whose dwelling is in the invisible. Ye are the guardians of the Gates of the Universe, be ye also the guardians of this mystic sphere. Keep far removed the evil and the unbalanced! Strengthen and inspire me so that I may preserve unsullied this abode of the mysteries of the Eternal Gods. Let my sphere be pure and holy so that I may enter in and become a partaker of the secrets of the Light Divine."

As she completed the invocation, the room flared white and the archangels disappeared. When the light faded, the walls displayed the elemental symbols for each quarter and the four Enochian tablets.

The chamber was now balanced between the four elements, as was her aura. A remnant of the four archangels remained to stabilize the chamber throughout the ritual. No elemental being would dare attempt to infiltrate the temple with the archangels protecting it.

Lena picked up the Talisman and announced: "In the name of ELOHIM TZABOATH, and by all the powers and forces invoked here this night in the hour of Mercury and the Full Moon, I proclaim that I will form a true and potent link between this Talisman and HOD, the Sephira of Splendor.

"To this end, I have formed and perfected this Talisman, bearing the necessary seals, sigils and symbols. I proclaim that the Talisman shall be charged in order that Malak, also known as Shadrack, may be drawn back into the realm of Enya. I desire this boon so that the forces of Light may be reunited on this plane, and the forces of darkness contended. May the powers of HOD witness my sacred pledge."

With the Talisman still in her left hand, she moved to the west of the circle, facing away from the altar. With the stiletto, she drew an invoking hexagram of Mercury before her. The hexagram was a vivid orange, pulsing with life. It consisted of two interlocking triangles, one upright and one pointing downward. She traced both triangles in a clockwise direction, the first beginning from her left hip, forming an apex at her head and then down to her right hip. The second started from her right shoulder, reached a point at her groin and then up to her left shoulder.

When she completed the hexagram, she said: "ARARITA! One is God's beginning! One principle is God's individuality! God's permutation is One!"

The hexagram vibrated vigorously.

"I now invoke the powers of HOD into this temple. In the name of ELOHIM TZABOATH, be here now! Know that all is in readiness to consecrate this Talisman. Aid with thy power that I may cause the great archangel MICHAEL to give life and strength to this creature of Talismans."

Moving clockwise around the circle, she reached her previous position behind the altar.

"I invoke the powers of ELOHIM TZABOATH. Through this Talisman, draw Malak into the realm of Enya!

"By the powers of Mercury, draw Malak into the realm of Enya!

"Holy art Thou, Lord of the Universe, who works in Silence and nought but Silence can express!"

She removed the covering from the Talisman and held it aloft. The vivid blue sigils on the surface vibrated with urgency, as if straining against imprisonment.

"Come, oh BENI ELOHIM, angelic choir of HOD and servants to God. Surround, consecrate, and charge this Talisman!"

As she forcefully vibrated the name of the angels, she traced the proper sigil above the Talisman. The corresponding sigil on the surface of the Talisman responded, glowing with a powerful light.

"Oh MICHAEL, help thy humble servant to consecrate and charge this Talisman!"

She traced the sigil, and the name of Michael pulsed with energy on the surface of the fire opal.

"I invoke the power of ELOHIM TZABOATH! Charge and consecrate this Talisman for thy Name's sake!"

White light flickered around the Talisman now, and blue sparks leaped from its surface. The entire chamber glowed with an eerie orange light as the power of Hod suffused it.

"Forces and powers of HOD, be friendly unto me, for I am a Servant of the same, your God: a true worshipper of the Highest!"

She moved around the circle to the west, carrying with her the Talisman, once again covered and bound. At the West she started to vibrate the Fourth Enochian Key.

Her voice was deep and sonorous, and soon the chamber vibrated with the sound of her voice. As she intensified the rhythm of the chant, her astral body reverberated with the alien words. The foundations of the chamber shook with the force.

As she reached a climax, the entire chamber held its breath for a second, before her tone gradually wound down. When she turned to face the altar, it was hidden by three columns. On the left was the Black Pillar of Severity, on the right the White Pillar of Mercy. Positioned centrally and slightly behind stood the Pillar of Equilibrium.

"The consecration is complete! The Talisman lives!" Lena affirmed. "It will now be duly initiated."

With the Talisman unveiled, she moved toward the Black Pillar. A huge, black-robed figure suddenly materialized before her. He held before him an immense two-handed sword, his eyes burning a fiery red.

"I AM THE MIGHTY HIEREUS. CREATURE OF TALISMANS, UNPURIFIED AND UNCLEAN, THOU CANST NOT ENTER THE GATE OF THE WEST!" the figure boomed.

Lena bowed her head and moved backwards.

"Dadouchos and Stolistes, please come forward."

A red-robed figure approached Lena from the south of the chamber. There was an upright equilateral triangle on his sternum, and within his hands he held a red and green wand of flame.

"I am the Dadouchos," he said. "Creature of Talismans, I purify thee with fire."

Lena removed the cover from the Talisman. It pulsed with intense energy. The Dadouchos passed the wand of flame over the Talisman; it turned a deep red color.

The Dadouchos moved back to his position in the south, and a blue-robed figure approached from the north. Upon her sternum was a downward pointing triangle, and in her hands she held a blue and orange chalice.

"I am the Stolistes," she said. "Creature of Talismans, I purify thee with water."

She dipped her fingers into the chalice, and flicked a few drops of water onto the surface of the Talisman. The Talisman cooled, turning back to the vivid orange color. The Stolistes moved back to the north.

With the Talisman held before her, Lena once again approached the Black Pillar.

"BEFORE ALL THINGS ARE THE CHAOS, THE DARKNESS, AND THE GATES OF THE LAND OF THE NIGHT," said the Hiereus. "I AM HE WHOSE NAME IS DARKNESS. I AM THE GREAT ONE OF THE PATH OF THE SHADES. I AM THE EXORCIST IN THE MIDST OF THE EXORCISM. YET FEAR NOT THE DARKNESS OF THE WEST, FOR THERE IS NO PLACE THAT GOD AND THE LIGHT OF GOD ARE NOT. THEREFORE, TAKE ON MANIFESTATION BEFORE ME WITHOUT FEAR. FOR IN THE WEST IS HE WHOM FEAR IS NOT. AND NOW THAT THOU KNOWEST THIS, PASS THOU ON TO THE GATE OF THE EAST."

Lena bowed and moved backwards. She approached the White Pillar. A huge white-robed figure materialized before her to bar her way. His eyes were a deep blue. In his hands he held a huge red and gold sceptre surmounted by a crown.

"I AM THE MERCIFUL HIEROPHANT. CREATURE OF TALISMANS, UNPURIFIED AND UNCLEAN, THOU CANST NOT ENTER THE GATE OF THE EAST!" the figure boomed.

Lena bowed and moved away.

"Dadouchos and Stolistes, please come forward," she said.

The red-robed Dadouchos and blue-robed Stolistes approached and consecrated the Talisman with fire and water for the second time. Lena advanced upon the White Pillar again.

The Hierophant said: "AFTER THE FORMLESSNESS, THE VOID, AND THE DARKNESS, THEN COMETH THE KNOWLEDGE OF THE LIGHT. TO BECOME A TALISMAN,

STRONG AND TRUE, THOU MUST PASS FROM DARKNESS INTO LIGHT, FROM DEATH INTO LIFE. TO DO THIS REQUIRES THE LIGHT THAT SHINES FROM WITHIN THE DARKNESS, THOUGH THE DARKNESS COMPREHENDETH IT NOT. BY THE WILL OF GOD, I CAN CONTROL A SPECK OF THAT LIGHT THAT ARISETH IN DARKNESS. REMEMBER, CREATURE OF TALISMANS, FORM IS ALIKE INVISIBLE IN BLINDING LIGHT AS IN IMPENETRABLE DARKNESS. TAKE ON MANIFESTATION BEFORE ME, FOR I AM THE WIELDER OF THE FORCES OF BALANCE. THOU HAST NOW KNOWN ME, SO PASS THOU ON TO THE CUBICAL ALTAR OF THE UNIVERSE."

The Dadouchos and Stolistes stepped forward to baptize the Talisman a third and final time. Lena stepped through the twin pillars of Light and Darkness.

"CREATURE OF TALISMANS!" said the Hiereus and Hierophant together. "LONG HAST THOU DWELT IN THE DARKNESS OF UNLIFE. QUIT THE NIGHT AND SEEK THE DAY!"

The Talisman in Lena's hand vibrated in understanding.

"Let the white brilliance of the Divine Spirit descend upon this creature of Talismans, and fill it with the glory of thy majesty!" Lena proclaimed. "Behold all powers and forces that are here in attendance. I am pure. I am pure. I am pure. Take witness that I have duly exorcised, purified, initiated, enlivened, consecrated, and empowered this creature of Talismans!"

An aura of power surrounded the Talisman; she knew that the ritual had been successful. She covered it with the black silk wrap and placed it upon the altar. She now had to banish the forces she had evoked, and close down the temple. Yet she found it difficult to concentrate, for she knew that soon she would be reunited with her husband. With resolve, she pushed the thought from her mind and began the ritual closing.

Come to the edge
He said. They said:
We are afraid.
Come to the edge
He said. They came.
He pushed them, and
they flew. . . ."

—Guillaume Apollinaire

20

Tellus
Malkuth of Assiah
Saxon mid-lands

In the moonlit confines of his chamber, Shadrack groaned and lashed out in sleep. His mind passed from one dream to another, never finding stability. He knew he wasn't awake, yet every time he tried to force himself out of sleep, he awoke within another dream.

His dreams were of Enya. A beautiful sky of deep amethyst. Golden-barked trees with blue-green leaves. A dark forbidding tower, studded with the light of the stars. A sleek black panther with green intelligent eyes. A huge astral vortex spinning above a decimated forest. The black soulless eyes of Dethen. Lilith in her seductive form, attempting to lure him back into her grasp.

Throughout the chaotic haze of broken images and experiences, there was Lena. He remembered only fragments of their time together, yet he recalled every detail of her face and voluptuous body. He knew her fiery, stubborn personality but couldn't remember experiencing it. He knew beyond a doubt that he loved this woman who haunted his dreams, and that she had once loved him. Might still love him. The thought frightened him. As he was, he had nothing to lose: he simply wished to evade the clutches of Lilith. But if this woman still cared for him, he had a great deal to lose.

He struggled fiercely to break away from the alluring image of Lena. She slowly faded from his consciousness. He now rushed through impenetrable blackness at incredible speed; the sensation disorientated him.

The source of the hallucinations confused him He had always been prone to lucid dreaming, yet it usually occurred at Dark Moon when Lilith's hold was at its greatest. To happen at Full Moon was unheard of, and he felt certain that some force must be propagating the experience.

Gradually his speed tapered off until it was difficult to tell whether he was moving. He still floated in darkness, alone in an eternal void. Here the perceptions of Lena were much stronger; he felt he could almost grasp her essence. The void reverberated with the deafening sound of her heartbeat, and he desperately wanted to meld into the sound; though he heard no voice, he knew she called him. She was reaching out to him, grasping for his hand across the dimensions of space and time.

In the far distance, he suddenly saw something. An orange speck of light approached rapidly. He watched in fascination as it rocketed toward him. Within a few seconds he saw it was a small, flat square. It spun on its axis as it flew at him. He only had time to register the strange, vivid blue symbols on its surface before the object pierced him through the chest.

His body instantly exploded. A moment later he spasmed on the bed as he experienced astral whiplash. When he saw the familiar sights of his personal chamber, he forced himself to calm. His body gradually relaxed, and he made himself inhale slowly and deeply. It took a few seconds longer for his erratic pulse to fall back to normal.

His mind whirled with the effect of the collision; stray thoughts and feelings surfaced like flotsam under a waterfall. Yet one thought dominated everything: he had to return to Enya. He felt the call in his blood, like the craving for an addictive drug. Nothing else mattered; he had to return now. He knew the impulse had been triggered by the strange orange object of his dream, yet this was unimportant. Somehow, he knew the object had been Lena's creation: it had been infused with her spirit.

He reached over to the bedside drawers and lit the oil lamp. He quickly dressed, pulling on clothes to protect him from the winter weather. Even though snow lay on the ground outside, the climate was still warmer than a summer day in Nippon.

He knew where he had to go. To return to Enya, he had to reach the witch stones. A gateway between worlds, Ghalan had told him. He had no idea how the gateway would transport him, or how to activate it, but he had a new-found faith. Tonight was right for him to return to Enya, and nothing would stop him, not even Lilith herself: he knew she desired his return to the sub-plane of Yesod anyway.

Extinguishing the oil lamp, he slipped quietly out of the door and into the corridor. A glint of moonlight on steel caused him to turn, and he stared in bewilderment. Leaning against the wall outside his door were his katana and wakizashi. There was also a backpack. When he explored its contents, he found a supply of food and water, plus an oil lamp and some tinder.

"I thought you might find the items useful."

He spun around in surprise, cursing his zanshin for being so weak. Ghalan stepped out of the shadows.

"How did you know?" Shadrack asked.

Ghalan shrugged. "The effect of the Talisman is very strong. Lena charged it well. I felt its effects on the astral."

"Talisman? What's that?"

"A part of your magical studies you haven't yet encountered. It has caused this effect within you. When you are drawn into Enya, you will arrive near the time the Talisman was charged."

Shadrack slipped into the backpack and thrust the swords through his belt. It was the first time he had worn them as a *daisho* pair, in true samurai fashion, since his possession by Lilith.

"How will the transit to Enya occur?" he asked.

"Don't worry. The Talisman will take care of such things. It will clear all obstacles so it can complete its purpose. Things will fall into place."

Shadrack nodded. "Then I must leave," he said. "Thank you for your help, Ghalan."

Ghalan's gaze suddenly softened, his eyes gaining such compassion, tears came to Shadrack's eyes. Shadrack hugged him, and for once Ghalan returned the affection.

"Good-bye, my son. I look forward to our paths meeting again."

"Will I see you again?"

"In my future, yes. But not in yours. However, our spirits will be one if you cross the Abyss to become Magus of Enya."

Shadrack nodded sadly. "I must go." The effect of the Talisman burned in his veins.

"Good fortune, Shadrack. And do yourself justice in the coming battle. Do not disappoint me."

Shadrack felt a poignant sadness, knowing he would never see the old man again.

"Good-bye, father."

He turned sharply and headed for the stairs. Ghalan's inhuman gaze followed him until he disappeared from sight.

Shadrack passed through the dark, snow-covered gardens of the cathedral and approached the main gate. He felt a twinge of apprehension. In his year at the temple, he hadn't once left its sanctity. It was like leaving the warmth and protection of a second womb, but he brushed the thought aside; he was eager to fulfill his mission at the witch stones.

Even though no one had disturbed the tranquility of the temple since Ekanar's arrival, there was always someone guarding the entrance day and night. The Sentinel came out of his hut and wordlessly opened the huge iron gate. His suspicious gaze made no secret of his distrust for Shadrack. The Sentinel was one of the few initiates who had seen the ronin in his possessed condition.

Shadrack nodded an acknowledgment and stepped out into the barren world. The gate crashed shut with an echo. Suddenly he felt very alone. The temperature seemed to plummet, and already he missed Ghalan's comforting presence.

A foot of snow covered the ground, and the heavy flakes continued to fall, dancing and whirling on the light breeze. The city of Prenzlau was like a scene from a faery tale. The shattered buildings and decaying cars looked softer and less threatening under the white blanket of snow. The harsh, sharp corners were replaced with feminine curves and the cars became gently undulating snow drifts.

Shadrack started to walk northward, in the direction of his objective. The Full Moon glared down on the surreal landscape; the snow glittered like powdered diamond.

As he trekked along his route, he found the snow completely undisturbed. Even the scavengers had abandoned the city, where the specters of the dead hovered in the shadows of once-colossal buildings. Shadrack felt anxious, as if trespassing on holy ground, disturbing the graves of long-dead ghosts. Nothing moved in the alien landscape. His breath crystallized in the air before him, lingering before being caught by the breeze.

He was awed by the sheer size of the city. He walked along twisted, ruptured roads and clambered over piles of rubble, made precarious by the coating of snow and ice. Walking at a respectable pace, it still took him over an hour to reach the limits of the town. The metamorphosis occurred gradually as the buried buildings and cars became less frequent, merging into the surrounding countryside.

Eventually the vehicles were left far behind and Shadrack's mood lightened. The snow-covered landscape reminded him of Nippon and the temperature was comfortable. Bushes and trees whispered to him in the wind as he passed. He smiled. He was going home. Enya was Malak's world, and that made it his home also. There he could discover who he truly was, and most importantly of all, he would have a chance to see Lena. The thought caused his heart to hammer painfully.

He struggled across the hilly landscape, his mind dwelling on the obstacles he would face with his return. He knew little of what would await him, but two words immediately sprang to mind: Dethen and Lilith.

From Malak's memories, he had a good perception of Dethen and he knew what the Black Adept was capable of. He didn't look forward to facing Dethen, but despite the Adept's incredible strength, he didn't fear him. It would be difficult, for he would not fight the magician; Ieyasu's principle of pacifism was embedded too deeply. He would only defend himself if his life was in danger, for he knew he wouldn't be able to stop that reaction. Many samurai had died due to the effectiveness of his instinct for self-preservation.

Then there was Lilith. He couldn't pretend he didn't fear her, for she sent shudders of terror through his soul, but he vowed to himself that he would never cower before her again. She might own his soul, but she would never again possess his body. He would not be a puppet to her evil cause. Once he had returned to Enya, he knew Lilith would have an even greater hold on him.

As he slipped over the brow of the next hill, he knew his destination loomed only moments away. He didn't know if it was the effect of the Talisman, but the stones called him with a passion. He felt their power within his bones, and though he'd only set off vaguely in the correct direction, he'd found the megaliths easily, drawn to them like a moth to a candle.

He saw them now, standing on the hilltop before him. They were incredibly ancient, older even than the megaliths of the Rose Circle on Enya. They were weathered and corroded, with a myriad of cracks and fissures from frost heaves.

The moonlight glittered off their surfaces as Shadrack approached, half running. They stood out against the starry skyline like broken teeth, gnarled and useless. Yet Shadrack felt their venerable power surge as they sensed him near. They seemed almost sentient, and they appeared to recognize him. Suddenly he knew that everything was in place. The circle would transport him itself. He would have to do nothing, for the Talisman had warped reality itself. The megaliths knew their task and they would perform it well.

He grasped the scabbards of his swords with one hand and a strap of his backpack with the other. Within a few seconds he had scaled the side of the hilltop, his legs sinking thigh-deep where the snow had drifted. He plunged thoughtlessly into the center of the circle, triumphant at last.

The effect was immediate. An incredible pain exploded in his chest as his heart suddenly ceased its rhythmic beat. He collapsed in agony, writhing in the snow. And then the pain disappeared.

He watched his corpse from above. Already, the snow began to cover it, destroying all traces of his existence.

The glowing chord that attached him to the cadaver snapped as if sliced by a knife, then he was spinning, spinning. He saw flickering lights around him and felt the incredible build-up of astral energy. The physical world faded from view as he spun faster. His astral body convulsed spasmodically as electricity surged through it.

Suddenly it was all behind him, and he was shooting through a tunnel of light. His body still buzzed, but it was no longer of human shape; it had flattened into an oblate sphere.

He emerged from the tunnel of light into an indigo sky. There was a great feeling of inertia and restriction here; the symbol of Saturn dashed past him. In the distance was a giant prolate necklace made up of many beads like pearls. Within it was a beautiful woman, semi-naked. Above her head was a crescent, and within her hands she held two rods, one white and one black.

Shadrack dashed toward her, passing through the necklace of pearls. As soon as he entered the gateway, blackness overcame him and he hit a cold and soft surface. With shock, he realized he had a physical body again, and that his backpack and swords were still present. He couldn't believe he had failed.

Yet the part of him that was Malak rejoiced in recognition. Shadrack opened his eyes. He wasn't lying on a snow-covered hill, and neither was the sky black, though it was studded with stars.

He rose unsteadily from the grass, and looked up at the three huge megaliths that surrounded him.

The inner ring of the Rose Circle, he thought. He stared in disbelief at the tree line of the Enchanted Forest, only a hundred yards away. And above him, the dark purple sky slowly turned amethyst as dawn advanced.

Finally, he was home.

One man with courage makes a majority.

—Prince Cassius Hawkin[5]

Epilogue to Regeneration

Enya
City of Sophia

Lena's eyes snapped open as she passed from deep sleep to wakefulness in a heartbeat. She held her breath in dreaded anticipation, expecting her hope to be dashed at any moment. But she could feel the truth in every tingling cell of her body: Malak had returned. A wave of joy mixed with disbelief rushed through her.

She rolled from the huge four-poster bed and onto her feet, her thoughts eddying. She stood in shock, unsure of what to do. Her mind struggled to energize itself.

She slipped her hand underneath her pillow and gasped. She pulled out the black silk wrap that had held the Hod Talisman. The object had disappeared, vaporized without a trace. It was true; the Talisman had performed its task. Within three days it had drawn Malak through to Enya and then dissipated back into the elements and forces that constituted it.

Something touched her mind, a gentle caressing sensation. She spun around to see Bast watching her. With the Full Moon the familiar now stood above Lena's waist, her powerful muscles conspicuous. Her green eyes glittered with pleasure.

"You know, don't you?" Lena asked.

Bast nuzzled against her thigh and loped over to the door. It took her only a second to work the door handle and slip out of the room.

5 Andrew Jackson

Lena went to follow Bast, excitement building within her. She had to tell Cassius; he would be as euphoric as she was. She suddenly realized she wore nothing but her negligee. It would be unladylike to roam the palace in such attire.

Turning back into the room, she yanked open the door to her wardrobe. She pulled out a white robe and quickly donned it, muttering about the outdated apparel. The robes the palace provided were less than practical in her estimation. The material was fine, but the cut was restrictive, preventing the use of legs in self-defense. The robes had been specially produced for her, and she hadn't had the heart to tell them that she was just as comfortable in a tunic and trousers.

Once dressed, she rushed from the bedroom and through the corridors of the palace. Though the tingling feeling had passed now, it had been enough to tell her what she needed to know. She forced herself to slow down as she attracted worried glances from the patrolling guards.

She strode quickly past the pair of soldiers outside Cassius' council chamber. The door was partially open, so she knocked once and entered.

Kira sat behind Cassius' desk, and two soldiers stepped from behind the door.

"What's this?" Lena asked as the guards moved to block her escape.

Kira stood up. "I'm afraid my father has asked me to detain you, for your own protection."

Lena's eyes flamed. "How dare he?! Do you really think these two soldiers will stop me? Malak has returned and I must find him!"

"I know. My father explained everything to me. He knows that Shadrack has returned to Enya, and he has gone to the Rose Circle to intercept him. He is adamant that you don't go, for your own safety."

"Fine," Lena said.

She had barely said the word before she launched an astral burst. Kira was smashed into the wall to fall to the floor, the wind knocked from her. The two guards moved forward to grab Lena. She fired another attack, stronger than the first. The energy deflected around the two guards, ripping the door from its hinges. Lena stared in amazement, too shocked to react. The guards grabbed her, exerting just enough strength to restrain her.

Kira pushed herself from the floor. "These guards were picked carefully, Lena. Your magick will not work against them. They share my father's secret."

Four more guards entered the room. Lena knew it would be pointless to resist physically. Someone would be badly hurt.

A growl came from behind the six soldiers. Everyone turned to see Bast, set ready to pounce.

"She doesn't like seeing me held," Lena warned.

"Call it off," Kira said nervously. The soldiers reached for their swords. "Or we'll have to hurt it. We're supposed to be allies."

Lena laughed. "Some allies. You think you'll hurt Bast?"

The familiar clawed the floor, leaving deep grooves in the stone. Lena knew Bast couldn't fight six armed men without seriously injuring one of them.

"No, Bast," she ordered. "Malak. Find Malak. Keep him safe."

Bast growled again, her eyes staring down the soldiers. She seemed hesitant.

"Go!" Lena ordered. "Malak is the one who needs you."

The familiar turned and ran down the corridor.

"Bring him back to me," Lena whispered.

Enya
Black School subterranean lair

Widowmaker whistled through the air as Dethen advanced, parrying and striking as he moved. There was no illumination in the chamber, and *Widowmaker* cast a harsh but dim scarlet light. The atmosphere was cold and malignant, though Dethen didn't feel it: they were his own vibrations.

Parry, strike. Parry, strike. The blade moved so quickly it left a red trail in the air like a sparkler. The ancient runes on the sword vibrated with desire: *Widowmaker's* purpose was to cleave flesh, not the wind. Though she didn't resent practice, because any use was better than none, she hadn't tasted blood for several days now. The sword possessed an unholy thirst after being buried in a millennium of dormancy.

As Dethen spun around to reverse direction, parrying high, he received the first perception. *Widowmaker* trembled slightly, her acute senses straining to the limits. Dethen felt it too: the cells of his body tingled. And then he realized.

"Ahhhhh! Malak! My twin brother returns."

He caressed the hilt of his sword.

"Perhaps here is the bloodshed you desire. Malak we will take alive, but as for his allies…"

Widowmaker hummed with satisfaction as her master sheathed her. Dethen's black eyes burned ferociously as the fire of his soul ignited.

Part II

Resurrection

They said to Him: Shall we then, being children, enter the Kingdom? Jesus said to them: When you make the two one, and when you make the inner as the outer and the outer as the inner and the above as below, and when you make the male and female into a single one, then shall you enter the Kingdom.

—The Gospel of St. Thomas

As far as we can discern, the sole purpose of human existence is to kindle a light in the darkness of mere being.

—Carl Jung

21

Enya
Black School
subterranean lair

Dethen stroked the blade of *Widowmaker* with a whetstone, his eyes focused internally. He sat in the lotus posture, facing the eastern wall. Behind him, Bal patiently awaited his master's attention.

"Malak has returned," Dethen said, his voice as deep and emotionless as ever.

Bal frowned. "To Enya?"

For a while, only the sound of the whetstone sliding along *Widowmaker's* blade answered him. It was a pointless task, since the blade never lost its keenness, but Dethen considered it his responsibility and the sword reveled in the attention, its blood-lust temporarily forgotten.

"He was drawn through the Rose Circle only a few hours ago. It is imperative we intercept him before anyone else. He now holds the key to our Purpose."

"But Master, is he not our enemy? He can surely not aid us?"

Dethen paused for a moment; he lifted the sword to check the alignment of the blade. It glowed scarlet, casting a cruel light over his features.

"Malak's soul is now one with Lilith's," he said. "His physical body can now act as a gateway to free the Arch-Demon and release her full might into Enya."

Bal's eyes glittered with excitement; he was as committed to the Purpose as his master. "How can we achieve this? Surely Malak will resist our efforts?"

"Malak's wishes are irrelevant. He is a weakling, unable to resist my power. I need to make preparations. A powerful ritual will be required to draw Lilith from the depths of his soul."

"Will Lilith not be able to smash through his mind herself, Master? Surely Malak will be no match for her might?"

"Normally so. But she is buried so deep it is almost impossible for her. However, there is a fragment of her force that has taken control of him before. It is the instinctive part of her nature, and if it runs amok on Enya there is a possibility that her full power could smash through. And if this occurred at Dark Moon, when her strength is many times amplified, Malak could not possibly resist."

Bal stroked his beard thoughtfully. "So if we fail to capture him, the demon will smash through of its own accord in two weeks?"

"Yes." Dethen rose to his feet and whirled around to face his disciple. "But we will not take that risk. It is possible that Malak has allies on this plane, perhaps even White Adepts from the old Council. Regardless, Lena is sure to be here. She is intimately connected with the karmic web."

Bal nodded. "What do you wish of me, Master?"

"Kalinda is waiting?"

"Yes, Master. She stands outside the door," Bal said.

"Bring her in, and await us outside."

Bal bowed from the waist and left the chamber. A few moments later Kalinda stepped inside. She was a woman of about forty winters, yet with a hard, well-muscled body that barely maintained its femininity. She wore chain mail armor; her sleek legs were tanned and bare. Fitted into a scabbard on her back was a huge sword, a dai-katana. Its blade was over six feet in length; its point almost brushed the floor and the hilt towered over her right shoulder. It was one of the most barbaric-looking swords Dethen had seen, yet she certainly had the biceps to wield it.

Kalinda's hair was dark and close-cropped, her face scarred in places and uncomely, but despite this she exuded sexual magnetism. Her eyes were brown, intelligent, and sharp; they viewed their surroundings with a predatory stare.

She seated herself on the floor as Dethen indicated.

"So, Felmarr, you were the Warlock all this time," Dethen said.

Kalinda smiled, a crooked lopsided smile with more than a hint of arrogance.

"I haven't used that name in nearly a thousand years. I am much more used to the idea of being female now."

Dethen noticed she still bore some of Felmarr's mannerisms, such as the way she sat, but a great deal had changed. Felmarr had been very talented, but would never have challenged his Master. Dethen knew that Kalinda wouldn't think twice about it if given the opportunity.

"What happened to you?" he asked. "I trusted you."

Kalinda shrugged. "I got tired of waiting for you to return. I rebuilt the Black School after the devastation of the Summoning in preparation for your return. I grew old and died waiting for you to come back. In my next life I was born as a woman, and I fought my way to the top of the School again. But it was too dangerous. Too many Adepts wanted to displace me, and almost succeeded. Imprisoning the dragon was my only chance of controlling things. I made it seem as if the Warlock had thrown me from power. Using the dragon's power, no one could stand against me."

"A dangerous game."

"It paid off. I still waited for you. For hundreds of years I waited for you. Then my loyalty turned to anger, and I gained ambitions of my own. I decided that if you ever did return, I would be the Master."

"Only your plan has failed, and once again I am the Master," Dethen said, studying her. "Will you serve me again?"

Kalinda gave a patronizing smile, obviously undaunted by his power. "I will do your bidding, but I will not serve you. I have an agenda of my own. After you have released Tien Lung, I must find some way to defend myself before she returns. Her power is too great."

Dethen nodded. He realized that although Kalinda had lost the dragon's power, she had not lost everything. She still had a thousand years of experience to draw on, and she had no lack of confidence.

"Leave me," Dethen said. Kalinda smiled and slowly stood up; she sauntered from the room.

"Bal! Come in here!" Dethen commanded.

"I want you to take a large group and ride to the Enchanted Forest," Dethen said. "You will be in command, and Kalinda will be your second. There I want you to search for my brother, Malak. I want you to bring him back alive. This is most important."

"Yes, Master. But is it wise to take Kalinda?"

"She is too valuable a resource to waste, but do not trust her. I want you to watch carefully to see how she behaves. She must be tested. You ride immediately. I will follow soon afterward to conduct my own search. But time is of the essence."

"I understand."

"One other thing, take Mendaz with you as captain of the guard. The action will do him good. He only mopes about here. I want you to keep him at your side at all times. Make sure no harm comes to him."

Bal scowled. "Why me? Why can't Kalinda babysit him?"

"You're not babysitting him, damn it!" Dethen snarled. He hesitated, surprised by his outburst. "He can look after himself. It is only as a precaution. I can't trust Kalinda, but I can trust you. So the job is yours."

Bal bowed his head. "As you wish, Master."

Even as he agreed to Dethen's wishes, Bal knew there would be unforeseen consequences to the assignment.

Enya
City of Sophia

Cassius paused to glance behind him as the azure city of Sophia slid from view. With a last pensive look he urged on his white stallion. Before him lay a great stretch of open countryside. Three hundred miles to the west lay his destination, the Enchanted Forest.

His mood was somber and reflective. He had waited many years to be reunited with Shadrack—too many. The weight of shame lay heavy on his shoulders. He had no idea how Shadrack would react to him. To Cassius, a lifetime had passed, yet to Shadrack it was only a few years. Would the ronin feel betrayed and treat him as Lena had?

Cassius was unsure whether he would reach Shadrack in time. He knew Dethen would be aware of his brother's return. There would be a myriad of Black Adepts and Black Guard soldiers combing the Enchanted Forest, and since he could not match their inflated numbers without weakening the defenses of Sophia, one man was more innocuous than several. Besides, this was his personal battle and at least he had faith in his abilities on that level.

He rode in full battle armor, a modified form of *haramaki*; it was a design he had borrowed from his memories of Nippon. The armor gave the right balance of protection and mobility. His breast plate was decorated with tiger lilies, just as his *yoroi* armor had been in Nippon. For the first time in many years, he wore his katana and wakizashi together as a daisho pair, in samurai style.

He hoped he wouldn't have to face Dethen. Though he didn't fear the confrontation, he feared the consequences of failure. Shadrack's life, and the very existence of the plane, would hang on the result of that battle.

He placed a scarred hand on the hilt of his katana. He would not fail.

The real voyage of discovery consists not in seeking new landscapes but in having new eyes.

—Doctrine of the White School[6]

22

Enya
The Enchanted Forest

Shadrack sat within the Rose Circle, tears rolling down his face. He had returned to Enya, and he was euphoric. There was no conscious reason for his sentiment; the emotion erupted from within, and despite the omnipresent emptiness inside, he knew he had come home.

He spent over an hour just feeling his way back into the plane, making it a part of him once again. At this point, his elation began to subside. He felt a tremendous, ominous difference in the nature of the plane. In his last life the Boundary had already started to weaken, but its condition was now incredibly frail, and it had left the plane lacking in defense—Shadrack could feel the signatures of alien essences that had penetrated through from Yesod.

One cognition that hit him with force was the fact that once again he was a magician. As he focused his mind, multi-colored lights appeared before him, dancing joyously in the air. It was something Malak had been unable to perform with ease due to the effect of the Boundary. Though he was once again able to wield magick, Shadrack was still not an Adept. He would not attain that honor until he defeated Lilith and re-established the link with his Higher Self.

Malak's memories seemed much closer and more real to him now. Poignant memories of the Rose Circle elicited a deep emotional

6 Marcel Proust

reaction. It was here that he had last seen Lena, as she threw herself forward in self-sacrifice, embracing certain death. The memory pierced him to his core.

The huge stone megaliths stood exactly as he remembered them, untouched by time. He felt the powerful currents of energy cast out from their forbidding, enigmatic forms, but they also comforted his mind, which strove to latch onto anything familiar.

He wondered what year he was in. Desperate fear and loneliness gripped him. This was not the Enya he knew—perhaps he was separated by hundreds of years from anyone he had known, mistakenly drawn into the wrong era. He remembered Ghalan's affirmation—he would be drawn through to the time when the Talisman was charged. There was a complex karmic web to be resolved. He, Lena, and Dethen must have therefore incarnated within the same time frame.

He wondered where he should go. Naively, he had expected to be delivered into Lena's arms. He was thankful now that this had not occurred, because the thought perturbed him. From Malak there was nervousness at the thought of reconciliation; to him, the separation seemed like an eternity. From Shadrack there was anxiety; Lena was not his love, and he was not yet one with Malak.

Checking through the contents of his backpack, he made a note of his food provisions. In addition to food and water, there was also an oil lamp, a tinderbox, a hundred feet of rope, warm clothing, a compass, and a hunting knife.

He ate a light meal of bread and cheese, then slung the backpack over his shoulders. He sighed pensively and slipped his katana and wakizashi through his belt, samurai fashion. It was now midmorning and he wanted to start moving, though he was unsure of a destination. There seemed only one obvious choice: the Celestial Tower. Though Lilith now possessed the Tower, he hoped Lena would assume it to be his objective. There was no other clear meeting point.

Pulling out his compass, he took a bearing. He then started walking north through the forest. Several hundred miles ahead lay the Wyrmspine Mountains and the Celestial Tower. Just possibly he would also find Lena.

By late afternoon Shadrack had walked twenty miles, halfway to the border of the forest. The sun hung low in the sky, and dusk was less than half an hour away. His body was tired, and he knew he would have to find shelter for the night—he didn't welcome the idea of sleeping in the open, unprotected. Intuition told him that night in the forest would be an unpleasant experience.

As he continued his trek, he realized that finding shelter would be difficult. The undergrowth was thin and only the huge golden-barked trees offered possible refuge. The idea of sleeping some distance above the ground perturbed him—he did not wish to roll over and plummet to the forest floor, no doubt being fortunate enough to break his neck on impact.

Due to their sheer size, many of the trees were difficult to climb because their branches began a dozen feet above the ground. As he walked, Shadrack glanced up continually, looking for a suitable tree. Kyoto Village had been situated in the middle of a forest and he had often climbed trees when younger. He was therefore confident of his tree-climbing ability.

The sun dipped below the tree-line horizon and he noticed a rope dangling from a tree to his left. He frowned and stopped to investigate. He was shocked when he looked up to see what could only be a treetop village. It extended for some distance in all directions, with simple wooden bridges linking the gargantuan trees together.

The structure was almost two hundred feet from the ground, interwoven with the middle branches of the trees. The blue-green leaves almost succeeded in camouflaging the village, and Shadrack was sure he would have missed it, had the rope not aroused his interest.

Shadrack possessed tremendous upper-body strength—he grasped the rope and was able to ascend hand over hand, his legs barely needed. He could not see anyone from the ground, but he was sure that the village was still inhabited. It didn't cross his mind that they might not welcome him—this was Enya, where fear and paranoia simply did not exist.

The rope was tied securely to a sturdy branch, designed so that one could literally step onto a wooden platform. From the platform, rickety bridges of wood and rope spanned the distance to three other trees. From these trees, more bridges branched out, and a whole network had been formed.

Shadrack stepped onto the platform and surveyed his surroundings. Still no one could be seen, but some distance away he heard the sound of children's laughter and clapping. Below him, through the gaps in the platform, he saw the forest floor. His head spun momentarily—though heights didn't usually bother him, the distance disturbed him. He began to question the stability of the large wooden platform that supported him, even though it had obviously survived the rigors of life longer than he had.

The platform stretched back to the main trunk of the tree, and Shadrack realized the village people actually lived within the trees. A sizeable archway was cut into the trunk of the tree, covered with a heavy brown fabric to shield against the elements. The other trees were similarly hollowed, with the bridges and platforms linking the community together.

Shadrack hesitated for a moment, and then decided to take a chance. If the people of the village refused him hospitality, he would simply move on and seek other shelter. He walked toward the main trunk and reached for the blanket that protected the entrance.

Only his zanshin allowed Shadrack a chance to respond to the trap. As he heard a minuscule creak of wood, he spun around quickly, his reflexes prepared for defense. He froze in place as his gaze traveled down the loaded quarrel of a crossbow.

"I wouldn't move none too quick if I was you, stranger," the man said, his accent thick with an unrecognizable dialect.

He was a huge man, dressed in a ragtag assortment of dirty animal furs. He had the build of a grizzly bear, with immense dirty arms and a barrel chest. His skin was pale and flaky, his hair receded to oblivion. Shadrack held his gaze, noting the intense paranoia and suspicion. But more than either of these was fear.

There was a swishing sound to Shadrack's left, followed by several more. He realized that men were descending from the upper branches of the tree. He had obviously been tracked by these people for some minutes before he had been snared.

"We get demons and all sorts in these parts, but they've never been able to climb before," the man continued, talking to the dirty male adolescent who stood next to him.

To Shadrack, the language was strange. He was more used to speaking in Nipponese, but this was part of a language he had understood since birth. It seemed different, though. The sentences were fractured and abbreviated, the dialect strange. He had to concentrate to understand. There was no doubting he was in serious danger; the village inhabitants were obviously not convinced by his apparent humanity.

"I say we kill him now!" shouted one of the men, leering towards Shadrack.

There were now five or six men clustered around the ronin. Shadrack's right hand rested on the hilt of his wakizashi, but there was not enough space to wield his katana. He forced himself to remain calm. He had vowed never to kill again. And he would fight whatever instinct sought to preserve him at the expense of other lives.

"Kill him now!" another voice agreed. Shouts of agreement resounded across the platform. From other trees, people crossed the bridges to investigate the excitement.

The first man in front of Shadrack grinned maliciously and aimed his crossbow.

"Nothing personal, friend," he said, "but we have to kill you."

"No, wait, I..." Shadrack choked on his words as someone slipped an arm around his throat from behind, making him a prone target.

Shadrack forced himself to go limp and he stopped struggling to breathe. He watched the man's trigger finger, ready to throw his assailant over his head the instant it moved. The assailant would shield him from the bolt as he was thrown in its path. If he then grabbed for the rope that he'd climbed, he might reach the ground by sliding in free-fall. He would lose the skin from his palms, but he might survive.

"Lughn! No!" A female voice sliced through the atmosphere, the unmistakable sound of a leader.

Lughn's finger poised on the point of disobedience, urged on by the silent encouragement of his peers. But his gall failed him; his finger relaxed, and he lowered the weapon slightly.

The woman pushed her way through the crowd of onlookers and cast her gaze disapprovingly over the scene. She was a large, chubby woman with a homely but experienced face, perhaps forty winters of age.

"There'll be no killing until we know who he is!" she said. Though there were quiet mutters, no one questioned her decision.

Shadrack was released from the throat-hold and he fell to the platform, gasping for breath. The headwoman scrutinized him carefully.

"Bind him," she said.

Shadrack had no time to react as several men converged in an instant, wrestling him to the deck. He struggled frantically, almost throwing one off the platform. But all further resistance ceased as something hard and heavy crashed into his cranium. Then there was only blackness.

The Kingdom of God is within you.

—Luke 17:21

Ye are the Temple of the Living God.

—II Corinthians 6:16

23

Enya
The Enchanted Forest

Shadrack awoke with a painful throbbing headache. Contrasting the dull ache, the sharp pain of a considerable gash lanced across the back of his head. He tried to reach up and check it, but his movement met resistance. The clink of metal and the numb feeling in his wrists revealed the sturdy iron shackles that bound him.

He was blindfolded, with his back against a firm but supple surface. The chamber seemed moderately sized, perhaps fifteen feet in diameter, he estimated from its ambience. There was a warm, pleasant atmosphere like lying within the womb; he realized he was sitting within the trunk of one of the trees. He felt its protective, benign influence wrapped around him and it helped dissipate his anxiety.

He felt the presence of other people in the room, though no sounds reached his ears. He groaned and shuffled to capture their attention. Though he was unsure, he guessed it was early evening, just after dusk.

"Mother, he's awake. Can I remove the blindfold?"

It was a young girl's voice, with a lesser accent than what characterized the violent men. The lack of dialect somehow made her seem more intelligent and reasonable.

He felt the soft brush of young skin and the blindfold was slipped over his head. He was grateful that the girl carefully avoided aggravating the gash at the back of his head. The light in the chamber was dim, but it still took Shadrack's eyes several seconds to adjust.

A pretty blonde-haired girl of perhaps seven knelt before him, her alert blue eyes inquisitive. Like others in the village she wore animal fur, mostly wolf skin. She held an orange clay cup out for him.

"Are you thirsty?" she asked, her voice loaded with childhood naiveté.

Shadrack held her gaze only fleetingly before glancing across the room to the second figure. She sat facing him, intent on stitching a garment. Her head was held low, but he recognized her instantly. She was the woman who had saved him having a crossbow quarrel buried in his chest. She was probably a headwoman, he decided.

She paused as she felt his gaze on her. Her hand reached out for a barbaric-looking knife that lay next to her. With a sharp, fluent movement, she hurled the weapon. Shadrack didn't flinch as the blade buried itself in the wood two inches from his right ear.

The woman looked up. "I am Althea, leader of this village. Do not cause any trouble, because I never miss twice."

The voice was deadly serious, like the severe blue gaze, but Shadrack saw he had gained a mental advantage in the lack of fear he showed. This surprised Althea, because she realized it was not pretense. There was curiosity in her eyes, but mixed with a great deal of wariness. He hoped fervently that the wariness wouldn't develop into paranoia.

"I bear no threat to anyone," he said lethargically.

"We shall see," Althea said, reaching for his katana. "And these are harmless ornaments, I suppose."

She grasped the hilt to unsheathe the blade.

"Please! Don't draw the blade!" Shadrack gasped.

Althea paused and looked at him suspiciously.

"It is a sacred weapon. To unsheathe the blade without drawing blood is to dishonor the sword."

Althea paused for a second in indecision, then laid the sword aside.

"Ursula, leave us," she said. "Join your uncle Lughn for the night. Tell him to send word to the Temple that we need a healer. Ask if Philip is available."

With a last curious look at Shadrack, the girl slid quietly out of the chamber and into the night.

"Despite first impressions, we are not barbarians," the headwoman said. "However, you live only because you didn't draw your swords in defense. What is your name, stranger?"

"I am Shadrack."

Althea frowned. "A foreign name."

"It means 'strange one.'"

Althea regarded him with distrust; only one language had ever been spoken on Enya.

"You are a warrior, Shadrack. Even without these swords of great quality, it is obvious. You have the face of a predator, like the hovering eagle. And your eyes show no fear. What manner of warrior are you? Your clothes are strange, and you wear no armor."

"I am samurai. A warrior of honor."

Althea mouthed the alien word.

"What master do you follow, samurai?"

"None. I am ronin, an outcast from my people."

The woman nodded, accepting this as likely.

"You speak with strange words, Shadrack. I won't ask from where you fare. But your injuries show you to be a man. Are you hungry?"

"No, ma'am. But I am tired."

"You may rest here, Shadrack. For now, at least, you will not be harmed," Althea said. "Philip will heal you when he arrives."

Yellow School sanctuary
The Enchanted Forest

Philip sat in perfect posture in the main hall before the statue of the goddess Maat, his breathing undetectable. He opened his eyes as the door opened behind him.

"What is it, Yhana?" As ever, his voice was totally devoid of emotion.

"A peasant has arrived from the tree village. They have need of a healer."

"Is noone else available?"

"You are the only healer left among us. The others are preparing for the Ascension."

Philip bowed to the goddess. He stood up and turned to face her.

"We should do more work on your wounds, too," he said, his cold eyes studying her face.

Yhana reached up to the ghastly scars that disfigured her.

"I prefer to keep them. As a reminder. When I get hold of my daughter and that damned panther, they'll pay for ruining my face!" Her tone was bitter with rancor.

Philip smiled, a gesture that always seemed patronizing. "You were hardly attractive beforehand," he said, then quickly added: "We must depart quickly. If I am to go to the village, I must not delay. My presence is required here for the Ascension."

He strode past Yhana. She swallowed her retort and followed him, her eyes watching him as a hawk studies a dangerous meal.

"You are the senior Adept now that the Master has died," she said. "In all the temples, there are few Adepts with your experience."

"This is true," Philip said, his voice noncommittal.

Yhana walked faster to keep up with his brisk pace as they stepped out of the sanctuary and into the forest. She pulled her hood over her head to hide her face.

"I have heard it said that you are favored to be the new Master. They say that you will be chosen by the goddess at the Ascension."

Philip raised an eyebrow. "The death of our Master is a tragedy for the School. She served it well. I will not use such an occurrence for the advancement of my own ambition."

Yhana scoffed. "Do you even have any ambition, Philip? Doesn't the prospect of leading the most powerful force on the plane cause your blood to rise in passion? Just think what this School could do with a strong leader!"

"We have a policy of non-interference. It has always been so. But the Master reigns supreme. Whatever he or she declares must be followed. However, it is unlikely the goddess will choose anyone with such delusions for power."

A look of disappointment passed over Yhana's face. "You think you will be chosen?"

Philip shook his head. "I do not believe so. I have spoken with the goddess and she has already made her choice, though it may seem strange to us."

"Strange?" Yhana's interest suddenly perked up.

"Her choice is the last one anyone would have imagined." He turned his face to see Yhana's eyes narrowed in thought. "Don't even think it. You are the second last person anyone would choose," he said dryly.

He stopped and looked up. "We are at the edge of the village. We can climb up here."

He started ascending the rope, his stringy muscles surprisingly strong. Yhana scowled at him and followed much more awkwardly —she had never had any use for physical exercise.

When she reached the platform a few minutes later she was breathless. Philip watched her dispassionately, arms enclosed within the sleeves of his yellow robes.

"Some help would have been appreciated," she said through gritted teeth.

Philip smiled. "I'm sure the exercise will be beneficial."

He turned and walked toward Althea's tree. Yhana struggled after him, worried she might miss something important. Philip brushed back the curtain and stepped into Althea's abode, Yhana close behind.

"Thanks for coming, Philip" Althea said. "His wounds are not serious, but they are best tended to."

Philip nodded, his eyes resting on Shadrack's sleeping form. His eyes narrowed as if in recognition.

"How long has he been sleeping?" he asked.

"Several hours. We drugged his drink," Althea said. "He doesn't appear quite normal and some of the men were paranoid he might be one of Lilith's demons."

"There is something strange about him," Yhana said. "I've never seen an aura like it. Such dormant power. . . ."

Philip nodded and crossed the room to kneel beside the sleeping ronin.

"I have seen his coming. The goddess Maat warned me." He turned to look at Althea. "The Warlock's agents must not hear of this. There will be Black Adepts combing the forest for him. They must not find him." He reached out his hands and started healing the injury to Shadrack's head.

"Black Adepts?" Yhana said, her heart suddenly beginning to hammer. She had loved only one person in her life, and he had been a Black Adept.

"I should think most of the Black School's Adepts will be searching for him. They desperately want this man."

Yhana's eyes glittered as an idea took shape in her mind.

"What will we do with him then?" Althea asked. "Surely the village is in danger as long as he stays."

Philip nodded. "I will send a message to Sophia. It is imperative that Prince Cassius Hawkin be informed of his location."

"How the hell do you know that?" Yhana asked.

"It is Maat's bidding," Philip said. "The role of our School is about to change." He suddenly looked very thoughtful. "About to change more than anyone would have imagined."

He worked for a few more moments, Shadrack's wounds healing under his skillful hands.

"That will do it," he said, standing up.

"What shall we do then?" Althea asked.

"Allow him to remain here in the meantime. Do not remove the shackles; he is indeed dangerous. Tell your people to avoid all contact with Black Adepts. I will attend to contacting Cassius Hawkin at Sophia."

The curtain was brushed back and a Yellow School initiate poked his head through.

"Frater Philip, the Adepts from the other sanctuaries have begun arriving. You are needed at the Temple. The Ascension will begin soon."

Philip nodded and turned to Yhana. "I must leave. I want you to stay here and ensure everything stays well."

"All right."

Philip raised an eyebrow in suspicion. "You are not worried you will miss the Ascension?"

Yhana shrugged. "As you said, I haven't a chance of being chosen anyway."

Philip studied her for a second, searching her eyes for an ulterior motive. "Very well. I will return when I have attended to my duties."

He stepped through the curtain to follow the initiate.

"I must give instructions to my people," Althea said. "Please excuse me, miss."

Yhana didn't bother to acknowledge her as the head woman left. She sat cross-legged on the floor, studying Shadrack's face. She didn't recognize it, but there was something vaguely familiar about the predatory hawk-like face. Suddenly she realized he looked like the paintings of the Magus Ghalan.

Obviously a coincidence, she thought.

She closed her eyes and tried to focus. It was difficult because she felt tremendous excitement building within her.

Most of the Black School's Adepts will be searching for him. Those were Philip's words. And Bal was prominent even among Black adepts. Was it possible he was in the forest seeking for the thing she had found? The thought of a reconciliation with her only lover thrilled her. She started to seek him with her inner vision.

If the doors of perception were cleansed everything would appear to man as it is, infinite.

—William Blake

Enya
The Enchanted Forest

Bal sat in the shadows against a tree, some distance from the fire around which the Black Adepts and Black Guard soldiers grouped. The men drank strong ale and told sordid jokes across the fire, eating venison and fresh fish. Bal had no stomach for their company. Like his Master, he preferred his own company to the company of fools.

He watched Mendaz as the warrior stepped over to the fire, cutting a strip of meat from the deer with his knife. The other soldiers watched him as they talked, resentful of an outsider in their midst, especially one in command. Bal smiled cruelly; he knew what was about to happen. The Black Guard were tough and totally lacking in conscience. Officers only survived if they had strength.

Mendaz walked back over to where he had been sitting. A soldier had moved into his place.

"Is there a problem, sir?" the soldier asked, giving a toothless grin.

Opposite Bal's position, Kalinda also sat alone; she watched with interest.

Mendaz stared at the soldier, the strip of venison still in his hand.

"I asked if there was problem," the soldier said, louder.

Mendaz muttered under his breath. The clearing went quiet as everyone focused on the incident.

"What was that?"

Mendaz's boot crashed into the soldier's face, sending him sprawling onto his back. He didn't rise and Mendaz kicked his body out of the way.

"I said you're in a stupid position to challenge me," he repeated. He sat down and started eating his meal. Suddenly the men started laughing. Bal cursed under his breath. Mendaz was tougher than he'd thought. The men hadn't accepted him yet, but it seemed it would be only a matter of time. Mendaz was unstable, but he was a born leader: he knew how to handle men.

Mendaz sensed he was being watched and he looked up at Bal. He smiled sarcastically, his eyes brimming with hatred. Bal returned the stare. In one way he didn't give a damn about Mendaz, but in another he had to admit he felt jealousy—it was obvious that Dethen felt affection for the bandit, something he rarely showed anyone. Never before had Dethen been protective over anyone or anything. Yet everything had changed now that Mendaz was here. It was even more bitter to Bal that Mendaz was Dethen's father. He had been sure that his own seed had given birth to his Master, but it seemed he was mistaken. It perplexed him as to who the child was that Yhana had given birth to. A girl, Mendaz had said.

Suddenly Bal felt something probing his mind, a gentle sensation but growing stronger. It was almost as if someone was scrying for him. He wondered if Dethen was seeking to make contact. He stood up and walked around the other side of the tree and knelt there, facing the darkness.

The feeling intensified and he received an impression of Yhana. He tried to shake it from his mind; he was sure it was because he had just been thinking of her. But Yhana's essence definitely seemed tangible to him. He saw no image, but words drifted into his mind.

I have the one you seek. Come alone to me at the village.

Bal saw an image of the tree village in his mind and as he concentrated, he felt the location of the scryer to the east. The link evaporated, leaving him alone once more. He had no idea of whether it was Yhana or not. There was no logical reason to presume it was, but intuition told him differently.

Dawn approached and he had to slip away quickly. He cursed as he remembered Dethen's instruction to keep Mendaz with him at all times. Even though he despised the bandit, he wouldn't disobey his Master.

He walked into the clearing and over to Mendaz. The captain stood up as Bal approached, ready in case he attacked.

"Come with me," Bal said quietly.

Mendaz stared at him. "I don't take instructions from you."

"I know where our quarry is," Bal said. "And though I'd rather go alone, Dethen told me to stay with you. If you decide not to accompany me, it is you who disobeyed him. As long as that is clear, you can do what you want."

"I follow Jaad," Mendaz snarled. "I'll go with you only because he ordered it."

"Suit yourself," Bal said. He turned and walked away from the clearing, not waiting for Mendaz to follow.

Kalinda watched from the shadows as Mendaz trailed Bal. Her eyes narrowed in suspicion. She attracted the glance of the Black Guard lieutenant and signaled for him to follow. The soldiers knew she had once been the Warlock, and Kalinda was widely feared. The lieutenant obeyed immediately, melding into the shadows to follow the two men.

Bal climbed the rope up to the tree village slowly, his body not as fit as it had once been. Behind him, Mendaz ascended more easily, his physique still hard and well muscled. He stepped onto the platform only a moment after Bal.

Bal stood with his eyes closed, searching with his inner vision. He gut tightened as he sensed Yhana's presence in a hut close by. He realized that if Mendaz saw her, he would kill her immediately.

"Wait here," he said, moving across the nearest rope bridge. Mendaz sat on the platform and watched as the Black Adept crossed the bridge and entered one of the huts. Then he stood up and followed him.

Bal brushed back the curtain to Althea's abode. The first thing he saw was Shadrack's drugged body, chained to the wall. His eyes widened in surprise.

"Is that the one you seek?" Yhana stepped out of the shadows.

Bal didn't even turn to face her. "His resemblance to the Master is...remarkable."

"I'm pleased you are satisfied," Yhana said, her voice icy.

Bal turned to face her.

"You have lost your hair and become fat," she said.

"I am older," Bal said. "Perhaps you should lower your hood and allow me to see how time has treated you."

He didn't miss the hesitation before she brushed back the hood. Unprepared for the horrific scars, he couldn't hide his shocked expression.

"Who did this to you?" His voice was tinged with anger.

"Our daughter, dearest. And her pet cat."

"We have a daughter?"

Yhana glared at him. "What would you care? She obviously didn't turn out to be your precious Master! But she was more trouble than enough!"

"I didn't know you didn't carry the Master," Bal said. "My plan failed. But he has returned anyway."

"And that is it? That's your apology?!"

"I didn't mention anything about an apology, Yhana. I'm here for Malak, not for you."

Yhana glowered, but didn't retort. Bal had not changed, and as ever, the fact that he used her excited her. She turned as Shadrack groaned, gradually awakening from drugged sleep.

"We should go outside," Bal said, pulling back the curtain and stepping outside.

Yhana pulled her hood across her head and followed him. Althea and her daughter stood waiting outside. Althea's eyes widened in shock as she saw Bal.

"You may go inside and tend to the prisoner," Yhana said haughtily.

"Philip said we were to avoid his type," Althea said.

"What would you know?" Yhana taunted. "Take your child and get out my sight!"

Althea's eyes hardened. "This is my village," she said, putting her hands protectively on her daughter's shoulders.

Undetected to anyone, Mendaz slipped closer along the cover of the tree branches, desperately trying to peer into the depths of Yhana's hood.

Yhana stepped in Althea's direction but Bal grabbed her arm. "We are wasting time. I must take Malak to my Master now."

"And what about me?" Yhana demanded bitterly. She pulled back her hood. "You don't want me now that I look like a hag?"

Bal opened his mouth to reply, then twisted his head sharply. "Soldiers!" he hissed.

It took him only a second to realize Kalinda had trailed him. There were Black Guards everywhere.

"Bring out the prisoner quickly!" Bal ordered.

A scream pierced the air, followed by several others. Soldiers swarmed over the rope bridges and into the trees, killing indiscriminately.

"They're killing my people!" Althea said, her face pale.

"Get the prisoner!" Bal hissed. "Or your village won't survive!"

Ursula clung to her mother, crying loudly. Althea pushed her gently away and rushed into the tree to unbind Shadrack's shackles from the tree.

From the nearby tree branch came the unnoticed sound of a dagger being drawn from a leather sheath.

"I want him, Bal!" a voice shouted. Bal turned to see Kalinda rapidly approaching across a rope bridge, several soldiers walking before her.

"Malak is mine!" Bal bawled. "I will deliver him to the Master!"

Kalinda laughed. "I'm afraid you won't be alive to do that."

Bal knew the soldiers would obey her. They feared her presence more than his own. He turned to release an astral burst at the rope bridge, intent on killing her.

Suddenly Mendaz leaped from his place of concealment, bearing down on Yhana with his dagger.

"Found you, you bitch!"

Yhana was taken completely by surprise. She stood in shock as Mendaz lunged with the dagger.

"No!" Bal shouted. He leaped into the path of the blade.

The dagger bit deeply into his kidney. He gasped in agony and fell to the platform, half of his body lying on the rope bridge.

"Bastard!" Mendaz snarled. He reached down and yanked the dagger from the Black Adept's body.

Shocked to action by Bal's injury, Yhana came to her senses. She released a blast of astral energy. It collided with Mendaz, stunning him and sending him sprawling across the platform. He lay still, barely conscious. Yhana bent down to comfort her dying love.

"Funny," Bal said, grimacing. "The Master made stopping a dagger seem so easy."

Kalinda was halfway across the bridge now, making ground quickly. Chaos reigned in the village—the peaceful inhabitants were sliced as they ran or begged for mercy.

Althea emerged from the tree holding Shadrack, who still had his hands bound. He blinked groggily in the bright light. Two of the village men, armed with axes, arrived to help Althea restrain him.

Kalinda pointed at him. "I want that man!" she shouted. Shadrack frowned in confusion, still fighting the mind-numbing drug.

All the troops began to converge on Shadrack's platform via the rope bridges. Shadrack groaned to himself as he recognized the insignia on their armor—a broken image of the Qabalistic descent of power. They were soldiers of the Black School, Dethen's minions.

"I'm sorry, Shadrack," Althea whispered in his ear. "Once I hand you over, they will stop this madness!"

Behind them, Yhana cradled Bal's unconscious form as his life's blood leaked away.

Althea pushed Shadrack onto the bridge Kalinda now crossed with four soldiers before her. When Shadrack was a few yards from the first guard, Althea shouted: "He is yours. We want no trouble. This is a peaceful village."

"Peace is not an option," Kalinda's snarled. "There will be no survivors, or witnesses!"

Althea stood for a moment in shock, before shouting, "Back!"

She grabbed her daughter and ran back toward the platform; Ursula started to cry. The two men restraining Shadrack followed her, ready to wield their hand axes in defense of the village. Shadrack was left with only the iron shackles to restrict his movement. He held his ground—if he ran, he knew the soldiers would cut him down from behind.

Ursula's crying reminded him of Saito's children on his last fateful day in Kyoto Village. The smell of burning assaulted his nostrils and the villagers' screams made him shudder. He knew that these soldiers would kill Ursula, just as the samurai had killed Saito's daughters in Kyoto. He could not allow it to happen again, but neither could he break his vow of pacifism—it was the last vestige of honor he possessed.

The bridge was only wide enough to accommodate men in single file. The first soldier reached Shadrack and started to draw his wakizashi. Shadrack reached forward and grabbed his wrist clumsily, the shackles making the act awkward. His gray eyes were focused and grave.

"I cannot allow you to do this," he said, his voice slurred from the drug.

The soldier glowered and punched him across the jaw with his free hand. Shadrack's head recoiled backward, but otherwise he didn't move. His eyes darkened in anger, a slight red tinge appearing.

Seeing the unnatural gaze, the soldier became fearful and he threw another punch, even harder than the last. He drew blood from the side of Shadrack's mouth. The ronin's eyes began to glow. His grip tightened on the soldier's wrist, and the man gasped in pain.

Shouts came from the troops behind the soldier urging him to deal with the ronin, but the troups were unable to see the gradual metamorphosis taking place. As a last desperate attempt, the soldier rammed his knee forcefully into Shadrack's groin. Shadrack bent forward slightly as the blow impacted. His eyes burned a ferocious scarlet. The soldier screamed as his wrist crumbled under the enormous pressure of the grip.

Shadrack inhaled sharply as he realized what was happening, but he was too late: the possession had advanced too far. Like a tidal wave of force, it immersed his personality and mind, utterly extinguishing his individuality. Intense, nefarious hatred coursed through him and he completely lost control.

The creature yanked its wrists apart; the shackles literally exploded from them. The soldier tried to draw his wakizashi, but he was too slow. The creature seized him by the throat and hoisted him into the air. Choking for breath, the soldier kicked and flailed like a madman. But the beast was oblivious to the impotent attacks—with a twist of the wrist, the soldier spun toward the ground and certain death.

The creature roared a howl of triumph and blood-lust, a noise to freeze the soul of the hardiest warrior. The sounds of the forest silenced as the cry pierced through the trees. On the platform behind, Ursula screamed as soldiers approached from two other bridges.

The beast lunged forward with a front kick, its technique incredibly quick and vicious, yet perfectly formed. The kick struck the second soldier with tremendous power, crumpling the breastplate of his armor and breaking his sternum. He was blasted backward, knocking another soldier down and another entirely off the bridge. Behind them all, Kalinda slipped athletically away to avoid the domino effect.

The creature turned and ran for the platform, where a soldier bore down on Althea and Ursula. The beast spun the man around, striking his suprasternal notch above his sternum with *tetsui-uchi,* the hammer fist strike. The man gasped once before the death strike took effect. His collarbones instantly dislodged from his sternum, collapsing his shoulders and puncturing his aorta and superior vena cava. His sternum split and his hyaline cartridges penetrated his esophagus and trachea, destroying his windpipe. Within seconds he was dead.

The creature saw Shadrack's katana lying on the platform, where Althea had dropped it. With a fluent movement, it retrieved the weapon and drew the blade. Two soldiers attacked. The beast sliced them to the ground without a chance of retaliation. A third attacked with a wakizashi. The creature parried and attacked again with *tetsui-uchi,* striking down at the soldier's jaw.

The jaw was instantly dislocated and the beast grabbed the soldier by it, twisting sharply. The man screamed in agony before being thrown across the platform. He rolled as he hit it, slipping off the platform to plummet to his destruction.

Yhana watched the beast in horror. She stayed low, cradling Bal to her breast.

In the upper branches of the tree, something large and black flitted back and forth, observing the battle as it unfolded.

A hail of crossbow bolts whipped past Shadrack on all sides as the Black Guard opened fire from a distance. The creature sliced the nearest from the air with his katana, then made a sweeping gesture with its arm. The glow of its scarlet eyes intensified. Suddenly every bridge exploded into green flames, incinerating the soldiers.

Yhana shouted and yanked Bal away from the bridge as the flames scorched his robes. She looked around quickly, realizing few people were left alive. She grabbed Bal and slung him over her shoulder, using magick to take his weight. She slipped off the platform and started the precarious descent to the ground, burning her hands on the rope as she slid. Mendaz watched her groggily, his eyes almost blind. A moment later he followed her, his body shaking from the blast she had released.

Hidden in the upper branches, the green-eyed black entity scrutinized the battle carefully, choosing its moment.

Kalinda saw Shadrack's magical attack before it struck. She hurled herself from the bridge. Concentrating her powers of visualization fiercely, she glided to a nearby tree branch. Camouflaged by the leaves, she slowly made her way toward the platform, her huge dai-katana drawn.

The creature spun around now, its blood-lust not yet sated. There were no Black Guards left, so it advanced upon Althea, Ursula, and the two men who guarded them. The men attacked with axes, trying to cleave the beast in two. It parried the blows easily. It attacked one man with a ridge hand technique across the temple, dropping him instantly. The second it kicked in the groin, then punched along the coronal suture, the joint across the top of the cranium. The force was enough to split the man's skull apart.

The beast advanced upon Althea and Ursula, murder in its eyes. Ursula sobbed loudly. The creature hesitated for a moment; its red eyes dimmed in intensity. It moved forward again, and then stopped. It snarled. Ursula cowered behind her mother, watching as the creature's eyes slowly turned to a neutral, nondescript gray.

"No!!!" Shadrack screamed, falling to the platform in exhaustion, but triumphant in wrestling control from the creature.

"Inside, now!" Althea said, pushing Ursula inside the tree.

Shadrack lay helplessly on top of his katana, too fatigued to move. Tears of anger and remorse flowed down his face as he realized the extent of the destruction he had caused.

Behind him, Kalinda reached the edge of the platform and advanced cautiously, her dai-katana raised and prepared to strike. Shadrack saw her approach, but couldn't find the energy to push himself to his feet. Kalinda realized his problem, and raised her sword to deliver a death-strike.

She said, "If Dethen wants you alive, I want you dead!"

From the upper branches, Bast sprang. She knocked Kalinda across the platform to fall on her back. Shadrack recognized the panther instantly. She stood over him protectively, growling vehemently at Kalinda.

Kalinda grabbed her sword and attacked. The blow deflected harmlessly off Bast, and the panther pounced on her, nearly ripping out her throat. Kalinda quickly used her magick to deflect the familiar. She jumped for a nearby branch before the familiar recovered, leaving her sword behind.

Bast growled in triumph, showing her three-inch canines. She loped over to Shadrack and lay down for him. Still hanging onto his katana, Shadrack slid onto her back. He gripped her neck tightly. With a last impressive roar, Bast leaped from the platform. She sprang from branch to branch, rapidly descending the tree. Even though he had no strength left, Shadrack was able to maintain his grip on the giant feline. Though her powers were more subtle than those of an Adept, Bast was still a magical creature and therefore capable of warping reality.

Within seconds she reached the forest floor. With Shadrack clinging tightly to her, she loped into the depths of the forest.

Behind Bast, Yhana's eyes followed the familiar with demonic hatred. She self-consciously touched the wounds on her face and swore. Turning back to her task, she picked Bal up again and started staggering back to the sanctuary, her magick only just allowing her to carry his weight.

Yhana didn't notice Mendaz drop to the ground behind her. Still shaken by her attack and half-blind, he half crawled after her, his hand clutching his dagger.

Verily, I say unto you. Except ye be converted and become as little children, ye shall not enter the kingdom of heaven.

—Matthew 18:3

Verily, verily, I say unto thee. Except a man be born again, he cannot see the Kingdom of God.

—John 3:3

Enya
The Enchanted Forest

Bast loped through the forest for five minutes before stopping before a slow-flowing stream. Shadrack patted her thankfully and slid from her well-muscled back. Looking at Bast's size, he realized it must be close to Full Moon, otherwise she would have been unable to carry him. He remembered how her size fluxed with the rhythm of the moon.

He groaned as he lay on his back, staring at the pink midday sky. Bast watched him with concern, her green eyes shining with alien intelligence. She moved forward and licked him across the face, her black sandpaper tongue almost ripping off his skin. Shadrack screwed up his face and pulled away. Bast purred, a noise more like a growl, and padded off into the forest to search for food for her master.

Shadrack lay without moving. Despite the intensity of the shock and pain, it all seemed terribly familiar—he had walked this path before. Apathy once again grasped hold of his mind. Everything he had striven for had been undone—when it mattered, he had been unable to suppress the demon within.

He rolled onto his stomach and wriggled forward to stare into the stream. At the edge, the water was calm, allowing him to see his reflection. His face was begrimed and cut, his hair filthy and matted. Yet despite this, his gray eyes were clear. He realized that he had achieved a triumph of sorts. When Lilith had first possessed him, his mind and body had been shattered and the demon had left him of its own volition. This time, he had wrestled control back from the beast. And although he felt very weak, he was otherwise unaffected by the possession, mentally and physically.

He also remembered his actions while possessed, unlike the previous occasion. He knew what it felt like to be the beast; he had felt its terrible hatred and aggression. The creature did not think in the normal fashion: it reacted purely on instinct. It was not actually Lilith that possessed him in these moments, but a splinter of her demonic essence. It was pure, unthinking, archetypal force. He knew that his vow of pacifism was futile while this demon had the ability to seize control in moments of emotional stress.

He splashed water onto his face, cleaning away the grime. The cuts on his face stung as the cold water touched them. As the liquid washed away the dirt, it also dissolved his apathy. The emotion gradually subsided into relief as he realized he might have killed both Althea and Ursula. As it was, he had killed two score of Black Guard and two village men, who had both attacked him with axes. The crime was serious enough, but not as bad as it might have been. It seemed he had killed so many in his life that a few more hardly mattered. His capacity for guilt had been exhausted.

As he lay staring into the stream, his mind lost in thought, a deep threatening growl came from the other side of the brook. Momentarily, he froze. Then he slowly raised his head to look into the red soulless eyes of Graymist. The wolf pulled back its jowls to reveal vicious yellow canines. Saliva dripped from its mouth as it considered its prey.

Shadrack's eyes widened in shock and fear. He reached for the hilt of his katana. As he did so he realized that along with his backpack, his wakizashi had been left behind in the tree village. No longer were his swords a daisho pair, but it was the katana that was important: a samurai should never be without his longsword.

He struggled onto his knees, moving slowly and maintaining eye contact with the creature all the time. Though his strength was gradually returning, he knew he was still too weak to defend himself. Neither was he in any condition to run.

Graymist sank down, its muscles preparing to spring forward. It launched itself through the air, fangs searching for his throat. Shadrack's body moved too slowly as he tried to leap sideways;

he could only throw up his arms and brace himself. There was a mighty roar as Bast intercepted the demon in mid-air, throwing them both into the stream.

The two creatures regained their feet in the stream, glaring at each other as they prepared for battle. Bast growled a challenge, a call for a rematch after their ill-matched battle at the *Murky Chasm* in Gorom. Graymist snarled uncertainly. This time the demon didn't have the advantage of physical size.

Suddenly Bast pounced. Shadrack watched the battle, desperately searching for a way in which he could aid his familiar. But Bast needed no help—her sleek muscles overpowered the demon. Graymist tried to use his demonic essence to manipulate her mind, but Bast's will was too strong. They thrashed about ferociously for half a minute before Bast clawed deep wounds into the demon, receiving only minor cuts herself.

Suddenly Graymist leaped from the stream, running into the forest. In a second, Bast pursued him and soon they were out of eyesight.

"I see your familiar has returned, Malak."

Shadrack's blood solidified in his veins. The voice was slightly different, but the manner was unmistakably Dethen's.

"A strange and exotic beast that one, far more intelligent than my own," the voice continued.

Half-expecting to feel a sword pierce him, Shadrack turned slowly in his kneeling position. As ever, Dethen was dressed in black robes. His face was still hawk-like, in many ways similar to his last incarnation, and the eyes were just as sinister. He had grown his hair long, and he had a Van Dyke beard, neatly trimmed compared to Shadrack's unruly full beard. By Dethen's side, *Widowmaker* pulsed with animosity, but Dethen's expression was softer, almost affectionate.

As he turned, several Black Guard soldiers advanced on Shadrack but Dethen signaled them to fall back. They obeyed immediately. Dethen reached out a huge hand toward the ronin.

"I'm quite capable of standing," Shadrack said. He rose unsteadily, ignoring the offered hand.

Dethen smiled. "It has been a long time, brother."

"We have not been brothers for thousands of years, Dethen. You are no ally of mine."

Shadrack's voice was bitter. His body's strength gradually returned and he knew he would need it. One way or another he had to escape this situation.

The two men held each other's gaze for a few moments. Dethen's was deep and menacing, but Shadrack didn't flinch from it. His own gaze was steely gray, hard and unrevealing.

"We are more alike than you think, Malak," Dethen said. "We were once twins in the flesh, and we will always remain twins in the spirit. Both of us have suffered greatly through no fault of our own. And both of us have been deprived of the women we loved."

Shadrack couldn't hide his surprise. It was unlike Dethen to emotionally open himself to anyone, and it was obviously a gesture of trust. It was an attempt to initiate the first step in a reconciliation, not unlike the time at the Celestial Tower so many years ago. Shadrack found it eerie to face a specter from his distant past like this. For so long there had been antagonism between them, and they now enjoyed a civil conversation.

"Neither of us is as we once were, Dethen," he said. "You have utterly changed since I knew you as a brother, with Ghalan as our father. And I don't even possess a soul anymore."

There was the barest glimmer of sympathy in Dethen's expression as he listened.

"We have both suffered," he affirmed. "But only one individual is responsible for this terrible mess, and that is Chronzon. He rules everything below the Abyss, instigating pain and sorrow everywhere. There is only one solution. He must be utterly destroyed!" For a moment intense desire flickered within Dethen's eyes.

Shadrack stood perfectly still, his face unreadable. Yet doubts rose in his mind. Once again, he felt the almost intangible but undeniable bond between himself and his brother—they were still kin.

"Join with me, Malak! Together, we can draw the force of Lilith through to this plane. She will smash through into Yesod, and the tumultuous battle with Gabriel will destroy the Sephirah. The resulting imbalance will annihilate the Tree of Life, ending the Universe as we know it! Only the higher plane of formlessness will survive!"

Shadrack frowned. "You think that death is the solution to our problems? Lilith has put you up to this."

"Malak!" Dethen's voice had reached fever-pitch, and was almost pleading. "Are we not immortal beings?! The human race will be reborn in the higher planes, far above the demolished realms of Chronzon! This may be Lilith's plan, but I owe no loyalty to her. The Purpose is my only care!"

The two brothers stared at each other for a long time as Shadrack pondered his twin's words. Dethen saw that he had penetrated Shadrack's mental defenses, but now there was nothing left to say. Shadrack simply had to make his decision.

"Malak?" Dethen prompted after a while.

The ronin looked up and shook his head sadly. "My name is Shadrack."

He raised his arms and a blinding flash of light appeared around him. Dethen and the soldiers were forced to shield their eyes. Some seconds later, when the after-image had passed, Shadrack was gone.

"Capture him!" Dethen spat, fuming with wrath. "And I want him alive!"

The five guards dashed off into the forest in different directions, swords drawn and ready. Dethen stood still for a moment, his eyes closed. He sought Shadrack's direction with his inner vision. In a few seconds, he found his target. He leaped over the stream and started to sprint. He knew that one of the Black Guard had run in the same direction, and might therefore apprehend his brother.

Dethen was impressed with Shadrack's stamina. At the stream, it had been obvious he was not in perfect health, yet he still almost outran his pursuers. His brother had obviously received some sort of training.

Dethen forced himself to pick up speed again as a cry sounded from ahead. He thought that Shadrack had fallen, but in a few seconds he came upon the body of a Black Guard. Dethen slowed as he passed, observing that the man had been killed by a sword strike, delivered from some height. His eyes narrowed in suspicion, and he scanned the trees for concealed enemies as he ran; the work was not that of Shadrack. Close by, he made out the sound of horse's hooves, but the trees were too densely packed to see anything.

For a moment, he had a clear line of sight on Shadrack and he acted immediately. He formulated an intense blast of astral energy and fired. Shadrack was blasted off his feet and landed face down in the foliage, stunned. His sword flew from his grip on impact, landing some distance away.

Dethen made up the last fifty yards quickly; he drew his sword as he neared. He stopped suddenly as a huge white stallion reared up in front of him, hooves kicking forward. Dethen fell backward in an attempt to avoid the lethal kicks. He rose a few seconds later, his pupils like pinpoints.

Cassius dismounted and knelt over Shadrack's prone body. Dethen advanced and loomed over him with his huge, intimidating build.

"You will die for this," he said. He released a tremendous blast of astral energy. The energy deflected around Cassius' aura, scorching trees in a wide radius.

Dethen stared in shock. He fired a burst of lightning and again observed the same effect. The tree behind Cassius was almost split in two by the blast.

"What manner of demon are you?" Dethen asked.

"I am a simple warrior, Dethen, nothing more."

Dethen's eyes widened at the use of his name. "Stand aside, stranger. This is my quarry," he said, his voice edged with menace. "You may deflect sorcery, but my sword will be harder to contend with."

Cassius straightened and turned to face him.

"I am Cassius Hawkin of Sophia. I have no wish to fight you, but Shadrack is coming with me."

Dethen smiled humorlessly. "Your wishes are irrelevant. You are obviously a man of honor. Are you familiar with *iai?*"

Cassius gave a twisted, unnerving smile. "More familiar than you can know. Honor, first blood or…."

"Death," Dethen interrupted. "We fight to the death."

Cassius bowed in acknowledgment. "Unnecessary, but as you desire."

Iai was a samurai tradition, though Dethen was unaware of this. Two opponents would kneel facing each other, and either opponent could draw his katana and attack. The defendant would attempt to parry the strike and then counter-attack. Historically, it had been used to settle disputes or feuds between samurai.

Hands by their sides, the two men knelt. Their eyes locked in a battle of wills. For Cassius, this verified the stories of the black mage's power. Dethen's black gaze sought to snare him, hypnotizing him like a cobra preparing to strike. Cassius felt his emotions flow away; his pale blue eyes became calm and detached, unruffled by the torrent of force seeking to swamp him.

For several minutes no one moved. The midday sun crawled lazily across the sky, and the sound of bird-song continued unconcernedly. Gray squirrels skipped back and forth through the tree branches, chattering excitedly. They sensed the mounting tension between the kneeling warriors.

A few yards away, Shadrack pushed himself up to watch. He was disorientated and confused from his loss of consciousness. He had not seen Cassius arrive, but he now lay watching in awe. There was something incredibly familiar about the warrior: his style and mannerisms were unmistakable. He was also wearing haramaki, a form of samurai armor, and he wore his swords as a daisho pair. Shadrack would not interfere in the iai. It was a sacred ritual, and as a samurai he had to respect it.

For the two dueling swordsmen only the mental battle existed. It intensified to the breaking point. The squirrels became silent, certain that one of the men was about to attack. They were right.

With incredible speed, Dethen grasped the hilt of *Widowmaker* and drew her. His attack sliced diagonally down toward Cassius' shoulder, with enough strength to cut through to his left hip. Cassius reacted instinctively. In an instant he drew his blade and parried the attack. Without a pause his blade then sliced across Dethen's abdomen.

His eyes wide with disbelief, Dethen waited for the excruciating pain. But there was only a sting. With embarrassment, he realized that Cassius had cut only through his skin, as the law prescribed. Once unsheathed, a katana must draw blood. It had been the perfect counter-attack.

"That was very, very foolish," Dethen said, his voice trembling with repressed anger. "The duel was to the death. You have insulted the honor of the agreement."

He rose and assumed an attacking posture, *Widowmaker* held horizontally above his head, the other hand held forward to counter-balance. Cassius stood up and calmly took up a stance to neutralize his posture, his sword raised and ready.

"My intention was not to dishonor you or the *iai*, but I had no intention of losing," he said, his voice level. "Push the incident further and I will be forced to defend myself." He paused. "You don't want me to have to do that."

Dethen snarled and sprang into action, attacking aggressively. Widowmaker bit through the air, hungrily seeking the taste of flesh. Cassius was forced backward, parrying forcefully. But he varied his tactics, moving from linear movements to circular and back again.

Dethen's blows were vicious, raining down with incredible force. Yet Cassius moved to use a minimum of force to deflect the attacks. Dethen became more and more infuriated; he began to overreach his attacks and leave significant gaps in his guard. Cassius moved like a blade of grass in a hurricane, being bent this way and then that, but never in any real danger.

Unused to fighting with anger, Dethen's excessive emotion caused his concentration to slip. Cassius counter-attacked with speed and vigor. Surprised and caught off balance, Dethen fought for his life as he was pushed back. Sparks flew from both swords at the force of the impacts.

The outcome of the battle was suddenly decided as Cassius sliced to Dethen's side, preparing for the death strike. The dark mage blocked the stroke and there was a loud crack as the blade of Cassius' sword shattered, overcome by the essence of *Widowmaker*. Cassius stood in shock, staring at the broken blade.

"The spirit of a samurai," he muttered under his breath. "Broken."

Dethen stopped for a moment and their eyes locked. Cassius waited for the death strike but Dethen seemed to be debating with himself, embroiled with internal conflict. He lowered *Widowmaker*, who whined in complaint.

"You are a noble adversary, Cassius Hawkin," he said soberly. "You had the upper hand. I will not take advantage of your misfortune. I concede defeat." He bowed formally.

His eyes flashed over to Shadrack.

"I will return for you, brother," he said, before turning his eyes back to Cassius. "And this time I will not be stopped so easily."

He sheathed the angry Widowmaker, then turned and strode towards the tree village. He quickly disappeared from view behind the curtain of trees.

Cassius barely noticed his opponent recede. He stared at the shattered blade of his sword. Over ten generations the weapon had existed and now it had been destroyed. Tears rolled down his face at the thought of the dishonor he brought on the Hawkin name.

He turned as Shadrack tentatively approached him.

"A thousand years of history," Cassius said disbelievingly.

Shadrack nodded sympathetically and held out his own sword.

"Then let me offer this to you, as you once offered it to me. My own sword, *Retaliator*, still lies within the Celestial Tower. This sword was forged by the father of Yoriie Saito, the finest sword master in Nippon. You do remember, Ieyasu?"

Cassius stared in amazement. "You know?"

Shadrack nodded, tears appearing in his eyes. "It is good to see you, father."

The two men embraced silently; there was no need for further words.

Strength with compassion,
Honor with chivalry,
Steadfast purpose with harmonious balance,
Dignity with humility.
The Knight Templar must temper all these qualities."

—Prince Cassius Hawkin

26

Enya
The Enchanted Forest

At the edge of the Enchanted Forest, Shadrack helped Cassius unload the stack of firewood they had collected. The sun had fallen below the horizon some time ago and already the air temperature began to plummet.

The two men had had little time to talk since their reunion. The large contingent of Black Guard soldiers had forced them to ride hard throughout the day, requiring a great deal of concentration from Cassius. His white stallion had performed admirably, weaving in and out of the huge golden trees with speed and grace.

"Is it safe to light a fire?" Shadrack asked, concerned it would draw the enemy to them.

Cassius nodded and sat himself down on the ground.

"We've put over fifty miles behind us. They won't see a small campsite from that distance, and the smoke will be invisible in the dark."

Shadrack nodded tiredly and sat down on the other side of the piled wood. Beside him Bast lay in restless sleep. It disturbed Shadrack; he couldn't remember Bast sleeping like this before. He noticed the claw wounds that covered her chest and back, and wondered if they affected her.

"Can you light it for me?" Cassius asked.

Shadrack frowned, surprised by the request. "Do you have tinder and flints?"

Cassius nodded. "I have, but I would have thought that you wouldn't need them."

"Ah." Shadrack stretched his hands out toward the wood. Flames vaulted into life.

"Surely you have the ability, too?" he asked. "A focused mind and good visualization will produce simple effects."

Cassius shook his head. "The Art Magick is forever forbidden to me. In my last life I was a samurai, and in this one all magick is forbidden to me. But I will explain all this to you later. First you must tell me what has happened since our separation."

The remembrance of Tanaka's suicide hung in the air between them and Shadrack's face became pained. He stared deep into the fire, as if the answers he sought lay within it. An intense, harrowing guilt lay within him. He had killed over fifty men and still had no control of the demon within. If he was forced to admit this to Cassius, would he disown Shadrack again as had Tanaka in Kyoto? But Shadrack knew he could only tell the truth—anything else would only serve to deepen his dishonor.

The fire burned vigorously now, casting its amber warmth in a respectable radius about them. The moon, two days past full, hovered over the horizon like an omniscient opal eye; its low height caused the atmosphere to magnify its image, making it sinister and intimidating.

When Shadrack started to speak, it was as if he relived the tale he told.

"After the demon possessed me in Kyoto, my body was left shattered, my mind incoherent and splintered. I have a vague memory of crossing a great sea in a boat with Ekanar. Everything from that period seems to be very dream-like and vague. I wasn't truly conscious.

"Ekanar took me to a Temple of Yellow Adepts in Saxony, beyond the continent of Azia. There I was treated both physically and psychically by Ghalan, but in his incarnation before he was Magus of Enya."

Cassius looked shocked. "Yes, I've heard of Ghalan, of course. Who hasn't? Enya no longer has a Magus, and Ghalan is revered as the last one we had."

"It seems very peculiar that it was Ghalan I was taken to," Shadrack said. "Almost unbelievable. Yet here I am again with you once more, father. My faith in the existence of coincidence will never be the same."

Cassius nodded in agreement. "It seems to me that though we do possess free will in some measure, there is little of our destiny that isn't already planned out. But continue. Ghalan helped to heal you?"

Some of the denizens of the forest, mainly squirrels, pushed forward now to enjoy the heat of the fire. They eyed the two humans suspiciously as they approached, their swelling numbers lending them courage.

"Yes, over a period of a year or so, Ghalan taught me to regain control of myself and to shake off the apathy that gripped me. Very gradually, he taught me to resist Lilith's strength and to fear her less. In return, I instructed him in the martial arts that you revealed to me."

The eyes of the two men met over the flickering flames of the fire. Cassius frowned.

"History records that Ghalan was the first to introduce martial arts and Oriental philosophy to Enya through his two sons Malak and Dethen," he said. "Are you telling me that his knowledge and skills originally came from me?"

Shadrack smiled, pleased that he had someone else with whom to confide the incredible paradox.

"So you taught him budo-kai so that he could then teach you in your past life, which would be his next life!"

"That's about it," Shadrack said.

"And now I'm here, a thousand years later, and I'm the source of it all!" Cassius laughed gruffly, a sound his throat didn't seem used to making. "Now I see just how much I've been tangled in this karmic web between yourself and your brother. When I battled him today, he was using martial arts that originally came from me."

"He was at a distinct disadvantage," Shadrack agreed, seeing the inherent humor.

The squirrels now grouped around the fire in numbers, sure the two warriors would not harm them. The creatures were quite brazen; one of them hopped into Shadrack's lap and offered a half-eaten nut in recompense. Shadrack declined the gift, but tickled the creature affectionately around the ears. The squirrel enjoyed this immensely and started to rub its head against his hand.

"So how did you return to Enya?" Cassius asked. "Surely not a simple task?"

Shadrack shrugged as he continued to stroke the squirrel. "It was actually quite easy. According to Ghalan, it was due to Lena. She charged a Talisman that gave me the motivation to return. But it was the witch stones that transported me. They were very much like the stones you found me in as a child."

Cassius shook his head. "Shadrack, I still think of you as my son, but you have to realize that the event at the stones occurred a very long time ago for me. For you it might only be fifteen years or so, but I have lived an entire lifetime since then as Cassius Hawkin. The memories are not nearly as fresh for me as they are for you."

"I understand," Shadrack said, feeling mildly rebuked.

"Don't misunderstand me," Cassius said. "My experiences as Ieyasu Tanaka forged me into what I am today, even if the mistakes were more important than my achievements."

"Mistakes are painful," Shadrack said quietly, then added: "Father, I must tell you. I have almost no control of the demon that possesses me. Just as in Kyoto, I cannot avoid violence if provoked."

He held his breath as he awaited cold condemnation. But Cassius was staring into the fire. He didn't speak for some time.

He finally said: "Do you realize what I did today?"

"Father?" Shadrack was caught off guard by the conversation's change of direction.

Two squirrels climbed onto Cassius' lap, seeking affection. The warrior's gaze was distant, however, and he seemed oblivious to the creatures.

"I fought Dethen," he said. "And though I wasn't prepared to kill him, because it is you who must finally face him, there was always the possibility that it could occur. This is most unlike the Ieyasu Tanaka that you knew, would you agree?"

The shock of the earlier event struck Shadrack—his father had always upheld a vow of pacifism when in Nippon.

"You see my life as Tanaka was characterized by extremes. When young I was arrogant, aggressive, and obnoxious. As you know, this is no way to behave in life. But in later years when I raised you, I was full of mercy and advocated pacifism. My death was not the act of honor which I thought it, but the act of a coward even though I felt no fear."

Shadrack stared at Cassius, utter disbelief in his eyes.

"Hari-kari is terribly wrong," the old warrior continued. "I should have fought tooth-and-nail for my life that day because I was not in the wrong. Together we might have defeated the Shogun's men and averted the following tragedy.

"Though I was wrong to be aggressive, pacifism can be just as dangerous. If we do not fight against evil and for what we feel is right, we are a part of that evil. Pacifism is wrong, Shadrack. It is wrong.

"And I was wrong to disown you. Terribly wrong. I have carried the shame of that secret within me for over forty years. It was I who betrayed you, not the other way, as I once thought. But in my own self-righteousness I couldn't see it."

Cassius tried to blink back the tears as he tried to control the lifetime of shame. They rolled down his face, the firelight glinting off them like translucent gems of amber.

Shadrack was oblivious to him.

Pacifism is wrong.

He should have listened to Ghalan—the Magister Templi had tried to warn him. Pacifism is wrong, he repeated, but the phrase held no meaning for him. After believing the opposite for so long, he could barely grasp the meaning of the phrase.

"I hope you can forgive me, Shadrack," Cassius said.

Shadrack barely heard him, lost in his own thoughts. Cassius became even more pained. He suddenly had no further desire to talk.

"Get some sleep, Shadrack," he said. "I'll take the first watch for four hours. I'll wake you then. We have to start early in the morning. We have a long journey ahead of us, and Lena will be anxious to see you when we reach Sophia."

Shadrack lay down like an automaton, his eyes clouded. He lay on his side, staring into the flames of the campfire. A terrible anxiety descended upon him. With the reunion with Lena now imminent, he was terrified to the core. After seeking it for so long, he would now do anything to avoid it.

Yhana dropped Bal's obese body and collapsed beside him, coughing violently. Up ahead lay the Yellow School sanctuary, its light hidden by magick from those who would seek it.

Yhana shivered, gathering her robe tightly about her. Bal's face was deathly white, and she knew he had little time left. The dagger had punctured his left kidney and he had lost a great deal of blood. She could expend no mana on healing him—she had exhausted her magick carrying him through the forest. Besides, she wasn't a healer. Only Philip would be able to treat such a serious wound.

By now the Ascension would be under way. The goddess Maat would be about to choose the next Master of the Yellow School, and Philip would be involved in the sacred ritual.

Damn him, Yhana thought bitterly. *His precious ritual comes second to Bal.*

She heaved the Black Adept's body onto her shoulders. Her magick was almost expended, but the proximity of the sanctuary gave her the final impetus she needed to stagger forward.

Somehow Bal now meant far more to her. She had been besotted with him once for the way he used her, because she respected power and arrogance. But the fact that he had leaped in front of the dagger, saving her life, cast a completely different light on him. The act was something she would never have imagined doing for anyone, and it shocked her that Bal had done it for her. She could barely believe it, but she definitely liked the feeling it gave her. Bal had saved her because he *felt* for her, not because she was useful. She grimaced as she shifted his weight on her shoulder; there was no way she would allow him to die now.

Behind Yhana, Mendaz stumbled after her, now almost upon his quarry. He rubbed his eyes, still suffering from double vision.

Yellow School sanctuary

The main hall of the Temple reverberated with chanting as the senior Yellow Adepts focused on the statue of Maat in the center of the room. The statue, once a lifeless silver, now shimmered with a yellow aura. The eyes, once painted and dead, started to glimmer with frightening intelligence.

Philip stood before the statue, within the circle of forty-two chanting Adepts who knelt around him.

"We summon the goddess Maat into our midst," he intoned, his voice carrying a peculiar authority. "Daughter of the mighty Ra, consort of the wisdom of Thoth, wielder of the force of Balance. Revered patron of our School, appear amongst us and inform us of your Will."

The chanting intensified, each Adept using his visualization to transform the statue into a suitable vehicle for the goddess to manifest. The air glittered with sigils as Philip traced with his lotus wand.

"Goddess MAAT, thou who art the Divine Order in our universe, the Word of All That Is. Weigh our hearts against your feather and find them to be worthy! Manifest here before us, as we will before you after death in the Hall of Double Justice!"

The skin of the goddess radiated a golden color as it gained life. Her chest moved as she started to inhale. She looked at Philip, her black eyes deeper than infinity. The circle of Adepts bowed in respect as the awesome power of her aura rippled over them.

Philip went down on one knee.

"Thou who art Maat to the Egyptians and Themis to the Greeks, the Yellow Council greets thee and thanks you for your presence!"

The goddess' face was beautiful in a cold, clinical way, the expression incredibly tranquil.

"You have called and I have come, as it has been since the beginning of time."

"Goddess, have you chosen a worthy successor to our deceased Master, whose heart we recently bequeathed to you to be weighed?"

Maat held out her right hand. A shimmering pure white feather appeared in it.

"My choice is made. Once this feather is accepted from my hand, the new Master's word is my law. Only the new Master may touch it."

"By your Will," the circle of Adepts agreed.

Maat became immobile, staring at the door to the hall as if expecting something to occur. Philip frowned, suddenly feeling uncharacteristically nervous. He waited, sure the goddess would choose someone from the circle. But Maat stared at the door, expectant.

Suddenly Yhana fell through the door, dropping Bal to the floor. As one, everyone in the room turned to look. Yhana's eyes simmered with hatred when no one moved to help her. She swore under her breath and heaved Bal's body up. She staggered into the circle, falling again in front of Philip.

Her eyes became alarmed as she suddenly noticed the goddess. Maat's expression didn't change. She stared intently at Yhana.

"What are you doing?" Philip hissed, outraged. It was the first uncontrolled emotional response Yhana had ever seen from him.

"He is dying," Yhana said. "You must heal him. Quickly, or he won't survive!"

"What is this? Get out of here, and take this vermin with you!" Philip scalded, barely holding his temper in check.

"Do as she asks." Maat's voice sheared through the hall.

"Goddess?" Philip could hardly believe what he was being asked.

"Heal the student of the Left Hand path."

Philip bowed, confused. He had known the rite would be unusual, that much he had been forewarned, but he hadn't expected such unpredictable behavior, especially from the goddess herself.

He laid his hands on Bal's chest and started to channel energy down from his crown chakra. The air around his fingers sparkled, and Bal's bleeding slowed. Philip grunted, straining to invoke enough energy: Bal was on the verge of death. Slowly, the Black Adept's aura began to brighten.

"I can't continue," Philip grunted. "He is too badly hurt."

"You must!" Yhana said, grabbing his hands and holding them to Bal's chest. Their eyes locked over Bal's body in a contest of wills. The goddess watched impassively as the Black Adept's eyes flickered and opened.

Suddenly Mendaz burst into the room; he gazed around slowly, his eyes still seeing double.

"Stop him!" Yhana yelled in panic.

The Adepts turned to the goddess for direction, confused. Maat stood unmoving, the feather of Ascendance still in her hand.

"Venomous bitch!" Mendaz shouted. He hurled the dagger with all his strength, falling forward on his face. Yhana could only stare in shock: she had no magick left to deflect the blade.

It whistled past her head as if in slow motion, burying itself in Philip's heart. Philip gasped and fell backwards.

Stunned to their senses, two of the Yellow Adepts broke the circle to capture Mendaz, using their magick to restrain him. He put up no fight as he realized he had missed. The Adepts started to drag him away.

"I'll be the death of you yet, bitch!" he shouted.

Yhana stared at Philip. She had hated him for so long, yet she felt a twinge of remorse as he drew his last breaths. She looked up in shock as Maat moved forward and reached out her hand with the feather.

"For me?" Yhana's heart pounded at the thought of the power in the goddess' hand.

She reached out quickly, grabbing for the feather. Her hand passed straight through it. She swore viciously, thinking Maat had tricked her. But the goddess stayed as she was, feather outstretched.

Slowly, Bal reached out his hand. His arm trembled from his weakness. Yhana and the Adepts watched in fascination as his fingers closed around the feather. His hand glowed and the light expanded to embrace his body, then faded. Immediately the body of the goddess stiffened, becoming a statue once again.

Everyone stared in amazement. Bal chuckled feebly as he remembered the Warlock's prophecy.

It seems that you will rule one of the schools of magick after all.

He smiled, lapsing into unconsciousness again. The Yellow Adepts sat dumbfounded. One of them rushed to aid Philip.

Philip fended off the feeble attempts at healing and grabbed the Adept's arm.

"Maat has spoken," he wheezed. "Send word to the other sanctuaries that we have a new Master."

He shuddered and fell limp, saliva dribbling from his mouth. Perplexed by her own sadness, Yhana reached over and closed his lifeless eyes.

Turn your face to the sun and the shadows will fall behind you.

—Maori Proverb

27

Enya
City of Sophia

Lena lovingly stroked the neck of her stallion, admiring its shining coat. Though she didn't know its real name, she had secretly named the horse Raven after a stallion she had owned a long time ago.

The horse gratefully accepted the affection, a rarity in the royal stables even though the beasts were well looked after. Lena had always loved animals dearly and had no trouble in handling them, though she had never possessed Malak's unique empathy.

Lena had had several days in which to cast her mind back and she now clearly remembered her last days spent with Malak. The memories were vivid and joyful, full of vibrant colors. In her memory, both she and Malak seemed to have been mollycoddled; they had also been incredibly naive. Both had been too wrapped up in themselves and in each other to pay attention to the world at large, regardless of how much it needed them, and they had paid a heavy price. She wondered if she could ever feel joy again, whether she could ever feel truly happy.

In the end they had both proved themselves courageous enough, but how wise had they been? She had sacrificed herself to appease Lilith, not simply to save the plane but also to save her husband. Thinking back, her actions almost seemed selfish. She had known that she had to perform the act—if Malak had done it, she could not have lived to mourn him, knowing he existed within the depths of the Qlippoth. Almost certainly, she would have made a pact with Lilith similar to her husband's.

She could never forget the terrible, endless time she had spent within Lilith's domain. It had left an eternal and ineffable mark upon her. Yet Malak's soul was now one with this hideous embodiment of evil. She longed for the return of her husband. Though in retrospect the action did not surprise her, his sacrifice for her had touched her deeper than she could express. But when he returned to her, would she be able to stand his touch, knowing his soul? Every time he touched her it would be Lilith's demonic essence striving to retain her.

Cassius had been gone seven days now. It was easily enough time to ride to the Enchanted Forest and return to Sophia. Lena tickled the ebony stallion behind the ear. Once again she considered whether to ride after Cassius, a thought that had occupied her continuously for the last few days, but she knew she had left it too late. The longer she waited, the more she wondered if she wanted to hasten her meeting with Shadrack—even his name seemed alien to her, and Cassius had no idea what memories he would have of his life of Malak.

Lena looked up as she sensed someone standing in the doorway. She recognized Kira, captain of the palace guard. Kira was always conspicuous with her vivid red hair and boyish looks; she was potentially quite attractive, but her behavior was too masculine for this to be obvious.

"You are dwelling on your husband," Kira said.

Lena shrugged. "It's difficult to think of anything else. We've been separated for so long."

"My father will bring him back."

"You have some trouble getting along with Cassius, don't you?"

Kira sighed. "He is very stuck in his ways. But we have come to a better understanding now that he's explained his past, and his relationship with Shadrack."

"You should have let me go after my husband."

"I may have some problems seeing things as my father does, but I trust him with my life. He won't fail. He'll bring your husband back to you."

The pair fell silent as Lena groomed the horse, then she spoke a few moments later.

"Kira, tell me. What is it that Cassius hides? I've noticed his aura is resistant to magick, and he's not the only one in Sophia. Those guards who restrained me were resistant too."

"Have you not asked him yourself?"

Lena shrugged her shoulders. "Your father and I do not see eye to eye at the moment."

Kira stared for a moment and then nodded. "It is part of Jeshua's plan to combat the Black School. After the Summoning, there were no White Adepts left alive except Jeshua. Instead of rebuilding the White School with Adepts, he decided to do it with soldiers. Over the centuries, he honed an organization of warriors called the Knights Templar."

"What does this have to do with his resistance to magick?"

"Cassius is leader of the Knights. They are like a spiritual brotherhood, with a very definite code of conduct. They take oaths to be admitted and have to survive terrible tests. Everyone on Enya uses their thoughts and emotions as magick to some extent, even those without talent. However, this is forbidden to the Knights. But by keeping their vows they gain a specific power that is much more useful: resistance to all forms of magick."

Lena nodded. "Ah. That makes sense. Jeshua was very wise to form the Knights. They will make a powerful weapon against the Black School."

A guard appeared at the stable door.

"Captain, a runner has just delivered news of the prince's return. He has Shadrack with him."

"Very good," Kira said, dismissing him.

She turned to Lena. "I told you everything would work out. It is time for you to be reunited with your husband."

Lena smiled hesitantly. Kira didn't miss the look of apprehension that appeared in her eyes.

It was midday when Cassius and Shadrack rode through the main gate and into Sophia. A runner was immediately despatched to warn the palace of their impending arrival.

Shadrack was still bruised and aching from his recent ordeals; likewise, Cassius' scarlet cloak was ripped and torn, his armor begrimed. Despite this, his people instantly recognized him as he rode by, Shadrack seated behind him. Shadrack noticed their lukewarm reaction and it amused him—Ieyasu Tanaka had never been the most charismatic man. He had always been a very private individual.

Shadrack was impressed by Sophia. Though it was dwarfed by the colossal city of Prenzlau on Tellus, it was far larger than any Enyan city from the Aeon of Dreams. Even so, Cassius told him that Sophia's walls would barely extend beyond one suburb of Gorom, which was rapidly becoming regarded as the plane's capital city in preference to Miosk.

Sophia's architecture was simple: strong, square buildings of one to two stories with wide, spacious streets and trading squares. The buildings were formed from blocks of local ore, the bricks fused together to produce perfectly smooth surfaces. The ore was a beautiful deep green, fading into dark blue where heavy weathering had taken place. The overall effect was aesthetically stunning.

More breathtaking than the city, and easily discernible as the jewel of Sophia, was the royal palace. The glittering purple citadel was captivating, with its gently twisting faery-tale spires and deep exotic hues. Shadrack noticed the central column, and recognized it as a replica of the Celestial Tower. It left a bitter taste in his mouth, for he knew that his final objective would lie within the true Celestial Tower, once the center of the White School's power. For now the structure was an extension of Lilith's domain, hell on earth. And it was there he would have to ultimately face the Arch-Demon.

Retainers rushed from the palace as Cassius and Shadrack dismounted. Cassius patted the white stallion appreciatively before he was led away. For three days the horse had borne two riders without complaint, and he thoroughly deserved his rest.

Inside the palace Cassius was greeted by Kira.

"Welcome back, father."

"Hello, Kira. How does the city fare?"

Kira smiled. "It barely noticed your absence."

Cassius rolled his eyes irritably. "I might have guessed. Nice to be needed." He turned and motioned toward Shadrack. "This is

Shadrack. Perhaps you could arrange a guest room with a bath. He has an important date ahead of him."

Cassius gave a twisted smile. Shadrack immediately felt embarrassed.

"The Lady Lena is…anxious to be reunited with you, Lord Malak," Kira said.

Cassius realized the ronin's uneasiness.

"No formalities, Kira. He prefers to be known as Shadrack. For now at least. After all, it was his given name."

Kira nodded. "Then please follow me, Shadrack."

Shadrack bathed meticulously for almost an hour as he tried to occupy himself, seeking to avoid the uneasy thoughts that swamped his mind. He found he couldn't abate his nervousness. He had no fear of battle and little of death, except that it would throw him into Lilith's deadly embrace. But he couldn't banish his fear at the thought of being reunited with Lena.

As he dried himself his hands trembled with anticipation. Though it could have been his imagination, a sense of foreboding gripped him. Something was bound to go wrong. Either he would be rejected outright, or he would make a fool of himself. Verily, he possessed Malak's memories and personality within him, but would Lena be expecting her husband, a man who had died a millennium ago? He knew he could not live up to such an expectation.

Neither could he imagine what Lena would be like, though he readily recalled her physical likeness. He had received impressions from her at a very early age, at first in wispy dream fragments. He had first thought of her as his mother, since to this day his conception and true parents remained a mystery. Gradually he had realized his feelings were different—though he yearned for her company, she was not his mother. She was his soul mate. And nothing could take that away, regardless of how long they had been separated. Still, he was extremely uneasy.

He rubbed his face. He had decided to shave off his beard, and it felt strange to be clean shaven.

Now dried, he walked into the palatial bedroom. Oriental trimmed and styled clothes of the finest quality lay on the bed for him, the satin shirt and trousers obviously tailored specially for him. He had not seen their style anywhere else on Enya. He had to admit that he approved of the dark blue garments with silver trim. He had never had the chance to wear such finery when in Nippon —the severe cold and poverty of Kyoto prevented that.

Five minutes after dressing, a knock at the door shook him from his brooding. He sighed.

"Come in."

The door opened and Cassius stepped in. He studied Shadrack carefully, his eyes full of concern.

"It is time, son," he said.

Shadrack looked up and nodded. Since their conversation around the campfire some days ago, the relationship between the two men had been tense. Cassius had tried to talk the situation through with him but Shadrack, though not abrupt, made it clear that he had no wish to talk. It was what Cassius had feared for so many years, but at least it was not outright rejection.

"Are you ready?" Cassius asked.

Shadrack shrugged and stood up. "As I'll ever be, I suppose."

Cassius gave him a reassuring squeeze on the shoulder.

"Come on. I'll take you to her," he said. "Believe me, she's as nervous as you are, but she's very good at hiding such things."

The veteran warrior led Shadrack out of the room and through the ornately decorated corridors of the palace. The ronin's head hung low and he stared at the floor as they walked. In his mind he recalled much time spent with Lena, yet it was never quite he who was with her—it was the ghost of Malak who he both was and was not. Again he wondered whether Lena would be bitterly disappointed. Perhaps they had nothing in common after all.

The two men ascended a beautiful marble staircase that twisted toward the upper heights of one of the towers. Shadrack found himself counting the steps through nerves and he forced himself to focus, but every atom of his being urged him to bolt down the stairs and away from this subtle, pressing danger.

They stopped on the third landing and Cassius led him up to a pair of dark mahogany doors, one slightly ajar.

Shadrack turned to Cassius, and the warrior nodded.

"She's waiting for you," he said. "I'll return to my duties in the council chamber. Come and see me in the morning to let me know how things are."

Shadrack attempted a confident smile, but it died on his lips. He stood for several seconds as Cassius disappeared from sight. He looked longingly in the direction of the staircase. He listened but no sound issued from the door. With a sigh he pushed the door open and tentatively entered.

The room, very much like his own—spacious and expensively decorated—contained a four-poster bed that had been slept in recently, and various bits of clothing scattered around. This slightly comforted Shadrack—for some reason he knew Lena had never been an advocate of tidiness.

The chamber, dimly lit by an array of white candles that gave it a homey feel, smelled of molten wax mixed with the subtle hint of perfume. Outside, darkness had descended some hours ago and the sky was clear. Staring out of the window, outlined by twinkling stars, stood Lena.

Beside her sat Bast. The familiar growled softly with satisfaction as she saw her master and mistress in the same room together after so long. She loped out of the door, leaving them in privacy.

Shadrack walked forward. Lena stiffened as she sensed his presence. She turned, her beautiful evening gown swishing around as she did so.

The sight of Lena took the breath from Shadrack's throat. She was exactly as he remembered her, but even more stunning in the flesh. Her face, perfectly balanced as ever, was framed by her long black hair. The gown, tailored for her, drew Shadrack's eyes down the length of her flawlessly proportioned body. The low-cut black gown gave the barest hint of her heaving breasts and flowed down to accentuate the curves of her hips. The dress reached to the floor, with a slit that climbed up to her right thigh.

"Hello, Malak," she said.

She moved like a feline to stand only a foot away in the center of the room. Their eyes locked and Shadrack was suddenly taken with intense passion. Lena's pupils dilated and he realized that her reaction was the same—she was satisfied with his physical resemblance to Malak, at least.

Lena's eyes fascinated Shadrack—a deep, deep brown, her personality shone from them, stubborn and strong. The irides were embellished with tiny flecks of gold that glittered in the low light. Yet despite the obvious physical passion, there was something else on display—anxiety. Shadrack was unsure whether he was pleased about this or not. It seemed she was nervous too.

"It is…good to see you again, Lena," he said, struggling awkwardly to find words.

Lena moved even closer, so that her body almost brushed up against him.

"It's been a very long time," she said.

Shadrack's breathing became ragged with the intensity of his passion, though they still had not touched. Almost involuntarily, he raised his palm toward her. Lena smiled and slid her palm up to touch his, their fingers interlocking; it was a manner in which they had held hands many times.

Lena's electric touch sent a surge through his system that caused him to shudder. The ecstatic feeling instantly swept away his misgivings, and he knew beyond any doubt that he and this woman were meant to be. He loved her with every fiber of his being. He felt he could drown within her eyes, which sought to devour him with their depth and intensity.

"Malak?" Lena said.

"Yes?" Shadrack gasped. It seemed natural to answer to the name, even though it was not his own.

"Are you going to kiss me, or what?"

Suddenly the tension of the spell was broken. He slid his arms around her and leaned forward, searching for her lips. She responded ardently as he kissed her, his tongue pressing into her mouth. He closed his eyes, his head spinning with the intensity of his feelings. Submerged under such a potent flood of love, his sexual desire paled into insignificance. Though he had cared deeply about Ieyasu and Ghalan, it was the first time he had felt genuine love in his present life. It was exhilarating.

But the unexpected intensity of emotion lowered his guard. It triggered something dormant deep within him. Lena froze in fear as she sensed the condensing essence of evil within her husband. She frantically pushed herself away, her eyes wide with alarm.

Shadrack snarled as he was pushed backward and a dull, red malevolent light appeared in his eyes. For a moment it seemed as if he would attack, lunging to rip out her throat. Then Shadrack regained control and he shouted out in frustration. The red glow faded away and tears of raw emotion spilled down his cheeks.

"God, I'm sorry…" he muttered. "I'm so sorry…."

Lena regained her composure slightly and took a step forward.

"It's all right, Malak," she said gently. "Come here…."

She reached out her hand, but there was still fear in her eyes—she had recognized Lilith's essence. Shaking his head, Shadrack backed off from her. He knew he could not stay, could not see her ever again. Even now he had to fight the beast with every ounce of his strength, otherwise it would break through his psyche and tear her limb from limb. He had to get out of Sophia.

With a cry he turned and bolted out of the door. Lena watched him helplessly, tears flowing from her eyes.

Happiness is an attitude of mind, born of the simple determination to be happy under all outward circumstances. Happiness lies not in things nor in outward attainments. It is the gold of our inner nature, buried beneath the mud of outward sense cravings.

—J. Donald Walters

28

Enya
City of Sophia

Dethen ran his eyes over the formidable walls of Sophia. He had to admit that he was impressed with the city's defensive capabilities. The walls, high and sturdy, with battlements from which missile weapons could be fired, were designed to make scaling and the use of siege equipment almost impossible. There was no moat or ditch, but the city was set onto high ground that made attack difficult. It had a commanding view of the surrounding countryside.

Next to him lay Kalinda and four more Black Adepts.

"I would have preferred Bal for this mission," Dethen said.

Kalinda smiled crookedly. "I told you. Bal is dead, and so is Mendaz. They died fighting each other."

Dethen stared at her. He could read most people, but a thousand years as the Warlock had taught Kalinda much. He couldn't tell whether she lied. He could only accept that Mendaz and Bal had not returned, and that every soldier had backed Kalinda's story up.

The night was clear, the air sharp and fresh. The stars glittered coldly in the heavens and the moon, now a thin waning crescent, cast out its harsh illumination.

"We approach as discussed," Dethen ordered. "I will tolerate no mistakes. I must take Malak alive. Follow my orders exactly."

Kalinda smirked. "I have no idea how you could doubt me."

Dethen scowled and walked toward Sophia, fading into the air as he did so. Kalinda and the Adepts stood up and followed, using their magick to draw a cloak of invisibility about them.

The palace was easily found in the center of the city; it was visible from almost everywhere, the moonlight glittering off its surface. It was simple for the Black Adepts to sneak through the main entrance; even in the late hours of the night, the palace was bustling with activity and the sound of their passage was masked.

Once safely inside, Dethen signaled to drop the veil of invisibility. There were numerous guards patrolling through the corridors but Dethen decided to take the chance—the curtain of stealth they used to conceal themselves was taxing. Anyone unfortunate enough to discover them would be succinctly dealt with.

He sought Malak with his inner vision but he could find no trace of his brother; after journeying across almost the entire plane, it frustrated him. After a few minutes he conceded defeat, and he started to seek Cassius' essence, since he had last seen his brother with the warrior. He also found Cassius difficult to track, but he did receive a vague perception of the warrior. This aroused Dethen's suspicion—for a man of Cassius' strength of character, the signature should have been much stronger. The problem had to be related to the warrior's apparent resistance to magick.

With hand signals he communicated his intentions to the rest of the group. They stalked through the corridors, moving slowly and carefully. Within a minute, the footfalls of a patrolling guard could be distinguished up ahead. Kalinda flicked her wrist and an Adept slipped ahead. There was a quiet, choked cry and then silence.

Dethen smiled grimly. The palace troops were well trained but they were no match for Black Adepts.

In a few minutes they reached the door to Cassius' bedroom. Dethen led the way, quickly moving toward the door. Two guards tried to intercept him. He sliced the first to the floor with *Widowmaker*. The second tried to run him through with a long sword, but he parried the blow and grabbed the guard by the throat. He signaled for the Adepts to storm the room.

"I want him alive," he ordered.

The Adepts burst into Cassius' bedroom. In an instant, two sprang onto the bed to seize him. Cassius was instantly awake; he crashed his elbow into the first assailant and rolled over to grab his katana. The second attacked and Cassius sliced him across the belly, spilling out his intestines.

"Wait!" Kalinda shouted. The men leaped out of the way as she released a powerful blast of astral energy, enough to knock over several men.

The blast deflected around Cassius' body, only nudging him slightly. Kalinda stared in shock.

Cassius' *mae-geri* front kick sent her reeling across the room and the flash of his blade cleaved open another Adept.

"Stop!" Dethen bellowed with such intensity that everyone did as he commanded, including Cassius.

"Give yourself up, or this man will die!" he said.

Cassius hesitated. Dethen held one of the palace guards in a headlock. It would be instantly fatal if he applied pressure.

"Give yourself up and you will both live," Dethen said. "Believe me. I will not break my word."

Cassius held Dethen's gaze; he knew the Black Master was deadly serious in his threat. Cassius slowly lowered his sword. Immediately, Kalinda placed her sword against him, ready to skewer him should he move.

"What is it you want, Dethen?" Cassius asked, his voice bitter.

"Where is my brother?" Dethen demanded.

"I don't know," Cassius said. "He left the palace some time ago, after seeing Lena. He ran off into the wilderness."

The two men still held eye contact. Dethen was suspicious for a moment, but then nodded. Cassius was a man who would not betray his word.

"Lena?" Dethen was surprised. He closed his eyes and searched for her. "Ah, her essence is very strong. She is above us in one of the towers. Thank you for your help."

Dethen released the headlock on his hostage. The man immediately lunged for the door, seeking to raise the alarm. One of the Adepts thrust his sword toward the man, but Dethen grabbed the palace guard and twisted him away from the sword. In an instant he drew *Widowmaker* and sliced the Adept to the ground, his eyes cold and merciless. He would not break his word, nor allow any other to do it for him.

In the distraction, Cassius lunged for his sword. Kalinda stabbed him through the abdomen. He fell to the floor, gasping.

"I knew I would deal with you eventually," she whispered in his ear. It amused her that Cassius had no idea she had been the Warlock.

Dethen's gaze scorched over Kalinda, but then he turned to Cassius.

"Your death was your own doing, Prince Cassius Hawkin," he said. Sadness tinged his voice. "It was foolish and unnecessary."

His gaze lingered on the dying warrior for a moment. He then twisted his hostage into a sleeper hold, grasping him by the neck. In a few seconds the soldier fell to the floor, unconscious. Dethen looked up as the sound of running feet rapidly approached.

"We must move quickly," he said to Kalinda. "Hold these guards off while I seek Lena."

Kalinda smiled, a malefic expression that twisted her lips.

"No problem," she said. She used the bed linen to wipe Cassius' blood from her sword.

Dethen ran out into the corridor and towards the tower.

Jeshua stared mournfully out the tower window. "I really hate this view, you know."

"Something bothers you, Jeshua?" Lena asked.

"I see him lying there, his body broken. At least this will perhaps be the last time I see him. A thousand years the vision has haunted me. Perhaps now I will gain some peace from it. So often fear of a thing is worse than the thing itself."

Lena frowned. She had hoped that Jeshua had called her to give her some useful information on how to find Malak, not to mutter about his phobia of heights. She had scoured everywhere around the city but her husband could not be found. She forced back her tears. It seemed she had cried so much of late, she had no more tears to offer. She hated crying, but the agony of losing her husband after being so close was just too much to bear. She could think of nothing else.

"Strange, Lena. Once I wasn't afraid of death, but it seems I've lived so long. You get used to living, and it terrifies you when death once again looms into your life."

"Jeshua, why are you torturing yourself in this way? I'm sure you'll still be here long after we've all gone," Lena snapped. She cursed herself for being so sharp, but she was too drained to offer any sympathy.

Jeshua shook his head sadly. "No, he comes for me. It is too late now."

"Who com. . . ."

Suddenly Lena fell silent as she sensed something she had not felt for a very long time. She closed her eyes, reaching out with her inner senses. She recoiled, alarmed, and suddenly she knew what Jeshua feared.

Her hand grabbed her ebony bo-staff, her knuckles white from the strength of her grip. "He *is* coming," she said, her voice shaking with the rush of adrenaline. "It is Dethen."

She barely finished the sentence before Dethen's huge physique loomed into chamber. His aura flickered, a sign he had recently defeated the guardians of the tower.

Lena stood up but Jeshua put out his hand to restrain her.

"So, we meet at last, Dethen," Jeshua said.

Dethen's ebony eyes raked over him.

"Do I know you?"

"No. But I know of you. I have been a member of the White Council for more centuries than you have lived on this plane."

"Then you are my enemy," Dethen said. He formed the Sign of Horus, hurling his energy at the White Adept.

The movement was so quick, Jeshua didn't even attempt to deflect it. The force collided with him, blasting him through the arched tower window. He plummeted toward the ground, his heart pounding as death accelerated toward him. Suddenly he smiled in satisfaction as he looked down. For the first time, he didn't see a lifeless, broken body below him. His astral form floated from his body before impact, watching as his own body became the vision he had suffered for so long. He started to ascend the planes, relieved his nightmare had ended.

"You bastard," Lena snarled.

Dethen raised an eyebrow. "Really, Lena. It is not like you to use such language."

"Things change." She moved away from the window to a space where she could defend herself. Her eyes met with his in a contest of wills. Neither Adept flinched.

"You will come with me," Dethen growled.

Lena smiled, a gesture so devoid of warmth that even Dethen paused. She launched a white-hot fireball of astral energy. It impacted with Dethen's chest, almost blasting him through the doorway. He lashed out and grabbed the frame. He grunted with the pain of the flames—his robes blazed and his hair and beard smoldered. Vibrating the Enochian name of water, a spinning cloak of blue suddenly surrounded him, dowsing the flames. With a loud hiss, clouds of steam billowed up toward the ceiling.

Dethen's eyes flamed more than the fire he had dowsed. He hurled a blast of energy at Lena, throwing his tremendous willpower behind the attack. Lena only just had time to make the defensive Sign of Harpocrates before the blast hit. She dissipated most of the force, but it still flung her across the width of the room to crash against the wall. As she rebounded, she performed a forward roll and found her feet in time to dodge Dethen's second blast.

The Black Adept advanced upon her, expecting the fight to be knocked from her. He realized his mistake when a chair rose and hurled itself at him. Dethen's fist connected with it, smashing it into a thousand splinters. He drew *Widowmaker*.

"Resist too strongly and I will be forced to kill you," he said. "Believe me, that is not my intention."

Lena attacked suddenly, using both ends of the staff to strike. Dethen backed off—it was difficult to deflect the blows with a sword without attacking. Swords were useless weapons for taking prisoners—they were designed only to kill. He didn't feel endangered, however, by this woman who was so much smaller than himself. With that thought, he defeated himself. Lena disarmed him with a deft sweep of the staff and then rammed the butt into his groin.

Dethen groaned in pain and shock as he fell to the floor. Lena immediately made a dash for the door. She was amazed when Dethen grabbed her ankle. The dark mage hauled himself up, the groin injury only slowing him slightly. Lena knew she had infuriated him—his black eyes burned ferociously.

He slapped her so hard that she hit the floor before she saw his hand move. She lay for a moment, stunned, before trying to rise, blood trickling from her mouth. A red mark spoiled one side of her face, quickly turning a dark, unwholesome purple.

Dethen grabbed for her hair but his grip found her neck because she was rising. Lena struggled vigorously but Dethen pulled her in toward him, his huge physique dwarfing her feminine frame—making it seem almost childlike. He forced his weight down on her to quell her struggling body. This was a mistake. Lena shifted her own weight slightly and used his to throw him forcefully to the floor.

Taken by surprise but possessing lightning reactions, Dethen performed a break-fall roll as he hit the floor. He rose quickly, reaching for Lena before she could grab her staff. He slammed *haito-uchi,* a ridge hand technique, into the upper vertebrae of her neck. Lena hit the floor hard. Dethen paused a moment to regain his composure, then checked her breathing. He nodded with satisfaction—she was unconscious.

"It was not my wish to harm you," he said, as if she still listened. "But you are a match for three men!"

He retrieved *Widowmaker* and hoisted Lena over his shoulder. As he walked toward the door, he slowly faded from sight.

Kira sprinted toward her father's room, a contingent of palace guards behind her. Ahead she saw a guard outside Cassius' room fall, run through by a huge dai-katana. The female Black Adept pulled her sword from the dying man and turned her head to see Kira rapidly approaching with reinforcements. Kalinda gave an oily smile and slowly faded from sight.

"Try and follow her!" Kira ordered the guards. "I want her alive!"

She ran into Cassius' chamber. The first thing she saw was the unconscious guard. She automatically bent down to check his pulse and realized his condition wasn't serious. Then her eyes found Cassius. He had crawled into a corner and he stared at her with a severely pained expression. She gasped at the vivid red stain on his cerulean dressing gown. He sat doubled over in agony, both hands clutched over the site of the wound. She immediately knew it was critical.

She ran over to him and knelt.

"How grave is the wound?" she asked, her voice calm but her eyes not.

Cassius attempted a smile but could only twitch his lips.

"Trust me to be stabbed by a dai-katana."

Kira knew then that he would not survive—dai-katana were immense swords and Cassius was trying to convey the seriousness of the injury without drama. Palace guards gradually accumulated at the entrance to the chamber, where they stood in disbelief at the sight of their dying monarch.

Kira whirled around and to the nearest. "You! Go and get Jhion, the palace healer. And you lot…" she made an embracing gesture with her hand, "get out!"

As the guards left the room, Cassius shook his head.

"You know, Jhion's art will be useless on me. I am resistant to all magick, both evil and benign. He will be unable to heal me. It will just deflect off my aura."

Kira closed her eyes for a moment, momentarily losing her iron composure.

"You cannot die." She paused as she tried to verbalize her affection for him. Instead she said, "Sophia needs you! You have no heir to replace you!"

She cast her gaze down, embarrassed and frustrated with herself—she had never been able to express her emotions to anyone. Cassius took her hand weakly. As he did so, she realized how quickly he was losing blood.

"Don't worry, Kira. I know how you feel, and I feel the same way for you. We were both too stubborn to admit it. But before I die, I must ask you one thing now."

"You will not die, father! You will recover!"

"Kira, you are not listening to me."

She paused, tears in her eyes. "Speak it, and it shall be done."

Cassius nodded. "You must discover Shadrack's whereabouts and bring him back to Sophia. If I have already departed, then you must inform him of Dethen's deed. He went to seek Lena and I fear he has kidnapped her."

Kira's eyes widened in shock. "We can assault his lair in the west, Lord. I could lead the Knights Templar against him and retrieve her."

Cassius shook his head. "We are not ready to face the Black School yet. The Knights are still in preparation. And this battle is not ours. If Shadrack does not face his karma now, he never will. Lena's fate must be in his hands. It is between him and Dethen. Now you must promise to do this for me."

"Of course. I will leave as soon as you are healed."

Cassius grunted. "No. You must leave now. Jhion will do what he can for me, but you cannot now aid me. You can only help Lena by finding Shadrack."

"Yes, father." Kira felt the urge to break down, but soldier's pride wouldn't allow it.

Cassius hesitantly brushed away one of her tears. "Be strong for me, Kira. You are my heir."

"I will not disappoint you, father."

Cassius nodded. "I know. Go now. You have no time to lose."

She stared at him for a moment and then stood up. She left the room without looking back.

It is no good casting out devils. They belong to us, we must accept them and be at peace with them.

—Doctrine of the Yellow School[7]

29

Enya
The Boundary

Shadrack sat on a boulder, staring nonchalantly at the flickering colors of the Boundary. It was early morning and the blades of grass were coated in dew drops. The bloated purple orb of the Enyan sun hung over the horizon, partially obscured by pink-tinged clouds.

Shadrack was unaware of all this. He watched the Boundary in its perpetual advance. It had been some distance from him last night; now it was only a few feet away and it seemed nothing could halt its advance. It was a curtain of destruction, and once it claimed a piece of land, it could never be returned.

The Boundary was semi-transparent from this distance, but there was little to see beyond it except a shimmering blue gray continuum in which terms such as "up" and "down" were meaningless. Shadrack picked up a rock and hurled it through the barrier. The rock immediately lost cohesion as it penetrated the veil, dissipating into formlessness within seconds.

Shadrack knew it was Yesod of Yetzirah, the astral plane, that lay beyond the Boundary. That dimension had its own forms but they were extremely malleable. The forms of Enya were alien to Yesod. They would only maintain their structure while within the Boundary—otherwise they would simply dissolve into the material of Yesod that had once formed them.

---

7 D. H. Lawrence

Until now, despite several incarnations on Enya, Shadrack had never seen the Boundary. In past Aeons, the Boundary had existed hundreds of miles away from civilization, too many days' journey for simple curiosity. Seeing it for the first time had shattered his perception of Enya. In many ways the plane was designed to duplicate Tellus, with relatively minor differences, such as the color of the sun. Enya was even slightly curved to give the illusion of a planet and a limited horizon, but the carefully designed forms and factors seemed totally illusionary to Shadrack as he sat next to the Boundary.

He hurled another rock through the shimmering curtain. He was sick of boundaries and limitations. As he sat before the invulnerable, untouchable monstrosity, it represented to him all the restrictions on his own life. Was he to be eternally bound by his past? To constantly suffer for a naive mistake, an impulsive action to save his love?

A love that no longer exists, he thought bitterly—the demon within had almost forced him to tear Lena limb from limb.

Hatred and bitterness consumed him. Lena, Ghalan, and Cassius, none of them mattered to him. He had betrayed them all now and he simply didn't care. Their aid and advice had not helped, it had only hindered him; he no longer had any need for them, as they had no need of him. How could they care for a demon who craved to cleave living flesh from bone, to destroy anything that lived?

Even now he felt the beast stir within as if invoked. He felt a malignant glee. He could release this demon, let it loose across Enya. He had the power to annihilate this petty plane.

But no, he did care. He cared far too much and it was agony to him. He had to shut it out because he was impotent to change matters and the pain would destroy him.

The sound of a galloping horse penetrated his shell of isolation. He looked up, annoyed. No one ever journeyed this far out to the Boundary—the rider was obviously looking for him. He wondered how he had been found; they must have been scrying for him at the palace. The last thing he wanted was company. He hoped that it was not Cassius, or even worse, Lena.

The horse skidded to a halt beside his own grazing mount, which looked up for a moment in interest and then returned to the grass. Kira dismounted fluidly and walked over to him. Shadrack stared at her in defiance.

Cassius has put her up to this, he thought bitterly.

"What do you want?" he asked.

"Lord Malak, I would speak with you," she said.

"It seems I have no choice."

Kira's eyes narrowed. "I am here under orders, not of my own free will. Believe me, I would just as soon leave you to rot in this place and let the Boundary claim your body."

"Then leave me in peace!"

Kira took a deep breath to calm herself. "Malak, my father has been mortally wounded. Even now he lies at death's door."

Shadrack couldn't hide the shock in his expression, but he recovered quickly. "You expect me to care?"

Kira regarded him with undisguised contempt.

"Lena has also been taken by your brother, Dethen."

Shadrack cast his gaze down to the ground.

"It is not my problem," he muttered. "I can do nothing. I can't defeat him, and if I surrender then Enya will be destroyed."

He looked up but Kira had already mounted her horse. She made no attempt to hide her anger.

"By the hells, I don't give a damn what you do, Malak! Why Cassius ever had faith in you, I'll never know!"

Shadrack winced slightly at the sting, but Kira had already turned her mount and was galloping back to Sophia.

"And my name's not Malak!" he shouted lamely after her.

Within seconds she had disappeared from sight as if she had never arrived, but the evidence was left within Shadrack's turbulent psyche. The pain, frustration, and anger had built up to such a point that something had to give. Memories of Ieyasu Tanaka bombarded him, memories of the samurai's commitment, intense training, and the gruff affection. Shadrack knew without a doubt that Cassius was the man who had once adopted him as his son. There was a link between them that could not be denied.

There were also memories of Lena, all vivid and emotionally charged, forced upon him by the part of him that was Malak. The memories from all his incarnations began to intermingle, merging incoherently together to form a terrible cacophony. He was torn between his present identity and his previous one—Malak was striving to express himself.

The world about him started to spin and he began to lose contact with reality. His consciousness was dragged further and further into the depths of his own mind. The identity crisis was not new by any means, but this time external events had propagated it and it was far more powerful. The problem demanded to be solved once and for all.

"I don't care!" he snarled as he pushed himself away from the boulder, staggering. "I don't care!"

A variety of emotions flowed through him simultaneously, splitting his psyche into dissociated shards. He struggled wildly to hold onto his identity, to maintain some sense of coherency. He knew that if he failed, he would utterly lose his sanity. Fear and confusion rapidly displaced all other emotions, growing at a frightening pace.

And then he began to feel the first stirring. Like a beast bounding off the walls of a cage, the demon careened off the fragments of his mind, searching for the weakness that would allow it to explode from its prison. Shadrack's body shook violently, mirroring the intense mental battle. He knew he would be unable to restrain the demon—he was barely able to hold his mind together. It continued to fracture, a myriad of personalities with the beast tearing its way through them.

Tears flowed from Shadrack's eyes, further blurring his disorientated view of the world. His consciousness hung at the center of the mental battle, unsure of its own identity as the many options flowed before him. Perhaps he was the demon, a terrifying being of immense evil and power. He desperately tried to repeat his own name to himself, but it started to lose meaning, an empty word from another world that lay a thousand years away.

His body convulsed and his heart spasmed. Pain wracked through his chest. He knew that soon his physical body would die. The conflict had to be resolved. If he failed and the demon gained control, he knew there would be no hope for Enya. He had to stop it, regardless of the consequences to himself.

"This...ends...now!" he shouted through gritted teeth.

He staggered forward toward the Boundary, which he barely saw through his blurred and spinning vision. His head pulsed erratically and he thought it would explode, but he had to keep a grip on his consciousness. The demon rose like a tidal wave, seeking to drown his insignificant will in its terrifying power.

Four more steps, he thought desperately, three, two....

He swerved sideways, staggering as his impaired balance threw him first one way and then the other. He froze for one final moment as the demon almost quenched his will. He screamed at the agony of its touch.

"No!" his voice echoed back from the Boundary.

With a last burst of willpower, his last action before being swamped, he hurled himself through the Boundary and into Yesod.

Shadrack screamed as skin flayed from his body and his blood began to boil. Agony coursed through every cell of his being. He knew he was dying. He could no longer see the Boundary—one step had carried him through, hurling him a million miles from Enya. There was no hope of return. His vision saw nothing but impenetrable blackness.

A fierce chill froze his body, while inside his organs were so hot he thought they would melt. He felt layer after layer of skin being ripped from his body. He darted back and forth in the void, using his thoughts to propel him, but there was nothing to be seen.

Slowly the void crushed him. He cried out as his limbs began to distort, slowly mutating and shortening. Ironically, the demon had fled from him. As Shadrack approached death, the beast had sensed its own demise and bolted.

Shadrack's memories became more coherent as the personality splinters were ripped away like his skin. As death progressed, Shadrack became more lucid with every second. Each memory became clear, dropping into its correct place. He was no longer Shadrack, son of Tanaka—he was the sum of all his incarnations. Yet two identities in particular were very distinct.

I am Shadrack-Malak, he thought, and he knew it to be true. The pain intensified, becoming unbearable, but he remembered every facet of his identities, past and present. He remembered the difficulties he had overcome in his many lives, the courage he had shown in the face of impossible odds. For the first time he remembered his original battle with Dethen, now three incarnations ago. And he had been triumphant. The memory boosted his confidence and strength. He knew his heritage.

I will not die sobbing, he thought. *At least my death will be a brave one.*

He stopped struggling and opened himself, embracing the dimension. Wave upon wave of pain flowed through him. He accepted it, laughing as it coursed through him. His body shook as if it would explode, and still it intensified.

I have no enemy in pain, he realized triumphantly.

And suddenly the pain was gone, and with it his body.

He hovered in a beautiful blue-gray continuum, completely at peace with himself. With surprise, he realized that his body was now a gently glowing sphere of white light. He was elastic, able to stretch himself into any shape or length. Strange beings, also appearing as globes of light, darted past him on all sides.

He realized he had only been in danger of dying because he believed it. His body had simply been losing its form, the plastic astral material melding itself into a sphere. Only his resistance to the process had caused the pain, along with the state of his mind, which had greatly intensified it. A feeling of great joy surged through him—here he was free of all restrictions, and he knew that his destiny was his own to forge.

His mind was like steel, focused and invulnerable. At last he was one identity. Cassius and Ghalan, both of them were his father. And now his memories of Lena were not vague and distant. He was Malak, and she was his wife. Intense feelings of love flowed from him. Suddenly he remembered her predicament.

Dethen. Beware, brother. Once again, my power will destroy you.

His astral form could travel fast distances in a moment. As he focused his mind upon Enya, he felt the sensation of great speed. And then he was there. The Boundary flickered before him, oddly colorless on this side.

He passed through it easily. While doing so, he visualized the spot from which he had left the plane. He materialized exactly at that site. He concentrated fiercely and his body flowed into its natural shape, once again assuming corporeal form.

Shadrack galloped toward Sophia's gates. The guards recognized him and allowed him to careen through, almost knocking over an unfortunate peddler. He waved an apology as he sprinted on toward the palace.

Even at high speed he handled the horse well. He dodged in and out of side streets as he picked the shortest route to the palace. He remembered the training he received from Gorun Tzan, once samurai of Kyoto village. He had been taught how to gallop through the forest at full speed, and the skill now became useful for his breakneck urban excursion.

He vaulted from the mount as it skidded to a halt in front of the palace's main entrance.

"Lord Malak! Can you…" a guard shouted, but he was already tearing through the palace toward Cassius' bedroom.

At every corner a guard moved to intercept him, then respectfully moved back as he was recognized. He raced past them all and reached the entrance to Cassius' bed chamber in under two minutes, then stopped himself to regain his composure. His pulse quickly dropped to normal.

He nodded to the two guards outside the room—they looked very alarmed for a moment and then saluted smartly. It caused him to pause for a moment in consideration—had he physically changed since his ordeal in Yesod? He thought it possible, since he had had to reform his body. But it was impossible to be sure because he had no way of knowing without asking.

He entered the bedroom to find Kira seated on the bed next to Cassius' supine body. For a moment he feared the worst, but he realized that the warrior was merely sleeping. He was not too late.

Kira rose as she heard him enter.

"Shadrack?" There was a hint of disbelief in her tone and again he received the perception that something was wrong.

"Yes, but I prefer the name Malak. I have had that one for longer."

She shook her head, confused. "I will leave you two alone. Jhion says he has little time to live. He has lost a great deal of blood and his strength is waning."

"Thank you, Kira."

She raised an eyebrow as she heard his voice. It was deeper, firmer, more commanding. She gave a slight bow and left the room, closing the door behind her.

Malak walked over to the bed and sat on the edge. Cassius stirred and opened his eyes lethargically. He frowned.

"What has happened to you, my son?" There was concern in his voice.

"I am my true self, father. My personalities have at last merged. Is there something wrong?"

"The mirror. Look in the mirror. You must see for yourself."

Malak scowled and put his hand up to his face, expecting to feel a disfigured mess. But it felt completely normal, though perhaps slightly different.

Cassius nodded to him. "Go on. Look in the mirror."

He stood up and walked over to the wall mirror, tension building within him. He was suddenly fearful of what he would see. Would it be Lilith's face staring back at him? Or some abomination from the Qlippoth? He peered into the mirror. What he saw was infinity. His eyes, recently bleached and colorless, were now like hemispherical mirrors. They perfectly reflected their environment, preventing anyone from reading the slightest thing about him. They were hard and impenetrable, as his personality had now become. Looking into the mirror, he saw another mirror in the reflection of his eyes, and within that mirror he could again see himself; the effect had no end.

He walked back over to the bed. "My eyes are silver," he said.

Cassius nodded. "What happened to you? You are Malak again?"

"Yes."

"Then I should no longer call you Shadrack?" There was remorse in the old warrior's tone.

Malak smiled. "I will always be Shadrack to you, father. But I am all identities now, and Malak is a name that I have borne much longer than Shadrack. On Enya, it is the name I should be known by."

Cassius relaxed at this explanation. "It is good you are whole again."

"I am not yet whole. My emptiness is deeper and more painful than before, because I now feel the absence of my soul more sharply than before. I am simply closer to my true self. Two things drive me now. First to be reunited with Lena, and second to defeat Lilith. I *will* regain my soul."

Cassius grasped him by the arm. "Lena, she...."

"I know. I'll ride after Dethen soon. He won't have reached his lair yet, and I might yet catch him in time. After all, he'll be expecting me. But what has happened to you? I didn't think I'd live to see you wounded like this."

"It is a mortal wound, Shadrack. I'm afraid I will be forced to leave you for a second time."

Malak stared at him for a moment, his eyes completely unreadable. "It was not the right time to die when you took your life as Ieyasu Tanaka," he said.

"It was wrong," Cassius agreed.

"And it is wrong now, father. You said that you betrayed me the first time. Do not do it again."

Cassius gaped at him in disbelief. "Shadrack, you do not understand. The wound is mortal. Nothing can be done for me. Magick will not work on my aura. I have a few days at most, perhaps as little as a few hours...."

"This is not Tellus, father. You may not be a magician, and magick may even be taboo for you, but on Enya we warp our own reality. This is how Jeshua lived for a thousand years—he would not submit to death. If you desire to live and your will is strong enough, you will find a way."

"No, Shadrack, I...."

"I must leave now, Cassius. Do not allow this to be a final parting. It will take me over a week to return from Dethen's lair. I dearly hope to see you then."

He bowed and walked toward the door, some of the luster fading from his silver eyes.

Things of a day! What are we, and what are we not? A dream about a shadow is man; yet, when some God-given splendour falls, a glory of light comes over him and his life is sweet.

—Pindar

Sell your cleverness and buy bewilderment.

—Jalal-Uddin Rumi

Anya
Black School
subterranean lair

Dethen entered the Warlock's throne room and dismissed the pair of guards with a casual gesture of his hand. They bowed deeply and departed; since his ascension to power, there had been no challenges against Dethen's authority. His defeat of the Warlock had ensured that.

Heavily chained against the far wall was Lena, her white robes torn and dirty. Her face was bruised and cut, but her eyes were focused and dangerous. A flickering etheral shield surrounded her. Constructed jointly by Dethen and Kalinda, the shield was vampiric—it continually drained Lena's vitality. In this way she was prevented from using her magical abilities.

The chamber reverberated frequently as blasts of lightning detonated above ground—the storm was slowly intensifying and the chamber vibrated more strongly with each boom of thunder. The noise made Dethen uneasy—there were few things that made him anxious, but lightning was one of them.

He strode up to his prisoner. "You are being treated well, I trust?"

Lena stared at him with hatred and contempt.

"Cut your head off, Dethen. The world will be a better place."

Dethen smiled thinly but there was no humor in the gesture. Lena's presence was another thing that made him nervous. Her resemblance to Anya was painful. He craved some form of recognition from her, and that, he knew, was incredibly dangerous for him.

It could be his undoing, yet he still felt the need to reason with her, especially considering the act he was about to undertake.

"I'm not quite as evil as you think, Lena," he said. "I have no more wish for people to suffer than you, only I do something about it. Destroy the world, and you destroy the suffering."

He knew immediately from her expression that he had made a mistake. She glowered at him. "Oh, how very noble! And what gives you the right to end everyone else's lives? If you're not man enough to live, at least give others the chance. Just what level of decadence will you sink to in order to achieve your goal?"

Dethen's black eyes simmered with anger. It frustrated him that her words had an effect on him. Had it been anyone else, he would have paid no attention.

"There are always sacrifices. Nothing is ever gained without sacrifice."

"Sacrifices?" Lena's voice was incredulous. "Do you remember Tara? The girl from Oaklan village whom you took to the Rose Circle? Was it your sacrifice or hers when you offered her life to appease Lilith? You rob others of their lives, but what do you offer of your own in sacrifice?"

"I offer my very existence! For three incarnations I have worked toward the Purpose! I am the only one with the courage to oppose the lie that we live, this petty game of the so-called gods. I will relieve the people of their suffering, on all planes of existence!"

Lena smirked. "And that is your motivation? Truly, Dethen. You almost believe yourself." Her voice was suddenly quiet and insidious.

"Meaning?" Dethen's tone was loaded with menace as he edged closer to her helpless form.

"You use such noble notions to describe your so-called Purpose. But what truly motivates you? Revenge, perhaps?"

"What do you mean, wench?" he repeated, his self-control beginning to slip.

"Malak told me of your past, Dethen. There was a woman called Anya whom you killed when possessed by the Arch-Demon Chronzon. Since then your only desire has been to bring the demon to his knees."

Dethen forced himself to be calm as he realized how he was being manipulated; she knew the effect she had upon him. He grimaced and shook his head; there was great sadness in his eyes. "Do you know why I've come here?"

He started to draw *Widowmaker*. He was surprised by the look of fear in Lena's eyes—she obviously had a loathing for swords. He advanced upon her. Another bolt of thunder shook the chamber.

"I'm sorry, but I must end your life now, regardless of Malak's intentions. You remind me too much of things that should remain buried. And you are too powerful a mage for me to have mercy. No threat I could make would stop you from joining my enemies."

"You're damned right," she snarled.

Her eyes moved up from the sword to hold his gaze. He was shocked by the intense hatred in her stare.

"So," she said, her voice bitter, "we find ourselves in the same position again."

Dethen paused; another blast of lightning detonated overhead. "Meaning?" He was sure she played for time and he wanted to finish the distasteful act as quickly as possible.

She laughed, but the sound choked in her throat. He saw the enmity she bore for him burning her up, a hatred as powerful as his own for Chronzon.

"Do you remember, Dethen? It was a night very like this one," she motioned with her head to indicate the thunder.

Dethen's eyes narrowed and his pulse quickened. "No. No, you cannot be."

"Cannot be what? Your beloved Anya? No, I shall never be that again, Dethen. Or should I call you Michael?"

"No. No." Dethen backed off, shaking his head. "That is not possible."

"Impossible?" she snarled. "Your blade pierced me through the womb and then you twisted the blade. For that I will curse your name for eternity. I will not rest until your very soul is destroyed!"

Widowmaker fell to the floor with a dull ring. Dethen's eyes were wide with panic and incredulity.

"No, I didn't mean to. Don't make me suffer any more...." He moved forward to grab her hand. "You must forgive me...."

She stared into his black eyes, a haven for evil where no light could ever penetrate. It was a gaze that extinguished all hope, all righteousness that existed in the world. She snatched her hand back.

"Crawl away and die, Dethen. Because if you don't die by your own hand, you'll die by mine! A thousand times over!"

Tears rolled down Dethen's face, but he had been pushed too far. He picked up *Widowmaker.* When he spoke there was terrible bitterness in his tone.

"Then if I am to suffer eternally with no hope of forgiveness, I will commit the crime twice."

Lena struggled wildly against her shackles. Her gaze followed *Widowmaker* as if hypnotized and her abdomen tensed involuntarily. She started to shake in fear. It was not death that terrified her, only the method. Like Dethen, she could not face living the nightmare again.

Suddenly another blast of thunder shook the room, but this one emanated from within the chamber. Dethen turned in shock to see Malak standing in the door frame, the heavy oaken door shattered in splinters. Two Black Guards lay dead at his feet.

"You!" His voice was disbelieving—he had thought his brother too weak to achieve such a feat.

"Malak!" Lena cried in relief, once again struggling to break free of her chains. She hadn't dared to hope her husband would attempt to rescue her after their parting.

Malak walked into the chamber and Dethen immediately noticed the difference in his adversary. Malak's eyes, once almost colorless, were now like quicksilver; they reflected all light that fell upon them. Dethen saw his own cruel face within them. As the two men met in the middle of the chamber, they seemed complete opposites. Dethen's eyes were pools of infinite darkness, swallowing all light that touched them; Malak's were hemispherical mirrors through which nothing could penetrate.

Dethen raised *Widowmaker.* Malak was unarmed; he simply stood there, holding his twin brother's gaze.

"You need me alive, Dethen," he said. "I suggest you sheath your weapon."

His voice was level and completely unemotional. Dethen's eyes narrowed—there was something wrong here. He had an intense feeling of déjà vu and it concerned him. But he knew Malak was correct—he would not take his brother prisoner by running him through with *Widowmaker.*

"It ends here," Malak said, his tone final.

Dethen threw his head back to laugh. "I see. I see. You are no longer Shadrack, or even the Malak of your last incarnation. You are once again the Malak of old, the great warrior who once defeated me! How amusing! You are right. It will end here."

Malak smiled. "I have grown even beyond that, Dethen. For now I have the training of Ieyasu Tanaka to augment my strength. Shadrack's suffering has taught me."

"Do you think you are the only one who has grown and suffered?" Dethen's voice was goading. "When you defeated me last, I was a pale shadow of my present power. Now no man can stand against me. Cassius may have defeated me with sword play, but my will is indomitable. I am the only challenger ever to battle the mighty Chronzon and survive! No mortal can achieve this. Already I have grown beyond the shackles of a mere mortal. You cannot defeat me, Malak!"

Malak remained silent for a few moments. Tension started to build between the pair.

Then he smiled and said: "Perhaps no man can defeat you, Dethen, but I am no normal man. I possess an advantage that you are perhaps unaware of."

Dethen's face was stoic. "Then I suggest you use it now, for you will not receive a second chance."

He grabbed Malak by the throat. "Call it a test of strength."

Malak knew he was not in serious danger—Dethen was simply goading him. He grabbed the black magician's wrists and shifted his own body weight, using it as leverage, and flipped Dethen head over heels, but he landed easily on his feet.

"Strength is very overrated," Malak said. "I prefer a more subtle approach, personally."

Dethen turned slowly to face his opponent. "Now the true battle begins," he said, advancing.

"Be careful, Malak!" Lena screamed from her prison, still struggling frantically.

Dethen sprang forward with a flying kick aimed at his opponent's sternum. Malak suddenly snarled and his eyes changed in a split second. The reflective quality disappeared and was instantly replaced with a deep red gaze, dangerous and powerful. Yet this time Malak's intelligence was controlling the power.

Moving like the demon had in its killing sprees, Malak slipped sideways with incredible speed, timing his *tai-sabaki* perfectly. Dethen's kick missed by a substantial distance and Malak grabbed him in mid-air, his body exhibiting incredible strength. Dethen was sent crashing head-first into the stone floor.

He lay there for a moment before starting to rise. Intense pain throbbed in his head, though he was unaware of the multiple skull fractures.

Dethen released a blast of purple and black lightning but it deflected harmlessly off Malak and back into himself. He gasped and sank to the floor again, his chest badly burned and his robe smoking. He had put enough energy behind the blast to kill several men and its shock on his nervous system was incredible—he could hardly breathe. He knew he was close to death.

Malak realized also, and he walked over to where Lena was being held, keeping a watchful eye on his brother. The red color faded from his eyes and they reverted back to their silver state. He easily negated the magical shield around Lena and melted her shackles. She fell into his arms.

"No! My Anya!" Dethen gasped, consumed with jealousy.

The couple started to walk toward him.

"Stay down, Dethen," Malak warned him, his voice threatening.

The black magician, his breathing irregular, managed to push himself to his knees. Malak saw he intended to attack and he kicked Dethen with *mawashi-geri*, the roundhouse kick. The technique connected forcefully, shattering Dethen's right cheekbone. Dethen skidded across the room, his face bloody and half-collapsed, but he immediately turned and started to crawl back. He barely looked human, his heart still beating erratically

"For God's sake, Dethen. Give up!" Malak snarled; he had no wish to torture his brother further. His feelings of anger had gone now that Lena had been returned to him. Much more than Lena, he was able to feel a glimmer of compassion for Dethen.

Dethen hardly seemed aware of his brother now; he was crawling toward Lena.

"Anya! Anya!" he sobbed. "You must forgive me! I loved you more than my life!"

Lena scowled and her first impulse was to vent her hatred, but she resisted the urge to kick him in the smashed cheek. She saw his condition and regardless of her enmity for him, she could not bring herself to strike him. Instead, she glared venomously at him.

"You're pathetic, Dethen. You can forget any hope of forgiveness. I will always hate you with every fiber of my being!"

She huddled closer to Malak and they walked toward the door. Malak used his magick to cloak them and they faded from sight.

Dethen lay on the floor for some time, his face blank and his will broken. His defeat was nothing, but being spurned by Lena had destroyed him.

Gods, all this time and I never actually suspected!

The resemblance had been obvious, but he had never believed in the possibility for a moment. He felt totally hollow—even his hatred had evaporated. He was nothing but a shell.

Malak, you have taken everything from me.

His magick had been slowly returning and he had begun to heal some of his injuries. He stood up and stared at the ceiling, shaking his head.

Then he screamed, a vociferous wail that echoed through the entire lair. He raised his hands and jagged streaks of lightning lanced into the chamber's ceiling. He made no move to protect himself as a hundred tons of rock collapsed upon him.

Man enter into thyself. For this
Philosopher's Stone
Is not to be found in foreign lands.

—Angelus Silesius

37

Enya
The Enchanted Forest

Malak and Lena rode through the storm for several hours on Cassius' mount. Lena clung to Malak tightly, her head resting between his shoulder blades. They didn't try to talk—the wind and stinging rain made it impossible. Besides, neither felt inclined to begin a conversation.

Lena was exhausted from her confrontation with Dethen, which had roused memories she had tried to bury long ago. Malak was sullen and he brooded as he tried to keep his eyes open against the relentless onslaught of rain that drenched both of them. They took a modicum of comfort from each other's company, however.

They reached the outskirts of the Enchanted Forest about three hours before dawn. This far east there had been no rain, but the temperature was not as mild. It was another indication of the rapidly approaching winter.

It took Malak only a few minutes to find a suitable clearing. They dismounted and he tethered the horse, then started setting up a camp fire. He hoped they were far enough from the Black School lair to avoid pursuit.

Lena shivered as she stood watching her husband, the cold biting into her injured face, still cut and bruised from her battle with Dethen.

"Malak?" she asked quietly.

He didn't answer. She started to shiver more violently. She knew she was mentally and physically exhausted and her body was soaked from the storm.

"Malak?"

Again, he didn't seem to notice her. The campfire started to burn now as sparks leaped from his fingers. Lena wondered what was wrong with him. His silver eyes unnerved her greatly, isolating him from everything, including her.

"Is it me, Malak? Have I done something wrong?"

He turned as if hearing her for the first time. She suddenly realized just how preoccupied he was.

"Huh? No. No, of course not," he said. He noticed her shivering. "You're cold. Come over here."

He spread some blankets over the forest floor next to the fire.

"You should take that robe off," he said. "It's soaked through, and you look pale."

She hesitated, as if the request had come from a stranger, and then nodded. She pulled the ragged apparel over her head, leaving her only in undergarments, and lay down as he indicated. His eyes lingered on her body for a brief moment before he looked away, embarrassed. He covered her with two heavy blankets and lay down next to her. He sighed dejectedly.

Lena rolled onto her side to face him. "It's Dethen, isn't it?"

A sad smile came to Malak's lips. "After all this time, you still know me well."

She had noticed him pause when they left the Black School lair—they had both heard the massive cave-in that killed Dethen.

"You grieve his death?" she asked. "You know, he would have killed both of us in there if you hadn't…"

The thought of Malak's semi-possession hung in the air between them.

"Maybe. But Dethen couldn't help what he was. I realize that now. And he truly thought he was right, that the Purpose he revered would deliver us from evil."

"But his methods!"

"I know. But Dethen has always been incredibly intense. And with his past, the episode with Anya…."

Lena lay back and was silent for a moment.

"I'm sorry that I never told you."

Malak lay on his back, staring at the stars. They glittered coldly, totally indifferent to the hardships of mere mortals. After a while he spoke again.

"I knew there was some hidden reason behind your hatred of Dethen. It was just too strong and long lasting. You would often hold a grudge against someone, but nothing ever drove you to hatred. Ah. And *Retaliator*. You always disliked her because of your death as Anya at Dethen's hands. You loathed all swords."

"Michael," Lena whispered. "His name was Michael."

"What was he like?"

Almost like old friends to Malak, the gray squirrels gathered around the fire to listen to the discussion. Their black eyes glittered, partially from the firelight and partially through mischief.

Lena reached for Malak's hand. He didn't seem to notice her touch and she withdrew.

"He was a fine man," she said. "Almost the opposite of what he finally became. He was extremely spiritual, and he loved God with a passion. In some ways, he was very much like you. But his dedication to God was absolute."

"He must have felt deeply betrayed the night he battled Chronzon in the Abyss," Malak said.

Lena sighed uneasily. "Yes, I suppose so." She rolled to face him again. "Do you blame me for not forgiving him?"

She could see the fire and clearing behind her reflected in Malak's eerie eyes. The effect was unnerving and she felt uncomfortable.

"Oh, I don't blame you, Lena," he said. "No more than I blame Dethen for not being able to forgive himself, or to let go of his hatred for Chronzon. But I would ask that you try and let go of your hatred now." He rolled over to face her. "This cannot continue. It must end somewhere."

For the first time he met her gaze. She watched in fascination and delight as the mirror-like effect faded, to be replaced with incredibly deep blue eyes.

"Your eyes! They're changing!" she gasped.

He raised an eyebrow in surprise—it had not been a conscious decision.

He smiled. "It seems I can seclude myself from everyone except you."

Lena smiled, and for the first time it reached her eyes. "I'm glad."

The simple change in his eyes alleviated a great deal of her anxiety. It confirmed to her that this was the man she had once loved, and that they were still linked. Through his eyes it seemed she saw through to his very soul. This both elated her and saddened her, for she saw the terrible emptiness where his soul had once resided. And somewhere within that darkness, she knew, was his link to Lilith.

Malak raised his hand to brush the bruised side of her face with his fingers. Though the touch was uncomfortable, she didn't try to pull away.

"Dethen did this?" he asked.

She nodded. "We had a disagreement. I gave him a good run, though. I'll never forget the look on his face when I caught him in the groin with my staff."

"Stay still," Malak said.

He closed his eyes and channeled energy down from his crown chakra and through his heart chakra. The energy emerged from his fingers and the air around them glittered with white sparks. Lena's facial injuries started to fade, gradually disappearing altogether. He then started to channel energy directly into her heart chakra, progressively vitalizing her aura.

"Malak, don't...."

"Shhh. It's okay," he said. "Strength is one thing I have enough of now."

When he finished, her face was completely unblemished and the fatigue had been washed from her limbs. He seemed unaffected by the loss of energy.

She smiled and ran her fingers through his hair. "Thank you."

Their eyes locked. He took her hand from his hair and kissed it.

"I..." he said, before changing his mind. "We should get some sleep."

She moved so that her body was pressed up against his and her face was inches from his own.

"I'm not tired...."

"I was hoping you'd...." The rest of the sentence was lost as their lips merged.

Suddenly there was only desire. After what seemed an eternal separation, their passion made up for lost time. As they kissed long and hard, Lena started pulling off his clothes, her movements urgent. He broke off the embrace to help her, his breath rasping.

He slid underneath the blankets to join her and they kissed again, their embrace intense and passionate. He slipped off her undergarments and she moaned softly as he caressed her bare breasts. She trembled as he ran a cold hand down her stomach towards her labia. He then paused and drew back slightly to gaze into her eyes. She smiled and nodded her acquiescence.

Lena was, of course, a virgin, but she was aroused enough not to feel any pain at penetration. She tensed and drew in her breath sharply, but she relaxed as Malak paused and kissed her on the forehead. She then held him tightly as his gentle motions pleasured her body.

The squirrels sat and watched, wide-eyed in fascination, whispering to each other, as though they wondered what the couple were up to.

Though it was also Malak's first experience, it seemed to him the opposite. It was as if the lovers had never been parted—he knew exactly how to move and where to touch to cause her to arch in pleasure. When the final release came, they shuddered together and lay in a satiated embrace.

A few minutes later they made love again, this time vigorously and wantonly. They fell asleep then, but were reunited again once before dawn, this time their movements tender and loving. As the waning moon gradually sank over the western horizon, Lena's soft moans drifted through the forest on a gentle breeze.

The next day they lay snuggled together for most of the morning. Neither had had much sleep in the night. Lena lay with her head on Malak's chest, her arm wrapped around him. He knew they couldn't lie together all day, however, much as they wanted to. There were concerns on his mind that demanded attention.

"What is it?" Lena asked him, her eyes still closed.

To Malak's surprise, he had discovered that Lena could sense his innermost feelings with amazing accuracy. Her intuition seemed totally unaffected by their long separation.

He sighed. "It's Cassius, Lena. He was wounded by Dethen's soldiers when you were kidnapped."

Her eyes snapped open and she stared at him tiredly. "I had no idea. Is he seriously hurt?"

He could hear the concern in her voice and it gave him some comfort.

"The wound was mortal. When I left, he was expected to die within a couple of days."

"Then he could be...."

Malak nodded and she squeezed him reassuringly. His unearthly silver eyes stared blankly at the midday sky. In them she could see the bright pink color mirrored.

He was quiet for a moment, before saying: "You know, there is something else that bothers me. Before I returned to Enya, Ghalan told me...."

"You met Ghalan?!" Lena interrupted.

He suddenly realized how much about each other they didn't know. After one night, it had seemed almost as though they had never been parted. Lena would find amazing parts of his life that he merely took for granted.

"Yes, I knew Ghalan," he said. "But it's not straightforward. It's difficult to explain. I'll fill the gaps in for you later."

She nodded. "So, what did he tell you?"

Malak sighed. "He said that if I was on Enya at Dark Moon, then Lilith would smash through my mind and become fully manifest."

Lena's expression became serious. "I thought you had her under control now."

"No. That's just the splinter that resides within me. At Dark Moon, her entire force will try to smash through."

"Because at Dark Moon her power is greatly magnified," Lena said, realizing that Ghalan had been right. "But it's Dark Moon tonight. If she smashes through, the entire plane will be destroyed. Dethen's Purpose will be fulfilled even after his death."

Malak nodded. "As far as I can see, there is nothing I can do."

"We never get simple problems, do we?"

"No."

"I mean, many lovers get separated for a few months at the most, and by a few hundred miles if unlucky," Lena said. "We had to be thrown a thousand years and several dimensions apart! And now this!"

Malak laughed and pulled her close; being together seemed to make the problem somehow less serious, though it was a dangerous illusion. There was silence for a few moments before Lena spoke again.

"Is there no way to stop it?"

"I don't think so. Ghalan said that I had to defeat Lilith in the Celestial Tower. It was the only way it could be done. If she tries to break through, nothing on Enya will contain her force."

"Nothing?" Lena frowned. "There must be something?"

They stared at each for a few seconds before making the cognition simultaneously.

"The Rose Circle!"

The couple spent three days within the Rose Circle, waiting until the new moon formed. They spent the time becoming reacquainted with each other, both mentally and physically. By the end of the third day, they once again knew each other as well as they knew themselves.

Lilith didn't show herself in any form during this time. If she attempted to break through, Malak knew it would rip him apart due to the extent of her power. There was no question of subtlety. He felt her stirring deep within him, far below his conscious mind. But nothing further occurred. He knew she was waiting for him to step beyond the protective haven—she knew exactly where he was.

The Dark Moon passed relatively uneventfully. Though an acrid red mist appeared at its peak, the substance did not enter the Rose Circle. Likewise, neither did the wolf-like denizens of the forest who hunted at night. Squint occasionally appeared during the three days, and he would beg Lena to sing for him.

It took Malak and Lena four days to make the journey between the Enchanted Forest and Sophia. In all this time there was only one thought on Malak's mind, and that was the condition of Cassius.

Man's desires are limited by his perceptions; none can desire what he has not perceived.

—William Black

32

Enya
City of Sophia

Malak and Lena dismounted thankfully as they reached the Sophian palace. It was immediately apparent that something was wrong; there was a morbid atmosphere that seemed to affect everyone.

Malak frowned as no one appeared to meet them. The thought of losing his father twice seemed too much to bear.

Lena laid a hand on his shoulder. "It doesn't mean the worst," she said.

Malak nodded somberly, but his urgent stride betrayed his deep anxiety. The couple quickly made their way toward Cassius' bedroom.

Outside the bedroom two soldiers stood guard. They stood to attention as Malak and Lena approached. Malak didn't speak a word to the guards. He had to see Cassius for himself, whether living or dead.

Malak sensed his father's aura even before his eyes recognized the old warrior. Cassius was still bedridden, but fit enough to be sitting up. He set down the book he was reading, still self-controlled despite the immense joy in his eyes.

"Malak! I've been waiting for you both."

Malak strode forward and wordlessly embraced his father. Lena watched, her eyes sparkling with delight; she knew how much Cassius meant to her husband.

"I feared you were dead," Malak said, finally releasing his grip on the warrior.

"I couldn't leave you a second time, Malak. There will be no premature separations in this life." He looked over at Lena. "For any of us."

Lena put her arm around her husband. Cassius looked at her inquiringly.

"So, am I forgiven by you also?" he asked.

"Whatever pain you caused Malak before has been cleared today," Lena said. She leaned forward and kissed Cassius on the cheek. "I never knew my father. From today you'll be like a father to me too."

Cassius smiled, and for the first time the gesture seemed completely natural to him.

That night Malak and Lena made love twice, but Malak was distant afterwards. It was poignant to Lena. Though he was responsive to her actions and words, his mind was focused elsewhere.

"What is it, Malak?" she asked after a while, her voice tinged with annoyance.

He sighed. "It's her."

Lena frowned. "Lilith?"

"She's here."

A shudder passed down Lena's spine. "She can't be. I'd feel her. Besides, it's approaching Full Moon and her power will be weak."

Malak grunted. "She is here. And she's gloating."

Lena's eyes narrowed and she scanned the lavish moonlit chamber. Everything seemed to be in place, yet could she also feel a fragment of an unwholesome force? As ever, the air shimmered where astral entities passed, but there seemed to be something else present, something more sinister than the harmless astral beings.

Malak lay on his back, staring nonchalantly at the ceiling. Since his transformation he had lost, or overcome, the ability to feel fear. He now only desired peace and his nonchalance stemmed from the impossibility of obtaining it. To defeat Lilith, he knew he would be pitting his mortal will against that of an eternal being, a dark goddess of immeasurable power. He saw little chance of success.

Lena slipped out of the bed covers and into her dressing gown. She was now convinced that Malak was right. Something distinctly menacing lingered by the far wall. Nothing could be seen; it was more an ambience that she couldn't put her finger on.

She walked tentatively over to the wall, looking for the source of her uneasiness. There was only one possibility: the mirror. As she looked into it, Malak moved up behind her.

She half expected to see a terrible wraith or banshee, but there was nothing except her own reflection, tinted silver by the waxing moon. As Malak's reflection loomed up behind her, she gasped in shock. Instead of his face, the reflection was of a woman, one side of her face incredibly beautiful, the other corpse-like and maggot infested. The eyes were deep purple, the gaze incredibly powerful and forbidding, their malevolence terrifying. Lena forced herself to stay still, fighting the urge to spin away from her husband. She knew the image in the mirror was false; due to the strength of the moon it was the only way Lilith could appear to them. Intense fear gripped Lena as images of her time in the Qlippoth flowed through her mind.

"Hello, my plaything," Lilith said, her voice both deeply melodious and hoarse as she smiled, an action simultaneously alluring and repugnant.

"What do you want?" Lena asked, her throat suddenly dry. She could only stare in terror at the image before her.

Lilith giggled, a sound contrasting her sinister eyes.

"Freedom, of course. I want Enya. And a return of my favorite play toys."

Lena shivered in horror but she took comfort from the fact that the voice came directly from the mirror. Malak stood behind her, his arm slipped around her waist for reassurance. His alien, mirror-like eyes gazed at Lilith's image with irreverence.

"I am coming for you, Demon," he said, his voice level. "I will reach the Celestial Tower by Dark Moon."

Lilith smiled callously. "You poor child. You will do exactly as I wish you to. Try to reach the Tower, and you will perish in the Wyrmspine Mountains. Your soul will then reside in my domain forever. Do nothing, and I will smash through your mind at Dark

Moon. Once again, your soul will eternally abide in the Qlippoth. There is no escape."

"And if I do reach the Tower to challenge you?"

The Arch-Demon giggled. "Well, that will be interesting. Think of the tortures I can bestow upon you. Remember, the Tower is now my domain. You will be challenging my full might, which no mortal can defeat. There is only one power greater than mine, and that is the Lord Chronzon. You see, Malak, regardless of your decision, you will be trapped in my realm. There is no hope for your soul."

Malak glared at her. Their inhuman eyes clashed in a contest of wills. He knew he could not hope to win such a mental confrontation—already he felt her essence crushing him. But he would not submit, never again.

Lena realized her husband's difficulty. "Lilith?" she said.

"Yes, my dear?"

Lena raised her right hand. "Go to hell."

The mirror imploded under Lena's magick. Lilith snarled, a hideous unnatural noise, but in a second, the Arch-Demon's power dissipated.

Lena turned in her husband's arms and hugged him, almost crushing his ribs. "I'm coming with you," she said.

Malak knew there was no point in arguing with her. She was incredibly stubborn, and once she made a decision it was impossible to reason with her.

"There is no escaping it. I must go," he said. "Even without the threat to Enya, I must defeat her. Until I reclaim my soul, I will only be a shadow. There is nothing within me except emptiness."

Lena nodded. "I know. We'll face it together."

"No. You can come with me, but only I can face her. Alone." His reflective eyes glittered with determination.

A diamond cannot be polished without friction, nor the perfected man without trials.

—Chinese Proverb

Fire is the test of gold; adversity, of strong men.

—Lucius Annaeus Seneca

33

Enya City of Sophia

Lena and Malak obtained no further sleep that night. The time was spent preparing and packing provisions for the journey ahead. Their plan was to set off at dawn, but when Malak went to inform Cassius, the warrior insisted they should be accompanied by a small escort. Malak was set against the idea, but he had to confess he had no idea what dangers lurked in the Wyrmspine Mountains. He grudgingly agreed that Kira and two palace guards could accompany them. Bast didn't require an invitation; she refused to leave Malak's side.

Two pack horses were taken to carry the provisions and cold weather equipment, and Cassius had had several snow coffins made in anticipation of the journey. The Wyrmspine Mountains, once relatively warm and hospitable, were now permanently covered in deep snow. The temperatures were bitter and some of the passes were unnegotiable. Though people strayed into the mountains on occasion, none ever returned because the mountains were rife with demons.

The contingent departed just before noon. All five riders had chosen strong mounts from the royal stables—the horses would require fantastic stamina in the deep snow of the passes. Other than their riders, the horses carried no equipment—all additional weight was loaded onto one of the two pack horses. Malak expected a difficult and prolonged journey and he had no intention of running out of supplies.

The parting with Cassius was emotional for Malak, because it was he as Tanaka who had given Malak the discipline to succeed in the coming battle.

"You've prepared all your life for this, Shadrack. Don't sell yourself short now," Cassius said. "I once told you to fear no man, but what you face now is an evil we can't comprehend. Lilith is as old as the Tree of Life itself."

Malak nodded. "I don't fear any man, Cassius. And neither do I fear anything else. I've run in fear all my life, but never again. I may not be able to match Lilith's power, but she won't match my willpower. I will not yield, and I will not fail."

Cassius looked at his son's disconcerting silver eyes. "I think you're right, Shadrack," he said. "I think you're right."

Three hundred miles of terrain lay between Sophia and the Wyrmspine Mountains. With the strength of the moon phase, this part of the journey was largely uneventful. It took seven days of hard riding, with only one unforeseen ordeal. This occurred when they were forced by the time limitation to ride between the cities of Miosk and Legth.

With the Black School in chaos over Dethen's death, Miosk was involved in a raging civil war. Many parts of the city were severely damaged or burning and the defensive walls had collapsed in places. Black School troops issued from nearby Legth to aid their side in the bloody skirmish. Fortunately, Kira knew the area well and she was able to lead them safely between the two cities. If the group was noticed, both sides were disinterested in their presence.

Once the two cities were left behind, the Wyrmspine Mountains glittered in the distance, their white peaks deceptively enchanting. Only two days later the group reached the foot of the mountain range.

From this point, the journey became very difficult. An unwholesome atmosphere surrounded the mountains and it made the group tire very easily. Due to his memories of the mountains and his experience with deep snow, Malak acted as the guide. He carefully led the group along the safest routes, avoiding the quicker but more dangerous passes. The horses became exhausted very quickly—only a couple of hours in the deep snow was enough to sap their strength. Only six days remained before Dark Moon. It worried Malak, but he still made certain that the horses rested frequently.

The mountains were bereft of life and the group began to suspect that the tales of demon infestation were erroneous. But they started to find bizarre, perturbing tracks in the snow. Many of them seemed to be from bipedal hybrids, while others bore no resemblance to anything the group had seen before. The tracks varied in size from an inch to over two feet in size. None of them were even remotely human.

By nighttime the horses were suffering badly. The strange ambience of the mountains continually sapped their strength, and Malak realized they would never survive the journey. The two palace guards were also beginning to show signs of illness, whether from the hostile conditions or something more sinister. Malak suspected that Lena and Kira were suffering also, though neither was prepared to admit to this.

They slept in twos within the snow coffins for warmth. Constructed from the design used in Nippon by the samurai, the coffins were designed to be buried under snow for insulation. Composed of many layers of material, they trapped air between laminae to produce a warm, soothing environment. Malak slept with Lena, and the two palace guards also shared a coffin. Kira slept alone. She preferred to brave the freezing weather rather than compromise her personal space.

During the night they heard creatures snuffling around the campsite. Bast chased many of them away, but more appeared when she disappeared to hunt the first batch. Malak realized after a while why they weren't attacking. They felt his presence, and they knew that he was one with Lilith. They feared him, and they would not attack as long as he was there. The sounds disappeared just before dawn, but when Malak and Lena burst through the morning snow from their coffin, the horses had been silently killed and dragged away in the night. Already the trail of blood was half covered by falling snow.

The entire group was dejected at the loss of the horses, but Malak was angered more than anyone: the animals had died on a journey that he should have undertaken alone. The two palace guards felt much worse in the morning, and Malak insisted they return to Sophia. Once beyond the range of the mountains, he knew they would recover. Kira refused to return, but Malak was adamant she should take care of the guards: it was possible they would not make it alone, and he was not prepared to risk anymore lives, either human or animal. Kira grudgingly agreed and Malak ordered Bast to accompany her. The familiar growled her displeasure, but Malak was concerned about her also. The wounds that Graymist had inflicted on her were not healing and she seemed to be getting sick, as if the demon had given her a disease.

When Malak turned to Lena, she stared at him intensely. "No," she said.

He shrugged. Once again, he knew that it would be pointless to argue with her: she felt too strong for that. And he knew that if he failed to reach the Celestial Tower in a few days, Lena would be killed anyway. The thought should have horrified him, he knew, but he was too numb to feel any emotion. The mountains had an effect on him, also. All that mattered was reaching the Tower.

Before the group separated to go their different ways, they collected together what was left of the supplies strewn around in a small radius of the campsite. Fortunately, most of them were still intact. They divided the rations before an impersonal parting. Kira still resented having to turn back—Cassius had told her to accompany Malak to the Celestial Tower. But Malak was sure he had made the right decision and he was in no mood to argue. He was unhappy enough about Lena continuing; he knew she was losing strength.

Over the next couple of days the temperature became bitter and the wind fierce. It blasted the fine snow up from the mountains and pelted Malak and Lena. It often hailed and Lena's strength waned further. Though his stamina was drained by the strange, unholy power of the mountains, Malak did not suffer from the cold—he had felt worse in his years in Nippon. It was only his experience in Nippon that kept them alive.

At night the couple snuggled close together for warmth, trying to ignore the growling beasts that prowled around the snow coffin. Lena was exhausted and she fell asleep almost immediately. She curled up against her husband for warmth and reassurance. There was no talk between them and the idea of lovemaking was inconceivable; their limbs were freezing cold and leaden, even after a night in the coffin.

Within a few days Lena suspected they were hopelessly lost. The Wyrmspine Mountains were huge, extending for dozens of miles in every direction. She had lost track of time as well as direction, and her compass spun on its axis when she tried to use it, as if mocking them.

But Malak was certain of their heading. He had an innate sense of direction and Lena knew she had to trust it. Every day that brought them closer to the Tower, Malak became more and more withdrawn.

At night he was haunted by terrible nightmares where Lilith taunted him. He knew they were more than simple dreams—the Arch-Demon was indeed playing with him. He would wake up in a cold sweat, calling out incoherently. In these times, Lena would try to cradle him and talk soothingly but he rejected her sympathy. He was eager to face Lilith once and for all, to end the cat-and-mouse episode that had started so long ago. The Arch-Demon had once elicited the most terrible fear from him, but no longer would he bow to her. He remembered her diabolical tortures so well—they were burned into his essence. But he also strove to remember the words of Ghalan. There was a way to undo his fate, and he would find it. The survival of Enya depended on it.

Malak and Lena had been in the mountains seven days when finally their destination appeared in the distance. The sight was just in time: at dusk, the Dark Moon would rise over the eastern horizon. The Celestial Tower loomed over the next hilltop, a tall, dark, and forbidding column. Extending around it for miles in each direction was Mishmar Lake, frozen solid. A light covering of powder snow coated its surface.

Malak worried about Lena's condition. Both her hands were frostbitten and she was suffering from the first signs of hypothermia. She was trying to use her magical ability to create warmth, but the mountains sapped all her mana. He decided he would set up the snow coffin for her before the rose quartz causeway, then bury it under the snow to provide insulation. He forced her to eat plenty of food.

His parting with Lena was painful. They had fought for so long to be together, it seemed unnatural to part for even a short while. With Lena's poor health, Malak found it heartbreaking.

He held her close. "I love you," he said. The words felt forced.

She closed her eyes. "Then come back to me."

He kissed her, but they both suffered with numb lips and it made the gesture clumsy. He hugged her, pressing his cheek against hers.

"I'll be back. I promise."

As he turned his gaze away from her, his deep blue eyes turned silver. They reflected the Celestial Tower, a pillar of void against the icy background.

It took some time to bury Lena safely under the snow. He told her not to emerge until he returned, no matter how long it took. If he failed, he knew she had no chance of making it back. But then, it didn't matter, because there would be no Enya left if he failed. It was powerful motivation for him to survive.

Malak waited for several minutes at the foot of the causeway. Ahead of him lay his fate, which would soon be decided once and for all. Since the first memory of his current life with Ieyasu Tanaka in the stone circle, he had been preparing for this confrontation. It seemed like ten lifetimes had passed, yet he was barely twenty years of age. He felt closer to a hundred.

As the caustic wind bit into him, his mind snapped back to the present. He sighed and started walking, the two-mile-long causeway stretching out before him. His grip was unsteady but the causeway was wide enough for him not to worry about slipping off. His feet left deep tracks behind him. Underneath the snow lay several inches of compacted ice, centuries old. It was as hard as rock.

The Tower loomed larger as he neared it and he became steadily more anxious. The wind howled about him, almost throwing him from the causeway. Thick snow started to fall. It whipped viciously into his face as if guided, obscuring his sight. He began to suspect a conspiracy among the elements.

He pushed himself on, lowering his head and arching his back, using his powerful legs to force his way through the storm. He felt etheral entities circling around him in curiosity, their essence even colder than the arctic waste around them. No one had dared to trespass upon the Tower before. Some had tried, but none had survived the mountains to reach the causeway. They orbited Malak in excitement, whispering in a strange arcane language that further chilled his icy blood. But he showed no fear, and that protected him—on all levels of existence, lack of fear was a powerful deterrent.

Malak shivered uncontrollably now; the temperature was far colder than even he could stand. It penetrated through his clothing and flesh, numbing his bones. He was so stiff it seemed a sharp blow would shatter his body.

He stopped suddenly as he felt the merest flicker of warmth from up ahead. He raised his head and squinted through the blizzard. The snow stung his eyes but he forced them open as he edged forward. Then he saw it, flickering in the air less than a foot before him. It was the barrier that surrounded the Celestial Tower, the demarcation that separated it from Enya. The Tower had always existed on a plane slightly removed from Enya, and the barrier was the crossing point. When he passed it, he would no longer be on Enya.

Though he could see nothing, somehow he sensed that the Dark Moon was just rising above the horizon. Enya trembled and he felt the stirring of something immensely powerful within, a being that dwarfed the splinter of Lilith that possessed him. He knew it was Lilith's full might rising from sleep within him.

He stumbled forward through the barrier.

The change was instantaneous. The wind and snow disappeared in a flash and he was left standing before the Celestial Tower, now only thirty feet away. It dwarfed him with its size and majesty. The surface was black, perfectly smooth and unblemished. It reflected nothing despite its polished appearance, and it seemed more like a gap in reality than a corporeal structure.

Even more spectacular was the landscape surrounding the Tower. The sky was a vivid red and the ground was brown and arid like a baked desert. The area outside the barrier had disappeared—there was only blackness. The ground around the Tower was suspended in an unending void.

Malak heard a terrible scream. Other voices joined it, forming a horrible, insane cacophony. Malak knew they were the White Adepts he had inadvertently imprisoned so long ago.

"Welcome, my plaything."

The last voice was feminine but powerful and resounding, blocking out all other sounds. Malak instantly knew it was Lilith.

"How brave you are, but alas, how foolish, Malak. You may turn back now, but if you enter the Tower there is no hope of return."

Malak paused only momentarily before walking forward to the Tower doors. Lilith's deformed minions scuttled out of the way as he approached. They were incredibly grotesque, but each was perfectly unique. Though they bore similar traits of sharp teeth, claws, and diseased bodies, no two creatures were the same. Malak paid little heed to them. They were Lilith's creations and subject to her every whim, but he was joined to Lilith and they would not think to attack their own mistress. He was given safe passage.

It took him several seconds to recall the password for the Tower doors, since he had not had occasion to use it for a very long time. The silver pentagram, normally invisible, flared into life and the doors obediently parted.

The hallway was lit with torches. There was a strong smell of decay. He noticed the bodies of two guards just inside the doors. After the Black School attack on the Tower, he had not buried the bodies and that now weighed heavily on his conscience. Some of the magicians were still trapped within the Tower—after physical death, the astral form stayed attached to the physical body in a dream-like state for several days, sometimes longer. The neophytes and Adepts would effectively be trapped within Lilith's domain.

Feelings of guilt assailed Malak, but he had lived with them for so long he refused to allow them to distract him. He knew he could never leave this place unless he defeated the Arch-Demon. Enya was now in the phase of Dark Moon and Lilith would be able to smash through his mind, destroying the plane and penetrating through to Yesod. No, he could not leave. Besides, he had nothing to lose; he had already forfeited his soul. He stepped forward into the Tower.

"No, Malak. You don't have anything to lose," a voice whispered to him. "But think of the pain that you have to gain. . . ."

And then he saw her, standing before the huge marble staircase that circled to the heights of the Tower and down to its depths. Her aura was so powerful it was painful to behold, but it was not an aura of light. It was something akin to light, but sinister; though visible, it cast no illumination around the chamber.

Malak moved forward. Lilith had once terrified him, but he would never again submit to his fear. Of all places in the universe, in this realm he could not run from her.

"You are right, my dear plaything," she purred. "In this place I am omnipotent. None would dare to cross swords with me. Tell me, Malak, why are you here?"

"I've come to challenge you for the return of my soul, Demon."

Lilith laughed, a sound to melt the confidence of any antagonist. "Then come forward and challenge me, little one."

Malak glowered and walked toward her, prepared for the thunder bolt she would surely hurl at him. Lilith watched him with amusement.

Within a few seconds Malak realized the air was becoming more viscous. It slowed him down as it gradually assumed the texture of a liquid. He pushed harder, straining with his legs to move forward. But the air became like thick gel, drifting back toward the Tower entrance. He fought for a few minutes as Lilith watched in amusement, before submitting and being carried back out of the Tower.

He heard Lilith's voice in his head: "You are helpless here, little one. Everything occurs here as I decree it."

He stood before the Tower, breathing deeply. Against the scarlet sky he saw the circle of the Dark Moon. There was no return to Enya for him now.

"Return, Malak. Return to Enya of your own free will. The alternative is pain. Pain upon pain. And then I shall hurl you from this place and into Enya myself."

"Never!" he snarled. "I will not betray those who trust me."

Lilith snickered inside his head. "We shall see."

The ground before Malak suddenly erupted and a huge serpentine dragon slithered into the air. Its ebony scales glittered in the scarlet light like plate-mail armor. Its head bore several broken yellow horns and its eyes flamed an iniquitous red. As it opened its mouth to release a deafening hiss, Malak saw the vicious array of teeth; there were several layers, all longer than a foot. A snake-like tongue flicked in and out of its mouth and fuming saliva flowed from its jaws. The pungent, acrid smell of hydrochloric acid assailed Malak and he gagged with the stench.

He backed away from the black dragon, his eyes wide in awe. The beast swayed hypnotically in the air. He frantically cast his eyes around. There was nowhere to run. Only the Tower offered the promise of protection, and the dragon blocked his path to the haven. With resolve, he firmly stood his ground, staring up in defiance at the abomination. Despite the terror it aroused from his primitive instincts, he refused to run.

The dragon lashed out, striking like a cobra. Moving almost too fast to follow, it seized him like a rag doll, its teeth impaling his flesh and the boiling acidic saliva stripping the skin from his body. He screamed as his organs were punctured, tears rolling down his face. Then the beast ground its jaws, ripping his body apart.

A moment later Malak materialized on the ground, still screaming. He lay there, gritting his teeth as the terrible pain slowly faded.

"You see, Malak," he heard Lilith's voice, "you cannot die here. Not for long. There is no limit to the pain you can endure before you submit." The serpent-like dragon reared above him, ready to strike again. "Would you like to reconsider your decision? The last time was very quick, but this time...."

Malak squinted up at the beast and saw its cold eyes gleaming with desire.

"Go to hell!"

He heard Lilith's laughter. "I'm afraid you're already here, little one."

The dragon seemed to smile, a terrifying gesture that revealed its barbaric array of teeth. Its body whipped forward and Malak was seized again, this time swallowed whole.

He fell into blackness, sliding along a slimy esophagus. With a splash he was submerged into boiling acid. It flayed away his skin and eyelids, more agonizing than any searing flame. He opened his mouth to scream but the acid entered his mouth, burning his throat and forcing its way into his lungs.

He lay in the beast's belly for what seemed an eternity, slowly drowning and dissolving away. He finally died when his heart and lungs were completely cremated. He regained consciousness some time later, lying on the ground once again. He could barely move; the memory of the death was so terrible that he just lay there in shock.

"No, Malak," he heard Lilith whisper, "there is no escape in insanity. You have made your choice and you will face the consequences with your full faculties. You see death has no meaning here. This is an extension of the Qlippoth."

Malak groaned and helplessness overcame him. He had no idea how to challenge Lilith, but one thing was clear: she was far too powerful for a direct confrontation. He looked over at the boundary that separated her domain from Enya. One step through and his torture would be ended. But he knew that that was a cruel illusion. He could not cross that barrier as long as the moon was still in its dark phase.

He looked up at the sky and received a glimmer of hope. The moon had moved some distance across the sky: almost four hours had passed since it had risen. He realized that it took a considerable amount of time for him to return to life after being killed here. It meant that Lilith could only kill him a finite number of times.

At least she doesn't control time, he thought bitterly.

He pushed himself up and checked his body. It seemed unaffected by his two ghastly experiences of death. Only his mind had been left afflicted. He knew this was Lilith's tactic, to break his mind by torturing his body.

He grimaced. *My mind is mine to control. It breaks only if I allow it to.*

He walked toward the Tower again. The monstrous dragon had gone and there was nothing but eerie silence. Now that he had some time to think, he remembered Ghalan's instructions to him. He had to reach the underground chamber in the Tower. It was there he had lost his soul, and it was there he had to somehow recover it.

"Come to me, Malak. Come!" the voice demanded inside his head.

He walked faster, his determination once again unshakeable. He drove the feelings of fear from his mind, banishing the memories of the dragon. He focused his mind purely in the present, allowing nothing else to penetrate except his purpose: he had to reach the underground chamber in the Tower.

As he walked, he realized the Tower was not getting any closer. He started to run, but the Tower stretched away from him, moving farther and farther into the distance.

"Give up, little one. You will never reach it!" Lilith whispered.

He ran faster, sprinting now toward his objective. The Tower kept pace, always moving away but never disappearing from his sight. It was tantalizingly beyond reach. He knew that Lilith would never let him reach it, but he refused to give up. He broke himself into a steady rhythm, running mile after mile across the bleak, featureless desert. Nothing tried to interfere with him as he ran, but he knew he was being observed. Lilith was fascinated by his behavior. Hours passed and nothing occurred. The Tower continued to retreat before his forced advance. Only the steady, monotonous rhythm of the run existed for Malak. And the goal—he had to reach the underground chamber.

After several hours he realized there was a figure gliding alongside him. He didn't need to turn his head to feel Lilith's compelling essence. She was within striking range for him to lash out but he didn't waste energy on the useless action. He merely concentrated on his run, paying no heed to the Arch-Demon.

"Why do you continue to run when you will never reach it?" she asked, genuine curiosity in her voice.

"I…will…reach…the Tower," Malak said through gritted teeth. His lungs burned and he had cramps in his legs, which were so saturated with lactic acid they felt leaden. Only his samurai training allowed him to continue. From the position of the moon, he had been running for almost seven hours.

"But why? The effort is pointless. Unless I allow it, you will never reach the Tower!" Lilith seemed angered by his lack of logic, as if she should be able to understand his every motivation.

Malak suddenly started laughing, even though his exhausted body made the action incredibly painful, and caused him to wheeze uncontrollably.

"There is something funny?" Lilith did not appear amused.

Malak laughed again. "No. It's…just that I'll…run indefinitely. I'm not…being eaten or…dissolved, you see." He started to laugh again, almost choking on his own phlegm. It felt so good to achieve a victory over Lilith that he couldn't stop himself from telling her. He turned his head to face her and grinned, the gesture calculated to be as irritating as possible.

Lilith's purple eyes darkened in anger. She smiled back, a chilling and malicious gesture that made Malak regret his audacity.

"We shall see just how much you wish to reach the Tower," she hissed venomously.

Malak suddenly found himself at the boundary to Lilith's domain again. Despite this, the Celestial Tower was closer than it had been. Lilith had ended her charade. Malak staggered to a halt, collapsing on the ground. He wheezed as he tried to regain his breath. Within a few seconds he vomited, and then lay still, utterly exhausted.

"Come, Malak. Come to me," Lilith whispered inside his head.

He groaned and looked up. Stretching from where he lay to the doors of the Celestial Tower, blue flames flickered hungrily from the ground. He felt the intense heat on his face from where he rested. The flames stretched across the whole width of the desolate desert; there was no way around them.

He stretched a hand out toward the flames and snatched it back. The fire was blistering enough to instantly destroy anything living. Staring up at the moon, he realized it was close to the western horizon. He laughed weakly and pushed himself forward into the flames. Scalding heat consumed his body. He bawled in agony before blackness seized him.

When Malak regained consciousness he lay on the ground with Lilith standing over him. The moon had disappeared from the west and now hovered over the eastern horizon. Malak sighed. It seemed he had only to survive for two more nights, since days did not exist in this hellish domain.

"Very clever, Malak. Very clever."

He stood up and stared at Lilith tiredly. Though he was mentally shattered, his physical body once again felt fresh.

"You are trying to spend time," Lilith said. "You think you will be safe when the three days are over? You must realize by now that your challenge is impossible—you will fail. And when the Dark Moon ends I will not simply allow you to return to Enya. No, you will remain here to be tortured. And when the next Dark Moon occurs, you will be more than eager to leap into Enya."

Malak stared at her with contempt. "Just allow me to reach that chamber...."

Lilith smiled and gestured with her hand. "Please, be my guest."

He looked at her suspiciously and then started walking toward the Tower. Nothing tried to intercept him until he had almost reached the doorway, but then they came hurtling toward him. A cross between men and demons, they were seven feet tall with vicious weapons ranging from morning stars to battle axes.

Malak stopped and waited. He was unarmed and there were over ten of them, but he knew there was nowhere to run. The battle was short but fierce and then he was slashed and bludgeoned to death.

"Problems?" Lilith asked when he materialized next to her.

Malak sat down in defeat, the fight taken from him. He knew he could not continue to experience such terrible deaths without his mind breaking. And if Lilith intended to keep him trapped when he didn't submit....

He stood up, the answer suddenly striking him.

"You can't hurl me from this place!" he shouted.

Lilith's eyes narrowed. "You are mistaken, little one. I am omnipotent here."

Malak laughed and shook his head. "You can't throw me out because I belong here! I'm a part of you!"

He turned his back on Lilith before she could respond and walked quickly toward the Tower. Once again, the man-demons appeared, grinning at his stupidity with weapons raised. Malak continued walking, his silver eyes dangerous.

The creatures rushed him. Malak snarled, and his eyes glowed red. As the first demon neared, he sprang forward with incredible speed, ripping its throat out with his bare hands. It gurgled pathetically and fell to the ground. Malak picked up its sword and turned on its comrades. They attacked without fear, but didn't stand a chance. He slashed one after another, cleaving open flesh and breaking bones with kicks and punches. Within half a minute, the last demon died with a cry of shock.

Malak threw back his head and roared in triumph. He was brought back to reality by the sound of Lilith clapping.

"Very good, little one. You used the splinter of my essence. And I can't take that from you, but remember, it is nothing but a splinter. Let me see how you deal with these enemies!"

Malak turned around and hesitated as he recognized the figures who approached him. They were all people from his past and they were advancing with swords raised. There was Ekanar, Yoriie Saito, Gorun Tzan, Cassius, Dahran and others whom he recognized but couldn't place.

"Let me see you cut your friends down, Malak," Lilith taunted him.

"They're not the people I know!" he said.

Lilith laughed. "No, but they're perfect replicas. In every way they are who you think they are. They live of their own accord, but they will obey my commands."

The doppelgangers moved to attack and Malak edged back. The man before him was an exact copy of Yoriie Saito, whom he had seen decapitated several years before. He was cloned in every detail—even the eyes seemed to hold the blacksmith's essence. Saito lunged forward to attack and Malak hesitated only momentarily before reacting. His eyes glowed an intense red and he slashed the replica to the ground.

I will not be defeated by your petty tricks, Demon.

The other clones rushed him but he was too quick and powerful. He destroyed each one, a look of anguish passing over his face as he extinguished each life. But when the last doppelganger stood before him he floundered. It was Lena.

"Go on," Lilith urged him, "kill her."

Malak raised his sword and hesitated again. Lena was dressed in white robes, holding an ebony bo-staff. Her eyes were the same deep brown that he remembered so well, flecked with gold. She spun the staff into an attack posture and advanced toward him. Malak lowered his sword and backed away. He stared deeper into her eyes, and though he was unable to distinguish the difference, he knew it was not his Lena. He knew her soul, and this was not her.

Lilith noticed his realization. "This may not be your Lena, Malak. But kill her and the real one dies!"

Malak swore viciously. "You're bluffing!"

"On the contrary, Malak. Does Lena not lie under the snow just before the crystal causeway? I have many creatures under my control in the mountains. Her death will be simple to arrange. Lower your sword and return to Enya."

Malak squeezed his eyes shut and lowered his sword.

"That's right, little one. Think of what Lena would want you to do. I'm sure she doesn't want to die."

Malak paused for a moment. "What Lena would want me to do?"

His eyes snapped open and he decapitated the clone of his wife with a single slice. In a moment he was running for the Tower, his sword left on the ground behind him. He heard a roar of anger behind and something flashed past him.

He sprinted faster and within a few seconds he was passing through the Tower doors. He slowed as he saw Lilith waiting by the marble stairway, his only means of access to the underground chamber. His eyes glowed a deep red and he accelerated, running straight for Lilith's body.

When he impacted he rebounded painfully to the floor as if she was a wall of iron. She bent down to him and lifted him into the air by the throat, just as he had done to the Shogun of Nippon many years ago. He struggled frantically to break the hold but his kicks glanced ineffectually off her body.

"You don't like your own medicine?" she asked, her terrifying purple eyes penetrating through his skull.

He gave a last desperate kick before she closed her hand, crushing his neck and throat into oblivion.

He materialized a few feet away, still inside the main hallway of the Tower. Lilith stood over him. He instinctively felt for his throat as he awoke, as if to reassure himself it was there.

"Tell me, Malak, will you not submit and return to Enya? This becomes tiresome."

"Why?" he said. "If I did, you would smash through my body, instantly killing me. Because you possess my soul, I would end up in your domain again, anyway."

She stared at him in surprise. "Of course, that is true. But what if I offered to release your soul? Your freedom for mine. I liberate your soul, and you grant me passage into Enya."

Malak looked at her with suspicion. "You'd never do it."

"I would give you my word."

"Your word means nothing!"

Lilith smiled sweetly. "Then I would swear a pact by my true name."

He realized she was serious. "But the effects of your...."

"You must weigh the deaths of the others against your soul, Malak," Lilith interrupted. "After all, what is physical death compared to eternal torment for the soul?"

He stared at her for a long time. Her offer seemed the only way out of the situation. Yet he remembered a similar choice he had made in the Celestial Tower over a thousand years ago.

"No! I won't make the mistake again!"

He pushed himself up and ran at her again. She caught him, this time gently but firmly enough to hold him still.

"Malak, we have been together for a long time," she said. "Perhaps now it is time we merged."

He struggled wildly as she leaned forward to kiss him. He was not fooled by the stunningly beautiful face or luscious lips. He had felt her touch before, and the memory was not a pleasant one.

As their lips met, Lilith poured herself into his body, her essence mingling with his own. It was a pain more intense than any he had ever felt, beyond any agony imaginable. He screamed and screamed. His body disintegrated with the force of her essence, the molecules rapidly decomposing.

He reappeared on the hallway floor again, his teeth gritted against the receding pain. He sobbed without shame as he vomited over the floor.

"Malak, dearest," Lilith said, looming over him. "Would you like to reconsider a final time?"

Malak stared at her groggily, thick saliva hanging from numb lips. His mind struggled to maintain coherency.

"The chamber," he mumbled. "Let me into the chamber."

Lilith snarled, a sound more menacing than an angered bear.

"It is the third day of the Dark Moon, Malak," she said. "Let us visit the chamber. When you realize the futility of your situation, perhaps you will be more cooperative."

She grabbed him by the hair and dragged him across the hallway. He grunted as she hauled him down the staircase, every step smashing his ribs. When they came to the reinforced door, it exploded simply from her glance. She hurled him into the center of the chamber, where he landed in an undignified heap.

His body was bruised and lacerated, but he pushed himself to his feet immediately. At last he'd reached his objective. It didn't matter that Lilith had brought him. He was here, and that was all that mattered.

From the doorway Lilith made a gesture and soft yellow light illuminated the chamber. Malak cast his gaze around. It was exactly as he remembered it. The protective circle and triangle of manifestation were still drawn on the ground, leftovers of his evocation of Lilith a thousand years ago. The four lamps were present, smashed at the edge of the circle. The altar stood in the center.

Though Malak took in all of this detail, his eyes were fixed on an object that lay beside the altar: his sword, *Retaliator*. He bent down to examine the sword, tears in his eyes. The blade had been shattered, its blue luster extinguished. The mystical runes inscribed on the hilt and blade were crusted with dirt and the star-sapphire, once the katana's heart, was empty and lifeless, its light forever quenched.

"You expected it to be whole?" Lilith's voice was mocking. "No, Malak. The sword represents the link to your soul, and will forever remain broken."

Malak stared in disbelief. He had expected it to be so simple when he reached the chamber. Hadn't Ghalan said so? But now his confidence was as shattered as the sword he now held.

"So there really is no hope?"

"None," Lilith said. "But cooperate with me and you will be saved a great deal of pain. The third day is almost over, Malak. After a month of torture in this place you will be eager to leave at the next Dark Moon. Why not save yourself the agony?"

He glared at her, his eyes full of hatred. "I will never submit to you, Lilith. If I can stand your tortures for three days, I can stand them for an eternity."

Lilith's aura darkened with her anger. "You think you can save this tiny plane? You see yourself as a savior, Malak? Then I think your heroics deserve a reward. There is only one true method of death for all saviors. Perhaps this will change your arrogance."

The stone floor behind Malak suddenly cracked and a large wooden cross broke through to stand erect. Malak found himself paralyzed, his limbs manipulated into the shape of the cross. Lilith motioned with her hand and he was thrown backward to be suspended against the cross. He screamed as nails pierced his wrists and ankles, pinning him to the wooden frame. Blood dripped from his arms and legs, forming scarlet pools on the dusty floor.

Lilith examined her work with satisfaction.

"You must realize now that there is no hope of defeating me. There is no way to undo the pact you made so many years ago. Only I can reverse it, and I will never grant your request unless you cooperate with me. It is very simple. Give me Enya, and I will give you your soul."

Malak shook his head limply. The strength had drained from his body and his mind was numb. Only one thing existed for him now, and that was pain. But it seemed that that was all he could remember. He could barely recall the time before he had entered Lilith's domain, only three days before.

"Then I shall watch you die. But this time it will be slowly, ever so slowly. And when you are dead you will awaken in my true domain, where tortures are beyond anything you can imagine."

Malak hung on the cross for several hours, slowly dying. It was not the blood loss that threatened his life, but drowning. With his arms locked into such an unnatural position his lungs slowly filled with water. This was how all victims of crucifixion eventually died.

Lilith watched him as his life slowly drained away. Terrible visions and hallucinations gripped his mind and he was almost oblivious to his surroundings. He was only aware of the pain and the difficulty in breathing.

After several hours he was close to death, and it was then that Lilith spoke gently to him: "Malak, there is barely a minute left to avert your fate. Dark Moon has almost ended. Cooperate now and you will be released from this torture, I swear it."

Her voice brought him back to the present and he stared down at her with his mirror-like gaze. Suddenly he laughed, a sound choked by the diabolical state of his lungs.

Lilith was furious. "What do you find amusing, mortal? Have you lost your sanity after all?"

Malak laughed harder, coughing up viscous, bloody phlegm as he did so. The words of Ghalan had returned to him.

"Speak, mortal. What amuses you?!" Lilith demanded.

Malak muttered something under his breath, but the Arch-Demon was unable to make it out. Nevertheless, it sent a shudder of apprehension through her essence.

"Repeat yourself!"

Malak flung back his head and bawled: "And on the third day, he was risen!"

Lilith snarled and leaped forward to rip him down from the cross. Just as she moved, a beautiful golden light descended on Malak. The chamber disappeared and his consciousness soared into the heavens, carried on a wave of ecstasy. The wave washed away his pain, fear, and every anxiety. He hovered over the universe like a bird of prey, every event and possibility visible to his eyes. He saw the way that all things were connected. There was only One source, and all things stemmed from it. And he was a part of the source, a part of the Oneness. It was something that would never change regardless of what happened to him.

A euphony of voices spoke to him, and he knew that they were the secret Chiefs of the Order, guardians of the White School of Magick.

"Malak, you have passed every test and temptation put before you. You hereby regain your Adepthood and the link to your higher self."

Malak gasped in pleasure as the vast emptiness he had suffered for so long was suddenly filled. He was whole once again. The sensation was an indescribable rapture, worth a million times the torment he had passed through. His trial had been nothing compared to the ecstasy of his prize.

Gradually the golden light dispersed and he found himself standing within the underground chamber. He was in front of the cross and his body was cleansed and uninjured. Standing across the chamber was Lilith, her eyes flaming with fury.

"You will pay for this, Malak!"

She launched herself at him, demonic canines reaching for his jugular. Malak held up his hand and she deflected off him as if he were steel. She landed hard on the floor. He grabbed her by the hair and pulled back her head to stare into her eyes.

She hissed and spat in his face, but even the saliva didn't touch him.

Malak smiled maliciously. "You have no power in this place." He gripped her hair tighter. "In the name of SHADDAI EL CHAI, God the Omnipotent, I hereby eternally banish you from this sacred place."

He launched a bright blue banishing pentagram. Lilith screamed as it hit. In a haze of green light, the Arch-Demon evaporated. As she did so, the cross dematerialized along with all other traces of her occupation.

The light she had summoned extinguished, but Malak was not left in darkness. A pulsating blue light lit the chamber. Malak walked over to the source to see *Retaliator's* star-sapphire flaming with azure light. The blade was once again whole. Malak retrieved the sword reverently. She vibrated with pleasure in his hand.

His attention was caught by an object glittering from deep in the chamber. He walked toward it, holding *Retaliator* aloft for illumination. When he reached it he bent down to scoop it from the floor. It was a silver pentagram, the badge of a White Adept. He remembered throwing it away before commencing his original evocation of Lilith. He cradled it to his heart. He had retained his Adepthood, and nothing would deprive him of it again.

Malak ran through the open doors of the Tower and along the slippery stretch of causeway. Already the snow storm was dying out; the evil ambience of the mountains was fading away.

He reached the spot where he had buried Lena's snow coffin and started furiously digging. Beside him, Squint materialized, jumping from foot to foot in anticipation.

"Lena?"

There was a dreadful silence, and suddenly Lilith's threat to Lena's life came back to him.

"Lena!"

He started digging again in panic. The wind whistled apprehensively. He was sure that the worst had occurred, that the Arch-Demon had carried out her threat. The thought horrified him—he couldn't face waiting another lifetime to be reunited with his love again.

He found the snow coffin. It seemed not to have been tampered with. He quickly unbuckled the coffin, his fingers fumbling with the catches. He yanked the coffin open.

Lena lay inside, her face deathly white.

"No, Lena. Come on!"

He felt for the pulse on her neck. There was barely a flutter. He pulled her from the coffin and held her in his arms, cradling her. He knew the life force was seeping from her body. The mountains were no longer draining her, but she was too far gone. She didn't have the strength to recover by herself.

Suddenly he recalled his words to Cassius. *This is not Tellus. On Enya we warp our own reality.*

He laid Lena's body on the snow and tentatively laid his hands on her sternum. He concentrated and drew energy down from his crown chakra, channeling it into her body. Her aura glowed as she warmed, her heart beginning to beat strongly again. She opened her eyes, and Malak fell back, exhausted. Squint jumped up and down, ecstatic.

Lena pushed herself to lie in the snow next to her husband. She ran her hand through his hair and smiled. Malak felt emotion swell within him. He would have suffered everything again just to see Lena's smile.

"I knew you'd do it," she whispered.

"You did?"

"No," she laughed, "but I lay for three days with my fingers crossed." Her expression became incredibly tender. "I love you."

She reached forward and gently kissed him.

"I love you too," he said, then smiled. "With all my soul."

She smiled. "Is it over?"

"It's over. We have no enemies now."

She wrapped her arms around him, holding him tight. Malak held her close, finally content to lie in his wife's arms.

Epilogue to Resurrection

The truth is that life is hard and dangerous; that he who seeks his own happiness does not find it; that he who is weak must suffer; that he who demands love, will be disappointed; that he who is greedy, will not be fed; that he who seeks peace, will find strife; that truth is only for the brave; that joy is only for him who does not fear to be alone; that life is only for the one who is not afraid to die.

—Joyce Carey

The Enchanted Forest
Yellow School sanctuary

Bal immediately retched and vomited over the floor as he returned to consciousness. He choked on the thick acidic saliva in his throat.

"Nice to be back," he muttered.

He felt a hand on his shoulder gently push him to lie down on the bed. Too weak to resist, he submitted.

"Yhana?"

"I'm here, Bal."

Bal stared at her. Her face seemed slightly softer than he remembered it.

"Where am I?" he asked, confused.

"In the Yellow School sanctuary. Do you not remember?"

Bal gasped as the memory of Maat returned to him. "Yes! Yes! I am the Master!"

Yhana's eyes glittered with pride. "Yes, you are the Master. But before you take up your position, I have some terrible news for you."

Bal paused. "What is it?" he asked suspiciously.

"It's Dethen," Yhana said. "Our contacts in the School say he has been killed, buried under hundreds of tons of rocks."

Bal's eyes widened. "No! That can't be! The Master can survive anything! The dagger that pierced me would be a pin-prick to him!"

Yhana shook her head. "They say it was suicide. That he has been lost for many days. It was his brother, Malak."

"That bastard will pay for this!" Bal snarled, his eyes dangerous.

"There is revenge here for your appetite," Yhana said. "We captured Mendaz in the hall. I have kept him alive so that you may take his life."

Bal smiled maliciously, but it slowly faded away. "No. I want you to release him."

"But he tried to kill me! And you almost died because of him!"

"No. The Master told me to ensure his safety. I will respect his last wish. Allow him to leave and go where he wants."

Yhana cast her eyes down, disappointed. "I thought you to be stronger than that, Bal."

Bal swung his legs quickly out of the bed and stood up unsteadily. "You want to see strength, my dear? You wish to see leadership? Then stay with me, for you're about to see the biggest upheaval Enya has ever seen. Today, the Yellow School policy of non-interference ends. Today we go to war!"

Yhana looked up, her eyes sparkling with dark ambition. "When we finish, my daughter and her husband will tremble on their knees before us!"

Black School subterranean lair

Dethen groggily opened his eyes and instinctively reached for his head, which pounded with a vengeance. He saw nothing but complete darkness and the air tasted foul.

"I am dead?" he asked himself, his mind struggling to remember.

"No, Dethen of Enya. You are very much alive."

Dethen turned to see two incredibly beautiful azure eyes staring at him. They glowed, lighting up the surroundings with an eerie blue light.

"Tien Lung? The Celestial Dragon?"

"It is I. The prophecy is fulfilled. Just as you saved me by freeing me, I saved you by entrapping you. It was not your time to die, Dethen of Enya. The debt I owe to you is now repaid."

Dethen looked around him, dazed. He realized that the dragon's huge body was twisted around him, holding the rock above at bay.

"I am not dead," he said, trying to grasp the idea. Suddenly he remembered his defeat by Malak, and the way Lena had spurned him.

My Anya!

It pierced him to the soul to think of his brother making love to Lena. A gentle ripple of anger started within him. Quickly it grew, augmenting at a frightening pace.

"I will destroy both of you," he snarled viciously. "Malak, Lena. I am coming for you."

Tien Lung shifted a section of his body away, leaving bare rock exposed. Lightning lanced from Dethen's fingers. Rubble exploded in all directions as he blasted a hole in the rock. He stepped through.

Tien Lung's words vibrated through his head as he escaped: "Tell Kalinda that the next time I come, it will be for my vengeance."

But Dethen barely heard the dragon. Black Adepts scattered from his path as he appeared. His black eyes burned with a hatred so intense it seemed they would incinerate anything they looked at.

One Adept failed to move quickly enough. Dethen lashed out, blasting him apart with a streak of lightning. He snarled in satisfaction.

He was alive, and it infuriated him. Malak, Lena, Lilith, even Tien Lung. He would destroy them all. There were no limits to his wrath. And once they were dead, he would cast Chronzon into a pit of eternal torture. He would cross the Abyss and challenge the might of the Godhead itself. This time nothing would stand in his path.

His black eyes simmered, mirroring the hell in which he eternally existed. His hand gripped the hilt of *Widowmaker*.

"Do not worry, my precious. This time the blood will flow freely. And Malak will have no Demon to protect him!"

Widowmaker vibrated with macabre anticipation.

The Nature of Magick

Magic. A word associated with the fantasies of children or the illusory tricks of stage magicians such as Paul Daniels and David Copperfield. A word that invites contempt and ridicule from contemporary society for those who consider the subject with a degree of seriousness. It belongs to the realm of fairy tales, its origins from an age when man's subconscious mind was dominant, his rational mind still in its infancy.

In the present age such concepts as magic seem to us ridiculous and almost abhorrent. We have science, which explains the universe in clear, rational terms without reference to such primitive notions as magic and the supernatural. It seems that humankind has grown beyond such notions, casting them away like an embarrassing aspect of his infancy.

Yet in this high-tech world where everything is rationally explained and superstition is forever banished, it is curious that many of us shiver in apprehension of the dark; amazing that once the comfort of daylight has passed and we are left alone, such words as "ghost," "spirit," and "demon" assume reality within vivid imaginations.

The problem occurs because we all innately believe in magic, as most psychologists will testify. Regardless of our profession or mental outlook, we all possess unconscious minds that are very similar below a certain level. This fact was first demonstrated by the Swiss psychologist Carl Jung. Our unconscious minds still believe that we live in a fairy-tale world of magic—in the concepts that we regard as ludicrous—and so we can never completely claim scepticism. Our unconscious minds compel us to listen to these fantastic tales, which is why the stories have existed for so long. They are an intrinsic part of us; to deny magic is to deny our own identity.

There are two major reasons our rational minds deny the existence of magic. As inferred earlier, the first is science. Science helps to banish the subconscious fears within us; it gives the illusion that we know what we are and that we control our environment. This is a powerful narcotic: humans loathe feeling helpless, though in truth we are more helpless than we realize. The thought of magic is a distasteful reminder of how little we actually know.

The second problem is our perception of magic in an age where the media controls almost all information. The public has preconceived ideas of what magic is, after watching sleight-of-hand trickery, absurd reports of ritual sacrifice and films in which magicians cast fireballs at each other with the flick of a wrist. But though the subject is vast, true magic resembles none of these. To distinguish the genuine article from sensational fiction, magic is often spelled "magick."

Magick is almost synonymous with the occult (a word that simply means "hidden," and has no allusions to evil as the Christian church would have us believe). In essence, it is the knowledge of humans and their relationship to the universe. As such it may be considered a precursor to science (indeed, mathematics and chemistry were once considered evil occult subjects for which practitioners were burned by the Church). Magick differs from science in its approach, however. In science objective phenomena are paramount and the scientist is irrelevant; in magick, the practitioner is everything. The center of its doctrine is that we are spiritual beings, with the potential to develop far beyond what we are born as. In this way there is a similarity to religion, but there is no emphasis on faith. The principles are clearly demonstrable to any open-minded individual, and the results occur in the present, not in some far-off realm when the individual is dead (though magick does not deny the existence of such realms).

It is an axiom of magick that man is a miniature replica of the universe: that the forces that flow through the cosmos are also to be found within man's psyche. There are several religions that declare that God made humans in his own image, but this is often taken to mean physically and is too literal an interpretation. Magick considers the universe (or macrocosm) and man (the microcosm) to be intimately linked. Therefore if a person has the skill to call forth a certain aspect of his psyche, he can affect the corresponding objective force. This is known as sympathetic magick, and is the manner in which such rituals as the rain dance work (such effects are often called natural magick, since it was used by native people all over the world).

In High Magick the universe is seen to be composed of many different planes, all inter-penetrating. The physical universe is the most dense and is the only one perceived by most individuals. The astral, mental and spiritual planes also exist simultaneously but are too fine to discern. The astral plane is what we enter every time we dream, and is a place of great emotional intensity. Even finer than this is the mental plane, where our thoughts are centered; above the mental plane is the spiritual plane, about which little can be said.

These planes are objective realities of the universe, but they are also the map of our unconscious minds. The images of gods, demons, angels, and archetypal heroes all stem from this great source and so all humans are irrevocably linked together. The planes may be thought of as a giant mind, of which our conscious minds are tiny growths, analogous to leaves growing on a tree. The planes emanate from Kether on the Tree of Life, the Source that may be considered God. The planes terminate with the physical universe and our physical bodies in Malkuth. Therefore man is intimately linked with the Divine Mind and the forces that govern the physical universe; by affecting the relevant part of his or her psyche, a magician can produce changes in the environment.

The explanation may seem far-fetched, but magick can explain a great number of mysteries. With some consideration it is possible to explain fairy tales, reincarnation, prescience, clairvoyance, out-of-body experiences, dreams, telepathy, telekinesis, ghosts, mediumship, auras, and countless other phenomena. I have given no evidence here to convince the reader of this doctrine; this essay is too short and it is not my intention to convince the reader of the reality of magick. Rather, it is my intention to hint at the comprehensive cosmology that lies behind it: in the end there is no need to resort to faith and superstition.

Science is gradually beginning to confirm these doctrines, which have existed for thousands of years. Science broke away from the occult subjects only a few hundred years ago. It now begins to return to its roots as scientists are baffled by the consequences of quantum physics. It is already accepted by many scientists that human consciousness can affect the universe on a quantum level. To Einstein, quantum physics had ramifications he refused to accept, but quantum theory remains the principal guiding light of physicists.

The acceptance of magical theory will be very slow. Just as the Christian church burned those who opposed its authority in the Middle Ages, scientists are now involved in their own witch hunt. Any scientist who steps outside of orthodox research is attacked with almost religious zealousness. It is unfortunate that science, as the establishment that once attacked stagnant religious ideas, has become what it once despised. Scientists have formed a belief system that they ardently cling to, turning viciously on those who would challenge it even when logic is against them.

In the magical philosophy, gods, demons and angels can be explained as fragments of our own unconscious minds. These fragments seem to possess their own intelligence. Whether or not they would exist independently of humans is a controversial question, but in some ways is irrelevant. Their significance comes from their relationship to us and each other, as told in the many mythologies of the world. By studying them, we also learn how the different aspects of our unconscious minds interact, and thereby learn about ourselves; much of magick is concerned with this goal.

There are many tales of magicians evoking fearful demons and devils, but this type of operation is extremely rare and is not concerned with "diabolical" creatures as such. A demon may be considered a negative character trait within an individual's character—for example, anger. To personify it and converse with it with a view to banishing the anger is the magician's goal. To many people, the "demon" never has an objective reality, and the process is basically one of self-psychoanalysis. The demons of horror films and novels are a long way from this type of beneficial operation, in which the entity is simply an aspect of the magician's character.

Though much of *Darkness and Light* concerns Lilith, an Arch-Demon, I would like to stress that this is a fantasy novel and is therefore as guilty of exaggeration as many horror films; the techniques, however, are quite legitimate. The talisman charging ritual in Chapter 19 is a good example of a magical ritual, though it is simplified for fiction (remember that it is performed on the astral plane, hence the spectacular effects). Occult work has little to do with "dark powers" or "evil," but because these concepts do belong to humankind's psyche, magick inevitably touches on them. It is unfortunate that the phrase "black magick" is so frequently used in the media, when "white magick" is a hundred-fold more common.

For anyone who is interested in magick, there are many excellent books available from Llewellyn Publications. A recommended reading list may be found at the back of this novel. To hint at the scope of magick, I will end with an extract from Mary K. Greer, taken from *Women of the Golden Dawn:*

"While some writers have regarded magic as psycho-therapeutic work (Francis King and Israel Regardie, for example), others have characterized it as the discovery of the unity within all duality, the truth behind all illusions. W. B. Yeats sought knowledge of what he called 'the single energetic Mind,' and its pole, 'the single Memory of nature,' both of which he believed could be evoked by symbols. But I like Florence Farr's definition of magic best: 'Magic is unlimiting experience.' That is, magic consists of removing the limitations from what we think are the earthly and spiritual laws that bind or compel us. We can be anything because we are All."

Glossary

Abyss, The: The Abyss is a spiritual and metaphysical concept; it is a great chasm that exists between the Qabalistic world of Atziluth and the world of Briah. In a sense it separates the mortal world from the immortal world. Below the Abyss we experience the illusion of isolation; we consider ourselves to be separate, isolated beings. Above the Abyss is the experience of being one with God: all illusions are cast aside and an Adept experiences his own divinity and Oneness with everything.

Adept: A man or woman who has obtained self-realization (relating to Tiphareth on the Tree of Life). Adepthood is referred to as Enlightenment in some traditions. An Adept has forged a link to his/her Higher Self and consciousness is thus greatly expanded.

Assiah: The last of the four worlds of the Qabalah. Assiah is the material universe in which we live. It is the most dense of the worlds.

Astral Plane: A plane more rarefied than the physical universe and interpenetrating it. It is equivalent to the Qabalistic world of Yetzirah. The ceaseless motion and forces of the astral give stability to the material universe. A magician can mold the astral material to his will, and because the physical plane takes its shape from the astral, this produces physical effects. Dreams and astral projection usually take place in the astral, and ghosts are also caused by astral phenomena.

Atziluth: The first world of the Qabalah. Atziluth is the most rarefied plane and is the world of Divinity. It exists above the Abyss, completely beyond our perceptions; despite this, the very core of our being resides in Atziluth.

Aura: A body of light around an individual, perceived only by those with psychic ability or under unusual conditions. It is caused by the ethereal body, and can reveal a great deal about a person, including health and current emotional state; these can be read by the brightness and color of the aura, respectively. Some psychics perceive the aura as a single variant color; more skilled psychics see a whole range of colors at any one time.

Bo: Literally "staff," a wooden stave approximately six feet long.

Bo-jitsu: Literally "the art of the staff." A martial art based on the use of a bo-staff. The staff is employed two-handedly and through variations in grip it can be used for long-range or close-combat. Techniques include striking, thrusting, blocking, parrying, sweeping, and holding.

Bokken: Literally "wooden sword." A bokken is a staff contoured like a katana, used mainly for practice.

Budo: Literally "military way." A word that encompasses all martial arts, especially those with emphasis on a spiritual approach.

Bushi: Literally "military person" or "warrior," used synonymously with "samurai."

Bushido: Literally "way of the warrior." A strict code of behavior followed by samurai. The code advised a samurai how to conduct himself in battle and how to find a meaningful place in society during peace. The code also contained ethical and religious concepts.

Chakra: One of the centers of power located in the astral/ethereal bodies of humans and animals. There are many hundreds of chakras, but only several are important for spiritual development; these are located in the soles of the feet, groin, solar plexus, heart, throat, forehead, and above the head. Chakras distribute energy to keep the astral body vitalized.

Daimyo: In feudal Japan, a samurai lord that other samurai were honor-bound to obey. A samurai without a daimyo was considered worthless, and was despised as a ronin.

Elemental: A low-ranking entity of one of the four elements, including salamanders (fire), undines (water), sylphs (air), and gnomes (earth). A skilled magician can bind an elemental to his/her bidding, though the task must suit the elemental's nature. It is also possible to create "artificial elementals."

Enochian: An ancient language used in magical rituals. Its origins are extremely obscure but fragments were rediscovered by Sir John Dee in relatively recent times. Enochian is said by some authorities to be the language of the angels.

Ethereal Plane: The ethereal plane may be considered as the densest part of the astral plane. There is no clear-cut distinction between the astral and ethereal, but in humans the astral body may depart from the physical, whereas the ethereal body remains behind to keep the physical body alive. Auras are seen when the ethereal body is perceived by sight.

Frater: A word used in occult orders, literally meaning "Brother." The feminine equivalent is Soror.

Gi: Literally "uniform" or "suit," a gi is the traditional apparel of a martial artist. Normally woven from cotton, or from cotton canvas (which is more durable).

Hari-kari: Literally "belly cutting," an excruciating form of ritualistic suicide performed by samurai. The formal name for the ritual is seppuku.

Iai: Literally "swordplay." Iai is also a type of duel in which two opponents face each other in the kneeling position before attacking. The first sword slice usually ended the duel, which could be for honor or to the death.

Iai-jitsu: Literally "sword drawing art," a martial art that perfected the initial movement of a sword and the instant striking of an enemy. Iai-jitsu was extremely important to samurai. The modern version of the martial art is iai-do, the "way of the sword."

Ipsissimus: An Adept who has crossed the Abyss to attain complete oneness with God. An Ipsissimus may not return to the lower planes once he has obtained this grade, for his essence is too vast. The grade corresponds to Kether on the Tree of Life. An Ipsissimus has become everything it is possible to become, and is beyond description and comprehension to us.

Jujitsu: Literally "the art of gentleness," a martial art used by samurai from the thirteenth century. Techniques include striking, kicking, throwing, choking, and especially joint-locking. The use of weapons is also a part of jujitsu.

Karate: Literally "empty hand," meaning a martial art used without weapons. Karate employs all parts of the anatomy to punch, kick, strike, and block. The style is generally more aggressive than jujitsu and aikido, which are more defensive arts (though still extremely effective).

Kata: Literally "formal exercise," a sequence of prearranged techniques against imaginary opponents. Kata is used to deepen concentration and awareness, and to perfect techniques.

Katana: Literally "sword." The katana was the long sword, always paired with the wakizashi short sword. Together they formed a daisho pair, which was the mark of a samurai. A katana was twenty-four to thirty-six inches long and was worn with the cutting edge up.

Kiai: Literally "spirit meeting." A kiai focuses the entire spirit and power of a martial artist into a single technique, and is accompanied by a loud shout to instill fear into the opponent.

Kime: Literally "focus." A martial artist concentrates his physical and mental power behind a single striking point (such as the knuckles) for maximum effect. Kime is used with every technique where power is required, and is devastating when used in conjunction with a kiai.

Magus: An Adept who has crossed the Abyss and realized his identity with God. A Magus is the grade before Ipsissimus. The difference between the grades of spiritual attainment is complex, but for the purposes of Darkness and Light, it is essentially that a Magus may return to Earth and an Ipsissimus may not. A Magus may be considered God incarnate on Earth, as many of our spiritual teachers have been.

Mana: Synonymous with magick.

Motsu: A form of meditation employed in the martial arts, performed kneeling on the insteps. The position is also employed in magical arts and is sometimes known as "dragon posture."

Neophyte: The lowest grade of initiation to a temple of magick.

Pantacle: A flat object, usually wooden, used in magical rituals and inscribed with a pentagram or pentangle. Pantacles often represent the element Earth.

Pentagram: A star with five regular points, employed in magical operations. With one point uppermost it is a sign of good, with two points uppermost it is a sign of evil. The symbol is very powerful when employed in either context and is very effective for banishing and invoking rituals, especially with elemental forces.

Qabalah: A system used for spiritual development by magicians and mystics. See the essay in *Lilith, Darkness and Light Volume 1*.

Qlippoth: The evil demons of the Qabalah, caused by unbalanced forces from the four Qabalistic worlds. The Qlippoth is also the name of the dark regions in which they reside.

Ronin: A masterless (usually dishonored) samurai.

Sensei: Literally "teacher" or "instructor," but the term conveys far more respect than these translations.

Sephirah: One of the ten spheres of the Tree of Life, which include: Kether, Chokmah, Binah, Chesed, Geburah, Tiphareth, Netzach, Hod, Yesod, and Malkuth. The plural of Sephirah is Sephiroth.

Sigil: A signature that represents a specific entity or essence. Sigils can be used to call forth the power they represent, and are very important in magick.

Soror: A word used in occult orders, literally meaning "Sister." The masculine equivalent is Frater.

Succubus: A female demon that visits men during the night to copulate with them. Traditionally under the presidency of Arch-Demon Lilith, the male equivalent is an incubus. Plurals are succubi and incubi, respectively.

Tai-sabaki: Literally "body movement," the principle of avoiding an attack by moving out of its path. Tai-sabaki employs circular movements and is especially common in martial arts like aikido.

Tellus: An ancient name for the planet Earth, named after the Roman goddess of the Earth.

Tree of Life, The: A glyph that represents the Qabalah as a diagram of ten spheres, linked by twenty-two paths.

Wakizashi: Literally "short sword," the wakizashi was identical to the katana except for the length of the blade, which was only sixteen to twenty-three inches long. Hari-kiri was performed using this weapon.

Yetzirah: The third world of the Qabalah, roughly synonymous with the astral plane. Yetzirah is associated with the Sephirah Yesod.

Yoi: Literally "prepare" or "ready." In yoi, a martial artist is ready for any attack and is in a state of zanshin.

Zanshin: Literally "perfect posture," a state of mental balance and ultimate alertness, utilizing all the senses.

Recommended Reading

This list is for readers interested in discovering more about the philosophy behind Darkness and Light. For simplicity, I have broken the titles down into three sections: General, Magick, and Qabalah. Readers without any occult/mystical background are advised to read books from the General list before progressing to whatever area takes their interest. Each list is in a suggested reading order, the latter books generally being more complex (though this is somewhat subjective).

General

Seth Speaks, Jane Roberts.
The Occult, Colin Wilson (Grafton).
Beyond the Occult, Colin Wilson (Grafton).
The Fourth Way, P. D. Ouspensky (Arkana).

Quabalah

The Mystical Qabalah, Dion Fortune (Ernest Benn).
A Garden of Pomegranates, Israel Regardie (Llewellyn Publications).

Magick

Modern Magick, Donald M. Kraig (Llewellyn Publications).
The Middle Pillar, Israel Regardie (Llewellyn Publications).
Astral Projection, Denning & Phillips (Llewellyn Publications).
Self-Initiation into the Golden Dawn Tradition, Cicero & Cicero (Llewellyn Publications).
The Foundations of High Magick, Denning & Phillips (Llewellyn Publications).
The Sword and the Serpent, Denning & Phillips (Llewellyn Publications).
Mysteria Magica, Denning & Phillips (Llewellyn Publications).

STAY IN TOUCH. . .

Llewellyn publishes hundreds of books on your favorite subjects

On the following pages you will find listed some books now available on related subjects. Your local bookstore stocks most of these and will stock new Llewellyn titles as they become available. We urge your patronage.

Order by Phone

Call toll-free within the U.S. and Canada, 1-800-THE MOON. In Minnesota call (612) 291–1970. We accept Visa, MasterCard, and American Express.

Order by Mail

Send the full price of your order (MN residents add 7% sales tax) in U.S. funds to :

Llewellyn Worldwide,
P.O Box 64383, Dept. K–356–5
St. Paul, MN 55164–0383, U.S.A.

Postage and Handling

- $4.00 for orders $15.00 and under
- $5.00 for orders over $15.00
- No charge for orders over $100.00

We ship UPS in the continental United States. We cannot ship to P.O. boxes. Orders shipped to Alaska, Hawaii, Canada, Mexico, and Puerto Rico will be sent first-class mail.

International orders: Airmail—add freight equal to price of each book to the total price of order, plus $5.00 for each non-book item (audiotapes, etc.).

Surface mail: Add $1.00 per item

Allow 4–6 weeks delivery on all orders. Postage and handling rates subject to change.

Discounts

We offer a 20% quantity discount to group leaders or agents. You must order a minimum of 5 copies of the same book to get our special quantity price.

Free Catalog

Get a Free copy of our color catalogue, *New Worlds of Mind and Spirit*. Subscribe for just $10.00 in the United States and Canada ($20.00 overseas, first class mail). Many bookstores carry *New Worlds*—ask for it!

THE DREAM WARRIOR
Book One of the
Dream Warrior Trilogy

a novel by D. J. Conway

Danger, intrigue, and adventure seem to follow dauntless Corri Farblood wherever she goes. Sold as a child to the grotesque and sinister master thief Grimmel, Corri was forced into thievery at a young age. In fact, at eighteen, she's the best thief in the city of Hadliden—but she also possesses an ability to travel the astral plane, called "dreamflying," that makes her even more unique. Her talents make her a valuable commodity to Grimmel, who forces her into marriage so she will bear a child carrying both her special powers and his. But before the marriage can be consummated, Corri escapes with the aid of a traveling sorcerer, who has a quest of his own to pursue...

Journey across the wide land of Sar Akka with Corri, the sorcerer Imandoff Silverhair, and the warrior Takra Wind-Rider as they search for an ancient place of power. As Grimmel's assassins relentlessly pursue her, Corri battles against time and her enemies to solve the mystery of her heritage and to gain control over her potent clairvoyant gifts...to learn the meaning of companionship and love...and to finally confront a fate that will test her powers and courage to the limit.

1-56718-169-4, 5 ¼ x 8, 320 pp., softcover $14.95